THE WAGES
OF DESIRE

THE WAGES OF DESIRE

AN INSPECTOR LAMB NOVEL

STEPHEN KELLY

PEGASUS CRIME

NEW YORK LONDON

THE WAGES OF DESIRE

Pegasus Books Ltd
148 W 37th Street, 13th Floor
New York, NY 10018

Copyright © 2017 by Stephen Kelly

First Pegasus Books paperback edition July 2017
First Pegasus Books cloth edition August 2016

Interior design by Maria Fernandez

ISBN: 978-1-68177-437-4

10 9 8 7 6 5 4 3 2 1

Printed in the United States of America
Distributed by W. W. Norton & Company, Inc.

To Cindy, Anna, and Lauren, with love.

ONE

—m—

AS THE VILLAGE OF WINSTEAD SLEPT BENEATH A LATE AUGUST sky threatening rain, twelve-year-old Lilly Martin settled herself in the grass of Lawrence and Alba Tigue's rear yard.

This was the fifth night running in which Lilly had come to spy on the Tigues. Although she had not been able to clearly hear most of what the couple said during their nightly rows, she knew from the volume and tone of their voices that neither was happy. Then, two days earlier, Mrs. Tigue suddenly had left Winstead to spend the duration of the war at her sister's in Chesterfield—or so Lawrence had said when some in the village missed Alba and inquired after her. But as far as Lilly knew, Alba Tigue had said goodbye to no one in the village. In any case, since Mrs. Tigue's departure, the nighttime drama at the couple's cottage had ended.

Lilly knew that she should not be so interested in the Tigues' troubles. *Schadenfreude.* That's what the Germans called it—the word that described the secret satisfaction one took in other people's problems and failings. She wondered if that was one of the reasons why she'd recently come to fancy crime novels so much, because crime novels allowed one a front-row seat into someone else's mistakes and downfalls. In crime novels, the people who fell from grace usually were wicked and deserved what they got. But though she'd never much liked Lawrence or Alba Tigue—she found them haughty beyond their station—she'd never considered either of them to be wicked.

In the last year Lilly had grown so enamored of reading crime stories that she'd decided that she wanted to become a crime novelist. She told herself that *this* was why she spied on the Tigues, who seemed to her a perfect pair of characters around which to build a mystery story. In appearance, Lawrence Tigue resembled Hawley Crippen, who thirty years earlier had murdered his wife, buried her torso in the basement of his London home, then attempted to escape to Canada with his young mistress. To explain his wife's sudden absence, Crippen had said that she had gone to the United States—just as Mr. Tigue now claimed that Mrs. Tigue had gone to Chesterfield. Neither Crippen nor Tigue looked anything like what Lilly thought a murderer should look like, which made them all the creepier. Both had round, soft faces and wore delicate-looking spectacles and looked more like accountant's clerks than cold-blooded killers.

Now, Lilly concluded from the dark cottage that Mr. Tigue had gone to bed. Intending to pack it in for the night, she stood and began to brush the dirt from her trousers. She had begun wandering alone at night only a couple of months earlier, in May, after her father was sent to the Mediterranean and her mother had taken a night-shift job in Southampton making, of all things, screwdriver handles. How long she stayed in any one place when she wandered the village at night depended on how she felt and if she happened upon anything interesting. She'd been surprised to discover how restless Winstead could be at night—as restless, and perhaps as lonely, as she.

To her right lay Mr. Tigue's henhouse and his garage, in which he kept his printing press and motorcar. The henhouse was fifteen meters from where she stood, enclosed by a low fence of chicken wire nailed to wooden posts. Lilly knew that Mr. Tigue made a bit of money on the side selling eggs to the officials at the POW camp for Italians the government was building on the abandoned farm just west of the village.

Just to the left of Mr. Tigue's henhouse, a narrow path led toward the road that eventually looped around to enter Winstead and become its High Street on the western side of the village. Lilly heard movement coming from along the path, near the rear of the henhouse. She crouched by the garden and made herself still. A spatter of rain began to fall.

A figure she instantly recognized materialized from around the side of the slant-roofed shack. Flora Wheatley moved slowly, her signature girth and waddle unmistakable. She wore a dark jumper and had pulled a kind of workman's cap down upon her head. She carried a basket looped in her right arm. She opened the rickety wire gate and trundled up the wooden ramp into the henhouse, causing the chickens to begin softly clucking. Two minutes later Miss Wheatley emerged, holding the basket delicately.

The hypocrite! Lilly thought.

She watched Miss Wheatley retreat up the path in the light rain. She went to the trail and saw Miss Wheatley crossing the meadow toward the small wood, beyond which she lived alone in a dilapidated cottage. Lilly followed, keeping her distance. As she came out into the meadow on the far side of the wood, she spied Miss Wheatley moving down the narrow path toward her cottage. She watched Miss Wheatley enter the ramshackle little house and wondered what the bizarre old woman was on about. She thought, too, that here might be a new mystery to investigate, one to replace the drama that had come to such an abrupt end at the Tigue place. By then, though, the rain had begun to fall harder, threatening buckets and softening Lilly's will to spy on Miss Wheatley any longer.

Feeling as if life intended to defeat her, Lilly gave up for the night and made her way back to the silent, empty house in which, not so long ago, she had been happy.

TWO

—m—

DETECTIVE CHIEF INSPECTOR THOMAS LAMB SAT IN THE PASSENGER
seat of the black Wolseley, staring out the window at the meadows,
farm sheds, and copses of trees that lined the southwest road out of
Winchester and wondering whether he should allow his nineteen-
year-old daughter, Vera, to see the dead woman's body. According to
what the vicar had told Wallace, the woman had been shot in the back,
meaning that a bloody mess awaited them in the village of Winstead.

Although Lamb had not yet discussed the matter with Vera, he
was sure that she *wanted* to see the body. He well understood that
Vera disliked the notion that he continued to believe it necessary to
protect her from life's harsher aspects—treating her, in other words,
as if she still were a child. But Lamb could not help doing so; the
desire to shield Vera had dominated and shaped his life since the day
of her birth. Still, he'd come to realize that, too often, he'd insisted

on playing the knight to his daughter-in-distress and that he must give up this role for Vera's sake.

He fished in the pocket of his jacket, withdrew from it a packet of Player's Navy Cut cigarettes, and lit one. He took a long drag from the cigarette and exhaled without removing it from his lips. The smoke traveled up to and tickled his right eye. He stole a glance at Vera, who sat behind the steering wheel dressed in the light blue shirt, trousers, and cap of an auxiliary constable, a rank that had come into existence with the war and the sudden shortage of men on the home front. The uniform fit Vera poorly—it was at least a size too big—because it had been cut for a man. Gamely, though, Vera had rolled up the cuffs of the shirt and trousers a notch so that they did not hang over her hands and boots, making her resemble something like—and here Lamb could not help but to conjure the word again—a *child* playing dress-up. She was a slender young woman with large brown eyes and brown-in-blond hair cut in a pageboy fashion. She stared ahead at the road, gripping the wheel, unaware that her father was appraising her.

The rain had come down steadily for a few hours during the night but let up by dawn as the storm had moved south and over the Channel. Now, the mid-morning sun was bright and hot, evaporating the puddles that had formed in the low places along the road. The summer had been hot and relatively dry, though nothing like the previous summer, when the rain had disappeared for weeks at a time, clearing the skies for the German bombers that had come to southern England from occupied France nearly every day, well into the middle of September. Lamb sometimes found himself surprised to realize that nearly a year had passed since then. It seemed like only weeks ago that the Germans had been dropping their bombs. They had destroyed much in southern England during the previous summer, including the horse racing track at Paulsgrove, which, in the end, Lamb came to consider a positive development because it had forced him to give up his less-than-salubrious habit of placing a bet now and again on a race at the track—a habit that had caused him to squander more money than he had collected. Since then, he had many times wished that he could give up his other ill-starred habit—smoking—as easily. But he had tried this often, employing many methods, from giving up fags outright to attempting to replace them with butterscotch drops, and every one had failed. He looked at the cigarette with longing, took a final drag from it, and tossed it, half-smoked, out the passenger side window.

Normally, he, and not Vera, would be driving; he preferred to drive, even though his rank meant that he needn't. Indeed, normally Vera would not be with him now, heading to the scene of a killing. But two days earlier, Lamb had sprained his left ankle falling off a ladder he'd ascended intending to clear the dead leaves and other detritus that had collected in the gutters of his house in Winchester. Lamb never had been comfortable with heights and so perennially dreaded the annual leaf cleaning and normally held off doing the job for as long as possible. But a spate of rain in the past week had made it clear that the gutters were clogged beyond ignoring any longer. Rain had spilled over the edge of the gutter at the rear of the house and down the pane of the window in the bedroom Lamb shared with his wife, Marjorie. The water had collected in the sill and seeped beneath the bottom of the window and thence down the wall to the floor of the bedroom.

Feeling his usual trepidation regarding heights, Lamb had gone to the shed and retrieved the ladder. He'd leaned it against the rear gutter and thought he'd made the thing sturdy enough to climb. But the ground beneath the right leg of the ladder was more saturated with rain than he'd suspected. He'd managed to climb to the height of the gutter and was just beginning to remove a first handful of sodden leaves when he felt the ladder begin to list sickeningly to port as its left leg sank into the swampy ground. He felt himself falling and grabbed at the gutter but was too late. His left foot struck the ground on its side; he yelped and lay on the ground, wincing. He sat alone for a couple of minutes massaging his swelling ankle and cursing his luck. Then he limped into the house, where Marjorie had made a cold water compress in a tea towel and forced him to sit in the kitchen with his left foot propped on a chair, the compress tied with twine around his ankle.

On the following morning, Lamb had gotten into the Wolseley, intending to drive himself to the Hampshire Constabulary. But when he'd depressed the clutch, he'd found that the pain that radiated from his tender ankle was too great for him to drive. When he'd limped back into the house intending to call Detective Sergeant David Wallace to come and fetch him, Vera, who had been at the table having breakfast with Marjorie, immediately volunteered to drive him to the nick. Vera had not been engaged in steady work for several months by then, a fact that worried Lamb and Marjorie because, during the previous spring, the government had begun to lay the groundwork for conscripting women into war duty. In April, the government had begun requiring every woman between the ages of eighteen and sixty to register their occupations. Since, the government had been interviewing the registrants and requiring those who were not gainfully employed to choose from a range of war-related jobs, a turn of events that had resulted in de facto, if not de jure, conscription for British women.

Thankfully, Vera had not yet been called for an interview. But Lamb knew it was only a matter of time before her moment came, and he intended to shield Vera from the call-up as long as he could. Although the government did not intend for women to bear arms, female conscripts could be sent to combat zones as nurses or other essential workers. At the moment, the Germans not only were rampaging through Russia but also held the upper hand in the Mediterranean and North Africa. The war could last years still, and Vera already had experienced one too-close encounter with combat when, during the previous summer, she'd taken a job as the sole civil defense employee in the village of Quimby, near Southampton, and been present on the evening that a German bomber, having overflown its target in the city, had dropped its bombs on the village, killing two people, including one whom Vera had known well. Since that time, Vera occasionally had told her parents that she was considering training to become a combat nurse, a job she defined as "relevant," as opposed to the safer jobs—typist, fire-watcher, Land Army girl— that her parents wished she would consider. And so, as Vera had driven him to work on the day after he'd sprained his ankle, Lamb had found himself blessed with an idea. He would ask Police Superintendent Anthony Harding if Vera could become his driver, at least until he figured out a more permanent way to keep the conscription act from sucking his daughter into the war.

Lamb had admitted to Harding that he was attempting to protect Vera from conscription with his request—though he said nothing of this to Vera. Harding had agreed to Lamb's idea, and since then Vera had been ferrying Lamb to and fro about his duties, dressed in her ill-fitting auxiliary constable's uniform. Now they were headed to the scene of an obvious murder, and Lamb admitted to himself that he had not counted on his bright idea placing Vera in a situation in which she might find herself standing over a dead body.

He glanced again at Vera and decided that he would spare her the experience of encountering the dead woman. For one, he wanted to limit the number of people who trod near the scene of the crime. But in truth he knew that he merely desired, yet again, to shield his daughter from the grim fact of death. This was stupid, he knew, and, under the circumstances of the war, probably unfair to Vera. And in that instant a small epiphany presented itself to Lamb: he sought to shield Vera from death because he feared exposure to it might somehow move the Reaper a step closer to her—that if he could somehow keep Vera out of death's sight, death would miss her. This, too, he understood to be stupid, indeed ludicrous. His time in the trenches on the Somme, in the previous war, had taught him the truth of death's indifference to whom it claimed, and why and when. But Vera's was the only death he was certain that he could not endure.

Having made his decision, Lamb allowed himself to light another cigarette as Vera headed the Wolseley down the road to the village of Winstead under a cloudless summer sky.

THREE

—⫘—

A STOUT, MIDDLE-AGED HOME GUARDSMAN ARMED WITH A BIRD gun stood by the front gate of the cemetery of Saint Michael's Church in Winstead, alongside a thin, balding man of average height who wore round spectacles, a well-cut brown wool suit, and a burgundy tie. Over his suit, the smaller man also wore a Great War–era Sam Browne belt that had attached to it a black holster containing a .455-caliber Webley pistol.

Twenty or so people from the village milled nearby, including a dozen unsupervised children who had climbed onto the waist-high black wrought iron fence that surrounded the cemetery, hoping for a better look at the dead woman. The men who had stationed themselves at the gate seemed at least to have had the good sense to bar anyone from entering the cemetery, Lamb thought as Vera pulled the Wolseley to a stop by the fence. An hour earlier, Wallace had taken a call at the nick in Winchester from the vicar of Saint Michael's Church, one Gerald Wimberly, who'd reported that he'd discovered a woman's body in the cemetery when he'd returned to the vicarage from his morning constitutional. The woman had a large bullet wound in her back, Wimberly had told Wallace, who immediately had passed the message to Lamb.

From the spot at which Vera had stopped the Wolseley, neither she nor Lamb could see the body. Lamb turned to her and said, "I want you to stay by the car, please."

Vera smiled. "Meaning that I can't see the body, then?"

Lamb returned her smile. He had gray eyes and short-cropped salt-and-pepper hair. He possessed a penetrating and sometimes remorseless intelligence that was softened by the genuine warmth he felt toward most people, except those he knew for certain had willfully and maliciously perpetrated an injury toward another, and particularly those who had purposely done harm to someone who was weaker than they. With such people he could be merciless.

"There's no reason for you to see the body, really," he said. "In any case, the fewer people who enter the scene at the moment, the better."

Vera touched her father's arm. "I understand, Dad," she said. "Don't worry."

Don't worry? Lamb thought. *She's seen right through me.* "If you get bored, you can help the uniformed men chase the gawkers away," he said. He tugged gently at her billowing left sleeve. "You've the uniform for it now, you know."

"I think I'll just watch for a bit," she said. "Learn a few things before I start throwing my weight about."

"Not a bad idea. See you in a bit, then."

Lamb exited the car and walked toward the cemetery gate. "Get those children off the fence, please," he said to one of the three uniformed constables who, with Sergeant Wallace, had followed Vera and him to the village in a separate car. Detective Inspector Harry Rivers and Cyril Larkin, the forensics man, had come in a third car. Lamb joined Wallace and Rivers by the gate, where they showed the two men who were guarding it their warrant cards and introduced themselves.

"Thank you for securing the scene," Lamb said to the pair. "Do you know if any of the onlookers entered the cemetery before you arrived?"

The thinner man stepped forward.

"We're sure no one got in, Chief Inspector," he said. He offered Lamb his hand. "My name is Lawrence Tigue. I am chairman of the parish civic council." Lamb reckoned that Tigue was in his late thirties or early forties, while the one in the Home Guard uniform clearly was a few decades older, beefy and red-faced, with black grit beneath the nails of his calloused hands.

"Tigue" rang a bell in Lamb's memory. Two weeks earlier, the *Hampshire Mail* had run a story detailing how the government was constructing a prisoner-of-war camp for Italians on a long-fallow farm near Winstead. Lamb had recognized the village's name as soon as Wallace had reported to him the vicar's story of finding the body in the cemetery of Saint Michael's Church. He recalled that, twenty years earlier, Winstead had been the scene of a disquieting suicide of a woman named Claire O'Hare—an incident that the *Mail* had been quick to remind its readers of in its story about the construction of the prison camp. At the time of the O'Hare incident, Lamb had been a uniformed constable assigned to Winchester and so had had nothing to do with the case. But, prompted by the story in the *Mail*, he recalled its basic details. Claire O'Hare had left a note saying that she had killed herself because her husband, Sean, had abandoned her and taken with him the couple's five-year-old twin sons, Jack and John. The last time anyone in Winstead had reported seeing the twins was on the morning of their disappearance as they walked down the narrow dirt road that led to the farm on which the government now was building the prison—a farm that, at the time of the O'Hare incident, had been occupied by a family named Tigue.

Lawrence Tigue nodded at his compatriot with the shotgun. "This is Mr. Samuel Built," he said. "He is a member of the LDV and our acting police constable. The police have yet to replace our former constable, Nate Goodson, who was killed in Belgium last summer."

Tigue smiled slightly. Lamb sensed that Tigue was not complaining about the police not yet having replaced Nate Goodson as much as he was merely informing Lamb of the fact that the village hadn't had a proper bobby for the past year, which was why he and Built had taken into their hands the matter of securing the scene of the crime.

"I'm sorry about the constable," Lamb said. "We'll have to look into correcting that."

Tigue smiled again. "That would be much appreciated, certainly, Chief Inspector."

"Which of you arrived first?" Lamb asked the men.

"I did," Built said. He nodded over his shoulder in the direction of the church. "The vicar found the body and called for me. I had to put my uniform on, so as to look official. Otherwise the lot hanging by the fence would have run all over the place." He paused, then added, "We haven't had a proper constable here since the war." Built looked at Wallace and said, "He were about your age, was Nate."

Wallace thought he knew what Built was implying. Since the war had begun, others also had implied it—or said it outright—when they first met him: *Why are you, an obviously healthy young man, not in uniform, as is my husband, son, brother, friend, lover?*

The idea that Britain might still require a functioning police force, despite the war, seemed not to have occurred to people such as Built, Wallace thought. Even so, Built's words stung his conscience.

"We're sorry about Mr. Goodson," Lamb said, coming to Wallace's relief. "I'm sure he was a fine man." Lamb also understood what Built had been implying with his remark to Wallace—that perhaps Wallace, as an obviously healthy young man, should have been fighting for England. Because he was a police officer, the government had granted Wallace and other men on the force of his age an occupational deferment from conscription, a fact that Built might have been unaware of or simply chosen to ignore, Lamb thought.

That said, Lamb had learned many years earlier, during his service in France, that no good way existed to respond to people who bluntly informed you that the war had snuffed out the life of someone they had known or loved. It was best to move on from the subject as soon as decorum allowed. With that, Lamb turned his attention back to Lawrence Tigue.

"I take it you arrived soon after Mr. Built, sir?" he said.

"Yes. Mr. Built called me."

"And where did you get your Webley?"

Tigue looked at the pistol as if he had forgotten he was wearing it. "Oh, this," he said. "I bought it secondhand shortly after the war began." He straightened his shoulders a bit. "It seemed a good idea, especially last summer, when there was no telling when or if Jerry would drop in."

"Yes, that's wise," Lamb said. "And where is the vicar now?"

"Vicarage," Built said. "The whole business has given his wife a shock."

"What exactly did the vicar tell you when he called you, Mr. Built?" Lamb said.

Built looked at Lamb as if he thought the answer to the question obvious. "He told me there were a dead girl in the church cemetery. Shot to death, he said."

"Have you seen the girl?"

"I glanced at her. I don't like dead bodies as a rule."

"Did you recognize her?"

"Well, I didn't see her face, like, as she were lying on her stomach. But no, she didn't look familiar to me."

"And you, Mr. Tigue? Did you recognize her?"

"Well, it's hard to know for sure, of course, as she was lying face-down, as Mr. Built said."

"Did the vicar tell you how he had found the body, Mr. Built?"

"He said he were just returning from his morning walk when he heard a gunshot from the direction of the cemetery. That's when he went there and found the girl, dead as you please."

Built's version of the vicar's story conflicted slightly with the one that the vicar had told Wallace on the telephone. According to Wallace, Gerald Wimberly had made no mention of having heard a gunshot from the cemetery; he'd said only that he'd returned from a walk and found the woman lying among the graves.

"Did the vicar say that he had seen anyone in the cemetery or that he'd found the gun used to shoot the woman?" Lamb asked.

"No. But then, I didn't ask him. Saw no reason to. Had he seen anyone or found the gun, I reckon he'd have told me."

"Did he tell you that he knew who had shot the woman, or that he suspected that he knew?"

"No."

"How far is your farm from the church?"

"Half mile."

"How long did it take you, then, to walk from there to here?"

"Less than ten minutes."

"So is that ten minutes for you to put on your guardsman's outfit *and* to get here? Ten minutes total, in other words?"

Confusion clouded Built's eyes for a moment. "No," he said. "It took me a couple of minutes to get into my uniform." Built nodded at Tigue. "And I telephoned Mr. Tigue and told him what were happening."

"So, can we say it took you fifteen or so minutes for you to get to the church from the time the vicar alerted you?"

"I suppose," Built said.

"And what did you do when you got here?"

"I went into the cemetery to look at the girl, as I said. It were the vicar who said we couldn't allow anyone from the village in to look at her. It'd become a circus, he said. Then he told me that his wife had had a shock and that I should guard the gate while he went in and called you lot and saw to her. I took my place at the gate, just as the vicar ordered. Then the people from the village started showing, as word spread. Then you arrived."

"And where is the vicarage, exactly?"

14

"Around the other side of the church, toward the back."

Lamb turned again to Tigue. "And when did you arrive, sir?"

"Shortly after Mr. Built and the vicar. When Mr. Built called I was still in bed, I'm afraid." Tigue smiled, as if this fact mildly embarrassed him.

"I wonder if you wouldn't mind turning over your pistol to us," Lamb said.

Surprise flared in Tigue's eyes. "My pistol?" he said.

Lamb smiled. "Yes, sir. Just so we can check it for forensics and eliminate it from our inquiries. It's merely routine, of course, but it would prove helpful."

Tigue smiled in return. "Of course," he said. He removed the pistol from its holster and handed it to Lamb, who in turn handed it to Larkin.

"Thank you," Lamb said to Tigue.

"Me, too?" Built asked.

"Please."

"I'll get it back then, won't I?"

"We'll keep it only as long as we need to."

Built broke open the shotgun and removed the cartridges before handing everything to Larkin.

Lamb nodded. "Very well, then, gentlemen," he said. "Thank you for your service. You may go home now."

"If you need assistance I hope you'll call on us," Tigue said.

"I will, sir, thank you."

Lamb turned from the two men and, limping slightly on his tender left ankle, pushed open the gate to the cemetery.

FOUR

—⁊⁊—

LAMB AND THE OTHERS FOUND THE POLICE SURGEON, ANTHONY Winston-Sheed, leaning casually against the rear fence of the cemetery and looking at the sky in a contemplative manner, a cigarette smoldering between the fingers of his left hand.

A woman's body lay on the ground to the doctor's left, in front of a weathered headstone. About fifteen meters further to the left of where the doctor stood, a gate in the rear fence opened onto a dirt-and-gravel footpath that came from around the rear of the church and led toward the center of Winstead. On the other side of this path lay a wood. About ten meters to the left of Lamb and his troop, as they crossed the cemetery in Winston-Sheed's direction, a freshly dug open grave yawned.

"Hello, gentlemen," Winston-Sheed said when Lamb and the others reached him.

Lamb nodded. "Doctor."

Winston-Sheed handed Lamb a small brown leather shoulder bag. "She was wearing this," he said. "I think you'll find its contents interesting."

"Thank you," Lamb said. He took the bag and found within it, among other items, a large sum of cash rolled into a kind of tube and secured with a rubber band. He removed the wad from the bag and held it up to the sun for a better look.

"How much?" Rivers asked.

"Fifty at least, I'd say," Winston-Sheed said.

Impressed, Wallace whistled. "If the killer was after money he bloody well bollixed it, then," he said.

"Maybe the vicar's approach interrupted him," Larkin mused.

Lamb handed the bag to Wallace, with a request to search its other contents for something that would identify the woman who lay at their feet. He then knelt next to the body to examine it closely.

The dead woman lay facedown next to the grave of a woman named Mary Forrest, who, Lamb noted, had parted the veil in 1927. Fresh foxgloves and daisies lay scattered between the body and the grave. Lamb wondered if the dead woman had known Mary Forrest and had meant to lay the flowers at Mary's grave. The woman was dressed in denim overalls and thick-soled hobnailed leather work boots—an outfit Lamb recognized as the type the government issued to the small army of citizens it had conscripted into the war effort. A bullet wound the size of a tea saucer oozed, blackish-red, just beneath her right shoulder blade. Blood and bits of body tissue stained her hair and shoulders and the weathered gravestone of Mary Forrest—some of it sticking to the moss that had grown in the stone's cracks and fissures.

"Preliminarily, it appears that she was shot in the back with a high-caliber weapon at point-blank range," Winston-Sheed said. He nodded toward the path on the other side of the fence. "The bullet exited her chest and is out there beyond this fence somewhere, I should imagine."

"You don't like the vicar's story," Rivers said to Lamb. Neither did he.

Lamb peered at the woman, nearly squinting, as if he hoped that something about the nature of her killing that he couldn't quite yet see might come into sudden focus. "I don't know," he said. "When he called the nick, he said nothing to Wallace about having heard the shot. And he had fifteen minutes between the time he called Built and when Built arrived." Beside the fact that the vicar, by his own admission, was up and about at the time of killing, and the girl had been killed in the church cemetery, next to the vicarage—two facts that put the vicar very much in the picture regardless of who found the woman—standard procedure insisted that you considered as a suspect whoever discovered the body and reported the crime.

Wallace held up an identification card issued by the Women's Land Army that he'd found in the bag. "Here we go," he announced. "Ruth Aisquith."

He handed the card to Lamb, who studied it for a few seconds. The woman in the photo had dark hair; a sharp, prominent nose; and intense, dark eyes. Her face was unsmiling. The card listed her date of birth as June 7, 1905, making her thirty-six years old. Lamb recalled how he and Marjorie had sought, unsuccessfully, to convince Vera to join the Land Army. Mostly, the Land girls did farm work, difficult but healthy labor. More importantly, though, the work was safe, far from combat. And yet here was Ruth Aisquith, dead well before her time.

"A Land girl, then," Rivers said. "Probably from the prison camp. But where does a Land girl come by fifty quid?"

"Maybe she comes from money," Larkin said.

"Yes, but why bring it to the bloody cemetery?"

"If she does work at the prison camp, maybe she didn't trust leaving it in her barrack. Too easy for someone to nick."

"Or she owed a debt," Wallace said. He nodded at Mary Forrest's grave. "Her grandmother, then?" he asked. "Or an elderly auntie?"

"Maybe," Lamb said. "Given that *this* was the grave she intended to visit. She might have been intending to visit someone else's grave. Or she might not have intended to visit any particular grave at all. She might have picked the flowers for herself or someone living."

Lamb asked Wallace to check the other grave markers in the cemetery to see if any bore the name of Aisquith.

—⁓—

As they spoke, the Rev. Gerald Wimberly fumbled in the kitchen of the vicarage as he endeavored to make a pot of tea for his wife, Wilhemina. He took the kettle from the boil and began to pour water from it into the pot; some of the hot water splashed onto the fingers of his left hand. He drew his hand quickly away from the pot and cursed. He went to the sink and put his fingers under a trickle of cold water, which only slightly eased the pain of the burn. He thought again of how thoroughly he despised Wilhemina. She'd always been a burden to him. All the same, he must make her bloody tea—must endeavor to calm her, especially now that the police had arrived. Using a pestle he'd crushed three sleeping tablets—more than he needed, really—in a small ceramic mortar, the contents of which he poured into the pot.

—⁓—

Lamb and Rivers rolled the dead woman onto her back, exposing the ragged exit wound just beneath her heart.

"Less than an arm's length," Rivers said, guessing at the range from which the killer had shot the woman.

Lamb checked her hands, pockets—in which he found nothing—and shoes, including the soles. He stood, turned, and limped a couple of paces from the woman's body toward the center of the cemetery. He gestured to Larkin.

"Come around here, please, Mr. Larkin, and stand in front of me." The forensics man did as instructed. Lamb turned to face the dead woman. "Raise your hand and pretend to shoot me in the back," Lamb said. Larkin raised his finger and said, "Bang!" Lamb took a couple of steps forward, which brought him again to the woman's feet.

"So she's shot and stumbles forward from the impact before she dies and falls against the headstone of Mary Forrest," Lamb said, thinking aloud.

Lamb bent to look at the grass at the place where he calculated the woman had been shot. The grass still was moist from the predawn rain. "Here are the impressions left by her boots," he said. He stood. "And what have we coming toward her, then?"

He took another two steps forward, then went to a knee to examine a small bare spot in the grass in which he saw what appeared to be a print left by a woman's shoe—though a shoe that was different from the government-issued boots the victim wore. The print had a distinct square impression at the heel.

Larkin kneeled next to Lamb and peered at the ground. "I see it," he said, squinting. Lamb pointed to another set of prints that appeared to have been left by a man wearing boots who also had approached the grave. These were roughly a foot away and parallel to the woman's prints.

"See if you can get photographs and casts of those, please," Lamb said. He stood and looked again at the dead woman. "There's nothing on her hands," he said quietly. "No sign that she struggled with anyone. I wonder if she had any idea that her killer was behind her."

Lamb turned in the direction of the vicarage and thought over several questions that needed answers, including why Ruth Aisquith had come to the cemetery so early in the morning, and alone. And why was she carrying nearly fifty pounds? And why didn't her killer take the cash? He wondered again about the vicar's story. Had Gerald Wimberly merely forgotten to tell Wallace that he'd heard the fatal shot, even though he had told Built and Tigue that he had? Most people became befuddled when forced to face sudden, violent death. Then, too, he had to consider the fact that lay at the foundation of most cases of murder: People overwhelmingly killed for three primary reasons—greed, jealousy, and vengefulness—and the most common triggers of these emotions were money and sex. They'd found a wad of cash, but what of the sex? Did it matter here? He thought again of the Rev. Gerald Wimberly, a man of God. Ostensibly, such men did not kill, and they especially did not harm innocents, which caused Lamb to ask himself two additional questions that he believed pertinent.

Had Ruth Aisquith indeed been an innocent?

And was Gerald Wimberly genuinely a man of God?

FIVE

—⟋⟍—

LARKIN REMAINED IN THE CEMETERY TO CHECK THE KILLING site for evidence, while Lamb sent Rivers into Winstead with a pair of constables to begin a door-to-door canvass of the village. He instructed Rivers to see what he could find out about Mary Forrest, the woman whose name was inscribed on the gravestone next to which Ruth Aisquith had fallen, and to ask if anyone had met Ruth Aisquith or knew of anyone in the village who possessed that surname.

Wallace reported that his search of the gravestones found that none contained the surname of Aisquith. That question settled, Lamb put the detective sergeant and a constable to the task of finding the bullet that had killed the woman. As Winston-Sheed had said, most likely the slug was lying somewhere in the luxuriant grass between the rear fence of the cemetery and the footpath that led into the village. Lamb then headed to the vicarage to speak with the Rev. Gerald Wimberly.

—⁓—

Vera patiently had waited by the car and not sought to get closer to the body. Nor had she taken any active role in helping keep the gawkers at bay. She had, as she had told Lamb she would, merely watched and observed. In the few days during which she'd acted as her father's driver she had done nothing resembling actual police work, nor was she meant to. She held no illusion that her job amounted to anything other than being a replacement for her father's sprained ankle. Still, she didn't mind the job, in part because it allowed her to be with her father; she'd always been curious about the mysteries and occasional dangers that seemed to fill his days. (She knew nothing of the paperwork and bureaucratic drudgery that the job also entailed.) And the pay was fair—five pounds for the week. Even so, she was glad the job was temporary. She didn't like the fact that her father had gotten her the job through obvious nepotism—and that everyone knew it—though its transitory nature softened the injustice of that. In any case, she didn't want people concluding that she got along in life thanks to her daddy.

She *had* wanted to see the dead woman and, as she had watched her father and the others enter the cemetery to begin the inquiry, she had contemplated why that was true. She decided that the human desire to confront the fact of death was natural, given that everyone had to die eventually, and that this probably became especially true during wartime, with death seeming to hover so much nearer than it normally did—though since the Germans had given up their bombing of southern England nearly a year earlier, she had not felt directly threatened by the violence and killing the war had wrought. She told herself that she should count herself lucky that she and her parents were so far from the actual war—the war as it was being fought in Russia and North Africa, and as it had been fought in Poland, France, Belgium, and Yugoslavia. And yet she did not feel lucky, exactly, but troubled that she remained protected when so many others were not.

After her father disappeared around the side of the church and headed to the vicarage, Vera eyed Wallace discreetly. She found him very good-looking and possessed of a kind of rugged charm, despite the fact that he tended a bit toward the peacock with his well-cut suits and shined black patent leather shoes. But she'd found him to be approachable and funny, too, and seemed genuine of heart. And she detected something else in him, something buried that, she thought, he endeavored to hide from the world—a kind of vulnerability and even a hint of anguish.

She contemplated lighting a cigarette from the packet she kept in her inner jacket pocket. She didn't *need* a cigarette exactly, but she felt that the time somehow was right for one. She had begun to smoke only a week earlier, mostly as an experiment to see if she liked it, a question she had not yet decided upon an answer to. In any case, neither of her parents knew that she smoked, and she was not prepared to tell them that she did until she *had* decided. She knew that her father hated his own smoking and that he had tried often to quit but always found that his normally resilient will failed him when it came to tobacco. In the end, she quashed the notion of a smoke for the moment, on the chance that her father might suddenly return and catch her with a fag dangling from her lips.

At that moment, two women and a girl approached the cemetery along the High Street, coming from the direction of the center of the village. Since the constables had dispersed the initial lot of onlookers, several people had come and gone in ones and twos—stopped and peered into the cemetery and gone on their way. Some of the children who'd earlier been climbing on the fence and been shooed away had returned, stolen another look, and run again when the constable shooed them a second time. Now, though, the constable had gone into the village with Rivers to knock on doors and Vera found herself the lone police presence by the front gate of the cemetery, a fact made all the more obvious by her ill-fitting uniform.

Because she had parked the car perhaps thirty meters to the west of the front gate, the three approaching women did not see her at first. They slowed as they passed the cemetery. One of the women was quite large—fat, really. She was dressed in a kind of countrywoman's getup of simple blue cotton frock and Wellingtons, her gray hair piled in a bun beneath a massive straw hat. The other woman was younger, perhaps thirty. She wore simple brown cotton slacks and a white blouse. Her hair was cut short, and she appeared to be wearing little or no makeup. She was quite pretty in an unadorned way, Vera thought. The girl was dressed in a simple tan blouse, blue shorts, and black plimsole shoes.

As they neared the cemetery, the older woman went to the fence and stared at the proceedings within. At that moment, Winston-Sheed was readying the body to be transported to Winchester for autopsy. The woman got onto the tips of her toes to better see the corpse. The other two stayed back a bit from the fence. The older woman turned to them and said, "But I can't see a thing! Not really!" She turned again toward the cemetery, as if hoping that the view might suddenly have improved in the instant during which she'd turned away from it.

"That's all right," the younger woman said. "Lilly and I will be getting off home now anyway."

The older woman left the fence and rejoined the other two. "But we must find out what happened," she insisted.

"We'll find out soon enough, Flora," the other woman said.

The older woman caught sight of Vera. "Oh, here's someone," she said and began moving very quickly toward Vera. The other two followed, though not as quickly. The woman in the lead waved at Vera. "I say, are you with the police?" Before Vera could answer the woman was in front of her.

"My word—a *girl* policeman," the woman said. She stared at Vera for a second. "You *are* a girl, my dear, aren't you?" Vera found the question rude. She hadn't thought her uniform *that* baggy and unflattering.

"Yes," she said without enthusiasm.

The woman smiled. "I say," she said. "*Good* for you, my dear. I've never seen a girl policeman—though it's about time. But that's what the war has done, hasn't it? Opened up things for us."

Vera forced a smile. "Yes, ma'am," she said.

The other two caught up and stood behind the woman named Flora. The young girl caught Vera's eye and ostentatiously whirled her right forefinger around her ear, signaling to Vera not to be alarmed—as if to say that the woman who stood in front of her was loony and that everyone knew it. The younger woman gently swatted at the girl's hand, but without vehemence or true censure. Vera did her best to suppress a smile.

"My name is Flora Wheatley," the older woman said, offering Vera a pudgy hand.

"I'm Vera Lamb." Miss Wheatley shook Vera's proffered hand with what Vera thought was needless vigor, as if Miss Wheatley was working a recalcitrant water pump. She realized that she had no rank to put in front of her name—only the baggy uniform.

"I say, my dear, can you tell us what's happened?" Miss Wheatley asked. "We only know that some unfortunate woman has been shot to death in our cemetery."

"I'm afraid that I don't know any more than that myself."

"Oh, but you must!" Miss Wheatley said. "You're with the police, aren't you?"

"I am, but . . ."

The younger woman stepped closer. "It's all right, Flora," she said, putting her hand on Miss Wheatley's shoulder. "I'm sure Miss Lamb would not be at liberty to discuss the case with us even if she did know anything." The younger woman smiled at Vera.

"Yes, that's right," Vera said, though she wasn't certain that it was. "Even so, I really *do* know nothing. I'm only just a driver, you see. It's a temporary job."

"I should think it would be a nice job to have," the girl said. "Exciting."

Vera smiled at the girl. "It's not bad. But to be truthful, it's mostly standing around waiting."

"Still, you get to go to the scene of the crime," the girl insisted.

"That's true."

"I'm afraid Lilly's on a bit of kick when it comes to detective novels at the moment," the younger woman said. She offered Vera her hand. "My name is Julia Martin, by the way, and this is my daughter, Lilly."

"I say, my dear, is your captain about?" Miss Wheatley interjected.

"Chief inspector, madam. And no, I'm afraid he's busy at the moment."

"Well, I wonder if you'll give him a message from me. I'm afraid we've a crime spree going on here in the village and have had for some time now."

Vera saw Lilly roll her eyes.

"A crime spree?" Vera asked.

"Yes, very much so. I've long said that the police should have been involved, but no one else in the village seems to care about the problem outside of me." She leaned a little closer to Vera and whirled her finger around her ear, just as Lilly had done. "Some in the village will tell you that I'm crazy, my dear, but I don't care. Those people have their *heads* in the sand. They don't want to hear the truth because the truth so often hurts. I'm speaking of the case of the nuthatch hereabout. The poor creatures are rare enough as it is, but with people stealing their eggs the poor things will never survive the war. They're cavity nesters you see, but they can't compete with the blasted starlings, which are so much more aggressive; I've built nesting boxes for them all around the village. But people steal their eggs from the boxes—and for *food* no less. And the worst of the offenders is our own chairman of the village parish council, Lawrence Tigue."

Julia touched Miss Wheatley's shoulder. "Now, you shouldn't say such things, Flora. You've no proof of that."

"Of course I have proof! He's in the egg-selling business isn't he? Besides, I've seen him."

Vera didn't quite know what to say. She didn't think she minded people taking birds eggs for food under the present circumstances.

"We must be vigilant," Miss Wheatley said. "But no one wants to hear it, least of all our very own local officials. They're all in it together, the lot of them."

Vera stole a glance at Julia, who raised her eyebrows slightly.

"Well I'm sure everyone is doing what they can," Vera said.

"Don't you believe it, my dear! Either way, I beg of you to inform your captain. He may call on me anytime he wishes." She nodded toward the wood beyond the cemetery. "I live just the other side of that wood. You can't miss my cottage; it's just off the trail."

"I promise that I'll mention it to him," Vera said. "He's my father, actually." She immediately wondered why she had felt the need to mention that. Was it from guilt that her father had obtained her position for her?

"All the better, then!" Miss Wheatley said. She looked at the sky, then back at Vera. "Well, it's getting on to midday, and I've duties to attend to."

Vera didn't want to say anything that might encourage Miss Wheatley to linger. To her relief, Miss Wheatley bade them goodbye and set off down the High Street in the direction of the village.

When Miss Wheatley was out of earshot, Julia said, "You must forgive her, Miss Lamb. She's harmless, really."

"No, she's not," Lilly said. "She's a windbag and a terrible gossip. *And* she's loony."

"That's no way to speak in front of someone we've only just met," Julia scolded Lilly. "And it's not fair to Flora."

"But she *is*, Mother."

"Nonetheless." Julia shot Lilly a stern look. "Apologize to Miss Lamb, please."

"Sorry," Lilly said. She shrugged slightly.

"It's all right," Vera said. Miss Wheatley clearly *was* a windbag, she thought.

"Well, I'm afraid that we also must be going," Julia said. "It was wonderful meeting you, Miss Lamb. It's terrible, what's happened here—this sudden killing—and I think it's shocked us all a bit more than we are quite yet willing to admit." She smiled again. "Good luck to you."

"Thank you," Vera said. She sensed a kind of sadness in Julia Martin and, as she watched Julia and Lilly leave, spent a moment guessing at its source. Something to do with the war, she concluded. After all, wasn't that the primary source of everyone's sorrow these days?

SIX

—⁂—

THE VICARAGE OF SAINT MICHAEL'S CHURCH WAS A MEDIUM-sized, white-shingled cottage with a green door and slate roof. Lamb had not much liked the majority of country vicars with whom he'd been acquainted; nearly to a man, he'd found them possessed of mediocre intellects and an unmerited self-regard. They tended to be plump, red-cheeked, self-satisfied men who ate and drank very well and often seemed entranced by the sound of their own voices.

He therefore found himself surprised by the man who answered his knock on the door. Gerald Wimberly was at least six feet tall, slender, and fit looking. Lamb judged him to be somewhere in the neighborhood of fifty. He had a full head of tousled gray-at-the-edges brown hair, blue eyes, and a strong, squared-off chin. He was a handsome man. He wore a gray shirt and white clerical collar, along with a pair of dark blue corduroy trousers that were stained slightly with mud at the cuffs and a pair of stout brown leather government-issued military boots that Lamb recognized as identical to those he'd worn during his time in the trenches of the Somme.

"The Reverend Gerald Wimberly?" Lamb asked.

"Yes."

Lamb showed Wimberly his warrant card. "I'm Detective Chief Inspector Thomas Lamb of the Hampshire Constabulary. I'd like to speak with you, please."

Wimberly stepped back from the door. "Yes, of course, Chief Inspector," he said. "I've been expecting you."

Wimberly led Lamb into a cozily furnished study that contained a large wooden desk that faced the door and stood in front of a wall that was full of shelved books. A pair of red-upholstered chairs situated on opposite sides of a small, round, polished cherry table faced the desk. The left wall also contained tall, brimming bookshelves, while the right was dominated by a large window that looked onto a well-tended flower and vegetable garden at the rear of the vicarage.

Wimberly sat behind the desk and gestured for Lamb to take one of the chairs. He was conscious of the impression of authority and control the large desk afforded him, and hoped it would work on Lamb.

"I understand that you found the body, sir," Lamb said.

"Yes, yes," Wimberly said. "A terrible thing. Terrible. It's given my poor wife the shock of her life, I'm sorry to say. I had to give her a sedative; she's upstairs sleeping now." He paused for few seconds, then added, "But I'm rambling, Chief Inspector. I'm sorry. I don't mean to say that my wife's condition is the only thing that matters in this business."

"Did you know the dead woman? We have reason to believe that she was employed as one of the workers who are building the prisoner camp just outside the village."

"No, I'm afraid I didn't know her, though with the prison construction we've had more than the usual number of strangers about the village in recent weeks."

"You've never seen her in the cemetery, then?"

"No, I'd never seen her until this morning."

"Can you tell me how you came upon the body?"

"I was returning from a walk—I always take an early morning constitutional—when I heard a gunshot. I could tell that it came from the direction of the cemetery, so I went there and found the girl. Unfortunately, my wife, who had been in the house, followed me, though I hadn't realized at first that she'd done so. She must have heard the shot, too. I'm afraid she went right to pieces. She's never seen anyone in that state before. I took her back to the house and got her into bed and mixed her a sedative. Then I called the Home Guardsman who acts as our law enforcement hereabouts. I understood that we could not have people from the village gawking at the poor woman; it would have become a mess, and I was worried that it might frighten some of the children and elderly people. So I left Mr. Built, the guardsman, at the gate and came in and called the constabulary."

As Wimberly spoke, Lamb pulled a notebook from his pocket and scribbled a few lines in it with the stub of a pencil. "And how long did it take you, sir, to get your wife calmed down?" he asked.

"A good fifteen minutes or so."

"So what time was it, then, when you heard the shot?"

"It must have been just before seven, perhaps quarter till. I usually go out to walk at about six and am gone three-quarters of an hour or so."

"Did anyone see you while you were walking?"

"No."

"And what was your wife doing when you heard the shot?"

"She was in bed, sleeping. She doesn't rise as early as I."

"You don't seem to have been much affected by the incident, sir," Lamb said. "You seem rather calm, given the circumstances. And you seem to have acted rather calmly. Most people who suddenly come upon a dead body—particularly one that has been shot—would find themselves at least a bit stunned and confused."

"Well, I daresay you're right. But I suppose I lost my shock at seeing the dead in the last war." He looked toward the window for an instant.

"Yes," Lamb said. "I noticed your boots."

"Yes, well, I've kept them. I've often wondered why. And yet they've served me quite well. All these years later and they continue to hang together. I suppose you were part of it, too, then?"

"Yes."

"Yes, well it was all a terrible business. I've often asked God why it was necessary, why any of it is necessary, including this war. And I've never received an answer."

"You were in the infantry?" Lamb asked.

"Yes, captain of infantry."

"Did you keep your service pistol, then, sir?"

"I did, as a matter of fact. There was a time when I used it to shoot the occasional rat about the place. But I'm afraid it was stolen about a week or so ago."

Wimberly already had calculated that it would be a mistake to claim that he had not owned a Webley Mark VI revolver; for years he'd displayed the gun in an open box on the bookshelf in his study, a fact Lamb could easily ascertain by asking anyone in the village. Indeed, Wimberly had met Lamb wearing his old combat boots on the chance that Lamb was of a certain age and would recognize the boots for what they were and quiz him about his service, thereby providing him with a plausible explanation of why he, a country vicar, had owned such a weapon.

"Stolen?"

"Yes, someone broke into the house." He nodded at the window. "They came in through that window, as far as I can tell. I left it unlocked, I'm afraid. But then, I always have done. They took the pistol, which I kept in a wooden box there on the bookshelf"—he nodded toward the shelf to Lamb's left—"and some coins I'd left lying on my desk."

"Nothing else?" Lamb asked.

"No, nothing else."

"Did you report this burglary?"

"Well, I didn't see the need; I didn't care much about the pistol, really." He glanced at the window again. "I probably should not have kept it in any case." He looked back at Lamb. "And the coins amounted to almost nothing—less than a shilling. Whoever broke in almost surely was from Winstead. I suppose I was hoping they might come to me and confess without the prod of the police being involved. Then we might have turned a sin into something redemptive, you see."

Wimberly purposely paused for a second, as if thinking, then added, "If you do find the gun you'll know it for certain. The thing has a small nick in the right side of the barrel." The vicar had concluded that should Lamb inquire in the village about the pistol, this bit of information also would come out and he therefore should not seek to hide it. Indeed, in telling Lamb about the pistol's eccentric defect, he would be seen to be cooperating fully. He knew that he must play the angle with the pistol straight ahead or not at all.

"I see," Lamb said. "Yes, that's helpful."

Lamb abruptly stood and walked to the window, turning his back on Wimberly as he stared out at the flower garden. "Is your wife the gardener, then?" he asked.

"Yes. She has a bit of a green thumb."

"What sort of shoes does your wife wear, sir?"

"Shoes?"

Lamb turned to face Wimberly. "Yes."

"Well, the normal shoes, I suppose. Women's shoes."

"I wonder if I might see them. I assume, from what you told me, that you must have helped her off with her shoes when you put her to bed and sedated her, so you would know which pair she was wearing when the two of you were in the cemetery."

Wimberly hesitated again before answering. He calculated that he had nothing to fear from giving Lamb Wilhemina's shoes. Her shoe prints would be in the cemetery, as would his. He'd said that she had followed him there. Even so, the fact that Lamb seemed to have at least slightly outmaneuvered him—taken him a bit by surprise—made him secretly angry.

Wimberly stood. "Well, yes, you're right, Chief Inspector, I do know the pair," he said evenly. He was skillful at hiding his ire. Even so, he found himself unable to merely surrender the shoes without hinting to Lamb that he would not be easily cowed or outdone again. "I wonder if you wouldn't mind my asking why you need them."

"It's just routine, sir. My men will check the cemetery for footprints, of course. And we'll want to know whose are whose, so we can eliminate the innocent from our inquiries."

Wimberly managed a brief smile. "Yes, of course. If you'll wait here, then, I'll be right back."

Lamb nodded. "Thank you."

With Wimberly gone, Lamb tried the window—it opened easily; someone *might* have come through it. He walked to the bookshelf on which Wimberly claimed he'd kept his Webley in a wooden box. He found a spot on which such a box might have lain.

Wimberly returned to the room carrying a pair of brown women's shoes with slightly raised, one-inch square heels. Lamb thought they looked like the shoes that had made the impression he'd found in the cemetery.

"Thank you," Lamb said. "I wonder if you wouldn't mind my taking these out to my assistant so that he can make a plaster impression of them." He could have sent Larkin to Wimberly, but he wanted to inconvenience Wimberly and to see how Wimberly reacted to this. Someone who had something to hide might not quite be able to hide their concern or, perhaps, even their irritation, at the request. But Wimberly seemed unperturbed.

"Yes, of course," he said.

"I wonder, too, sir, if you wouldn't mind giving me *your* boots as well." Lamb smiled again. "My man will bring them back to you as soon as he's finished with them."

Wimberly returned the smile. "Yes, of course. However, I'm afraid I wasn't wearing these on my walk. Too bulky, you understand."

"Of course," Lamb said. "Can I have the shoes you were wearing then?"

Wimberly briefly left the room and returned holding a pair of well-worn, mud-stained black brogues. "Here you are," he said.

"Thank you," Lamb said. He held a pair of shoes in each hand. "Just a few more questions, sir. Do you have a maid or some other domestic help about the place? Someone who cleans up or works on the grounds?"

"Well, there is Miss White—Doris White—who lives in the village. My wife normally handles the arrangements with her. But when Miss White heard about all of the trouble up here this morning she called me and I told her not to come in today, for obvious reasons."

"Yes, I see," Lamb said. "And I will want to speak with your wife, too, of course."

"I'm afraid that she's not up to answering questions at the moment. Indeed, she's sleeping. I'm sorry."

"I understand. Later, then. Also, sir, I noticed an open grave in the cemetery. Can you tell me who that is for?"

"Miss Lila Tutin, a village woman—an elderly spinster. Her funeral is tomorrow."

"And what time is the funeral?"

"Eleven."

"This morning, when you called the constabulary to report finding the body, you failed to tell my sergeant that you had heard the gunshot or that it had been your hearing the shot that had alerted you to the trouble in the cemetery. Why was that, sir?"

Again, Wimberly became briefly silent, then smiled slightly.

"I suppose I wasn't as unaffected by the thing as I thought, then," he said. "I can only say that I simply forgot to mention that I'd heard the shot."

Lamb nodded. "Very well, then."

Wimberly saw Lamb to the door. Lamb held up the shoes. "We won't keep these long, sir."

"Take as long as you like, Chief Inspector."

As Wimberly watched Lamb disappear from sight around the front of the church, he shook his head. *Did I really not say that I'd heard the bloody shot?* He thought that he must get rid of his service pistol as soon as possible—though the notion came to him that he wouldn't mind shooting Lamb with it first.

SEVEN

—ɱ—

LAMB WENT BACK TO THE CEMETERY TO COLLECT WALLACE. HE
wanted to go next to the farm on which the government was
building the prisoner-of-war camp. Someone there surely would
have missed Ruth Aisquith by now. Indeed, he was surprised that
no one from the camp had come into the village looking for her.

Winston-Sheed had left for Winchester with Aisquith's body and
the area surrounding the cemetery had grown quiet. Lamb found
Wallace and Larkin exiting the cemetery through its front gate. While
Lamb was interviewing Gerald Wimberly, Wallace had found in the
grass just beyond the rear fence of the cemetery the slug that had passed
through Ruth Aisquith, and handed it over to Larkin. Now the lanky
forensics man showed the bullet to Lamb; although mangled, the slug
was unmistakably a .455 caliber.

"Likely a Webley," Larkin said, touching the bridge of his glasses, which had slipped down his nose. "Not sure which vintage, though."

Lamb glanced back in the direction of the vicarage. "The vicar owns a Mark VI; he claims it was stolen a week ago, but that he never reported the theft."

"Do you believe him?" Wallace asked.

"I don't know," Lamb said.

Vera joined them at the gate, which made Lamb smile. "Ready for another drive?" he asked.

"Always."

"I hope it hasn't been too boring for you."

"Not at all. I actually had an interesting conversation with a few of the women from the village—well, a couple of women and a girl, really. One of them claimed there's been a rash of egg thefts from the nests of the local nuthatch population. Seems people are stealing them for food—or so the oldest of the three claimed. She was very strange, eccentric—sort of chaotic, but passionate. She made me promise to tell you, and now I have."

"We'll get right on that, then," Wallace said. He winked at Vera, who smiled at him warmly.

Vera's smile caught Lamb's attention. *My, my*, he thought. He well knew that women tended to fall for Wallace, who was tall, dark-haired, intelligent, witty, and confident. But even beyond these qualities, Wallace possessed *something* that was hard to define that attracted feminine attention. Lamb could not quite define this quality—he thought it had something to do with an obvious penchant for action over reticence. Lamb long had hoped that when the time came, Vera would truly fall in love with the man of her choice, rather than merely fall under his spell, though he understood that he possessed no power whatever to control any of this.

He hoped that Vera possessed sense enough to recognize what men offered to her and what they withheld, and why. Only a year before, she'd had a bad experience with a young man in Quimby who'd died in the freak German bombing in that village. She'd kept her relationship with the young man a secret from him and Marjorie, though after the boy had been killed, Vera had told them everything. The boy had been slightly older than Vera and had managed to convince her that he was a far different person than he actually was; in fact, he'd been jealous, controlling, and potentially violent. The story that Vera had told Lamb about the boy—he was a man, really; Lamb wondered now why he continued to think of Arthur Lear as a boy—had forced him to admit that he'd too long denied his daughter's natural adult desires and aspirations.

Lamb also knew of at least one of Wallace's darker aspects—his drinking. Though Wallace seemed to have given up the bottle, only a year earlier the detective sergeant had been on the verge of sinking into an alcoholic haze. But Wallace had managed to right himself, partly with Lamb's assistance and encouragement, along with a few well-placed threats about where Wallace would end up if he persisted in his drinking. Lamb had made it clear to Wallace that if he lost his policeman's job thanks to alcohol, as a man in his mid-twenties, he'd go right into the war.

That said, Lamb liked Wallace. Despite Wallace's overreliance on a kind of outward charm, he was dependable, a good detective, and physically courageous in a way Lamb knew that he himself never quite had been, unless it was in defense of his wife or daughter, someone crucial to *him*. But Wallace would think nothing of running into a burning building to save a bloody dog. Since the beginning of the war, Lamb had done whatever had been in his power to keep Wallace, Larkin, and the other young men who worked under him out of combat and danger, just as he was now doing what he could to keep Vera free of it. That said, he couldn't have his detective sergeant bird-dogging his nineteen-year-old daughter, especially while they were on the clock.

"Maybe you'd prefer that I put you on that nuthatch matter right now, David," Lamb said to Wallace without smiling.

Wallace seemed to get the message. He lost the charming smile and nodded.

"Sir," he said.

—m—

The farm on which the government was building its prison camp for Italians lay about a half-mile west of the village, just off the road that became Winstead's High Street.

A rutted dirt lane led from the main paved road to the farmhouse. Before the government workers had arrived a month earlier, the farm had stood vacant and unused for a decade, and its twenty-seven acres, along with its abandoned house, barn, and sheds, had become badly overgrown in a tangle of underbrush and young trees, all of which had to be cleared to make way for the prison. Before that, Lawrence Tigue had lived on the farm with his mother and younger brother, whose names Lamb could not now remember, though they had popped up in the newspaper accounts of the O'Hare suicide twenty years earlier. Lamb was surprised to see no guard posted at the head of the lane.

Vera drove slowly, carefully, down the pockmarked dirt road. The land on either side of the lane was roughly cleared; the soil was churned up, soggy and dark from recent rain and spotted with fallen trees, stumps, and piles of cut brush. In the field to their right, two women were tossing bits and pieces of vegetative detritus into the back of a battered lorry that nearly was up to its fenders in mud.

At the end of the road, two dozen large dark green canvas tents stood in two parallel rows, creating a kind of muddy street between them. The scene reminded Lamb of the rear echelon camps to which the army had sent him as a respite from the hell of the Somme. Since that time he invariably connected the sight of such tents with memories of hot food, ample cigarettes, relatively clean toilets, a bath, and a temporary relief from the ceaseless anxiety, backlogged sexual longing, and endless threat to one's life that constituted the primary fact of front-line combat.

Vera pulled the Wolseley to a stop at the edge of the encampment, which smelled of freshly turned earth and burning wood. About thirty meters to their left, a number of men were clearing away what remained of the stone foundation of the farmhouse, breaking the stonework into pieces with sledgehammers and hauling it away in wheelbarrows to a rubble pile.

A man dressed in the uniform of the regular army was the first to approach them as they exited the car; Lamb saw that the man possessed the rank of corporal. He asked them their business; Lamb flashed his warrant card and asked to see the camp's commander. The corporal took what Lamb thought was an inordinate amount of time to read his identification before handing it back.

"All right, then," he said in a northern accent. "I'll take you to Captain Walton."

Vera waited at the car as Lamb and Wallace followed the corporal down the lane that led between the tents—which, to combat the mud, had been corduroyed with lengths of old timber torn from the former house and barn—to its end, where they found two additional tents that were slightly larger and detached from the others, facing down the lane rather than alongside it. The corporal led them to the one on the right and asked them to wait outside.

A minute later a man dressed in the uniform of an infantry captain emerged from the tent. Lamb put the captain at perhaps forty and concluded that either he was a contemporary who had remained in the service after the first war or had volunteered again at the outbreak of the latest one. The officer nodded at Lamb and Wallace in greeting. "Good morning, gentlemen," he said. "I'm Captain Walton, the camp commander. How may I help you?"

Lamb introduced himself and Wallace. "I'm afraid we have troubling news for you, sir," he said. "We're investigating the likely murder of a woman whom we believe worked in this camp. Her name is Ruth Aisquith. I'm afraid she was found shot to death this morning in Winstead."

Lamb handed Walton Ruth Aisquith's identity card. "This was found in the woman's possession."

Walton stared at the card for a few seconds, then softly said, "My God."

"So she did work here, then, sir?" Lamb asked.

Walton looked up. He seemed genuinely stunned. "Yes, yes, she did, of course, Chief Inspector, I'm sorry. She was a conscript. A cook in the camp mess, and other duties, as needed. She was a Land girl." He looked again at the identity card, then at Lamb. "She also was a conscientious objector," he added. "Or, at least, she had been. She was shot, you say?"

"Yes," Lamb said. He didn't want to reveal too much to Walton yet. "She appears to have been shot while visiting the cemetery of Saint Michael's Church in the village."

"And you've no idea who did it?"

"I was hoping you might help me with that."

Walton straightened his shoulders. "Yes, of course," he said. "I'm sorry, but you can imagine the shock of hearing this. I can't think of any reason why anyone would have shot Ruth Aisquith, or anyone from the camp. We've only been here a month."

Lamb found himself surprised to hear that Ruth Aisquith had been a conscientious objector. Though he hadn't thought about it until that very moment, he realized that the newly instituted conscription of women must have led some women, as conscription had some men, to protest the call-up on religious or other grounds. He knew little about the fates of such people other than that they were required to plead their cases for exemption to local tribunals. In some cases the tribunals approved the request, though in many cases—most, Lamb thought—they did not. Those whose requests were denied but continued to defy conscription could be jailed, and some were. He wondered if Ruth Aisquith's refusal to serve the war effort, while others were doing so and dying in the process, might have caused someone to kill her, especially someone who had lost a loved one to the war.

"Was Miss Aisquith a Quaker?" Lamb asked.

"No," Walton said. "Not that I am aware of."

"Given that she was a conscientious objector, why was she here, then, sir? You said that she was a conscript."

"She was a conscript, yes. The camp is staffed by them, men and women both, and some contract workers. She originally had declared herself a conscientious objector but was one no longer, you see. She'd objected at first to performing fire-watching service on the grounds that she did not believe in military conscription. A tribunal rejected her plea and she was sent to prison for several months for her further refusal to comply. She then changed her mind at some point and agreed to go to join the Women's Land Army and was assigned here; we have six Land girls here. They work in the laundry or the mess or do other light duty. In agreeing to work here, Miss Aisquith effectively ended her objection to conscription. Basically, she changed her mind, as I said. That's the way I understand it, at any rate, though frankly I never questioned her on it and I treated her as I treated all the conscripts. It's rare, I grant you—a female objector—but she was a good worker." He looked a third time at the identity card and shook his head. "I find it impossible to believe that she's been shot."

"I take it that the men's and women's quarters are kept separate."

"Of course, though they take meals at the same time, to keep things simple."

"Was Miss Aisquith's status as a conscientious objector known to others in the camp?"

"As far as I know, yes. It's not the kind of thing that is kept secret. It's part of her official record."

"Did anyone object to her stance—perhaps someone who has lost a relative or loved one in the war?"

"Well, there was some grumbling, I suppose, as there normally would be in such situations, but nothing that would lead you to believe that someone here might want her dead. If there was, I should think I'd have heard about it."

"Do you know of anyone, specifically, who voiced objections to Miss Aisquith's attitude toward war service?"

"I'm afraid not, no, Chief Inspector. Frankly, you'd be better off asking Mr. Taney—George Taney—such questions. He's the main contractor on the job here; he's a builder from Southampton and has more direct contact with the workers than do I. We're not wasting prime military bodies on the construction of this place, you see. Nearly all of the work is being done by the less desirable conscripts—by women and by men who are either too old for combat service or who are at the low end of the fitness scale—along with civilians employed by Taney. All of them can handle a shovel or an axe well enough. Corporal Baker, who escorted you here, and I are the only regular army people on the site. My job is administrative—to see to it that the work is done correctly and on time and budget."

Walton likely kept a well-organized and up-to-date filing system in his tent, Lamb thought. Meanwhile, he'd not bothered to post a guard at the camp's entrance and had been unaware that one of the people for whom he was responsible had for several hours been lying dead with a bullet wound in her back three-quarters of a mile away. Walton didn't even seem to have known that Ruth Aisquith was absent from the camp.

"We have taken possession of Miss Aisquith's body in order to perform an autopsy," Lamb said. "And there will be an inquest into the cause of her death. But we will coordinate that with the correct military authorities."

"Yes, of course," Walton said.

"I also must ask you, Captain Walton, if you were aware that Miss Aisquith had left the camp this morning."

"I was aware, yes, though I assumed that she had returned by her usual time." He raised his chin slightly. "Perhaps I shouldn't have assumed."

"She left the camp this morning with your permission, then?"

"Yes. Everyone who works here is allowed a certain amount of leave. When she first arrived here, she told Mr. Taney that her grandmother was buried in the cemetery in Winstead and asked his permission to visit the grave on occasion. He in turned asked me, and I approved it. I saw no reason to reject her request. She was not troublesome in any way, as I said. She went into the village a couple of mornings a week and always returned by the proper time—seven thirty A.M."

"Did she give you her grandmother's name?" Lamb asked.

"No. And I'm sorry to say that I didn't ask. Perhaps I should have."

"Does the name Mary Forrest mean anything to you, sir?"

"No, I'm afraid it doesn't."

"How about Lila Tutin?"

"No."

Lamb didn't know quite what else to say to Walton. The captain seemed to have ceded much of his command of the camp to George Taney.

"Where can I find Mr. Taney?" Lamb asked.

"I'll have Corporal Baker take you to him." Walton summoned Baker and ordered him to escort Lamb and Wallace to where Taney was working. "If I can be of any more assistance, you only need ask," he told Lamb.

"I'll want to see whatever files you have on Miss Aisquith and to search her billet. We'll also want to question the employees here."

"You have my permission."

Lamb wondered how much weight Walton's permission actually carried.

"Thank you, sir," he said. Then he and Wallace followed Corporal Baker in the direction of George Taney.

EIGHT

—⁂—

LAMB AND WALLACE REJOINED VERA AT THE CAR. LAMB POINTED to the two women toiling in the field whom they'd passed as they'd entered the farm. Thus far, the two were the only women any of them had seen about the place.

"Why don't you try those two while I speak to Taney," Lamb told Wallace. "They would have billeted with Aisquith."

Wallace gazed in the direction of the women. "Right," he said.

Lamb found George Taney directing a green lorry that was backing up to the pile of stone rubble the workers had removed from the foundation of the farmhouse. GEORGE TANEY. BUILDER AND CONTRACTOR. SOUTHAMPTON was printed in white letters on the lorry's door. Taney was a well-built man, close to six feet tall, with brown, close-cropped hair and tanned, sinewy arms protruding from the rolled-up sleeves of a green cotton work shirt.

"Stop it there!" Taney shouted at the lorry driver. He gestured to a waiting trio of men in denim clothes who began to shovel the debris into the back of the lorry. Nearby, a half-dozen other men continued to toil in the rectangular space that once had formed the basement of the house. Taney noticed Baker approaching with Lamb and stepped away from the ruckus to meet them. Taney nodded at the corporal. "Baker," he said.

"Police want a word with you, Mr. Taney," Baker said. He nodded at Lamb then abruptly departed without saying anything more, leaving Lamb with the distinct impression that Baker didn't like Taney and probably resented having to take orders from a civilian.

Lamb showed Taney his warrant card and introduced himself. He detected no surprise or concern in Taney's eyes at the sudden appearance of a policeman. He thought that Taney must have known by then that Ruth Aisquith was absent and yet he'd apparently said nothing about this to Walton. Taney possessed a domineering physical presence that some people—including, perhaps, Walton—likely found intimidating, Lamb thought. Taney wiped grime from his hands on a yellow rag then vigorously shook Lamb's hand.

"What can I do for you?" he asked.

Lamb decided not to dawdle with Taney. He wanted to see if Taney expressed genuine surprise or shock at the news of Ruth Aisquith's death. "Are you aware that Ruth Aisquith is dead?" he asked.

Taney's face clouded. "Dead?" he asked.

"I'm afraid so. She was found shot to death in Winstead just a few hours ago."

Taney didn't answer for several seconds. He glanced at the surroundings, as if he'd lost something small and personal and knew that the bloody thing had to be somewhere nearby, he'd only just been holding it. He looked again at Lamb, as if he expected to find what he was searching for in the spot where Lamb stood but instead had found something different and unsuspected.

"Shot?" he said.

"Yes," Lamb said. "Someone shot her in the back as she was visiting the cemetery by the church there. I take it you knew she was absent this morning."

"Yes," Taney said. "Yes, I knew she was absent." He became silent again, as if thinking—trying to remember: Where *did* I leave the bloody thing? Even so, his seeming confusion and sudden vulnerability—which Lamb thought *might* be genuine—did not lessen his commanding presence.

"Did her absence not concern you? I've just spoken to Captain Walton and he had no idea that she was missing from the camp."

Taney shook his head slightly. "Well, he wouldn't, would he?"

Lamb repeated his question: "So Miss Aisquith's absence didn't concern you?"

Taney sighed heavily. He seemed to be trying to regain his composure. "No—no it didn't," he said. "I had given her the entire morning as leave; she wasn't due back to the camp until after ten." The time was a little past noon.

"Why did you give Miss Aisquith such generous leave this morning?"

Taney stood straighter. He looked directly down at Lamb, who believed that Taney was attempting to overawe him—to do what he'd done to Captain Walton and, perhaps, everyone he met.

"She'd earned it," he said. "She'd worked very hard the past week. And she liked to go into the village and pay her respects to her late grandmother. She normally went into the village very early and returned in time for breakfast and the start of the workday. Yesterday, she asked for the extra time and I granted it."

"Did she tell you her grandmother's name?"

"No."

"Did she have living relatives in Winstead or mention the names Mary Forrest or Lila Tutin?"

"No." Taney's face clouded slightly again, as if he'd just remembered the topic of their conversation. "You say Ruth was shot?" he asked. "But who in bloody hell would shoot her?"

"I thought that you might know, sir."

"Me? Why would I know?"

"You are as good a person as any. You were her boss."

Taney's face reddened slightly. He seemed to be getting angry; Lamb guessed that he'd learned to be free with his anger—that others rarely insisted he rein it in. "I barely knew her, other than from what she did here, on the job."

"Why did she want the extra time this morning?"

"I think she intended to buy a few things in the shops."

"What sorts of things?"

"I don't know."

"I assume you knew that Miss Aisquith was a conscientious objector," Lamb asked.

"Of course."

"Do you approve of conscientious objection?"

"I've no complaint as long as it's actually based in religious belief. I've no use for people who use it as an excuse for shirking their duty."

Lamb thought that Taney could have followed Ruth Aisquith into Winstead, shot her to death in the cemetery while the village and work camp still mostly were asleep, then returned to the camp without anyone knowing. The fact that he remained a civilian—along with the manner in which he seemed to have wrested control of the camp from Walton—would allow him nearly complete freedom of movement. His motive might have been that he despised Ruth Aisquith as a shirker, but Lamb doubted that. If Taney killed her, his motive likely was that she'd sexually spurned him. He thought that George Taney didn't much countenance being spurned. But he was merely guessing, of course, playing the odds. Behind Taney, the men continued to load dusty wheelbarrow loads of broken rock into the lorry.

"Do you know of anyone here who objected to her stance on war duties?"

"No."

"What did Ruth Aisquith do here?"

"Same as the other women—light duties, laundry, cooking, clearing brush, fetching and carrying. Someone has to do it, and there simply aren't enough men now. We have six women working here."

"Did you frequently allow her extra leave?"

Taney glanced back at the men wheeling the broken rock to the lorry, as if signaling that he was growing impatient. He turned back to Lamb. "No," he said. "This morning was the first time. But as I told you, she had earned it by working harder than most."

An empty lorry like the one that was backed up to the rock pile was coming up the dirt entrance road toward them. Taney turned toward the foundation of the farmhouse and whistled shrilly. The men who were working there looked up in unison. "Head off that lorry, Jenkins," Taney ordered. "The other one's nearly finished." The man named Jenkins nodded, dropped his shovel, hopped out of the foundation, and began to jog toward the lorry.

Taney turned back to Lamb. "Is that all, then?" he asked. "As you can see, I've work to do."

Lamb thought it odd that Taney suddenly had concluded that heading off a lorry was more important than discovering as much as Lamb was willing to tell him about Ruth Aisquith's death. But people showed their shock and grief in unique ways. Either that, or Taney felt no actual shock or grief.

"That's all," Lamb said. "For now."

—⁓—

Wallace lingered for a moment by the car with Vera. He lit a cigarette and leaned against the bonnet. He'd begun smoking a year earlier, as a substitute for drinking, which he'd sworn off, partly to save his job and—he'd eventually come to understand—probably his life. In hindsight, he was able to see how close he'd been to falling into a kind of abyss. Despite the effort he'd put into hiding his drinking—and the success he'd believed he'd had in that—he hadn't fooled Lamb, who'd picked up on his distress.

Then he'd bollixed an assignment and found himself in Superintendent Harding's doghouse. Lamb had pulled his arse from that sling and, in the process, presented him with a kind of ultimatum grounded in common sense. Lamb had made it clear that if he slipped too deeply into a bottle he would lose his job, and if he lost his job, he would find himself in the thick of the war. And it was Lamb who'd backed his application for deferment from conscription on the grounds that he was needed for police work. He was glad to have kicked drink and, yet, at the same time mourned the fact that being sober seemed to have drained him of some of the swagger and charm he'd long depended on to see him through. He couldn't help but feel that, over the past year, he'd somehow become softer.

As he leaned against the car, smoking, he wondered about the deferment. Earlier, Built had made a point of bringing up the death of Nate Goodson, Winstead's former bobby, making obvious reference to Wallace's protection from combat duty. Now, he'd found out that Ruth Aisquith had been a conchi. None of it seemed to him just, or fair, or to make any sense. At that moment, the world seemed to him to contain two basic types of people: those who did their duty by the country and those who didn't. Some who didn't had excuses for taking a pass, including himself, though his excuse was beginning to seem less and less legitimate as the war continued. He didn't agree with conscientious objection. The threat from Germany was too real to merely object and turn away from it, as if the bloody war didn't interest you. And yet, for some reason, Ruth Aisquith seemed to have had a change of heart—as he now seemed to be having. Or maybe she'd just discovered that she didn't much fancy prison.

In the spring of 1940, his first cousin—the youngest son of his mother's oldest sister—had been killed in France while waiting to be taken off at Dunkirk. Alan had been killed on the beach, waiting his turn to get aboard one of the transports home, by a pilot in a lone Messerschmitt who had shown up briefly one morning and strafed the beach a single time. Alan had been supremely unlucky—one of those who had been in the wrong place at the wrong time, and his death had crushed the boy's mother. He'd sent his condolences to his aunt, of course, but what bloody good were condolences? Wallace wondered if Nate Goodson had met a fate similar to Alan's—if his death had been freakish and spectacularly unlucky.

He knew that some of those who had qualified for an occupational deferment from conscription declined the pass and enlisted. He admired their courage and questioned his own. In the beginning, he had told himself that he could not go into the service because he struggled with drink; he now sometimes worried that going into the war might reignite his problems with liquor. And yet he had never been able to fully dismiss from his mind the idea that his unwillingness to enlist and take his chances with the others amounted to cowardice, purely and simply, and that his concerns about drink were nothing more than a cover for that cravenness. Although he understood and accepted, in an intellectual fashion, the argument that the country needed its policemen to remain on duty at home, he had once or twice in recent months considered quitting the police force to join the army, though he'd always drawn back in the end. Now, with his latest deferment due to expire in little more than a month, Wallace had begun debating with himself anew about whether he should make the leap—to make himself available for combat, for probable death or mutilation.

He leaned against the car for a moment, deep in thought, silently finishing his smoke.

Vera moved next to him and asked for a cigarette. Earlier, when her father had ordered Wallace to interview the two women in the field, she had been surprised to feel a twinge of jealousy that the women were soon to become the temporary possessors of Wallace's full attention, while she once again stayed behind with the car.

Wallace turned to her, frankly surprised, and smiled. "Since when do you smoke?" he asked.

She shrugged. "I don't know. A while." She returned his smile. "I'm of age, you know."

He wondered if Lamb knew that his daughter smoked and if giving Vera a cigarette was out of line. He didn't want to be caught corrupting the chief inspector's daughter.

"My father won't mind," Vera said, as if she'd read his thoughts.

"All right, then." Wallace fished a cigarette from the packet and lit it for her. She took her first puff like a pro and blew the smoke into the air in front of them.

"You've done this before, then," Wallace said.

"Did you think I was lying?"

"I suppose not." He smiled again.

"You were thinking that, because I'm the chief inspector's daughter, I couldn't possibly smoke. Is that it?"

That was it exactly—or, at least partially. He thought that, in some way, it might be hard to be Lamb's daughter. Lamb was one of those men whose favor other people sought. Besides that, he possessed an uncanny ability to root out other people's secrets.

"No," Wallace said. He smoked his cigarette down to where he could no longer hold it then dropped it into the grass and trod on it. "Well, back to work," he said.

"Can I go with you?" Vera asked. "I get bored just hanging about the car. I wouldn't mind seeing a little detective work—seeing how it's done."

Wallace glanced across the field, to where Lamb was interviewing Taney. Earlier, Lamb had cuffed him behind the ears for flirting with Vera. He looked at Vera, who was leaning against the bonnet, as he had been, casually smoking. Something about the cigarette made her seem older. She was a good-looking girl; her curves were easy to discern even beneath the ill-fitting, baggy uniform. And she had something else, too—confidence and wit. She was nineteen; he was twenty-five. It wasn't much of a difference, really, when one thought about it. Plenty of girls went off and got bloody well married at nineteen.

"Sure," he said and made a little gesture with his head, inviting her to fall in with him.

Vera dropped her cigarette in the grass and said, "Splendid."

"How are you liking the job, then?" he asked Vera as they walked into the field. "Aside from the boredom, I mean."

"It's not bad—though I know why my father has gotten me the job. He's trying to keep me from being conscripted, which is lovely of him, but it makes me feel guilty."

The words pierced Wallace. "Why do you feel guilty?"

"I don't know—nepotism and all that. Not everyone has a father who can set it up for them to stay out of it. It's obviously not fair. Besides nobody likes someone whose relative has paved the way. They resent it, and I don't blame them. I'd resent it, too. Anyway, it's not permanent."

Wallace looked at her. "I don't resent you."

Vera smiled at him. "Yes, but I didn't take *your* job."

"True."

They walked for a few seconds without speaking. Then Wallace said, "I know what you mean about the guilt, though. I feel it myself at times, with the deferral. I think, why should I be protected?"

He hadn't quite meant to say it in a way that sounded as if he were complaining. Indeed, he found himself surprised to find that he mentioned his guilt at all. He doubted that Vera wanted to hear his grievances.

"Well, you're a policeman and needed here," Vera said in a forthright way that made Wallace believe that she was sincere, which made him feel grateful. "Not everyone can go off to war. If they did, the country would collapse."

"Yes, but when you're a man my age, people wonder. They want to know: *Why are you here and my Johnny isn't?*" He looked at her. "It's especially bad with women, by the way. They hate that their husband or son or sweetheart has gone away while you're still here drinking tea and reading the Sunday papers."

"Well, I'm not that way," Vera said simply.

The women in the field left off from their labor as Wallace and Vera neared them. Wallace wondered where the other women in the camp were and guessed that they must be employed indoors at domestic labor, cooking and cleaning. Walton had said that Ruth Aisquith and the other women were members of the Land Army. Wallace didn't know much about the Land Army, though he'd thought that the girls who joined it did farm work. The women had been clearing away underbrush that a bulldozer had churned up, which, he thought, probably was close enough to qualify as farm work. Both wore denim coveralls, brown leather boots, and thick cotton gloves. The taller of the two wore a yellow bandanna on her head. She held a cigarette firmly in her lips and squinted at Wallace and Vera through a haze of drifting smoke. The other woman was shorter and heavier.

"Good morning, ladies," Wallace said. "I'm Detective Sergeant David Wallace of the Hampshire police." He nodded toward Vera. "This is Auxiliary Constable Lamb," he said, endowing her with an official rank that he made up on the spot. "We were wondering if we might have a word."

The taller woman removed the cigarette from her mouth. "About what?" she said.

She was, Wallace thought, in her mid to late twenties. She was slender—skinny really—with curly, disheveled, shoulder-length brown hair that had tiny bits of hay stuck in it. The smaller woman had straight, silky brown hair, cut short at the ears, and large green eyes. Wallace noticed the smaller woman glance at him, and then quickly look away. He concluded from the taller one's question that neither of them knew the fate of Ruth Aisquith. He thought that there was nothing for it but to plunge in.

"I've some bad news, I'm afraid. Ruth Aisquith was found dead this morning in Winstead."

Both women appeared to freeze; neither of them spoke for several seconds. The smaller one looked at Wallace with an expression on her face that seemed to say that she hoped that the news he'd just delivered to them was part of some bizarre joke. "What do you mean that she's dead?" she asked quietly.

"She died this morning," Wallace said. Something in the disbelieving way the smaller woman looked at him—almost as if she were a child for whom the fact of death still was alien—pierced Wallace and he decided that he must be gentle with her. "Can you tell me your name please, miss?" he asked her.

But the taller woman answered. "Her name is Nora Bancroft; I'm Marlene Suggs—Corporal Suggs, Women's Land Army, officially. How did she die—Ruth?"

"I'm afraid that she was shot."

"Oh, no," Nora whispered. She drew her arms tightly about herself; Marlene put her arm around Nora and said, "There now." Nora put her face in her hands and began to cry. The two women stood together for a minute, saying nothing, while Nora cried. Marlene squeezed Nora. "There, there," she repeated. She coaxed Nora into revealing her face and pushed a moist strand of Nora's brown hair from her forehead. Vera stood by watching, transfixed but uncomfortable. Nora seemed to have cared for Ruth Aisquith, she thought.

"I wonder if you're up to answering a few questions?" Wallace asked.

Nora wiped her eyes with her right hand, leaving a vague muddy streak on her forehead.

Marlene looked across the road to the place, about a hundred meters distant, where Lamb was standing with George Taney. "All right," she said.

"Did Miss Aisquith have any family in Winstead or any personal relationships with anyone there?" Wallace asked.

"If she did, she never mentioned them to us," Marlene said. She looked at Nora. "Then again, she didn't talk much to me and Nora, did she Nora?"

"No," Nora whispered.

"I always thought she considered us not quite good enough," Marlene said. "She had a haughtiness to her. Spent a lot of her time reading books." She shook her head. "Nah—me and Nora weren't up to her level, or so she thought."

"It sounds as if you didn't like her much, miss," Wallace said.

"Well, I had nothing against her, mind. I hardly knew her. But I'm not one to go begging attention from one who's got it in her mind that she's better than me."

"Did you know that Miss Aisquith had gone out this morning?" Wallace asked.

"We knew," Marlene said.

"Was it unusual for her to go out so early in the morning?"

"She went out in the morning to visit her grandmother's grave in Winstead. She went several times a week. Taney allowed it. She came back in time to help serve breakfast; that was one of her jobs here."

"Did she ever fail to return for breakfast?"

"Not that I remember," Marlene said.

"How about you, Miss Bancroft?"

Nora shook her head and sniffled. "No."

"Do you know if she ever visited anyone while she was in the village?"

"As I said, if she did, she said nothing to us about it."

"Did she ever mention the name Mary Forrest?"

"No, who is that?"

Wallace smiled. "It's not important," he said. "What about the other women in the camp—did she have friendly relationships with any of them, or perhaps some of the men?"

"Not that I could see. Some of the men try it on with us, of course, but we're not allowed to fraternize."

"Where was she found?" Nora asked.

"In the cemetery."

"Was it bad?"

"I'm afraid it was, yes."

Nora put her hand to her mouth.

"Did Miss Aisquith mention anything to either of you about someone she might have had a disagreement or row with?"

"No," Marlene said. "But it wouldn't surprise me if she did. She was pig-headed—a conchi. She went to prison rather than join the fire-watching service. Then she ended up here."

"Did it bother anyone here that she was a conchi?"

"A few, I suppose."

"Do you know who, specifically?"

"Some of the men, I suppose. Nobody talked about it. If you must know, I didn't much fancy the idea myself. Times such as these, everyone has a duty. Apparently she thought herself too fine to do hers. Let someone else do her duty and yet she reaps the reward, if you know what I mean."

"Did she ever talk about—mention—that someone might have threatened her because she was a conchi?"

"No."

"Did she speak to either of you about anything that might have been troubling her?"

"She hardly said good morning to either of us."

Nora stood with her arms still wrapped about her and looking away from Wallace toward the wood that bordered the field. Wallace concluded that he would get nothing more useful from either of the women for the moment. He would speak that day to many other people in the camp and some of them surely would know more than these two, he thought. He raised his hat and said, "Thank you, ladies."

As Vera and Wallace turned for the car, Marlene, clearly speaking to Vera, said, "I didn't know they let girls join the police."

Vera turned to Marlene and smiled. She didn't like Marlene and had concluded that Marlene sought to control and bully Nora and that Ruth Aisquith probably was nowhere near as bad as Marlene portrayed her. Class envy emanated from Marlene like heat from a fire, Vera thought.

"They don't," Vera said. "I'm only a driver."

"Meaning you know somebody in high places, then?" Marlene said.

The words stung Vera because they were true. But she retained her smile. "Something like that," she said.

—◊◊—

They found Lamb waiting for them by the Wolseley, smoking a cigarette. Wallace secretly was cheered by Lamb's unbreakable addiction to tobacco; it humanized Lamb, who seemed otherwise to be free of vice and weakness. Even so, Wallace felt a bit concerned that Lamb had returned to the car before he and Vera had, given that Lamb obviously now could see that Vera had gone with him to interview Marlene and Nora.

Vera spoke up first, hoping to blunt any inquiry into the matter her father might feel it necessary to launch. "I tagged along, Dad," she said. "I hope you don't mind. It was my idea." She smiled at her father warmly. "I was a little bored and decided I might get a little on-the-job training."

Wallace thought that Vera's sudden chattiness made her sound guilty, as if she were confessing to a crime before anyone could accuse her of one.

Lamb smiled. He also thought that Vera's explanation contained a hint of confession. He cast a brief, wary eye Wallace's way, which Wallace did not fail to notice.

"Did you learn anything?" Lamb asked.

"At least one of them—a Miss Suggs—disliked and envied Ruth Aisquith," Wallace said. "Otherwise, Aisquith mostly kept to herself— at least according to Suggs."

Lamb raised his eyebrows in acknowledgment of this information.

"Suggs said that Aisquith didn't get on well with most of the other women in the camp; called her haughty. The other one, a Miss Bancroft, seemed genuinely broken up at the news of Aisquith's death, though. If Aisquith had any family or close contacts in the village, she didn't speak to either of these women of them."

"All right, then," Lamb said to Wallace. "I want you to stick here for the moment. Search Aisquith's file and billet and talk to as many people as you can."

Lamb added that he and Vera would return to Winstead to check on the progress of the inquiry there and would pick Wallace up later in the day before heading back to Winchester.

Lamb thought for a moment on what seemed to be blossoming between his daughter and his detective sergeant. If Vera and Wallace were sending romantic signals to one another, he would have to keep an eye on that. He didn't want Wallace distracted or Vera hurt. He believed he had the right—even the duty—to step between them if their flirting compromised the inquiry. Otherwise, he would have to let Vera follow her path.

—⁂—

Late that afternoon, one of the men who were digging in the foundation of the farmhouse shoved the point of his spade into the moist ground and felt it strike something solid. The man's name was Charlie Kinkaid; he was thirty-seven years old and had lived all of his life in Winstead and had been glad to land one of the civilian jobs helping to build the prison camp. The job kept him close to his wife and three children, though since taking it he saw them on weekends only. The rest of the time he lived in the camp, with the other conscripts.

Believing he'd hit a stone, Charlie pulled back on the spade, worked its tip beneath the obstruction, and leveraged it into the daylight. A slender gray bone about two inches long came up in the loosened earth. It looked aged.

Likely from a dog or cat, Charlie thought, though he couldn't recall anybody ever having owned a dog at the Tigue place. Of course, he hadn't come to the farm much when Mrs. Tigue—Olivia—had run it; he'd found Olivia Tigue and her two sons to be rather strange and never had been friendly with either of the boys. Lawrence especially had struck him as weak and aloof, wholly unappealing—though now Lawrence was the bloody chairman of the Winstead parish council and head of the village's civil defense. At any rate, he reasoned, there must have been a cat or two around the place. Most farms had cats to keep away the mice and rats. And there had been that problem with the cats in the village, a year before the mess with Claire O'Hare. A few people had said then that they believed that the cats had come from the Tigue farm. But even as Charlie considered this scenario, another possible explanation for the bone's presence in the foundation crowded into his consciousness. He'd been seventeen when Claire had committed suicide and Sean O'Hare had run off with their twin sons, and he remembered the case well. He'd known Sean well enough and found the man to be a louse; he also had known, as everyone in the village had, that Claire had been a terrible mother to the twins and that Sean had beaten her. And even before the disappearance of Sean and the twins, whispers had gone around the village that Sean seemed to be spending an inordinate amount of time on the Tigue farm and that Olivia Tigue was hardly a saint.

He picked up the small bone and weighed it in his hand. He told himself that it couldn't be—that such thinking was macabre. He thought that perhaps he entertained such dark thoughts because the Aisquith woman had been shot to death in the village that morning. That had set the men's tongues wagging, and Charlie himself quietly had wondered whether Aisquith had upset Taney in some way. Either that or she'd been at it with someone in the village; all of her early-morning trips into Winstead hadn't been to visit someone dead, but someone very much alive, he and the other men had concluded. Then that little arrangement had gone wrong somehow and the result was that Ruth had ended up shot. That was the talk, at any rate.

Charlie looked at the bone and considered tossing it away but found that he couldn't quite. He would show it to Taney and see what the boss thought. The bell rang to signal that it was time to wash up for tea. Charlie put his shovel aside, put the bone in his shirt pocket, and went to his evening meal.

NINE

—ɯ—

THAT NIGHT, WINSTEAD CAME ALIVE WITH CLANDESTINE MOVEMENT.

At half past midnight, a short, plump woman named Doris White left her cottage in the village and walked toward Saint Michael's Church along the narrow footpath that led from the center of Winstead toward its western boundary. For three years Doris daily had cleaned the chapel and vicarage of Saint Michael's under the eye of Wilhemina Wimberly, the vicar's wife, who despised Doris.

In turn, Doris saw Wilhemina as a nasty *frau* who reveled in barking orders and criticisms. Gerald's collars must have exactly the right amount of starch to them; the tea service must be stored in the cupboard in just a certain way; the candlesticks in the chapel must never be smudged. The candlesticks must shine, Wilhemina once had told Doris, just as her husband shined every Sunday in the pulpit. Now, though, the triangular relationship the three of them shared was about to change for good and all, Doris thought as she headed up the path in the dark.

A nearly full moon shone in a clear sky alive with stars. Doris moved past the rear of the cemetery and behind the church to the vicarage. The bedroom on the second floor—*their* bedroom—was dark. The only light came from Gerald's study. She thought of moving to the window, to look in upon Gerald. But she could not risk him seeing her. Soon enough, he would come to her.

That morning, she'd been in the chapel polishing the candlesticks when she'd heard the shot. Everything that she was now about to do— the wheels that she intended to set in motion—had occurred to her in a kind of flash in that single, auspicious moment. She had put her plan into action almost immediately, surprising herself at her own ruthlessness. Then again, *was* she really being ruthless, given what Gerald and Wilhemina Wimberly had done to her? The more she thought about the Wimberlys, and particularly Gerald, the more the entire matter, even the shooting, made sense to her, and she wondered why, indeed, something like the murder in the cemetery hadn't come to pass earlier.

She thought again of how utterly predictable Gerald could be, despite the wild heart that beat within his breast. Although he could be a beast, one could almost set a watch by him. He sought control above all else, and losing control enraged him. He was a conundrum in that way—a man who sought domination but was addicted to risk. Gerald seemed to see life as a kind of dangerous game, and that excited Doris. She recalled how Gerald had thrown her onto her bed and actually ripped her clothes from her body and buried his face in her sex, conjuring within her a savage pleasure she hadn't known it was possible to feel. His passion in turn had fired within her an appetite to match his, so that their sex became like bouts—magnificent, thrilling battles—of which she'd loved every second. She had loved *Gerald*, too, though she knew him to be wicked. Indeed, she had loved him in part *because* he was wicked, and because he had taught her that she, too, could be wicked in her way and that power could reside in wickedness.

Once, before he'd abandoned her, Gerald had bought her a French perfume called *Desire*, which came in a tiny blue bottle. No one had ever before bought her perfume, and, until that moment, she had not considered herself worthy of perfume. But Gerald had made her feel worthy. He splashed her with it, all over, and the scent of it had set him aflame and he'd thrown her upon the bed, roughly, as always, and overpowered and transported her. But very soon after that Gerald's fire had seemed to go out as quickly as it had flared and he'd scorned her, left her alone again, though profoundly changed.

She moved away from the vicarage and back toward the cemetery. She *knew* Gerald—knew him better than anyone knew him, including Wilhemina. She knew that he set out each morning at exactly six fifteen to walk two miles around the environs of the village, and she was certain that he must have, on numerous occasions, seen the woman who visited the cemetery early in the morning and that he almost certainly had attempted to chat her up. He would not have been able to resist attempting to seduce the woman; his ego wouldn't have allowed him to resist doing so. In the end, he was almost without a conscience.

She knew that he'd lied to the police about the pistol and other things because he'd been left with no choice but to lie. And she knew that he would seek to rid himself of the gun as soon as he was able— as darkness fell. When, earlier that day, the police had fanned out in the village to take statements and a detective had arrived at her door and asked to speak with her, she had been careful to say nothing that might contradict the lies she knew that Gerald must tell. She had been guarded in her answers to the detective's questions and had tried to think as Gerald would think. Now she was on her way to see if she'd correctly guessed Gerald's next move—if she really knew him as well as she believed she did.

She moved along the rear fence of the cemetery and around to a spot that was just outside it and near to the place where Lila Tutin's grave lay open and waiting, a black rectangle in the moonlit grass.

She sat on the ground behind a broom shrub about a meter from the fence, from where she could see the grave.

She hoped that she had not left things until too late, though she doubted that Gerald would have risked moving too early in the night. He would wait until the village was long asleep. And indeed, fifteen minutes later, Gerald appeared at the cemetery gate, just as she suspected he would. From her hiding place, Doris watched him creep toward the open grave carrying a spade and a dark canvas sack with something heavy inside it that made the bag sag. He was dressed in black and used no torch. She did not have to see what the sack contained. She knew what it contained, just as she had known that Gerald would come to the cemetery. She had thought in the way Gerald would think and she had been right. She *did* know him best.

He put the shovel and sack by the edge of the grave and eased himself into it. He grabbed the shovel and began to dig. He dug only for a minute—a small hole, obviously. He retrieved the bag and, clutching it, bent into the hole, out of sight. He then began working the earth with the shovel again. Two minutes later, he was finished. He put the shovel by the edge of the hole and lifted himself out. He stood by the hole for a few seconds, staring into it as he rubbed the soil from his hands. Then he picked up the shovel and left the cemetery, the gate creaking as he opened it.

Once he'd disappeared into the shadow of the church, Doris emerged from behind the broom shrub and crept toward the grave.

—⁓—

An hour later, Lawrence Tigue moved—also unseen and with determined stealth—up the path from the village. His target was the thick tangle of blackberry bramble that grew in the northwest corner of the cemetery, by the grave of Mary Forrest.

Lawrence had impressed himself with how easily he'd kept his composure when Lamb had questioned him at the cemetery gate that morning. Throughout his life, people had considered him to lack backbone, but they were wrong. Even the woman whom he'd married had incorrectly concluded this about him, though he found that he hardly cared about that any longer. Even so, he felt himself sorely tried by recent events. He'd been on the verge of escaping, and now the entire bloody thing seemed to be crashing in on him. He was not yet sure what he would do to correct that, though he had begun to form the outline of a plan of action in his mind. At certain times during the difficult day that had just passed, he had felt as if he might cry—cry for himself and the injustices he'd endured. As he prepared to enter the cemetery he realized that his hands were shaking and, despite the cool dampness of the night, that he was sweating. He told himself that he must be cold and pitiless—calculating—as so many others had been cold and pitiless toward him.

He came to the bramble and knelt before it. He reached into the thicket, the thorns snagging the sleeve of his shirt, and put his hand on the small mound of loose earth beneath the bush. The place seemed not to have been touched. He began to clear away the thin layer of dirt and detritus until he felt the canvas sack. He thought again of how, once he moved it must be for good and all. There could be no turning back.

He grasped the sack and pulled it free from its hiding place.

—※—

Lilly Martin ventured into the sleeping village, though she hesitated doing so at first because the murder of the strange woman in the cemetery that morning had spooked her. But she found that, even with the macabre events of that morning, she could not stand lying alone in bed, in her dark room, listening to the obscure, moody sounds the empty house emitted. The sounds frightened her more than thoughts of the dead woman lying in the cemetery. Mother had tried to convince her that she wouldn't mind being alone in the house at night because she would spend most of the time sleeping. But she hated being alone in the empty house. Worse, she was beginning to believe that Mother was coming to prefer the long bus rides to and from her job in Southampton to being home. She couldn't help but think that Mother, too, was seeking escape from the lonely house, just as she herself sought escape in wandering at night. And so she screwed up her courage and went out, resolving that she would go nowhere near the church or the cemetery.

She decided that she would go to Miss Wheatley's cottage, hoping that she might again catch the old hypocrite pilfering Lawrence Tigue's eggs. She walked along the path she had trod the previous night and settled herself in the knee-high grass to the left of the trail, near Miss Wheatley's cottage, from where she had a clear view of the dark, thatched-roof house. She settled in to wait for the old cow to move. As she did so, she noticed that the moist air carried on it the vague smell of something dead—probably some poor animal Miss Wheatley had shot, she thought.

She had been waiting only ten minutes when she spied a dark figure emerge from the small wood that bisected the meadow, just down the trail from the cottage. The figure was coming from the direction of Mr. Tigue's house, and at first she thought that she might have come too late to Miss Wheatley's, that Miss Wheatley already had pilfered Tigue's eggs and now was on her way home. But she soon could tell that the approaching person was not Miss Wheatley; the figure was too thin and moved too quickly. She crouched and watched the figure pass Miss Wheatley's cottage and continue in the direction of the old O'Hare house. Even in the dark, she could tell by the figure's silhouette and the way that it moved that it was Lawrence Tigue. He wore dark slacks and a dark shirt and carried what seemed to be a kit bag or satchel tucked under his right arm.

Lilly glanced again at Miss Wheatley's dark cottage; nothing seemed to be happening there. In a snap, she decided to move onto the trail and follow Mr. Tigue. She still considered Alba Tigue's sudden departure from Winstead suspicious, no matter the excuses Mr. Tigue had offered.

She followed him, keeping a safe distance, for a hundred or so meters down the trail, until they reached the long-abandoned house in which Sean and Claire O'Hare had lived with their twin sons and in which, tragically, Claire O'Hare had hung herself. The house lay about twenty meters from the road that entered the western end of Winstead. The high grasses, brambles, and young trees of the adjoining meadow had consumed the O'Hare property.

Lilly had heard the story of the O'Hares in bits and pieces over the years. She knew some of the story, thanks to what other children in the village had told her—several macabre legends had grown up around Claire O'Hare's suicide—while the rest had come from her father and mother, who had, when she was younger, answered her questions about the family's fate in ways that, she now understood, had been designed to prevent frightening her. She knew for certain that Claire O'Hare had hung herself from an exposed roof beam in the house's cramped sitting room. One of the local legends of the case said that Claire actually had been murdered and that police had discovered, clutched tightly in her right fist, a note that named her killer that was not in her writing, but that the police had hushed up this fact for reasons people could only speculate upon. But when she had asked her father about this legend, he had dismissed it as "ridiculous" and "impossible" and touched her face, encouraging her not to "dwell upon" such morbid considerations.

To go along with the legends, the children of Winstead inevitably dared one another to enter the house at night; indeed, entering the house, even merely to step inside it, had become a kind of rite of passage for village children of a certain age, and the younger one was when taking the dare, the more respect one earned from their peers. Lilly had first taken the dare two years earlier, when she was ten, which was considered "old" to have done so. On that occasion she had entered the house through the back door, by the kitchen. The front door, as anyone who had tried to enter the house knew, was nailed shut and blocked by two decades' worth of undergrowth and detritus. Lilly had run through the back door and into the hall that bisected the house, then turned around and run right back out again. As she had passed the parlor in which Claire O'Hare had committed suicide, Lilly had allowed herself a quick glance into the room as she passed it on a run, despite the assertion advanced by some village children that anyone who dared gaze upon the room would be turned to stone on the spot.

Lilly watched Mr. Tigue leave the path and begin to make his way through the bramble and brush toward the rear of the O'Hare house. She followed through the growth in time to see Mr. Tigue move past a tire swing that hung from the branches of an ancient oak by a rotting length of rope—a swing the O'Hare twins had played on—toward the back door. By then Mr. Tigue had disappeared and Lilly reckoned that he must have entered the house. She looked toward the house and saw the faint glow of the light of an electric torch coming from the window of the parlor. She debated whether she should try to move closer to the window, to see what Mr. Tigue was doing, but could not bring herself to do so out of fear that Mr. Tigue might catch her out.

The torch light suddenly snapped off and Lilly saw Tigue's dark figure emerge from the rear door and head back toward the path, directly toward her; he had stayed inside the house for only a minute. Instinctively, she moved to the right, deeper into the brush. Tigue passed only meters away, close enough for her to hear his slightly labored breathing. She noticed that he no longer held the satchel he had been carrying.

She let him go, squatting in the brush and realizing that she, too, was breathing quickly, heavily. She longed to enter the house to see if Tigue had left something there. And yet she was afraid—afraid of the O'Hare house and suddenly remembering that a woman had been murdered in the cemetery only that previous morning. She wondered if she possessed the necessary fiber to be a crime novelist, or whether she was nothing more than another run-of-the-mill frightened young girl. Sadness suddenly threatened to overwhelm her—a sadness she had tried so hard for so very long to keep at bay—and she began to cry, alone in the dark. The whole world, she thought, seemed to have become more sad and selfish and deceitful and crazy.

Feeling defeated, she ran home to the dark, moody house and her lonely room.

TEN

—⋙—

LAMB AND HIS TEAM MET THE FOLLOWING MORNING AT THE NICK in Winchester. He lit a cigarette and called the meeting to order.

Police Superintendent Anthony Harding stood next to Lamb, looking vaguely dissatisfied. Before the meeting, Lamb had briefed the super on the events of the previous day, and Harding had not been pleased by Lamb's assertion that he didn't trust the vicar of Winstead.

"He found the body and had opportunity," Lamb had told Harding. "And when he called here to report finding the body he told Wallace a different story than he told the Home Guard man who acts as the village constable and that he later told me. He told me that his hearing the shot alerted him to the trouble, but he said nothing of this to Wallace. He claimed that he forgot to mention the shot to Wallace because finding the body confounded him, but he didn't seem in the least upset when I

69

spoke to him. And he owns an infantry officer's Webley but claims that it was stolen a week ago. On top of that, he never reported the theft."

"Yes, but what's his motive?" Harding asked.

"I'm working on that," Lamb said.

Harding sniffed and shook his head as if to show that he was less than awestruck by Lamb's progress thus far.

Wallace, Rivers, and Larkin also gathered for the briefing, along with Vera, who sat in a corner of the room in her ill-fitting uniform.

Larkin began by reporting that the soles of Wilhemina and Gerald Wimberly's shoes matched the plaster casts of the prints he'd taken at the cemetery and that he'd officially identified the slug they'd found at the scene as being a .455 caliber. Lawrence Tigue had voluntarily surrendered his .455-caliber Webley Mark VI to Rivers, and Larkin had sent it and the slug to Scotland Yard to be checked for ballistics.

Rivers reported that the door-to-door canvass of Winstead had turned up no one who had seen Ruth Aisquith in the village on the previous morning, though several people said they had seen her about the village in the past.

"The construction of the prison camp has meant there's been more than the usual number of strange faces in Winstead of late," Rivers said. "It's been a bit of a boon to the shops and the pub. Everyone we spoke to claimed not to have known her. We also spoke to a woman named Doris White, who is the vicar's housekeeper. She confirmed that Wimberly takes a regular walk in the mornings but said that she had not gone to work at the vicarage yesterday because of all the trouble, though she claimed to have popped up later in the morning to see for herself what was going on. As for Mary Forrest, she had a son, Roger, who left the village more than forty years ago, but no one we spoke to knew for certain if he'd ever married or had children, or even if he was still alive. No one had any familiarity at all with the name Aisquith."

Wallace took the floor to report on what he'd found in Ruth Aisquith's personnel file, among the personal belongings she'd kept in the footlocker at the end of her cot, and his conversations with others at the prison camp.

Ruth Aisquith had been born in Haworth, West Yorkshire, and was thirty-six and unmarried. The latter information, he said, seemed to nullify the notion that Roger Forrest might have been her father—and therefore that Mary Forrest might be her grandmother—"unless she lied about having never been married or changed her surname to Aisquith from Forrest for some reason."

She had been living in Haworth when she was conscripted into the fire service and refused service on the grounds that acceding to military conscription did not comport with her personal religious beliefs, though she was not a Quaker and her file did not list a specific religious affiliation. A military service tribunal heard her case and rejected it, after which she was ordered to report for duty with the Manchester fire brigade. She refused and was sent to prison in Manchester. A few months later she'd renounced her objection, enrolled for conscription, and asked that she be spared fire brigade work. This time she'd said that fire frightened her and that she doubted she would be much good at fighting it. The tribunal honored her request and sent her to work at the prison camp outside Winstead.

"According to the file she has no living relatives," Wallace said. "Before the war she made her living as a seamstress in Haworth." He paused, then added, "Funny thing, though. One of the women I spoke to at the camp said that she doubted that story—that Ruth didn't strike her as the 'seamstress type.' Those were her words. She seems to have been hardworking but aloof. When she had leave, she usually went into Winstead; most people were under the impression that she went there to lay flowers at her grandmother's grave, though if her grandmother *is* buried in the village we don't yet know the woman's name. None of the people at the camp had heard Ruth ever mention her grandmother's name. At night she often sat in her bunk and read until lights out. Her personal effects included a few books and toiletries and the like, rather Spartan. No one would admit to disliking her because she was a conchi, though most of them said they didn't agree with her. Men and women are kept segregated,

71

and of the half-dozen or so men I was able to speak with, all claimed to have rarely seen her outside the camp mess."

"Obviously, we've got some work to do on her background," Harding said.

"Yes," Lamb agreed. He then handed out the day's assignments. Wallace was to return to the prison camp with a constable to finish taking statements from the male workers, while he, along with Vera, Rivers, and a trio of constables returned to Winstead. Lamb intended for him and Rivers to interview Wilhemina Wimberly and had devised a plan for doing so that he would discuss with Rivers in detail as they rode to the village. First, though, he wanted to attend the funeral of Lila Tutin, the woman for whom the empty grave in the cemetery was reserved. During the funeral, he intended to study Gerald Wimberly more closely.

When the group arrived in Winstead, Lamb sent the three constables into the village with instructions to continue the house-to-house canvass. He and Rivers then went into the church to await the funeral, while Vera cooled her heels outside, leaning against the Wolseley.

Saint Michael's was a small, mid-nineteenth-century Anglican church of cut stone, stained glass, and polished wood. A faint light illuminated its interior, which smelled of lingering smoke and a kind of mustiness that emanated from its hard-to-reach corners. Miss Tutin's closed casket sat in front of the altar. Candles in gleaming brass candlesticks burned at either end of it. Three elderly people—two women and one man—sat in the pews, though apart from one another. One of the women bent over and coughed violently.

Lamb and Rivers sat in the rear pew, Lamb closest to the aisle. As they waited for the funeral service to begin, Lamb looked for a moment at the wooden Christ that hung from a crucifix at the back of the altar. Images of Christ, and especially those of three dimensions, made him uncomfortable. They never conjured in him the belief that, although life equaled suffering, peace and redemption waited at life's end. Instead, the paintings, statues, and icons tended to remind him of the reasons for the suffering and the necessity of redemption in the first place—of ancient human fears and passions, those aspects of humanity that had failed to evolve from their dark, primitive beginnings and never would.

No other mourners entered the church. A few minutes later, Gerald Wimberly, dressed in priestly robes, appeared and stepped onto the altar. He stood silently behind Lila Tutin's casket for perhaps a full minute, whispering prayers over it, before he launched into a brief service. He spent a few minutes extolling the kindness and selflessness of Miss Tutin in a manner that Lamb found bluntly stock; he wondered if Wimberly had even known the old woman. Then again, few people in Winstead seemed to care that Lila Tutin was dead, or that she had lived.

As the service neared its end, a quartet of men in ill-fitting suits entered the church and stood silently along the rear wall with their hands clasped in front of them. Lamb stole a glance at them. Each seemed to be trying his best to observe a solemnity imposed upon them by the setting that each understood was necessary but otherwise found alien. He concluded that they were village men who had volunteered to bear Miss Tutin's casket to its resting place. Perhaps they were the same men who had dug her grave. Lamb imagined them gathered in the cemetery on the previous Sunday afternoon, sweating beneath a warm late August sun and sharing a bottle of cider and the local gossip as they worked.

Wimberly gestured to the quartet, who moved to the front of the church and took their places on either side of the casket. On a second signal from Wimberly, they lifted the casket and began to carry it up the aisle. Wimberly followed, swinging a silver incense burner in their wake. As Wimberly passed them, the three elderly mourners in the pews each stood stiffly and followed, the man steadying himself on the edges of the pews. Wimberly did not look at Lamb as he passed.

Lamb and Rivers stood and followed the procession out of the church. They did not enter the cemetery for the burial, as the others did. Instead, they stood by the fence along the front of the cemetery and watched. At Lamb's feet were the two pairs of shoes he'd taken from Gerald Wimberly on the previous day.

The four men placed Miss Tutin's casket next to the open grave, then stood back. The elderly trio made their way to the edge of the grave; the woman who had coughed placed her hand against the other woman's shoulder and began to softly cry. Wimberly stood at the head of the casket and began to read from the Bible the usual verses beseeching God's forgiveness of human wickedness. Lamb wondered if Miss Tutin had ever been wicked. Even elderly spinsters could brim with dark, unrelenting urges.

As they waited for the funeral to end, Lamb noticed a woman walking up the road from the village. She came to the fence and stood by it, a few meters away, watching, as Lamb and Rivers were watching. Rivers also saw her and whispered to Lamb that she was the vicar's housekeeper, Doris White. Doris turned toward Lamb and Rivers and smiled.

Wimberly finished reading the Scripture and signaled for the quartet of men to begin lowering the casket into the ground. As they did so, he made the sign of the cross over the grave. The woman who had coughed wiped her eyes roughly.

The funeral was finished. As the men from the village removed their jackets, loosened their ties, and took up shovels, Wimberly escorted the mourners to the front gate of the cemetery, speaking quietly to them as they walked. He now looked directly at Lamb for the first time—a glance only. He shook the hands of each of the mourners, then moved to Lamb and Rivers and bade them good morning. "You're here to speak to my wife," he said.

"Yes," Lamb said.

"Well, I think she's up to it this morning—though I'd appreciate it if you'd allow me to be present when you speak with her."

"Of course," Lamb said. "We'll give you some time to change out of your vestments and then we'll be over to the vicarage shortly."

"Yes, that would be fine," Wimberly said, adding, "I see that you've brought back our shoes."

"Yes."

"And what did you find, if I might ask?"

"Yours and your wife's shoes match the prints that we found in the cemetery," Lamb said.

"Yes, well," Wimberly replied. "We were there together, as I said."

"Yes," Lamb said. He handed Wimberly the shoes.

Doris hovered in the background, watching and listening. Wimberly nodded to her but did not otherwise acknowledge her.

"I'll spend a few minutes speaking to Miss White now," Lamb said. "I won't keep her long, as I suspect she has some duties to perform around the vicarage. Oh, and I should tell you, too, sir, that we found the bullet that killed Miss Aisquith. It passed through her body and landed by the rear fence of the cemetery."

Wimberly thought that this piece of "evidence" was of no real consequence given that Lamb would never find the pistol that had fired the incriminating slug. "That's good news," he said. He nodded. "Well, I shall see you in a few minutes then, Chief Inspector." He turned toward the vicarage and went on his way.

—m—

Doris moved down the fence toward Lamb and Rivers. She was curious to know how much the police had discovered about the murder in the cemetery. She smiled at them again. "Good morning, Sergeant," she said to Rivers, deflating his rank.

"Good morning, miss," Rivers said. He turned toward Lamb. "This is Detective Chief Inspector Thomas Lamb, Miss White," he said. "He'd like a word if you don't mind."

"Not at all," Doris said.

Lamb bowed a little. "Pleased to meet you, Miss White," he said. "I wonder if I might ask you a couple of questions."

"Certainly," Doris said.

"Where were you yesterday morning between half-past six and half-past seven?"

"I was home, just as I told the sergeant when he interviewed me yesterday. I heard from one of my neighbors that someone had been found murdered in the village. I didn't believe him at first, but when I called the vicar he told me that it was true and that I needn't come in, though I did come up later to see for myself what all the fuss was about. I really couldn't quite believe it, you see. No one has ever been murdered in Winstead, at least not in my memory."

"And you are back at your duties today, then?" Lamb asked.

Doris counseled herself to be careful with Lamb. "Yes. My first job will be to clean up after the funeral."

"I see," Lamb said. "Do you also clean the vicar's study?"

"Yes. Once a week."

"Have you ever seen a Webley pistol in the study or anywhere else in the vicarage?"

"Yes," she said. She must be *very* careful now. Still, she saw no reason to deny knowledge of the pistol, given that Gerald long had displayed it in his study.

"When and where did you last see it?"

"Well, I must have seen it in the study, where the vicar keeps it. I'm sorry. I tend not to look at such things when I'm cleaning. I don't approve of pistols."

Lamb smiled again. "All the same, I wonder if you can think back. It might help immensely if you could tell me exactly when you last saw the pistol."

Doris glanced at the sky, as if she were giving the question her fullest consideration. She did not yet know the nature of the lie that Gerald had told Lamb to explain the pistol's absence, only that he certainly *had* lied to Lamb. "I don't *think* so," she said, treading as carefully as she dared. She paused, as if thinking again, then added, in a tone designed to impart the idea that she just *couldn't* remember, "I can't say for sure, because, you see, I simply don't otherwise notice it."

"Very good, then," Lamb said. "Thank you, Miss White." He tipped his hat. "I'm sorry to have kept you from your work."

She smiled a third time. "No trouble at all," she said. As she watched Rivers and Lamb walk toward the vicarage, she wondered how long Gerald would be able to fend off Lamb successfully and thought that, in the meantime, she must not dawdle.

ELEVEN

—∞—

LAMB AND RIVERS FOUND WILHEMINA WIMBERLY AWAITING them in the neat sitting room of the vicarage. She sat on a red sofa with her hands in her lap. Someone had set out things for tea on the table in front of the sofa. Gerald, who answered Lamb's knock, ushered them toward a pair of chairs that faced the sofa. Lamb felt as if Gerald was orchestrating the encounter, and that he had been orchestrating his and his wife's movements since the previous day.

Wilhemina briefly smiled at Lamb. She wore a blue dress adorned with white flowers and shoes that were similar to those that Gerald had turned over to Lamb on the previous day. Gerald had shed his vestments for a pair of brown corduroy trousers and his priest's shirt and collar. Lamb introduced himself and Rivers to Wilhemina.

She stood and gestured them to sit in chairs. "Would you like tea?" Wilhemina asked.

STEPHEN KELLY

"Yes, please," Lamb said. "Thank you."

"Detective Inspector?" Wilhemina said to Rivers.

"No, thank you."

Gerald sat on the sofa as Wilhemina served Lamb tea. When she finished, Wilhemina sat next to Gerald.

"Thank you for agreeing to speak to us," Lamb said to Wilhemina. "I understand that yesterday's events gave you a shock."

"Yes," she said. "Very much so, I'm afraid."

On the previous day, Lamb had come away from his interview with Wimberly believing that the vicar had sought to shield his wife from being interviewed, perhaps because she had received a shock—but also perhaps because he had wanted to have time to rehearse a story with her. Lamb intended to unbalance the pair of them and see what that produced. As part of that strategy, Rivers would conduct the interview, or at least its opening stage. Rivers made a show of retrieving a pencil and notebook from his pocket, leaned forward, and addressed Wilhemina. He and Lamb had discussed the first question he would ask.

"How often do you tend to your garden, madam?"

Wilhemina and Gerald looked at Rivers. Lamb saw that the question had befuddled them, as he hoped it would.

"I'm sorry," Wilhemina said. "How often do I tend my garden?"

"Yes, madam," Rivers said without emotion. "Especially given that at this time of year it can get quite hot, especially in the afternoon, thereby making mornings a more comfortable time to work out of doors."

Wilhemina glanced again at Gerald. Neither of them seemed to understand Rivers's question. As Lamb had guessed he might, Gerald immediately seemed to smell a trap and attempted to shield his wife from falling into it.

"I'm sorry, Detective Inspector," he said. "I don't understand the question."

"The question was directed at your wife, sir," Rivers said, his expression placid.

Wilhemina looked at Lamb, as if expecting him to explain, but Lamb merely smiled at her scantly. She smoothed her dress and turned back to Rivers.

"I'm sorry, Detective Inspector, but I'm afraid I don't understand, either."

"I was merely wondering if you occasionally rise early in the morning to garden, especially given that yesterday morning was a good one for gardening."

Wilhemina glanced at Gerald and then back to Rivers. Her confusion was evident on her face.

"Not often, no," Wilhemina said.

"Then you were in bed when Miss Aisquith was shot?"

Wilhemina hesitated a hitch before answering. "Yes."

"Were you asleep or just resting?"

"I suppose I was sleeping."

"So you did not hear the shot, then?"

She glanced again at Gerald. "No."

"But you did hear your husband come into the house?"

"Yes, I heard Gerald come in."

"According to your husband, he reached the house just as the shot was fired." Rivers made another show of flipping through his notebook. He stopped at a page and read aloud. "Quote, *I was returning from a walk when I heard the shot*, end of quote." He looked up from the notebook at Wilhemina. "That is what your husband told Chief Inspector Lamb yesterday, madam. He then said he went right to the cemetery and that you followed him there. So I was wondering, then, when exactly you woke up and what awakened you."

Lamb could sense Gerald Wimberly attempting to restrain himself from speaking.

"I suppose I must have heard something outside," Wilhemina said. "After all one doesn't always necessarily know for certain what has awakened one."

"But you are certain that it was not a gunshot?"

"I don't think so. In any case, I don't remember it as such."

"Do you normally wake up in the morning when your husband returns from his walk?"

"Occasionally."

"Is your husband sometimes rather loud, then, when he returns from his morning walk?"

"Is he loud?"

"Yes, madam. Does he normally make a racket?"

"I'm sorry, Detective, but I fail to see how such questions are relevant," Gerald interjected.

"I assure you that the questions are relevant," Lamb said. "I wonder if you wouldn't mind allowing your wife to answer, please."

Gerald Wimberly raised his chin in a small, almost unconscious gesture of defiance. "Of course, Chief Inspector. It's just that I don't see what my making noise in the morning has to do with anything."

Lamb ignored Gerald. "Mrs. Wimberly?" he said.

"Well, I suppose he sometimes is noisy."

"Was he particularly noisy yesterday morning, then, madam?" Rivers asked. "Did he shout something or call out to you?"

Wilhemina glanced a third time at Gerald. "No," she said. "I simply heard something—something outside, I suppose. And it awakened me. Most of the rest of it is a blur, I'm afraid."

"So you're certain, then, that the sound of the shot did not awaken you?"

"As I've said twice before now, no. Or at least I don't know that it did." Wilhemina's voice had become tinged with irritation. "I wasn't sure what had happened."

"I see," Rivers said. He paused, a slight look of apparent confusion on his face—a small, though subtle, gesture that impressed Lamb. Once again, Rivers made a show of searching his notebook. "Yes, here it is," he said, stopping at a page. He read aloud: "Quote, *Unfortunately, my wife came into the cemetery. I hadn't even known that she'd followed me. She must have heard the shot*, end of quote."

Gerald ran his fingers through his hair.

"That was your husband's statement to Chief Inspector Lamb yesterday, madam," Rivers said. "I wonder why your husband believed you'd heard the shot? Had you told him that you had heard the shot?"

"No," Wilhemina said. "I suppose he assumed that I had heard the shot. Anyone might assume so, given the circumstances."

"Yes, madam," Rivers said. "But if you didn't hear the shot, then why would you have thought it necessary to follow him to the cemetery? Indeed, why would you have thought it necessary to leave your bed and follow him at all, given that he makes a daily habit of coming and going in the mornings?"

Wilhemina looked sternly at Rivers. Lamb saw that she could not entirely hide her anger. He could almost feel Wilhemina restraining herself from chastising Rivers for his impertinence. "I merely sensed that something was wrong," she said.

"I'm sorry, madam," Rivers said. "You *sensed* that something was wrong?"

"Yes, *sensed*," she said. "Have you never heard of intuition, Detective Inspector? A woman's intuition?"

"Does that mean, madam, that you did not know for certain that your husband had left the house, but merely intuited that he had?"

"No. I heard him come in and then go immediately out again. I got out of bed and went to the window and saw him heading toward the cemetery and so followed."

"I see," Rivers said. "You saw him from the window, then, rather than merely intuiting that he had gone to the cemetery."

Internally, Gerald winced. Rivers was picking apart their story with ease. When he'd first seen the stolid, unimaginative-looking Rivers at his front door he had tabbed him as likely not bright. Obviously he was wrong. And he began to believe that he understood what Lamb was on about. Lamb intended to topple them both by pulling down the weakest of the pair first.

"Yes, I saw him from the window," Wilhemina said.

"And what did you do when you arrived in the cemetery?"

"I don't remember, exactly. I only remember coming into the cemetery and seeing the dead woman there and feeling suddenly very shocked."

"Where were you standing, exactly, when you first saw the dead woman's body?"

"Just by the gate."

"Did you approach the body at all, to see if the woman might still be alive?"

"No. One could see that she was dead. She had that terrible wound in her back."

"So you did get close to the body, then?" Rivers persisted.

Wilhemina narrowed her eyes. "As I just told you, Detective Inspector, I did not approach or touch the body. Perhaps you should listen more closely."

"And yet you also just said, madam, that you could ascertain that Ruth Aisquith was dead because of the seriousness of the wound in her back, which you called, 'terrible.' Had you not approached the body how would you have noticed such a detail?"

"Well, I suppose I was close enough to see, then," she said. "As I said, I don't remember everything exactly. No one could."

Gerald wished he could put a muzzle on Wilhemina. The stupid cow was stumbling badly—obviously lying. Even a bloody idiot could see that. He had told her that she must allow him to take control of everything—every detail—and, as usual, she had defied him. Now they were up to their necks in it.

"I'm afraid I'm to blame here, Detective Inspector," Gerald piped up. "I approached the body, to see if the woman was dead—just as you said. I later told Wilhemina that I knew she was dead from the seriousness of her wound. One could see the gore on the gravestone near which she fell from a fair distance."

Rivers paused again to look at his notes. He did not speak for perhaps fifteen seconds—a silence during which Gerald literally squirmed in his seat, adjusting his position on the sofa and crossing his legs. Rivers then looked at Gerald and smiled briefly at him. "I see, sir," was all he said.

Lamb now took up the questioning, Rivers having done his job. Lamb addressed Gerald. "Did you touch anything on the body, Mr. Wimberly?"

"No." Gerald told himself that he must be careful. They could afford no more damage to their story.

"Other than your wife, did you see anyone else in or near the cemetery?"

"No one."

Lamb paused, as if considering what he intended to say next. After a few seconds he said, "I wonder if you might tell us what you *believe* happened, Mr. Wimberly, given that you apparently were the first person on the scene, other than the killer."

Gerald shifted again and uncrossed his legs. "I'm sorry, but I'm not sure I follow you, Chief Inspector," he said. "I have no idea who killed that unfortunate woman, or why anyone would want to."

"Well, I was just wondering if you noticed anything out of the ordinary, sir—other than the body, of course. Anything that might have caught your eye."

Gerald pretended to seriously consider the question for a few seconds. "Nothing," he said. "I'm sorry. Just as I told you yesterday."

"So you didn't look into the empty grave, then?" Lamb asked. "The one that was awaiting Miss Tutin's body?"

"Why would I do that?" That Lamb had mentioned Miss Tutin's grave frankly shocked Gerald. Certainly Lamb could not possibly *know*. He counseled himself not to lose his head. *Of course* Lamb didn't know. There was no chance that he knew.

"Well, it's possible that whoever shot Miss Aisquith might have heard you coming and gotten down into the open grave to hide. It was deep and wide enough to hide a squatting man, for example. Then, once you were gone, it would have just been a matter of climbing out of the grave and running off."

"I see," Gerald said, trying to say no more than was necessary. "I'm afraid I didn't think of that."

"What did you do once you realized that your wife had followed you to the cemetery?" Lamb asked.

"She became distraught when she saw the body, as I have said. I tried to calm her. Then I took her back to the house and put her to bed. I mixed a sleeping powder and gave it to her."

"And how long did she sleep?"

"Four or five hours."

Lamb turned to Wilhemina. "I must ask you once again, Mrs. Wimberly, how far into the cemetery you walked."

"As I have already said, I don't remember." The peevishness in her voice was palpable. "I was quite shocked."

"Is it also possible, then, Mrs. Wimberly, that you are unsure of other aspects of the story that you have told us here today, given that you were, by your admission, sleeping at the moment the shot was fired and then in a state of shock and near collapse following it?" Lamb asked.

A desire to strangle Wilhemina nearly overcame Gerald.

"I have told you what I remembered to the best of my ability," she said.

"Did you also know that your husband kept his service revolver in his office?"

"Of course."

"And did you know that it had been stolen?"

Wilhemina glanced quickly at Gerald. He had told her that morning how he had explained the pistol's absence to Lamb. "Yes," she said, though without looking directly at Lamb.

Gerald decided that he must go on the offensive.

"Look, Chief Inspector, I know you've a job to do, but I must say that I believe you've crossed a line," he said. "You're harassing my wife, who has had a shock. As for the pistol, you know very well that I told you yesterday that it was stolen."

"I merely asked your wife to clarify her recollections on the matter, sir," Lamb said, turning to Gerald. "In the end, some of her recollections don't match the evidence found at the scene. And, unfortunately, you failed to report the theft of your pistol, so I've no way of independently confirming your story about its theft."

"Certainly, you don't believe us liars?" Gerald said.

Lamb didn't answer that question. "I think we've gotten all we need for the moment," he said. He abruptly stood, followed by Rivers. Gerald and Wilhemina remained seated, surprised by Lamb's sudden ending of the interview.

Feeling the need to regain his sense of self-possession, Gerald stood. "I'll see you to the door, then," he said.

As Lamb and Rivers were leaving, Gerald, his tone suddenly conciliatory, said, "I do hope you'll forgive my wife and me, Chief Inspector. We've both had a shock, and so I'm afraid we're still a bit cloudy. We want to help in any way we can to solve this terrible mess."

Lamb and Rivers walked back toward the cemetery. Although Rivers considered himself to be Lamb's opposite in some key ways—he sometimes found Lamb's reliance on instinct in solving crime a bit too capricious—he had discovered that, in other ways, their minds functioned similarly. The two were certainly alike in one key way, Rivers thought—both were naturally suspicious, quick to smell a rat.

When the two detectives were around the corner of the church and out of earshot of Wimberly, Rivers shook his head and said, "A bloody lying vicar."

"Yes," Lamb said. "And a bloody lying vicar's wife."

TWELVE

—⁂—

DURING MISS TUTIN'S FUNERAL, VERA STROLLED INTO WINSTEAD.
The High Street was quiet; she passed several people to whom she nodded hello and who nodded to her in return. The village struck her as like most country places, if a bit larger. In addition to a pub called the Horn and Claw, she passed an estate agent's, a tea shop, a shop selling food and general merchandise, and a primary school with a stone-fenced yard that was closed for the summer term. Farther up the street stood a collection of small, neat cottages with well-kept gardens in front. On the opposite side of Winstead, the village's western end, where the church and cemetery sat, the road moved about a quarter mile out of the village proper before it intersected with the footpath that led from Lawrence Tigue's property and past the cottage belonging to Miss Wheatley and the O'Hare house. Thus, the road and the trail, taken together, formed a kind of oval around the village's inhabited center.

Vera walked perhaps a half-mile along the road leading east, beyond the cottages and into the farm country, before deciding she had gone far enough and should turn back. On a hill in the distance, she saw a man walking behind a plow pulled by a pair of huge, shaggy draft horses. She found the scene beautiful, though tinged with melancholy. Even so, the walk suited her; for the moment she felt happy, optimistic about her future. She had begun to turn over in her mind what she would like to do from here out, given that she could not avoid conscription forever—no matter her father's machinations on her behalf—and had no desire to.

She thought that she might become a nurse; the idea of tending to wounded men appealed to her because it seemed a substantial contribution. The notion of avoiding hard duty made her feel guilty and irrelevant. She did not want to look back after the war and conclude that she had shirked, that someone else had performed the difficult or dangerous duty that she might have. She did not intend to spend her life scheming and figuring ways to avoid life's hard choices. Although her father's efforts on her behalf touched her—she had no doubt of his love for her, after all—she must eventually take her chances with the war, as so many others had.

She also thought of David. Before becoming her father's driver she had encountered David only a few times and always briefly; they hardly had spoken beyond having been introduced. And although she had always found him good-looking, she had felt no romantic tug from him. Mostly, he had struck her as just another of the men with whom her father worked, if a bit younger than most and more attractive and stylishly dressed.

Now, though, her feelings toward David had begun to change. He had several times flirted with her, at least a little, and in doing so flattered her. David was funnier and not nearly as impressed with himself as she had imagined he was. Indeed, he was surprisingly down-to-earth, if not exactly cerebral.

She'd been surprised to find, too, that he seemed to share her general feelings about avoiding the call-up, though in being a policeman he had a perfectly good reason to justify his deferment. Still, she liked that he seemed to have contemplated the possible consequences to someone else of his sitting out the war. In this he had shown her hints of a deeper character.

She'd been glad, too, when he'd so readily agreed to her suggestion that she go with him to interview the women at the prison camp, even though they'd both been caught off guard when they found her father waiting for them at the car. She knew that her father had noticed the signals that she and David had exchanged and that it had disconcerted him, though she did not believe that they troubled him overmuch. She *hoped* they hadn't, at any rate.

As she strolled back toward the center of the village, she noticed, to her left, a narrow, well-worn public path that led from the street between two cottages. The house to the left of the path was conventionally pretty, with timbered walls, a red door with brass knocker, and a slate roof with tin gutters. A pair of tall evergreen shrubs grew on either side of the door, like sentries guarding a castle gate.

Curious about where the path led, Vera followed it between the cottages to where it gave onto a meadow as it passed a rather large wood-slat garage and then a henhouse at the rear of the neat house with the red door. In front of the henhouse, a dozen or so chickens clucked and scratched within a small bare-dirt surface surrounded by wire fencing nailed to wooden posts.

Vera moved into the meadow behind the house, which was full of tall grasses and wildflowers, thistle and low bramble. Small birds flitted here and there as she walked toward the wood on the meadow's other side. As she approached the edge of this wood she spied, to her right, just off the path, a small rectangular wooden box mounted on a wooden pole. The box, which was about four feet from the ground, had a round hole in the middle of its side that faced the trail. Its top was slanted forward and hinged at the back so that it could be opened. Vera approached the box and found it to be built of thin pine slats hammered together with ten-penny nails. She noticed that the post on which it sat was wrapped with a strand of rusting barbed wire attached with u-shaped nails. The wire lent the contraption the aspect of some sort of ancient torture implement, Vera thought.

She listened for the sound of movement from within the box. It seemed empty. She lifted the roof and looked inside. Lying in the middle of the box was a compact nest made of summer grasses and bits of tree bark that was empty of eggs. She realized that the box was intended to provide a home for birds, which made it seem much less unpleasant, and she remembered Miss Wheatley mentioning that she had built "nesting boxes" around Winstead for the nuthatch.

Leaving the nesting box, she walked on, following the trail through the brief wood and into another patch of meadow. To the right of the trail, a thatched-roof cottage nestled in front of an extension of the wood through which she'd just walked; smoke issued from the chimney of the cottage and a low fence of chicken wire nailed to rotting wooden stakes paralleled the trail, seeming to mark the boundary of the property on which the cottage sat. A rough path led to the cottage through an unkempt meadow. The dark blue paint on the cottage's door and window frames was faded and chipped. Vera calculated that the church was somewhere beyond the wood that lay behind the cottage and that if she kept on along the trail she would make a kind of circumnavigation of the village and end up back where she had started. As she passed the cottage, she noticed that the air smelled vaguely of decay, as if an animal lay dead somewhere nearby.

Another hundred or so meters on she came to an abandoned house that sat to the right of the trail, facing it on a slight rise. It appeared that no one had lived in the house for some time. The white paint of its shingles was faded and peeling and its windows were broken out. The remnant of what had once been a stone walkway leading from the path to the house had all but disappeared beneath the brush and bramble.

She peered up the trail and calculated that the road leading out of the western end of the village, in the direction of the prison camp, must be ahead. Sure enough, she reached the road after walking another thirty meters. The place at which the trail ended at the road was tamped down and constituted a kind of lay-by at which motorists might pull off the road or walkers could gain access to the trail. Vera noticed several cigarette butts pressed into the moist ground at her feet as she stood in the lay-by.

She remained there for a moment to get her bearings. Should she walk down the road to her right she would find herself back by the church and cemetery; should she head left she soon would reach the prison camp site.

Enjoying the walk, she decided to walk back to the church by doubling back over the path she had just trod. She turned and headed back down the trail, passing the abandoned house, which, she thought, seemed to beckon her to come closer—a spooky notion she dismissed with an audible "Rubbish!" As she passed the rummy-looking cottage that sat off the trail by the wood, however, she heard someone call her name.

"Miss Lamb!"

She turned to see Flora Wheatley waddling up the path from the cottage toward her. Vera was surprised to see Miss Wheatley carrying a shotgun over the crook of her right arm.

"Miss Lamb!"

Vera could not quite take her eyes off the gun; it was the type with which one shot birds—pheasants and other fowl. She wondered what Miss Wheatley was intending by toting around such a weapon and was glad to see that the gun's barrel was cocked open and therefore could not go off. She thought, too, of her promise to Miss Wheatley; she *had* told her father about the nuthatches and therefore, thankfully, had no cause to lie to the old woman about that. Still, she felt no desire to chat with Miss Wheatley, whom she'd found pushy in their first meeting.

By the time Miss Wheatley reached the low chicken wire fence that marked the border of her property, she was nearly out of breath. "Miss Lamb, what a pleasant surprise," she said, briefly putting her hand to her heart. "What brings you this way?"

Vera smiled. "Just out for a walk."

"I say, I wonder if you've had a chance to tell your captain about the nuthatches," Miss Wheatley asked. "We must do something soon, you know, otherwise the nuthatches here about will be wiped out."

"Yes, I told him," Vera said. She left it at that.

"Oh, thank you, my dear. Perhaps now someone finally will do something about this problem before it's too late. I've put up a number of nesting boxes, but I'm afraid they've only made it easier for the thieves to steal the eggs. But I had to put up the boxes, you see, because the starlings also are cavity nesters and they push the nuthatches out of the natural nesting spots. The starlings are a much more aggressive species than the nuthatch. That's why there are so bloody many of them. Rats of the air, I call them."

"I think I just passed one of your boxes in the meadow," Vera said. She didn't want to engage Miss Wheatley in an extended conversation, but she was curious about the box.

Miss Wheatley gazed in the direction of the meadow. "Yes, they prefer to nest near meadows. Of course, you can't place the boxes too close together because they each need their own bit of territory, and they have a hard enough time coping with the starlings. Then, of course, too, you have predators—not the least of which, these days, is the human variety, Lawrence Tigue being the biggest culprit, as I told you yesterday. He has chickens, you know, and supplies eggs to the people at the prison camp, and I'm certain he's been padding his supply with nuthatch eggs. They represent pure profit to him."

Vera began to think of a way in which she might politely extract herself from the conversation.

"I've taken care of the natural predators in any case," Miss Wheatley continued. She smiled. "The barbed wire around the trunks of the nesting boxes keeps out the snakes. Horrible things. I don't like snakes—never have. When I find them around the cottage I chop their heads off; a single whack with a sharpened hoe is all it takes. Anyhow, without the barbed wire they slither right up the post and into the nest."

"Yes," Vera said, slightly taken aback by the blunt way in which Miss Wheatley described her method of dispatching snakes—and by the sudden and unwanted image of a serpent slithering up a pole to invade a nest of newborn innocents.

"The same goes for the starlings," Miss Wheatley said. "I can't tell you how often I find that a pair of the evil things have taken up residence in one of my boxes, thereby pushing out the nuthatch." She patted the gun lying in her arm. "I try to kill as many of the adults as I can with this. I keep it near the front door, in case I see one in the yard. I was just going out on a bit of a hunting expedition as you passed. Sometimes one must take the bull by the horns, as they say."

"Yes, well, I must be getting back," Vera said. "The captain will be waiting for me." She glanced down the trail in the direction of the village.

"I take the eggs, of course," Miss Wheatley continued. "Of the starlings, I mean—if I find the eggs in the nesting boxes in the place of the nuthatch's. Or, if the starling eggs have hatched I dispose of the hatchlings."

This last assertion surprised and troubled Vera. How did one "dispose" of baby birds, she thought. "What do you mean?" She couldn't help but ask.

"Just that. I dispose of them; twist their necks until they break. They're filthy birds, and their numbers have become madly out of control. As I said, they're more like rats than birds. If someone doesn't stop them, they'll ruin the nuthatch."

Vera tried to manage a smile but found she couldn't. "Goodbye, Miss Wheatley," she said. She didn't wait for a reply, turning toward the little wood.

Miss Wheatley waved at Vera's back. "Goodbye, my dear," she said. "Please come by again if you've the chance. We'll have tea."

No, we won't, Vera thought.

As she passed the barbed-wired nesting box on her way back to the village, she heard Miss Wheatley's bird gun explode somewhere on the other side of the little wood.

—⁓—

Doris White cleaned the chapel after Lila Tutin's funeral.

Not that she had much to do, really. Hardly anyone had come to bid old Miss Tutin farewell, which Doris found sad in part because she once had worried that her own funeral would be the same sort of lonely, empty affair. But she needn't worry about that any longer. She blew out the candles and put them in her bag.

Once upon a time, Gerald had come to her in the night, leaving Wilhemina lying alone in their marital bed. On those few occasions, she had lit her cottage with candles she'd stolen from the chapel, which Gerald had found romantic.

She left the chapel and walked to the vicarage. She did not bother to knock on the door. She entered the foyer and listened. No one seemed to be about. She concluded that the cow likely was upstairs sleeping—Wilhemina often slept during the day—and that Gerald was out, probably walking. He normally found excuses to leave the vicarage during the day because he couldn't stand being with his wife. Doris knew that Gerald was weak and strong all at once. His wickedness made him that way. She had lost her grip on him for a time. But the woman's murder had changed that.

The police—Lamb and the other detective—had only just left the vicarage a half-hour or so earlier, after having interviewed Gerald and Wilhemina. She wondered what the silly cow had told the policemen, especially Lamb, who was smart, a man to be careful with. She found that she liked Lamb. He was handsome and self-possessed, almost steely. She had noticed that about him right away.

She went into Gerald's study as easy as you please. She looked at the place on the bookshelf where he'd displayed the Webley in its box. Of course she'd seen it the last time she'd cleaned the study. Once again, she could only imagine what lie Gerald had told Lamb to explain its absence. Now, of course, Gerald had another secret that involved the pistol that would make him obedient to her.

She went to Gerald's desk and pulled from the top drawer a piece of his personal stationery, the one embossed with the words *The Rev. Gerald Wimberly, Vicar, St. Michael's Church, Winstead, Hampshire.* Gerald forbid anyone but himself to use the stationery, but she needn't worry about that now. Neither did she care if Wilhemina saw the note, because Wilhemina could do nothing about it. She would complain, of course, hector Gerald in her usual way, but that, too, meant nothing.

She sat at the desk, took up Gerald's pen, and wrote:

> *Gerald,*
> *I will see you tonight at my cottage at nine. Don't be late. The detective asked me about the pistol today and I told him that I really didn't know if you had the pistol last week. Aren't you proud of me?*
> *Lovingly,*
> *Doris*

Once upon a time, Gerald had forsaken her, as if she was of no more value or consequence to him than yesterday's rubbish. But she had a heart and mind and her own sense of dignity, and she knew things—secrets—that no one but she and Gerald knew.

THIRTEEN

—⚌—

WHEN SHE REACHED THE HIGH STREET, VERA DUG INTO THE TOP
pocket of her tunic and withdrew from it a packet of Player's Navy
Cut cigarettes—the same brand her father smoked—lit one, and began
to walk toward the church. She would have to smoke the fag quickly,
before she reached the car, in case her father and Rivers had finished
with the vicar and were waiting for her.

As she walked, she couldn't help but think of her encounter with
Miss Wheatley and concluded that Lilly Martin was right—the
woman was loony. She conjured, then banished, from her mind a brief
image of Miss Wheatley twisting a slender, fragile infant starling's
neck between her fat fingers.

As she neared the church, she saw that her father and Rivers were
still gone. She took a final drag of the Player's then ground it out
beneath the toe of her shoe. She heard the sound of someone pedaling

a bicycle coming up behind her and turned to see Lilly making for her. Lilly pulled alongside Vera and got off her bike. Vera smiled and said hello.

"Hello," Lilly said. "Back for more fun I see."

"Well, I wouldn't call it fun." Lilly seemed cheeky for her age, Vera thought. She wondered if *she* had seemed that cheeky to adults when she was Lilly's age.

"Everyone's talking about it now," Lilly said. They began to walk together toward Lamb's Wolseley, Lilly pushing her bicycle.

"And what are they saying?" Vera asked.

"That it's all a great mystery."

"And what do you think?"

"That the vicar did it, of course."

They reached the car. "Why the vicar? I would think he'd be the last person you'd suspect."

"Not if the killing takes place in a detective novel," Lilly said. "In detective novels, the killer's always the person you least suspect."

"Do you read a lot of detective novels, then?"

"Yes, I love them. I hope to become a detective novelist myself one day."

"Do you? Some detective novels get a bit bloody, don't they?"

"I don't mind a little blood. I'm getting myself used to accepting the fact that some people can be quite wicked. You have to if you're going to write detective novels."

Vera smiled. "I suppose you're right. You can't have a good detective novel without a bit of wickedness."

"A lot of wickedness, actually." Lilly gently laid her bike on the road. "I saw you come out of the path to Miss Wheatley's."

"Yes."

Lilly formed her fingers into claws, like a cat's, and pretended to scratch at Vera. "Did she get you, then? Try to put you in a pot and cook you?"

Vera laughed. She liked Lilly. "Yes, she very nearly did, as a matter of fact."

"She's like that. She's eaten several children in the village. I've managed to escape her clutches, though. Mother says I shouldn't talk about her in that way, but I think she's a hypocritical old cow in addition to being a tremendous bore, going on as she does about this and that. Her latest obsession is the nuthatches."

"So I gathered. I found one of her nesting boxes."

"Yes, they're horrible things—a blight, if you ask me." She shrugged. "Nearly the whole village is that way, though. They're all a bunch of loonies and hypocrites."

"I don't know," Vera said. "Your mother seemed all right."

Lilly shrugged again. "Mum means well. But since Dad went to North Africa, she's become a little loony, too. She has a job now in Southampton, in a factory, making screwdrivers. She works nights and so I don't see her much now. And she nags too much."

"Maybe that's because she's concerned about you."

"That's what *he* says in his letters—Dad. He says Mum's under her own kind of pressure and that I shouldn't be cross with her."

Vera thought she understood the source of Lilly's cheekiness a bit better now. Cheekiness was one way to mask emotional pain.

"Where is your dad, exactly?" Vera asked. With the war nearly two years on, the question no longer was considered to be prying.

"I don't know, *exactly*," Lilly said with what Vera thought was a brave nonchalance. "His last letter said he was near Cairo, but that was weeks ago. He writes me separate letters, though, addressed to me and just for me. He tells me not to worry, but I know that he's only trying to make me feel better. I read the papers. I know what's going on there. The Germans are winning."

"Which branch?"

"The infantry—the ones who get shot," Lilly said.

Vera didn't quite know what to say to this young girl who seemed to have so much weighing on her shoulders. Lilly's problems made her own seem puny in comparison. "What's it like here in the summers, then?" she asked. She was changing the subject, and that was not very brave of her, she knew.

Lilly shrugged. "Boring."

"What about the other girls in the village? There must be other girls."

"There are, but they're all so—I don't know. *Silly*, you know? At least the ones my age are. They only want to talk about this and that boy or how hard it is now to get decent shoes with any sense of fashion to them. I don't care about those things."

Vera smiled. "You don't like boys, then? I'm not sure I believe that." She thought she saw Lilly smile briefly.

"I don't hate *all* boys, of course. But I've no intention of hanging my happiness on the whims and wants of some boy."

"That's smart—and very grown-up of you," Vera said. "But it doesn't have to be either or, you know. There are some real rotters out there, I'll grant you. But there are nice ones, too. Decent ones."

"I suppose."

"Who looks after you at night, then?" Vera said. Though the answer was none of her business, she couldn't help but ask the question.

"Nobody," Lilly said. "I'm old enough to take care of myself and do."

"That's very brave."

"Not really. It's not that hard." She glanced at the ground for an instant, then added, "Sometimes, when I get bored or can't sleep, I go out and walk around the village." She looked at Vera. "I thought at first that I might be scared of the dark, but it's really not scary at all. Besides, I know the village so well."

"You go out in the middle of the night, you mean?"

"Yes. It helps me to sleep sometimes. I started after Dad left and Mum started working at night. I felt restless, I suppose." She glanced down the street, toward the heart of the village. "Sometimes I see things. It's why I'm so convinced that so many people around here are loony. You'd be surprised how many people in this village are up and about in the middle of the night. Miss Wheatley, for one."

"Miss Wheatley?"

"Yes. Only two nights ago I saw her sneak into Mr. Tigue's henhouse, well after midnight, and steal eggs. I followed her to her cottage."

Vera thought of the house she'd passed with the henhouse that was next to the path that led to Miss Wheatley's cottage; that must have been Mr. Tigue's place. She could very easily envision Miss Wheatley stealing eggs from Mr. Tigue's henhouse. The woman's head seemed to be utterly addled when it came to questions of birds and eggs and Lawrence Tigue.

"Is Mr. Tigue's the place by the path, with the red door, then?"

"Yes."

"Does he know that Miss Wheatley stole his eggs?"

"I don't think so. But he's a queer bird, too."

"What do you mean?"

Lilly hesitated for a couple of seconds, then asked, "Can you keep a secret?"

"I suppose, yes."

Lilly looked directly at Vera.

"I've seen and heard other things, too—besides Miss Wheatley stealing Mr. Tigue's eggs, I mean. I've heard Mr. Tigue and his wife arguing, and now his wife has gone off to Chesterfield to live with her sister—or so Mr. Tigue says. He's telling everyone that she left to get away from the bombing, to spend the duration in a safer spot, but there hasn't been any regular bombing down here in more than a year. They don't like each other, the Tigues—not at all."

Vera wondered if Lilly really had heard or seen such things or merely was saying so as a way of gaining attention. That was another reason to be cheeky—people noticed you for it. And Vera could see how Lilly, given her situation, likely needed more than the usual amount of attention.

"Maybe the bombing last summer frightened her," Vera said.

"But if that's the case, why wait a year to move?"

"There might be all sorts of reasons why she waited."

"Yes, but she didn't say goodbye to anyone in the village. She just left."

"Well, that does sound strange, I grant you. But you can't possibly know, really, if she said goodbye to no one in the village. Maybe she was in a hurry for some reason."

"I think she has left him—or she tried to leave him," Lilly says. "Mr. Tigue, I mean. At least I did think that anyway, until last night."

"What happened last night?"

"Last night I was out along the trail and I saw Mr. Tigue. I followed him, though he didn't know it; I thought it would be good training for me, to see how you followed someone without their knowing it—for my training as a detective novelist, I mean. Anyhow, I followed him up to the old O'Hare place; he was carrying something in a sack, which he left in the house. It's a ruin, a spooky place."

"I think I saw it on my walk today; is it the place by the road, near Miss Wheatley's?"

"Yes, that's it. That's where Claire O'Hare hanged herself after her husband abandoned her."

"That's terrible," Vera said.

Lilly shrugged. "It was more than twenty years ago. They say that if you go into the house and look into the room where it happened, you're cursed. But I saw Mr. Tigue go into the room last night. He only stayed a minute, though he left the sack in the house somewhere."

Vera didn't want to encourage Lilly if Lilly was merely gossiping. But something in the way Lilly spoke—something in her character—struck Vera as authentic. She probably *had* seen some of what she claimed to have seen, but might be exaggerating parts of it, tarting it up the way a detective novelist would. "What do you think was in the sack?" she asked.

Lilly looked at Vera, her eyes afire. "I don't know, but I've an idea."

"What's your idea?"

Lilly looked around, as if to make sure no one was near enough to hear. "I think it might be his wife—or bits of her," she whispered. "I mean, if he wanted to get rid of something why do it at the O'Hare place and why in the middle of the night, unless it was something he needed to hide? Something terrible."

Vera laughed—briefly and uncomfortably. "Oh my, you *have* read too many detective novels, Lilly."

"But it's the only explanation that makes sense," Lilly protested. "Have you ever heard of Dr. Crippen? He killed his wife thirty years ago. He was having an affair with a younger woman. He killed his wife and buried her in the basement. Except that he only buried bits of her there. They never found her head. He put it somewhere else, but never did say where. Hardly anyone goes into the O'Hare place these days. It's the perfect hiding place."

"You're being morbid, Lilly. I'm sure Mrs. Tigue is in Chesterfield with her sister."

"So *he* says. He could be doing it in his garage, you know. It's big enough. That's where he keeps his printing press and his car. Or he might even be doing it in his house."

"Doing what?"

"Sorting out the bits, like Dr. Crippen."

"You're being silly and you know it."

"I just find it strange, that's all."

"Well, it *is* strange—the skulking around in the middle of the night, I mean. But merely because it's strange doesn't mean that it's wicked. Some people might find your walking around at night strange, too, but that's not wicked."

"Yes, but I'm not hiding anything in a spooky old abandoned house, am I?"

Vera conjured for Lilly her best serious, motherly expression, conscious of the fact that she was aping the expression that *her* mother used when she was about to address some weighty subject with her.

"Look, Lilly, I believe what you're saying about seeing Miss Wheatley steal the eggs and Mr. Tigue going to the O'Hare house. But I do think you're allowing your imagination to run away with you. You can't very well go around the village telling stories about thievery and murder. It's too macabre."

"But I haven't told anyone else."

"Yes, but these things have a way of getting out regardless and before you know it you've lost control of them. I really think you should discuss these things with your mother. It might ease your mind a bit."

Lilly looked at the ground. She and Vera stood in silence for a moment.

"So," Vera said. "Will you talk to your mother, then?"

"I don't know," Lilly said. "I'll think about it."

FOURTEEN

—⁂—

AT THE POW CAMP, CHARLIE KINKAID AND THE OTHER MEN IN
his group had resumed their job of clearing away what was left of
the stone foundation of the farmhouse. On the previous evening,
in the mess, Charlie had mentioned to Taney that he'd found a
small bone amid the rubble. Taney had told Charlie to forget the
bone—that it certainly belonged to an animal.

"God only knows how many rats and other bloody animals have
scurried through that place in the past ten years," Taney had said.

Taney had a point, Charlie thought. The old basement probably
had attracted its share of rats, badgers, foxes, skunks, and the rest. But
he wondered, too, how much, if anything, Taney knew of the case
of the O'Hares.

Either way, Charlie had gone to work that morning feeling uneasy.
He knew that if he tried to tell Taney the story of the O'Hares, the

boss would only order him to forget it. Taney brooked no delays on the job. Not only that, but the news of Ruth Aisquith's death clearly had upset Taney. Indeed, news of the Aisquith woman's death had sent a rumble of unease through the prison camp generally and had been the main topic of conversation at tea on the previous night and at breakfast that morning, though neither he, nor any of the other male workers at the camp, had known Ruth Aisquith, really. She'd kept to herself.

As the morning wore on and he struck no more bones, Charlie felt better about his decision not to mention the O'Hare case to Taney. Then, too, he'd spent the morning helping to clear a different portion of the foundation than the one in which he'd found the bone on the day before. When he later moved to the place where he'd found the bone, Charlie had been digging only a minute when he felt the point of his spade bite into something hollow-feeling; he vaguely heard the thing crack as his shovel struck it. He eased his shovel from the ground and bent down to sort through the loose soil.

—⁊⁊—

Wallace spent the morning taking statements from the workers at the camp whom he'd missed on the previous day. Nearly everyone told him roughly the same story about Ruth Aisquith: They hadn't known her well; she'd kept to herself; they'd known she was a conchi but didn't hold it against her, necessarily, though they found the idea distasteful under the present circumstances, with the Nazis marching over nearly all of Europe and North Africa.

Wallace essentially agreed with that point of view. On the previous night, he'd sat alone in his flat for an hour considering the question of whether he wanted to continue his occupational deferment. He'd found that speaking to Vera about the subject had eased his mind a bit on the subject; the fact that she also seemed to believe in the idea of him being "indispensable" to the war while remaining home had comforted him. He liked Vera. She was nice-looking and smart, and had a kind of hardiness and confidence that he found attractive. Still, he'd found his thoughts turning from her to his cousin, Alan, whom the Germans had killed on the beach at Dunkirk. He continued to believe that Alan had performed a duty that he himself was avoiding, and he did not want to live through the war and its aftermath troubled by a sense of self-imposed ignominy. If he could manage it without it seeming foolish or weak, he would endeavor to speak again with Vera on the subject.

Now, though, he was walking down the muddy "lane" between the tents, nearing the last of the tents on his left, when he heard someone say, "Sergeant!" He turned to his left and saw Nora, the small, quiet woman whom he'd met the previous day in the field, standing between the tents.

"Hello," Wallace said. He smiled.

"May I speak with you?" Nora spoke in a near whisper.

As Wallace began to walk toward her, Nora turned and moved toward the rear of the line of tents. Wallace followed her there, where they were out of sight of the rest of the camp. He was glad to see that Marlene Suggs did not seem to be around. He hadn't liked Suggs and believed, as had Vera, that Suggs sought to control Nora through a veneer of "kindness" toward her. On the previous day, Nora had struck Wallace as uneasy and timid.

Nora held her hands together tightly and looked beyond Wallace, as if checking to ensure that no one had seen him follow her.

"What's the matter?" Wallace asked.

"I'm a little nervous, I suppose," Nora said. She didn't look directly at him.

"Why?"

Nora glanced quickly around—again, as if checking to ensure that they were alone. "It's about Ruth," she said. "I didn't tell you everything yesterday. I couldn't."

"Why couldn't you?"

"I didn't want Marlene to hear. Ruth didn't like Marlene, you see—though I suppose that really doesn't matter any longer. Also,

Mr. Taney mustn't know. If he finds out that I've spoken to you I could lose my posting. This isn't such a bad place to be, all things considered. It's better than fire-watching duty in London." She finally looked at Wallace.

"Why are you afraid of Taney?"

"He's the real power here; Captain Walton's not much more than a figurehead. It's Mr. Taney makes the decisions and runs the place. Everyone who works here knows that. You don't want to get on his bad side."

"Did Ruth get on his bad side, then?"

Nora looked at the ground for an instant, then at Wallace. "I don't know," she said. "But I heard them arguing once; they were behind the tents just as we are now. I was passing on my way from the latrine."

"What did you hear?"

"Well, I suppose that you might call it a lover's quarrel."

"Meaning that Taney and Ruth were at it?"

Nora looked away again. Wallace realized that the idea of Taney and Ruth "at it," as he had so gracelessly put it, embarrassed her. "Sorry," he said. "Do you mean that Ruth and Taney were lovers?"

"I don't know for sure. But he pleaded with her, like, and I've never heard him speak like that. Normally he's in charge, giving orders."

"Pleaded with her? About what?"

"He asked her to give him more time. That's how he put it. 'More time.' She said she'd try but couldn't guarantee anything. She seemed to have no fear of him. I hadn't suspected that she'd known him any better than the rest of us did, which is hardly at all. And he'd been generous enough to allow her to go into the village in the early morning to visit her grandmother's grave. That raised a few eyebrows around here, given that Taney is not a man who doles out favors. But she spoke to him as if none of that meant anything to her."

Nora glanced around nervously again. The voices of two men walking down the "lane" came from the other side of the tents.

"I have to go," Nora said.

Wallace touched her arm; she looked at his hand in surprise. "Thank you," he said.

"I thought I should tell you. I'm worried that Mr. Taney became angry with her and, well, you know."

"Yes, I know."

Nora smiled briefly then hurried up the rear of the line of the tents. Wallace stepped back into the muddy lane. As he did so, he saw Corporal Baker jogging toward him from the direction of the farmhouse. Baker reached Wallace red-faced and perspiring.

"Captain Walton sent me to find you," he reported. "He wants you to come to the farmhouse site as soon as possible."

"What's the problem?"

"One of the men digging there has found bones—human bones. A skull."

"A skull?"

"Yes, a small skull. A child's skull."

—m—

Miss Wheatley moved as quickly as her girth allowed up the High Street in Winstead toward Vera. Lamb and Rivers, having finished with Gerald Wimberly, had returned to the car a few minutes earlier, and the three of them had been discussing possibly having lunch in the pub.

"Miss Lamb!" Miss Wheatley yelled, waving at Vera. "Miss Lamb!"

Vera sighed. "Oh, no."

Her father looked at her. "What's wrong?"

"I've spoken to her a couple of times, the last time just this morning. She's a bit of a village crank. I told you about her yesterday; she's the one who's on the warpath about the nuthatch. She's put up a bunch of boxes for the birds to nest in around the village and has convinced herself that this man, Tigue, is stealing the eggs from them. She told me that when she finds starling fledglings in the boxes she wrings their necks and throws them away, as starlings are competitors of the nuthatch."

Lamb looked toward Miss Wheatley.

"Miss Lamb!"

Lamb, Rivers, and Vera moved down the street to intercept Miss Wheatley, who, when they reached her, pulled up and slapped her right hand to her heart. "Oh, Miss Lamb," she said, her bosom heaving from her exertions. "Miss Lamb, I'm so glad I caught you."

Lamb put his hand on Miss Wheatley's shoulder. "Slow down, please, miss," he said. "Are you all right?"

"Yes, yes," Miss Wheatley said. "Quite all right. I've just been running, you see."

"Yes, I see that," Lamb said. "Do you need water?"

"No, no, I'm fine." She looked directly at Lamb. "It's Mr. Clemmons, you see."

"Mr. Clemmons?" Lamb asked. Just as Tigue had rung a bell in Lamb's mind on the previous day, so now did the name Clemmons. After returning to the nick and before heading home on the previous night, Lamb had dug through the constabulary's newspaper archive and retrieved the story from the *Hampshire Mail* of about a month earlier that had reported the beginning of the construction of the prison camp on what the paper referred to as "the old Tigue farm"—a story that also contained a brief recounting of the suicide of Claire O'Hare, which the paper's editors considered the most newsworthy event to have hit Winstead. Lamb's recollection of Tigue's name earlier that day had caused him to return to the story and refresh himself on the details of the O'Hare case. And, indeed, in reading the story, memories of the case, which had engendered its share of coverage in the *Mail* in its day, had begun to flood Lamb's mind.

He recalled that DI Ned Horton had handled the inquiry and that Horton—who had retired many years earlier—had concluded that Claire O'Hare's husband, Sean O'Hare, had spirited the couple's twin boys to Ireland. He also recalled that, for a brief time, Horton had suspected that a farmhand who had worked for the Tigues and had a prior conviction for pedophilia might have fiddled with the twins in some way; the man had assaulted a thirteen-year-old girl in Southampton four years earlier and spent two years in jail. But Horton had failed to turn up any useful evidence to support his suspicions. The story on the construction of the prison camp had repeated this aspect of the old story, along with the man's name—Albert Clemmons. The story also asserted that Clemmons had left Winstead shortly after Horton had wrapped up the case and never returned.

"Do you mean Albert Clemmons?" Lamb now asked Miss Wheatley.

"Yes, yes. Albert Clemmons."

Lamb touched Miss Wheatley's arm, hoping to calm her. "I'm sorry, miss, but do you mean the same Albert Clemmons who worked on the Tigue farm twenty years ago?"

"Yes, yes, that's him," Miss Wheatley said in a tone that suggested that such ancient history meant nothing to her and that Lamb was not responding quickly enough to her plea for assistance. She pointed toward the village. "We must go! I must take you there! He lives in the wood behind my house."

"But didn't Albert Clemmons leave Winstead years ago?" Lamb said.

"He did—but he returned this spring. He normally comes to my back door, you see, usually at twilight, and I give him what I have left over. Scraps of this and that; fresh vegetables if I have them." She stopped and put her hand to her heart again. "Oh, my," she said.

"Are you sure you're all right?" Lamb asked. He was not yet entirely certain of what, exactly, had upset Miss Wheatley.

"Yes, yes, I'm fine." She looked at Lamb queerly for an instant. "Are you the captain, then?"

"Chief Inspector."

Miss Wheatley wiped her brow. "Oh, then you *must* come. I went to check on him, as I said, but couldn't find him. I called his name but no one answered. I thought perhaps he'd merely left for a while, as he sometimes does, though he likes it here and I've never begrudged him his place in the wood."

"Do you mean Mr. Clemmons?" Lamb asked again, just to be sure.

"Yes."

"And did you find him?"

"Yes, I did. Yes."

"And is he hurt?"

"No, he's not hurt."

"What is wrong with him, then?"

Miss Wheatley looked at Lamb as if she thought the question ridiculous. "Well, he's dead, Captain!" she said. "Dead!"

FIFTEEN

—ᘯ—

WALLACE STOOD ALONG THE EDGE OF THE RECTANGULAR HOLE IN
the ground that once had served as the foundation of the farmhouse,
looking down at a small, gray human skull. It lay on its side in the
clot of earth in which Charlie Kinkaid had shoveled it to the surface.
Captain Walton and Taney stood with Wallace.

Charlie also showed Wallace the bone he'd found on the previous
day. "I thought it belonged to an animal," he said.

Wallace had no idea what sort of bone Charlie Kincaid had handed
him, but figured that it was human. Given the skull, which clearly
was human, he couldn't assume otherwise.

"It's one of the O'Hare boys," Charlie said. "I'd bet my life on
it. I never did believe that Sean cared for the boys; he didn't give a
damn for them. Now that we've found the one, the other one has got
to be here, too."

"What in hell are you talking about?" Taney asked.

Kincaid delivered to Taney, Walton, and Wallace a brief explication of the O'Hare case and his long-held suspicion that Sean O'Hare hadn't cared enough for his sons to spirit them away.

"Bloody hell," Taney said. "This will bloody well hold things up."

Wallace turned to Walton. "You'll have to stop the work here until we figure out what has happened," he said.

"Of course," Walton said.

"But we can't do that," Taney protested. "It will put us behind."

Wallace turned to Taney. He thought of what Nora had just told him. He wondered if Taney had fancied Ruth Aisquith and Ruth had rejected him.

"I'm sorry, sir, but I'm afraid we have no choice but to stop," Wallace said, choosing diplomacy for the moment.

"But the bleeding Italians are going to be arriving by the boatload as soon as you please and we've no place to put them," Taney persisted. "Besides, you've no authority to close us down."

"You're wrong, there, sir," Wallace said. "This skull could be the result of a homicide, therefore making this pit a crime scene." He smiled, ever so slightly, as if to add, *so sod off.*

Taney turned to Walton. "You can stop this nonsense," he said.

Walton shrugged and turned to face Taney. "I'm afraid I can't, and even if I could, I wouldn't." He glanced down at the skull. "This is a child—someone's child. I think we can delay things around here for a few days to discover, if we can, why and how this child died."

Taney shook his head and made a hissing sound of displeasure. "You're bloody useless," he said to Walton.

—⁂—

Miss Wheatley led the way up the path from the High Street, past Tigue's house and through the meadow, to her cottage, with Lamb, Rivers, and Vera following.

Vera had asked her father if she could accompany him and Rivers to the scene. Once again, Lamb's first thought had been that he should not allow Vera to see Albert Clemmons's dead body. But as he looked at her, he found himself questioning what, exactly, he was hoping to shield her from, and why. She must face death eventually, and it was better that she do so with him in attendance. He surveyed her as she stood in the road dressed in her ill-fitting auxiliary constable's uniform; as ridiculous as the uniform was, Vera wore it with dignity. He thought of how young she continued to seem to him—how young she indeed was. But he saw in her eyes resilience and strength of character, traits he'd always known she possessed. Besides, he was her father, not her bloody knight in shining armor. He nodded to her and said, "All right."

As Miss Wheatley's cottage hove into sight, Lamb smelled decay on the air and immediately understood that encountering Clemmons's body was going to be more unpleasant than standing over the freshly dead body of Ruth Aisquith had been. Although he did not like facing dead bodies as a rule, he found the fresh ones bearable, but he could not stomach those that had begun to decompose. The smell was bad enough, of course, but the stench of decaying bodies also invariably reminded him—as it reminded Rivers—of the ten months the pair of them had spent together in northern France during the previous war. Rotting bodies had been a feature of the landscape there, along with mud, well-fed rats, and barbed wire. Despite the number of dead bodies Lamb had seen then and since, in his police work, the bloating and settling of the corpses, the buzzing flies and burrowing maggots, and the darkening of the skin continued to distress him. He wondered now if he'd made the right decision in agreeing to allow Vera to see the body.

They followed Miss Wheatley to the rear of her cottage and entered the wood behind it. Lamb realized that this wood was the same one that backed onto the cemetery and that they were entering the wood from its opposite side. As they walked, Miss Wheatley told them of her latest encounter with Albert Clemmons. Clemmons had grown up in Winstead, and she'd known him as a boy, she said. ("He was rather a nice little boy, actually. Very polite.") He was about thirty when the events involving the O'Hares had occurred. Until that time, most people in Winstead had not known that Albert had served time in jail for diddling with a young girl in Southampton. He'd managed to keep that a secret. But Horton's brief investigation into Clemmons's background had "let the cat out of the bag" and, soon after, Albert had fled the village in disgrace, Miss Wheatley said.

Then, during the previous April, a filthy disheveled man had built a lean-to in the wood behind her cottage. Miss Wheatley had, she said, "marched into the wood" to confront the man and run him off.

"I thought he was just another tramp, you see," Miss Wheatley said as she led them into the wood. "But as soon as I got close enough to really see his face, I *knew*, despite the years and the fact that he now had a full beard and was quite bedraggled. I *knew* that it was Albert. And so I allowed him to stay and gave him blankets and food when he needed it. He'd grown up here after all and I couldn't very well send him away. He lived by his wits, you see."

Immediately upon entering the wood they began following a narrow, well-worn trail. Miss Wheatley moved slowly but without stopping, huffing and puffing as she went. "It's just up here," she said, gesturing ahead of them.

"Why did he come back after so many years?" Vera asked.

"Well, I'm afraid that's the thing, my dear," Miss Wheatley said. "I know it must sound macabre, but he told me that he had come home to die. I think he believed that he'd run out his string. I told him that such thinking was rot, of course—one can't know these things, really. When one must die."

As they neared the scene, the smell of decomposition thickened and Lamb began to feel nauseated. He fought off the feeling and followed Rivers, who was directly behind Miss Wheatley, as Vera followed him. Through the trees Lamb spied what appeared to be the lean-to. He calculated that the church and vicarage were somewhere on the other side of the wood, though he was not sure how far the wood extended before it gave onto the church grounds.

They had advanced only two or three yards farther up the trail when Lamb found that he could no longer fight his rising nausea. He stepped off the trail and vomited. Vera also had been fighting a steadily creeping feeling of nausea; watching her father broke her self-control and she also turned from the trail and vomited.

Miss Wheatley turned around. The odor did not seem to bother her. "It's the smell, I should imagine," she said. "I have no sense of smell myself, you see, and haven't had for thirty years. I'm afraid I forget sometimes that others do." She went to Lamb and Vera.

"Are you quite all right, Miss Lamb?" she asked.

Vera, who was doubled over with her hand clasped over her mouth, nodded. She wasn't sure she was up to going on but told herself that she must not turn back.

"I'll go ahead, then," Rivers said grimly. The rancid smell troubled but did not sicken him, and never had, even on the Somme.

Lamb waved his right hand at Rivers to show that he'd heard. Vera straightened, pulled a handkerchief from the pocket of her trousers, and wiped her mouth. But Lamb doubled over and vomited again. Vera moved to him and put her hand on his back. "Are you okay, Dad?" she asked. She liked that she had outlasted her father and could comfort him, rather than the other way around.

"I will be in a minute," he said. "I've never been much good at this, I'm afraid."

"It's nothing to be ashamed of," Vera said, trying to be helpful.

"No," Lamb said. He straightened and steeled himself. "All right, let's go, then." He turned to Miss Wheatley. "It might be best if you went back to your cottage now, Miss Wheatley. I'll come by soon to take a statement from you. Thank you for alerting us."

To Lamb's surprise, Miss Wheatley acquiesced without even a small protest.

He and Vera moved up the trail, Lamb with a handkerchief covering his nose and mouth. The body lay in a small clearing in front of a lean-to constructed of a web of fallen branches and bits of lumber; a dark green canvas tarp covered the web. Two or three military-issue woolen blankets lay crumpled in a heap against the rear of the lean-to. Albert Clemmons's slightly bloated body buzzed with blackflies. Fully clothed, it lay near a fire pit that was ringed with stones and contained the damp, blackened remains of a wood fire that had burned down nearly to ash before expiring.

Vera looked at the body; she had never seen a corpse, not even an embalmed one. She had expected to feel something like pity for the dead man—and she did feel something like that for Albert Clemmons. Mostly, though, the sight of Clemmons's decaying body revolted her, though not in the stomach-turning manner in which the smell had. The fact of death itself, its squalor, revolted her—sickened her soul. She saw no sign of peace in Clemmons's gaunt, dirty face, which was nearly black with accumulated filth. His lips were swollen and scabbed, and his mouth lay open. A trail of dried yellow vomit led from the corner of his mouth and down his cheek. Flies flew in and out of his mouth like bats from a cave. He had only a few teeth, and those that he did possess were the color of strong tea. His clothes—he wore a green cotton shirt and green wool trousers—were filthy and ripped in places. His open eyes seemed to fix themselves on hers, and yet they contained no hint of life or light. For Albert Clemmons, death seemed to have represented a final misery in a life spent mostly in wretchedness.

The sight of Clemmons also revolted Lamb—though, as a matter for forensic investigation, the apparent condition of the body relieved him. Clemmons was not as far gone as he'd feared. Other than the swarming flies, insects had not yet begun to invade the body in force, and it appeared that the local animals had so far let it be. He saw no outward signs of trauma on the body and hoped that Clemmons's heart merely had given out or that some other natural cause had killed him. He was in no mood to take on another murder inquiry.

Rivers squatted by the body but did not touch it. Someone would have to search the man's fetid clothing. Rivers decided that he would do so and spare Lamb the duty. "No sign of anything," he said. "Might be natural. He's old enough by the look of it."

"Yes," Lamb said. He forced himself to move closer for a better look. Vera stayed where she was, watching her father.

Lamb squatted by the body, the handkerchief still covering his mouth and nose. The stench nearly overcame him, but he managed to stave off another wave of nausea. He saw nothing that indicated foul play in Clemmons's death, except that Clemmons had vomited. People who had been poisoned sometimes vomited. He stood and turned toward the lean-to, within which he noticed an upturned wooden box that seemed to have a slip of paper lying on it. Lamb moved to the box and found a single sheet of paper lying upon it that was weighted in place with a small stone. A short note was written in pencil on the paper.

Lamb picked up the note and read it.

> *20 years ago I kiled the O'Hare boys and so now have kiled my self. May god have mercsy on my soule.*
>
> *Albert Clemmons*

Rivers read the note over Lamb's shoulder. He swatted a fly from his face and said, "Bloody hell."

SIXTEEN

—〰—

LAMB LEFT RIVERS WITH THE BODY OF ALBERT CLEMMONS. HE AND
Vera hiked back to the village, from where Lamb began to organize
a response to the discovery of the tramp's body. It appeared possible
that Clemmons had committed suicide. But the fact that Clemmons
had vomited in his death throes bothered Lamb. Clemmons might
have poisoned himself, of course, though neither he nor Rivers had
found poison in or around Clemmons's lean-to during their brief
initial search of the site. In the meantime, Lamb wondered who else
in the village had known that the tramp living in the wood by the
church was Albert Clemmons.

He was not yet certain what to make of the apparent suicide note.
But since coming to Winstead on the previous day, Lamb had felt the
presence of the O'Hare family continuing to hover over, and even
oppress, the village.

As they walked back to the village, Vera reported to her father Lilly's story about Miss Wheatley's nocturnal thieving from Mr. Tigue's henhouse and Tigue's visit to the O'Hare house in the middle of the night, along with Lilly's macabre theory on what the bag Tigue had been toting at the time contained. She added the caveat that Lilly was about twelve, that her father was in North Africa and her mother worked nights in Southampton, and that Lilly clearly was lonely and seemed to have an active imagination. "She's desperate for attention," Vera said. "So she might be exaggerating some of what she claims to have seen, or even making it up. I feel rather bad for her, actually." She also told her father that Lawrence Tigue's wife apparently had left the village in recent days and that Lawrence had told those who asked after his wife that she'd gone to spend the duration of the war with her sister in Chesterfield because she was afraid the Germans would return to bomb southern England again.

The mention of Lawrence Tigue's name concerned Lamb slightly, given that Tigue had lived on the old farm with Clemmons during the time when the O'Hares had disappeared and so had a connection to the tramp. The idea of a lonely young girl wandering the village at night also concerned him. But he could not put much stock in Lilly's tale. He found it credible that Lilly might have seen Miss Wheatley steal eggs from Lawrence Tigue's henhouse; Miss Wheatley clearly saw Tigue as the primary villain in the drama she'd created around the village nuthatch population. He also thought that Miss Wheatley probably had intended to give at least some of the eggs she stole from Tigue to Albert Clemmons.

As for Lilly's claims about Tigue hiding something in the O'Hare house, Lamb was less certain. Lilly might not like Lawrence Tigue or might merely consider him odd and thus good fodder for a spooky story. He in no way believed, however, that if Tigue had hidden something in the O'Hare place, this something had been chopped-up bits of his wife. In any case, it would be easy enough to confirm whether Mrs. Tigue had indeed gone to her sister's in Chesterfield, as Lawrence Tigue claimed. Still, he spent a moment considering what the bag

Tigue had carried *might* have contained, *if* Lilly's story was true, and the germ of an idea began to form in his ever-skeptical, curious mind that might explain the bag's contents—one that, if true, might also explain why Ruth Aisquith had come to Winstead carrying fifty quid in cash. He asked Vera to keep him informed if Lilly said anything else that struck her as concerning. He didn't entirely discount the idea that Lawrence Tigue might have been skulking about Winstead in the dead of night, but for the moment he couldn't expend time following up on the likely tall tales of a lonely twelve-year-old girl.

In the Winstead village pub, as Lamb got Evers, the duty sergeant in Winchester, on the telephone to report the Clemmons matter, Evers immediately told Lamb that Harding had been trying to reach him and that he should stand by. A few seconds later, the superintendent came on the line. He allowed Lamb to explain the situation in Winstead before he dropped in Lamb's lap the news of the simultaneous discovery at the prison camp.

The rush of events left Lamb feeling mildly stunned. He and his team seemed suddenly to have found themselves saddled with the challenge of making sense of a grave and mysterious coincidence—the simultaneous discovery of a child's skull on the old Tigue farm and the seeming confession of Albert Clemmons, who had worked and lived on that farm, of his having murdered the O'Hare twins twenty years earlier. Lamb had learned not to discount coincidence, including those that on the surface seemed rather improbable or convenient. But neither did he trust coincidence, necessarily. He preferred to assess coincidences on their merits—or lack thereof—and this one seemed to him questionable.

"I've sent Larkin out to the prison camp to set up a proper dig of the foundation for evidence," Harding said. "Obviously, we'll also have to start an inquiry into Clemmons's death. I'll send the doctor to Winstead this afternoon." Harding added that he would put someone to the task of digging out the old files on the O'Hare case for Lamb, since that investigation now appeared, at least potentially, to be in the picture again.

Lamb stopped for a minute to consider what lay before him. He faced one certain murder inquiry, that of Ruth Aisquith; one of a possible suicide, Albert Clemmons's; and the probable reopening of the inquiry into the suicide of Claire O'Hare and the subsequent disappearance of her husband and twin sons. He found his packet of Player's, lit one, took a good long drag from it, and told himself that he must do as he always did, as he had no choice but to do—to approach the mess one step at a time.

He returned to Clemmons's campsite, where, by then, Rivers had gone through the tramp's pockets—in which he found nothing save a rusty folding knife—and begun searching the contents of the lean-to. In doing so, Rivers had found a small tin of rat poison by the pile of blankets and rags on which Clemmons apparently had slept.

"It's been opened," Rivers said. "He has no marks on him and there's no sign about of a struggle."

Lamb picked up the container; it contained arsenic, which induced vomiting when ingested in sufficient amounts. He replaced the container on the ground and wiped his fingers on his pant leg. Placing his handkerchief over his mouth and nose again, he waded into the disarray of the lean-to and began to search through Clemmons's scattered belongings—a pile of soiled socks and clothing; a metal cup, along with knife, fork, and spoon that lay inside a rusting iron pot; four or five tins of canned fruit and vegetables and one of sardines; a second large green canvas cloth; a half loaf of coarse brown bread that had begun to grow white mold.

He also found lying among the items of clothing a small satchel made of heavy blue cotton that was cinched closed with string. He parted the strings and looked in the satchel. It contained two shillings and five pence, a nearly empty box of matches, a dull stub of a pencil tucked within several folded pieces of unmarked paper (Lamb immediately wondered if the pencil had been used to write the suicide note) and—curiously—a three-inch-high leaden figurine of the American Civil War general Ulysses S. Grant. The toy was well detailed and carefully painted, down to the golden sash Grant wore around his waist and his signature brown beard. Indeed, the figure seemed almost too pristine, given its owner and the conditions in which he lived, and seemed to have been the only thing resembling a personal keepsake that Clemmons possessed.

He held up the figure so that Rivers could see it. "What do you think of this, Harry?"

"General Grant, then?"

"Yes, but why? He doesn't seem to have kept anything else in the manner of a keepsake. Why a toy soldier and why an American? And look how bloody clean it is."

"Maybe he fancied the American Civil War."

"Yes, but there's nothing else—no books or other personal items."

"Maybe his mum or dad gave it to him, a long time ago. Maybe our man"—Rivers nodded at Clemmons's body—"was a sentimentalist at heart."

Lamb stared at the figurine for another couple of seconds then, on impulse, put it into the pocket of his jacket.

"All right, Harry, keep at it," he said. He added that Winston-Sheed was on the way to examine and move the body and that a few uniformed constables also were due to lend him a hand.

Lamb retraced his steps along the path through the wood to Miss Wheatley's cottage. She answered his knock. Lamb thought that the distress at Albert Clemmons's death that Miss Wheatley had exhibited only an hour before seemed to have lessened.

"Captain," she said. "Come in."

Little natural light penetrated Miss Wheatley's small, close cottage, tucked, as it was, hard against the wood. The place was crammed with packaged and canned food, piles of newspapers and magazines that appeared as if they might go back years, even decades, along with bits of paper, empty bottles, and boxes and crates of various sizes stacked in corners. Upon entering Lamb could not see a clear place on which to sit.

Miss Wheatley moved a stack of newspapers from one of three chairs that surrounded an oval wooden table in the middle of her kitchen. "Won't you sit down, Captain?" she said. "I'll get us tea."

"That sounds fine, thank you."

As she brewed the tea, Miss Wheatley regaled Lamb with her tale of the sad fate of the local nuthatch and renewed her claim that Lawrence Tigue was the worst of the offenders. He allowed her to spin out her tale to its end and promised that he would look into the matter.

She sat opposite him at the table and poured the tea from a bone white china pot with matching cups and saucers. She offered no milk, nor made mention of possessing any, though she produced a small bowl of sugar. Lamb thanked her, sipped his tea, and, falling short of the truth, pronounced it delicious.

"I wonder if you know yet how Albert died, Captain?" she asked.

"It appears as if he died of natural causes."

"Well, that's a comfort. Poor man. I'm afraid he lived a very difficult life."

"Did you have reason to believe that he might have died in some way other than naturally?"

"Well, I don't know for sure," she said. "Given his past history with the village one couldn't know for sure."

"Meaning you believe that there are people living in Winstead who might have liked to have seen him dead?"

"Well, the mess with the O'Hares upset and frightened people here, as you might imagine. Some hereabout never fully bought into the idea that Claire O'Hare killed herself. Claire was no angel and an execrable mother, to be sure, but Sean was a bad sort, too. He drank and beat Claire about. In fact, the rumor had gotten around at the time that he was up to something with Olivia Tigue, the woman who ran the farm on which they're building the prison camp now."

"Lawrence Tigue's mother?"

"Yes."

Lamb could not recall hearing of such a rumor at the time of the O'Hare case—though his distance from the case would have precluded him from being privy to village rumor. He wondered, though, whether the rumor Miss Wheatley recalled was a product of her dislike and mistrust of Lawrence Tigue. He made a mental note to check the rumor when he looked at the O'Hare case files Harding had promised to pull from the vaults.

"You said that you knew Albert as a boy growing up here and recognized him when you encountered him in the wood in April," he said. "Do you know if anyone else in the village recognized him?"

"Well, I suppose they did." She paused to sip her tea, then added, "Though I don't know for certain. Most people just avoided him, as they normally do tramps."

"Did it not bother you that he'd been convicted of pedophilia?"

Miss Wheatley threw up her chubby hands.

"Please, Captain—that's a load of rubbish. Albert was no pedophile. He merely made a mistake with a girl who was too young. Some girls, as you know, can seem quite old at thirteen. And as for Ned Horton's suspicions of him regarding the O'Hare boys, he was cleared in that, and rightly so, though it cursed him for living here any longer. He'd been branded a pervert and that was that. He was an only child, and both his parents are long dead. He said he came back here to die, but I thought that rubbish, too. I believe he returned here because he still considered Winstead his home, despite the terrible thing that had happened to him here. I was glad to see that he'd returned, if you must know. He'd fallen so very far, you see."

"And how was it that you found his body this morning?"

"Well, I simply went up the trail to check on him. I hadn't seen him in a day or so and was worried that he might be sick."

Lamb sipped his tea and daubed his lips. "Why were you out in the village two nights ago, and well after midnight?" he asked as he replaced his cup in its saucer. "You were seen in Mr. Tigue's backyard—coming from his henhouse as a matter of fact."

Miss Wheatley's eyes widened and, for a moment, Lamb believed that he'd actually struck her speechless. Obviously Lilly had not lied about seeing Miss Wheatley steal the eggs, he thought.

"May I ask, Captain, who saw me?"

"I'm afraid I can't say."

"I see." She was silent for a few more seconds, then raised her chin. "*Yes*, I took the eggs and I'm not sorry," she said. "Tit for tat I call it. He takes from the nuthatch and I from him. If you must know, I intended to give the eggs to Albert—and to keep one or two for myself, of course."

She went to the crowded counter by the sink and retrieved a blue ceramic bowl covered with a yellow cloth. She put the bowl on the table and withdrew the cloth, revealing seven brown chicken eggs.

"You see, Captain, I still have them," she said. "I took them with me this morning when I went to check on Albert." She paused, then added, "That's when I found him." Her eyes suddenly began to fill with tears. "Poor Albert," she said.

Lamb considered returning the eggs to Tigue but decided to let the matter go. He was inclined toward believing that Miss Wheatley had nothing to do with Albert Clemmons's death.

"One other thing, Miss Wheatley. Do you know if Albert Clemmons finished school?"

Confusion briefly clouded Miss Wheatley's eyes. "Why, yes, he did," she said after a pause. "He made it through primary school at any rate."

Lamb stood.

"I'm afraid I've done a very naughty thing, haven't I, Captain?" Miss Wheatley said, looking up at him.

"Yes you have, Miss Wheatley. But I'm confident that you won't do it again."

"No, Captain," she said. "No, I won't. I promise."

SEVENTEEN

—⚏—

DURING THE AFTERNOON AND INTO THE EARLY EVENING, LAMB remained in Winstead as Winston-Sheed examined Clemmons's body in situ and then removed it for autopsy.

The doctor found no sign of trauma on the body—no one had bludgeoned, strangled, cut, or shot Albert Clemmons. Other than the suicide note and the rat poison, Lamb and his team collected no useful evidence from the scene. At the same time, Harding had taken care of negotiating with the army the bureaucratic necessities of shutting down work at the prison camp until the police removed whatever evidence the farmhouse foundation contained.

Lamb very much wanted to go to the prison camp to have a look at what the workers had unearthed in the foundation of the farmhouse. He also wanted to speak again with Lawrence Tigue, who had connections to the farm and Albert Clemmons. At the time of the O'Hare case, Tigue had lived on the farm with his mother and younger brother, and they had employed Albert Clemmons as a farmhand. Now Miss Wheatley had alleged that Sean O'Hare might have been having an affair with Olivia Tigue. Lamb feared that the small skull that had been found on the farm indeed belonged to one of the O'Hare twins, and that Larkin might soon turn up a second skull to match it.

If the bones did turn out to belong to one or more of the O'Hares, then someone who lived on the farm, or had access to it, had buried them in the basement. In any case, *someone's* remains had come to earth in the foundation of the building that Lawrence Tigue once had called home—though it was possible that the bodies had been buried in the house after the Tigues had left the farm and the house had lain abandoned.

Lamb wondered if Tigue had known that the tramp who'd taken up residence in the wood had been Clemmons. He also yearned to look at the O'Hare file and to track down and interview Ned Horton, the detective who had investigated the case more than two decades earlier. He also must track down Lawrence's younger brother, about whom he knew nothing, and, if she still was alive, Olivia Tigue. On top of that, none of his team had yet found an opportunity to thoroughly look at Ruth Aisquith's background.

As twilight descended upon Winstead, Lamb began to feel as if he needed to be in too many places at once and lacked time to get to all of them promptly enough. Before he left Winstead, he found Lawrence Tigue's cottage and rapped on its red front door. No one answered. Vera stood by her father's side.

Lamb rapped again with more vigor. "Mr. Tigue?" he said. "Police, sir. I'd like to speak with you."

Silence.

He went to the window of the sitting room but found it curtained. Frustrated, Lamb went around to the back of the house and knocked on the door to the kitchen. Still nothing. Here, too, he found a heavily curtained window. He turned his attention to the garage and the henhouse next to it. He found the double doors of the garage firmly locked—he could not even give them a good rattle—and its lone window shrouded with a blanket. Rivers had said that Tigue ran a small freelance printing business out of the garage. He hoped that he had not made a mistake in failing to focus more attention on Lawrence Tigue. He could see now how all of the digging and shoveling at the prison camp might have made Tigue nervous— though Tigue had not appeared even remotely uneasy when Lamb had interviewed him outside the cemetery gate on the previous morning.

Lamb closed his left eye and with his right peered through the narrow space between the locked double doors of the garage. He saw the front of a motorcar, though he could not identify its make in the fading, murky daylight that managed to pierce the garage's interior.

He turned to Vera. "Let's get onto the farm, then, before it gets too dark," he said. As Lamb and Vera drove away, Tigue risked parting the curtain on the window by the sitting room to watch them leave. He knew that he must not seek to dodge Lamb indefinitely—that he must keep from arousing Lamb's suspicions further until his preparations were complete.

On the previous evening, he'd taken the bus into Winchester to meet with his younger brother, Algernon, and had come away from that meeting certain that he was in control of the situation—though Algernon, of course, believed differently, as he always had. But it made no matter now what Algernon thought. Although the events of recent days had obstructed his plans, Lawrence believed that he still had enough time and opportunity left in which to salvage most, if not all, of what he'd originally sought. But he must keep his head and not lose the courage to act and to continue to risk. Once everything was in order he could forget Lamb, and Winstead, his wife and brother, and the O'Hares and Albert Clemmons and the whole sordid mess—a mess that had never been his doing but that he'd been forced to clean up nonetheless.

—◠◡◠—

Thirty minutes later, Lamb and Vera stood on the edge of the foundation of the farmhouse with Wallace, Superintendent Harding, Rivers, Taney, Captain Walton, Corporal Baker, and a dozen uniformed constables. Lamb lit a cigarette and stared down at Larkin, who was on his knees in the dirt, carefully unearthing a small human skeleton—one that appeared to have belonged to a child who would have been about the age that Jack and John O'Hare had been when they'd disappeared from Winstead. Darkness was descending and the forensics man was about to call it quits for the night and return to the job on the following morning. Harding had assigned two men to guard the scene through the night. The army had agreed to stop construction on the camp for three days only, which Harding believed was insufficient.

"We're going to have to get to the bottom of this quickly, Tom," the super said, as he stood next to Lamb and watched Larkin begin to pack up his kit.

"Yes," Lamb said, though he doubted that fulfilling such a wish was possible. Although a very neat solution to a crime he hadn't even known had been committed seemed almost literally to have fallen into his lap—Albert Clemmons had killed the O'Hare twins, buried their bodies in the basement of the house of the farm on which he'd been a laborer, and confessed to the murders, then killed himself in remorse—many aspects of that tidy scenario bothered Lamb, including the fact that Clemmons's apparent suicide note appeared to have been written by someone semiliterate while—at least according to Miss Wheatley—Clemmons had finished primary school, which meant that, at the very least, he probably had been able to spell simple words, such as *soul*, properly.

"It seems likely that Clemmons realized that the work here would unearth the bodies," Harding said, giving voice to Lamb's thoughts. "So he killed himself to avoid hanging."

Lamb took a drag from his Player's. "Yes, it's possible, certainly."

"But too neat. That's what you're thinking, isn't it, Tom? You love to bloody cloud things."

Lamb let the remark pass. He possessed not a shred of doubt that Harding trusted his instincts and usually yielded to them, and would now if he presented a strong enough case for his skepticism.

"I wonder why Clemmons felt the need to kill himself—if he did kill himself," Lamb said after a pause. "He was cleared of any connection to the O'Hare mess twenty years ago and was living nearly anonymously as a tramp in the woods in Winstead. I could see the suicide if there were more at stake for him—if an unmasking would have ruined his good reputation or left his wife and children shocked and betrayed. But he had no reputation and no family. He had very little to lose."

"Perhaps the guilt ate him up. He was exhausted—tired of the hiding, living as a tramp, the squalor and isolation, and this," Harding nodded at the hole, "pushed him over the edge."

"And yet his suicide note seemed to be missing any real sense of remorse or guilt. It read almost like a telegram. And it contained misspellings—*killed*, *mercy*, *soul*—that strike me as false, as if someone had written the note and thought, 'Well, here's how a tramp would write it.' Except that Clemmons was not a tramp in the usual sense; he wasn't uneducated or illiterate. He'd finished grammar school."

"The army has given us three days to clear up this mess," Harding said. "Then we're to clear out so they can make way for the bloody Italians."

Lamb dropped his cigarette in the mud and ground it out with the tip of his shoe. A slight shiver shot down his spine. The shiver wasn't fear, exactly—though neither was the sensation free of trepidation, unease, foreboding. He did not believe in ghosts. And yet he felt surrounded by distressed spirits reaching out to him, importuning, wanting justice and an end to their secret misery.

—⁂—

At a few minutes past midnight, Wilhemina Wimberly was in the living room when Gerald came in and told her that he was going to

Doris White's cottage. Gerald had shown her the note that Doris had left on his desk in the vicarage and insisted that they had no choice but to give in to Doris's demand that he come to her cottage that night. He promised Wilhemina that he would see to the problem but that she must give him time and, in the meantime, keep her mouth shut and not interfere.

He reminded her of how easily Lamb and Rivers had picked apart her story. He told her that, although the police had their little bits of evidence—their footprints and so on—and their suspicions, none of it amounted to anything worthwhile. Even though Lamb had found the bullet, he never would find the Webley. He'd seen to that.

Wilhemina stood in the living room, facing Gerald, a mixture of defiance and disgust on her face. She was about to give in again to Gerald, as she always did. Both of them had learned long ago that her defiance of Gerald was a pose designed to allow her to retain some dignity within her act of submission.

He reached for Wilhemina and touched her hand. "I'm doing this for you as much as for myself," he said. "I hope you realize that."

Wilhemina looked at Gerald's hand on hers. Once, she had loved him. She supposed she still did, despite the myriad times and ways in which he had betrayed and mistreated her. Now, though, she must depend on him. Gerald had a way of making problems disappear. He was never slowed, riddled with anxiety, or made tongue-tied by feelings of remorse or guilt, sorrow, or shame. Doris White had them by the hair, and neither of them could do anything about that for the moment, save give in to her, as Gerald said. Eventually, Gerald would act, as he always did. She did not delude herself that he would act for her sake, however, as he claimed. Gerald acted only in *his* interest.

"I'm off, then," Gerald said. He smiled. He seemed confident, Wilhemina thought. She could not fathom his iciness. "Don't wait up," he added.

Wilhemina turned her back to Gerald and wrapped her arms about herself. As Gerald closed the door behind him she began to cry.

—〰—

Gerald walked into the village along the path. He believed that he still held sway over Doris and could convince her to keep quiet until he figured out a permanent solution to the problem she represented. She was a stupid little cow, easily suggestible. Seducing her three years ago had presented him no challenge—which had caused him to become bored of her practically in the same moment in which he'd conquered her. He recalled that moment now with disgust and wondered what in God's name he'd been thinking when he'd seduced her. She was repellent, stupid and dull, hairy and pasty. She was worse than a cow, really. She was a kind of odious badger. But his sexual appetites sometimes led him astray.

At the time of his seduction of Doris, he'd quickly realized his mistake and talked his way out of the affair—again, quite easily. He'd spoken to Doris of his guilt in the eyes of God of the sin of adultery, and she'd swallowed that. Even so, he'd felt it wise to give her the job of cleaning up around the church to ensure her silence. Each day, when she came to the church, he had worked on her, a little at a time, like someone training a dog to sit or beg. Eventually she'd responded and he'd become satisfied that he had nothing to fear from her publicly revealing their affair. Her regular presence around the church had upset Wilhemina, of course, but that hardly concerned him. The insolent note that Doris had left on his desk that afternoon had surprised him a bit—her cheek had surprised him. But he told himself that it meant nothing. His job now was to discover how much she *actually* knew versus how much she was guessing at.

He did not knock on her door; he never had. He entered Doris's cottage to find the sitting room lit with at least two dozen candles he recognized as being from the church. He realized that Doris had nicked the candles from Miss Tutin's funeral.

As Doris emerged, Gerald immediately believed that he had little or nothing to worry about. She was the same loathsome, suggestible badger. She walked from the relative gloom of the kitchen, as if walking onto a stage. She was dressed in the same dull green dress she invariably wore to Sunday services and the same square brown shoes. She'd hideously painted her face with lipstick and rouge. He thought that she looked sick—even a bit mad—and thoroughly repulsive.

"Hello, Gerald," she said. "I'm glad you came."

"I received your note," he said. He made his voice sound gentle, conciliatory.

"I hope it didn't upset you."

"Why would it upset me?"

"Because you don't love me. I know that you don't. You said you did once. But you were lying."

"How can you say that? Look at all I've done for you. And I'm here now, aren't I?"

"You're here only because you're afraid of me. You're afraid of me because I know things." She stood, tentatively, on the threshold between the darkness of the kitchen and the soft candlelight of the sitting room.

He took a small step toward her. "I'm not afraid of you. I trust you."

"I know things," she said. She stood very still, watching him.

"I know that you do. But I trust you." He took another step toward her. "You look very beautiful. I'm glad you dressed up."

"I dressed for you. I don't know why."

"I know why. You haven't changed the way you feel about me." She took a step toward him; he held out his hand to her.

"I like what you've done with the candles," he said.

"I nicked them—from the chapel."

He smiled. In a low, conspiratorial voice, he said, "I know. That was very naughty of you, wasn't it? You haven't forgotten that I like it when you're naughty."

To his surprise, she took a step backward, toward the darkened kitchen. "I won't let you seduce me," she said.

"I remember how delicious you are."

"You can't seduce me," she repeated. "I know things. I know what you did with the pistol. I saw you. Last night, in the cemetery."

This shocked him. How could she possibly have known that he would bury the Webley in Miss Tutin's grave? A pang of fear shot through the depths of his gut. Nonetheless, he smiled. "What did you see, my darling?"

"I saw what you did."

"What did I do?"

"You buried the pistol in Miss Tutin's grave. Then, today, the grave was covered up forever."

"You're mistaken." He must be careful. He did not want to antagonize her. He must try to convince her that she did not see what she believed she saw. "That wasn't the pistol. It was Wilhemina's shoes. I knew that the police would ask for them so I buried them."

Doris stepped out of the darkness. "Do you like the candles?"

"Very much." He was uncertain what she was up to. Even so, he must remain patient—must not rush or upset her.

"It was naughty of me, wasn't it—to nick the candles?" She took another step toward him.

"Very naughty."

She stepped fully into the candlelight and put the palms of her hands on Gerald's chest. Internally, he recoiled. Outwardly, he smiled again.

"You're lying about Wilhemina's shoes being in the bag," she said, her voice suddenly husky. She playfully picked at a piece of lint on Gerald's sweater, then looked directly into his eyes. "I will tell the police all I know unless you do as I say."

Gerald fought an urge to strike the badger's hideous face. Instead, in a voice that made it sound as if he was merely playing a mischievous game, he said, "And what is it that you want?"

She lifted her sticky, painted lips toward his. He found the sensation of her breath on his face ghastly.

"For you to pretend that you love me," she said.

EIGHTEEN

—◊◊◊—

LAMB AND VERA ROSE EARLY, PAUSING ONLY LONG ENOUGH TO share with Marjorie a cup of coffee and a slice of toast with a bit of marmalade before heading to the nick. Lamb had awakened that morning still feeling a keen desire to learn as much as he could, as quickly as he could, about the O'Hare case. He intended to take at least a cursory look that morning at the dusty files of the case and hoped to track down and interview Ned Horton that day.

Also, the story he'd read in the *Hampshire Mail* a few months earlier that had detailed the government's intention to build the POW camp on the farm near Winstead had mentioned that the farm had been owned since 1917 by an estate agent from Winchester whose name Lamb could not recall. This man therefore had been Olivia Tigue's landlord. He intended to put Vera to the job of finding the agent's name, as the man might possess memories of the Tigues and the case. On the drive to the nick, Lamb filled Vera in on what he recalled of the O'Hare case, reasoning that the residents of Winstead would begin speaking about the case again and that one of them might say something to Vera or anyone else on the team—even in passing—that could prove valuable. He and Vera arrived at the nick to find that Rivers, too, had come in early; he was hunched over the typewriter at his desk, writing a report on the canvass of Winstead he'd led in the wake of the Aisquith killing.

On the previous night, Lamb and Harding had decided that the inquiry team needed an incident room in Winstead, from which it could coordinate its various inquiries. Lamb had noticed the small stone school in the village and thought that it would do nicely, given that classes were out for the summer term. Lamb now sat by Rivers's desk and explained to Rivers what he desired in Winstead. Rivers promised he would take a few constables to the village that morning and set up the incident room.

Rivers also had a bit of news that surprised Lamb. "I made a telephone call yesterday," he said. "The toy soldier—Grant—comes from a set manufactured by the W. Britain Limited toy company between 1900 and 1930 of field marshals and generals. Each set had six figurines, all generals, all made of cast lead."

In the rush of events Lamb had forgotten about the Grant figure. He was uncertain if the figure was significant, though it had been just odd enough—just enough out of place—to potentially be so. Lamb was glad to see that Rivers had been thinking along the same lines.

"I had a set when I was a boy," Rivers said. "Wellington, Napoleon, Edward IV, von Hindenburg, Johnny Burgoyne, and Grant. The man I talked to at Britain's said that, after the last war, they replaced Edward IV in the set with Haig. Keeping up with the times." Douglas Haig had led the British Army during most of the Great War.

Lamb smiled. "Nice work, Harry," he said.

"We'll see," Rivers said. "It might mean bollocks."

"Maybe," Lamb said.

Lamb again consulted the newspaper file and found the story on the prison camp that had been in the *Mail*. The name of the man who had owned the farm was Oscar Strand, an estate agent in Winchester. Because Wallace had yet to come in, Lamb sat Vera at the detective sergeant's desk and gave her the task of calling Strand and inquiring if he was free that day to speak to a policeman about his former tenants, the O'Hares. If he claimed to be busy, Vera was to push a bit and say that the matter was rather urgent. The story also contained the name of the younger O'Hare brother, Algernon, who, the paper reported, was the head of the mathematics department at the Everly School in Winchester. Algernon's and Lawrence's mother, Olivia Tigue, had died some years earlier, according to the story. Vera also was to call Algernon Tigue and arrange a time that day during which Lamb could speak to him.

"If he's seen this morning's *Mail*—and my guess is that he has— he'll understand why I want to speak with him," Lamb said of Algernon Tigue.

That morning's paper had reported on its front page the discovery of a child's skeleton in the foundation of the farmhouse near Winstead. Although Harding had made it clear to the press that the constabulary had not yet determined the identity of the child, the *Mail* once again had reminded its readers that Winstead had been the scene of Claire O'Hare's suicide more than twenty years earlier. The paper also had reported that morning the discovery of a body that police said they had not yet identified—likely that of a tramp, and likely a case of suicide, the story said—in the wood near Saint Michael's Church in Winstead on the previous day, though the editors had decided that this story merited only five paragraphs on page seven.

Lamb went to his office, where he found the files of the O'Hare case lying on the floor next to his desk in three cardboard boxes, and closed the door. He believed that he must treat the case as if it was fresh. And to do that, he must go back to the beginning and reconstruct the day on which Claire O'Hare was found hanging from the end of a rope tied to a rafter in her parlor.

He peeked into one of the boxes, which emitted a musty smell. The files seemed to be in relatively good order; Lamb had worried that a kind of volcanic mess of paper awaited him in the boxes. He also found on his desk a slip of paper, which Harding had placed there, on which was written Ned Horton's telephone number and address. Lamb sat at his desk and dialed the number. After a couple of rings, a voice answered, gruffly: "Horton."

"Mr. Horton, this is Chief Inspector Tom Lamb."

"I expected that you—or someone like you—would call."

"So you saw the *Mail* this morning, then?"

"I saw."

"We're not sure yet who the body belongs to."

Horton said nothing.

"I'd like to come by this morning and talk to you about the case," Lamb said. He decided that he would wait to tell Horton that he believed that the tramp who'd died in the wood by the church was Albert Clemmons.

"I'll be home all day."

"How about ten?"

"Ten will do."

"Thank you, Mr. Horton. I'll see you at ten, then."

Horton emitted a grunt that sounded like "Right," then hung up.

Vera knocked on the door and Lamb bade her enter. She laid a slip of paper on his desk with Oscar Strand's name, address, and telephone number on it and the notation that he was free that morning from ten to noon. She stood before her father in her baggy uniform, looking rather serious. He sensed the pride she felt in completing the assignment he'd given her.

"Nice work," Lamb said.

"Thank you."

Lamb thought he had heard Wallace's voice in the outer room. He checked his watch; if the detective sergeant hadn't yet arrived, he was past due.

"Is Wallace in yet?" he asked Vera.

"He's just arrived."

"Could you ask him to pop in and see me, please?" Lamb felt it slightly odd to be ordering around his daughter as if she were his secretary, but he thought it best that Vera stay busy during the time she worked for him and that she and Harding and the rest of the team came away from her tenure with the nick feeling as if she'd at least earned her keep.

"Of course," Vera said.

A minute later, Wallace stood in the doorway.

"Come in," Lamb said. He delivered to Wallace the same brief summation of the O'Hare case that he'd delivered to Vera, then handed Wallace the paper on which Vera had written the contact information for Oscar Strand and explained Strand's relationship with the Tigues. "He might recall something useful about them and the O'Hare case," Lamb said. "I'd like you to speak with him this morning, before you head out to the prison site."

Wallace took the paper. "Right," he said.

And steer clear of my daughter in the meantime, Lamb thought, though he merely nodded at Wallace in acknowledgment and watched the detective sergeant exit.

Again alone in his office, Lamb picked up the first of the boxes containing the O'Hare files and began to go through it. The file turned out to be deeper than he had expected, given that Horton's conclusion seemed to have been the obvious one—that Claire O'Hare had committed suicide and that her husband had abandoned her for parts unknown and taken their twin sons with him. He spent an hour sorting through the first two of the three boxes and found himself frustrated in his attempt to find Horton's first official report on the case, which he hoped would contain a narrative of Horton's initial call to the scene of Claire O'Hare's suicide and his discovery that Sean O'Hare and the couple's sons were gone. He found the absence of such a document troubling, though portions of old files sometimes went missing and were rearranged over time. Despite this missing piece, Lamb was able to cobble together a basic outline of the case through what the boxes contained—some of Horton's handwritten notes, witness statements, later official reports, and a few clippings on the case from the *Mail*.

An unnamed resident of Winstead had called the constable in the neighboring village of Lower Promise—Winstead had had no constable of its own at the time—to say that they suspected that some violence had been committed in the O'Hare cottage, though the file did not say what sort of violence the neighbor believed had occurred.

The constable, a man named John Markham, arrived a half-hour later, at roughly eight P.M., to find the door to the O'Hare cottage open. He entered the house to find Claire O'Hare hanging, dead, from a rafter in the cottage's parlor. He'd immediately gone to the pub to call the nick in Winchester and request a CID man, who turned out to be Ned Horton.

Horton determined that Claire O'Hare had stood on a chair she'd taken from the kitchen, knotted one end of the belt of her yellow dressing gown around her neck and the other around the rafter, then stepped off the chair into oblivion. She wore only the dressing gown itself, which lay open on her dangling body. Horton had found a brief suicide note on the kitchen table in Claire's handwriting that stated that she had killed herself in despair over her husband having abandoned her and taken their five-year-old twin sons with him. (In his search of the first two boxes, Lamb had not been able to find the note itself or a document that contained its exact wording, which also troubled him.) The cottage displayed no evidence of a struggle having taken place within it. The coroner had determined that Claire had hung herself at no earlier than noon of that day.

Sean O'Hare and his sons seemed to have disappeared from Winstead at some point during that morning. Horton seemed never to have determined with any certainty to where Sean had fled with the boys, though the primary rumor around Winstead was that he had gone to County Wicklow, in Ireland, from where, it was said, his parents had immigrated during the previous century. He and Claire both were known to drink and to regularly row loudly and violently.

The twins last had been seen at roughly ten fifteen on that same morning—Tuesday, August 17, 1919—by Albert Clemmons, who had been working in the front field of the Tigue farm. When questioned, Clemmons had told Horton that he'd seen the boys walking down the dirt road that led from the paved road toward the farmhouse, but that he had not seen them again that day. The twins often went to the Tigue farm because Olivia Tigue considered them to be neglected and often fed them. More than a dozen people in the village, along with Clemmons, testified that the boys often knocked on the doors of people whom they trusted and found to be kindly, seeking handouts of food. On the day they and their father disappeared, the boys were five years and ten months old and, according to Clemmons, wore matching tan cotton short trousers and white cotton socks; Jack wore a light blue cotton collared and buttoned shirt, while John wore a light green shirt of the same style. Sean, a sporadically employed carpenter and performer of odd jobs, was last seen on the evening before his disappearance by the men with whom he was working on a temporary road construction job near Winchester.

Several people to whom Horton spoke had described Claire O'Hare as an exceedingly negligent mother and said that, long before the boys' disappearance, she had faced general criticism in the village for failing to feed and bathe the boys properly and allowing them to wander too far from home without supervision at too young an age.

Horton seemed to have suspected Clemmons of having done something with the boys primarily because of Clemmons's previous conviction for pedophilia. Otherwise, Horton had found no connection between the boys and Clemmons—though Horton's revelation of Clemmons's conviction in Southampton two years earlier for having sexually toyed with a thirteen-year-old girl had ruined Clemmons's reputation in the village, causing Clemmons to eventually leave Winstead.

Olivia Tigue and her sons—Lawrence, who was sixteen at the time, and Algernon, who was thirteen—all claimed not to have seen the twins on the farm that day, and Horton seemed never to have seriously considered any of the Tigues as having any connection to the events surrounding the O'Hares.

Lamb felt dissatisfied as he finished his perusal of the first two boxes of the files. He considered taking a cursory look at the contents of the third, hoping to find within it Horton's original report and Claire O'Hare's suicide note, but time would not allow it for the moment. The apparent source of his frustration and suspicions—retired DI Ned Horton—was waiting for him in Southampton.

As he was about to leave, his phone rang. It was the police surgeon, Anthony Winston-Sheed.

"Preliminarily, your tramp, Mr. Clemmons, didn't die of natural causes, though I haven't quite finished the autopsy yet," the doctor said.

"What did he die of, then?" Lamb asked.

"A massive dose of arsenic, the kind of thing one finds in rat poison or common insecticides, and in a quantity far more than was necessary to send him to the hereafter. Either he was very determined to kill himself or someone else very much wanted him dead."

NINETEEN

—⚮—

NED HORTON LIVED IN A SMALL COTTAGE ON THE EASTERN EDGE of Winchester. The cottage's front yard featured a small, well-tended flower garden edged in stone, which was alive with a profusion of red roses, yellow carnations, and blue cornflowers.

Vera stayed with the car as Lamb went to Horton's door and knocked. The man who answered was of medium height, with a high, creased forehead, stubby pugilist's nose, and thin, uncompromising lips, all of which were offset by a full head of brown hair that was long enough to touch the tops of his ears, softening his otherwise severe countenance. An unlit pipe protruded from the left corner of his mouth, and he had not shaved that morning. Seeing the way in which Horton had aged surprised Lamb for an instant; Horton had left the police force within a year of the O'Hare case, and Lamb hadn't seen him in nearly twenty years. The picture he'd kept in his mind of Horton was that of the man's younger version.

Horton stepped back from the door and invited Lamb into a cramped but neat sitting room that, Lamb thought, his own mother might have been proud to call her own. A lime-green couch sat in front of a mahogany coffee table, and facing these were two upholstered chairs of the same color. The linen curtains behind the couch were of a contrasting light red that was almost pink. The table fairly gleamed, and Lamb detected in the room not a single speck of dust or stray cobweb. All that seemed to be missing were the lace doilies, Lamb thought. In the corner of the room was another highly polished table upon which sat a large wireless.

"Can I get you something?" Horton asked. "I've a couple of bottles of ale if you fancy that."

Lamb smiled. "A bit early for me, thanks."

"Tea, then? I've a bit of milk and sugar both."

"Tea would be fine, thanks."

Lamb waited in the living room for Horton to return with the tea. He noticed as he sat on the sofa that, despite the sitting room's neat and homey aspects, it contained no photographs. Horton never had married and had no children. Perhaps he preferred keeping his memories to himself, Lamb thought.

Horton returned with a tray containing tea in a small red ceramic pot, two matching cups, milk, and sugar. He poured Lamb and himself each a cup, then sat in one of the upholstered chairs opposite Lamb. "What do you want to know, then?" he asked.

"As much as you can remember," Lamb said. "Why don't we start at the beginning."

"You've seen the file?"

"I had a look at it."

Horton sat back in his chair.

"It was nine o'clock and bloody well nearly dark by the time I got to Winstead. I went alone at first, as there was no one else available in the nick at the time the call came in, and I didn't really know what I would find out there. You never do in these bloody little villages—though, of course, once I saw what I had I called in forensics and the surgeon."

Lamb withdrew from the inner pocket of his jacket a notebook into which he had jotted the notes he'd taken that morning while perusing the files. "The village bobby from Lower Promise called you," he said, glancing at the notebook. "A man named Markham."

"Was that his name, then? I'd forgotten. I remember that he was older—too old for a village bobby—and none too sharp besides. The whole thing seemed to have knocked him off his kilter, seeing the O'Hare woman hanging from the rafter like that, with her face in the way they get from a hanging, the tongue and the eyes bulging out, like. I knew right away that he wasn't going to be much use to me."

"Do you remember the name of the person from the village who called Markham? I would assume that person was the first to find the body."

"Anonymous; wouldn't give their name."

"Male or female?"

"Female, according to the bobby."

"Did you find that suspicious?"

"I did, yeah."

"Did Markham have a guess as to who it might have been?"

"Didn't have a clue. As I said, he was none too sharp."

"And no one ever came forward as the caller?"

"No—as I said." Horton's voice suddenly became tinged with irritation, as if he considered the answer to Lamb's question obvious.

"I'm sorry, Ned, but you didn't say," Lamb said. He looked evenly at Horton.

"Well, you said you'd seen the file," Horton said. "It'll be in the file."

"You found a suicide note," Lamb said.

"Yes."

"Where?"

"On the kitchen table."

"What did it say?"

"Well, I can't remember exactly. The gist of it was that she'd killed herself because her husband had left her and taken their sons."

"Can you remember anything specific about it—a phrase perhaps?"

"It'll be in the file."

"Probably, but I haven't found it yet. The file's large, as I'm sure you remember."

Horton looked at the ceiling, as if trying to recall the specific contents of the note. "Something about, 'He's gone and he's never coming back and I'll never see my boys again.' Along those lines."

"How did you determine that the handwriting was Claire O'Hare's?"

"I found some other things she'd written—notes and lists and the like—and they matched."

"Who else did you show them to?"

"Green, the forensics man."

"And he agreed with your assessment?"

"Yes, and so did the coroner."

"Did you not think to send the note and the other materials to the Yard for handwriting analysis?"

"Why should I have done?" Horton again sounded irritated. "What does the Yard know that I don't? I realize it's all the fashion these days to send your bloody evidence away to all the college-educated boys at the Yard. But in my day we handled our own inquiries. Didn't depend on outsiders. It was her handwriting—Claire O'Hare's. That was easy enough to see. Not only that, but a couple of people in the village told me she'd threatened to kill herself a couple of times before. She had a habit of announcing this every time she and the husband fought, or when she wanted something from him. 'Stop or I'll kill myself; give it to me or I'll kill myself.' That sort of thing. Emotional blackmail."

"What happened next?"

Horton sat back in his chair and lit his pipe. Aromatic blue smoke rose in a delicate cloud in front of his face, obscuring it slightly. Horton squinted at Lamb through the miasma, as if he was trying to see through fog.

"Well, as I secured the scene I sent Markham—the bobby—to see if he could find Sean O'Hare and the children. Although her note said they'd left, I didn't take that as truth, of course—at least not then." He paused to puff his pipe anew. "But it did turn out to be true. Markham never found them that night, and neither I nor anyone else that I know of ever saw them again. I concluded that he'd gone back to Ireland; he was bloody Irish—his people were from County Wicklow—and he hightailed it. Claire O'Hare was a lush and treated the bloody kids like dirt. Everyone in the village said so. So it made sense."

"Did you contact the Irish for help?"

"Of course. But he'd gone to ground on his home turf, more than like. You have to remember that this was just a few years removed from the Easter Rising. Nobody who knew him from the Auld Sod was going to give him away to a bloody British copper. Not a chance of that. Probably changed his name and those of the kids, too."

Lamb had seen no mention in the file of Horton having contacted the Irish police.

"Claire O'Hare was nothing in the way of a wife or mother, and her children suffered because of that," Horton said. "They had to go wandering around the village looking for a bloody handout if they expected to eat."

"They were last seen that morning on the Tigue farm, where they normally went for food," Lamb said.

"That's right."

"And Sean O'Hare last had been seen the night before, at his road job in Winchester?"

"Yes."

"What did you conclude happened then—that morning, I mean?"

"Sean came home from his road work job a bit after eight on the previous night; several people said they'd heard him and Claire arguing from about then until nearly ten. Eventually, everyone in the house went to sleep and the boys rose early, as they always did, and went to the farm looking for food. They seemed to have gone to the Tigue farm for part of the morning—or so Albert Clemmons claimed.

Sean O'Hare rounded them up and left. I think it took Claire several hours to even realize they'd gone. She was probably drunk or sleeping one off. Then, when she saw the truth of what had happened, she did what she had so many times threatened to do."

"Did no one besides Albert Clemmons report seeing either Sean or the boys around the village that morning?"

"No. It's in the file, as I said."

"Did Claire go out into the village looking for them when she realized that they were gone? Did anybody see her about?"

"If they did, no one told me about it. As I said, she was probably drunk at the time."

"You checked into Albert Clemmons's background. Why was that, if you didn't suspect that he might have had something to do with some aspect of the case—that maybe Claire O'Hare's suicide didn't quite explain everything?"

"Well, I had to check didn't I?" He looked directly at Lamb. "Otherwise, sharpies like you would have come up behind me, nosing around and asking questions. 'Why didn't you check this, Ned? Why didn't you check that?' I remember you, by the way, Lamb. You were a uniformed PC at the time. Eager beaver type. Just the type I mean. I was a damned good detective and I followed procedure. Clemmons had been the last man to admit having seen the twins, and so I checked his background and up came this conviction for raping a thirteen-year-old girl. But there was nothing to connect him to the disappearance of Sean O'Hare and his sons—not a bloody thing. If it turns out that the body you've found on the farm is one of the O'Hare boys and that I was bloody well wrong, then I was bloody well wrong." He looked directly at Lamb. "We all make mistakes."

"Did you interview the Tigues?"

"Of course. They all accounted for their whereabouts. Besides which Olivia Tigue was one of them who fed the O'Hare boys, took care of them when their own mother wouldn't. She had no cause to harm them."

"What about the older son, Lawrence? He was sixteen at the time."

"He'd spent the entire morning on the other side of the farm hunting rabbits. They owned a fowling piece, and I checked it and it had been recently fired. And they had three rabbits in the larder, waiting to be skinned."

"Did you speak to the younger son, Algernon?"

"Yes, but he was only a lad at the time. Like his brother, he was away from the farm that morning—off with his mates somewhere. His mother confirmed that."

"Did you confirm either of the brothers' stories with anyone else?"

Horton straightened in his chair. The question obviously offended him. "Of course," he said.

"So you spoke to their mates, then?"

Horton looked directly at Lamb. "I interviewed nearly everyone in Winstead. If you check the file you'll see that."

Lamb paused for a second, then moved forward in his chair, closer to Horton. "Did you see in this morning's *Mail* that we also found the body of a tramp in the wood by Saint Michael's Church yesterday?"

Horton crossed his legs. "Yes."

"That man was Albert Clemmons. He left a note admitting that he killed the O'Hare twins."

Horton seemed to freeze for an instant. Lamb saw genuine surprise in his eyes.

Lamb pulled the note from the inner pocket of his jacket and handed it to Horton, who read it, then handed it back. "How did he die?" he asked.

"A massive dose of arsenic."

Horton sat back in his chair and crossed his arms. "Well, as I said, if I was mistaken, then I was mistaken. If Clemmons did kill the boys then good riddance to him."

From the right pocket of his coat, Lamb produced the figurine of General Ulysses Grant he'd found among Clemmons's belongings. He was fishing now, but he sometimes had a bit of luck when he fished.

"Does this mean anything to you?" Lamb asked.

Horton peered at the figure for a second then pulled his glasses from his shirt pocket and put them on. He looked again at the tiny Grant. "Where did you get it?"

"I found it with Clemmons's things. It was in a little bag of what appeared to be his few keepsakes."

"First time I've ever seen one—General Grant." He handed it back to Lamb. "If it has significance I don't know what it would be."

"Did the O'Hares or the Tigue boys own toy soldiers?"

"I don't know. Most boys do."

"Did you search the farmhouse thoroughly, including the basement?"

"No," Horton said. "I'd no cause to." He removed his pipe from his mouth and leaned toward Lamb. "If you're asking me why in bloody hell I didn't find the body you've found, then the only answer I can give you is that I don't know why. I did everything that was required and then some."

"Does the name Ruth Aisquith mean anything to you?" Lamb asked.

"The woman who was shot in the cemetery? No, why should it?"

"How about Mary Forrest?"

"No. Who is that?"

"It's not important." Lamb paused for a few seconds, then said, "It sounds as if you didn't have much sympathy for Claire O'Hare, Ned."

Horton looked at Lamb sharply. "Why should I have had sympathy for her?"

"She'd lost her sons."

"Until then, she'd hardly noticed her bloody sons."

Lamb stood and offered his hand to Horton. "All right, then, Ned," he said. "Thank you for your time."

Horton stood and shook Lamb's hand. "Right," he said. He clamped his pipe in his teeth and failed to see Lamb to the door.

Lamb slid into the passenger seat of the Wolseley as Vera started the car. He thought of the obviously poor job that Ned Horton had done investigating the O'Hare case and how this was worse than a shame. It was, he thought, almost a kind of crime in itself.

TWENTY

—⟪⟫—

BEFORE SHE AND LAMB HAD LEFT THE NICK THAT MORNING, VERA had reached Algernon Tigue and arranged for her father to meet Algernon in his rooms at the Everly School, where he was head of the maths department, after Lamb had finished with Ned Horton. Algernon had sounded "rather pleasant," Vera had added when she'd informed Lamb of the interview.

In the meantime, Lamb's study of Horton's file on the O'Hare case, along with his subsequent interview with Horton, had added another person to the list of those to whom Lamb wanted to speak— John Markham, the former bobby of Lower Promise, who'd called Horton to the village after finding Claire O'Hare hanging from the rafters. In addition, the events of the past twenty-four hours had forced Lamb to temporarily put aside the problem of Ruth Aisquith.

Now, though, as he and Vera drove to the Everly School, he turned his mind again to the case.

Although he believed that Gerald and Wilhemina Wimberly knew more than they were telling him about Aisquith's death, he had collected no real evidence to connect either of them to any wrongdoing. He needed Gerald Wimberly's Webley, but was certain that Wimberly already had gotten rid of the pistol—that it now was lying at the bottom of some pond or buried in a nearby wood. He still knew very little about Ruth Aisquith, really, and that was a disadvantage. He decided that once Rivers had finished setting up the incident room, he would dispatch the detective inspector to the Ministry of Labour and National Service, in London, to have a look at Aisquith's government file and, hopefully, to learn more about her background and personal history.

Because it was out for the summer term, the Everly School, in Winchester, was mostly deserted. The only person Lamb saw on his way to Algernon Tigue's rooms was a lone gardener who was raking freshly cut grass into a sodden pile on the lawn in the school's small main quadrangle.

Algernon Tigue answered Lamb's knock on his door. He resembled his older brother in some respects, with the same narrow nose. But Algernon was several inches taller and more solidly built than Lawrence, huskier in the shoulders and heavier in the waist. He wore circular, metal-rimmed glasses and had combed his longish dark hair over his head in a way that Lamb thought foppish. He offered his hand to Lamb.

"Good morning, Chief Inspector," he said. His grip was firm. He stood aside to allow Lamb to enter. "Please come in."

Tigue's rooms were small and comfortably appointed. A high mahogany bookshelf dominated the left wall, while a large window on the right gave onto a view of the quadrangle. In front of the window was Tigue's writing desk, upon which a collection of books and papers was neatly arranged. A door at the other end led to an anteroom, presumably Tigue's bedroom. Along the far wall was a hearth, in front of which stood a small round table surrounded by two chairs.

It was to this place that Tigue led Lamb and offered him tea, which was waiting on the table. As Lamb passed Tigue's desk, he noticed a small military figurine beneath the lamp, as if it were standing watch there. The figure was of arguably the greatest field marshal of them all, Napoleon Bonaparte.

"Thank you," Lamb said to Tigue's offer of tea.

Tigue poured tea and sat opposite Lamb, crossing his legs. He pulled a silver cigarette case from his pocket, removed one, then offered one to Lamb, who declined. He lit the cigarette and said, "Now, how can I help you, Chief Inspector? If you don't mind my saying so, it sounds as if you've quite a mess on your hands in Winstead. What you've found out at the farm is quite shocking. Have you identified the skull you found on the farm yet, by the way?"

"Not yet, no. I was hoping that perhaps you might be able to help me with that."

Tigue exhaled and smiled. "Oh come now, Chief Inspector. How could I possibly help you with that? The only person who could help you with that is the person who buried the child there, and that certainly wasn't me."

"You and your mother and brother did live at the house for several years."

"Of course we did. But none of us ever buried a body there." He smiled yet again—confidently, Lamb thought. "You're making this all sound rather like a novel—the body in the basement."

"It is what it is," Lamb said flatly.

"True. Then, too, I'm sure you've considered the possibility that someone might have buried the child there long after my family and I left the farm. My mother died in 1932, and Lawrence left shortly thereafter. I had left several years earlier, to begin my university education. The place has been abandoned ever since. Anyone might have come along one foggy night and buried a body there."

"What is your opinion, sir? Do you believe that the skull could be that of one of the O'Hare twins? As I'm sure you recall, the boys were last seen alive on the farm."

Algernon shrugged. "Well, I don't know, as I said. I can only say that if the skull does belong to one of the twins, then Albert Clemmons must have been the culprit all along, just as Ned Horton had suspected. Albert had been convicted of pedophilia, as I'm sure you must know."

"So neither you nor your mother nor brother had anything to do with the disappearance of the O'Hare twins, or possess any knowledge of what happened to them or their father—or, for that matter, any knowledge of the death of Claire O'Hare?" Lamb spoke without emotion, maintaining his gaze on Algernon.

Tigue laughed, as if he found Lamb's question a kind of game and he enjoyed games.

"Ha! I suppose you're only doing your job, despite what I've just told you. But I'll play along. The answer, as I said, is no. I was a boy at the time, not much older than the O'Hares themselves, and my brother is incapable of violence. I assume you've met Lawrence, given the amount of time you must have been spending in Winstead of late; if so you've probably seen that for yourself. As for my mother, she probably treated the O'Hare twins with more kindness than did their own mother, who was a worthless lush. That's why the boys came onto the farm in the first place; my mother often fed them when they were hungry."

"Did your mother have an affair with Sean O'Hare?" Lamb knew that even if Olivia Tigue had been at it with Sean O'Hare, Algernon would deny it. But he wanted to see how Algernon would react to the question baldly asked—whether he could, in asking the question, perhaps crack Algernon's composure and cockiness.

"Ha!" Algernon said. "You are a prize, Chief Inspector." He smiled again, but Lamb sensed a rising irritation in Algernon's voice and body language, leading Lamb to believe that he'd scored a hit. "I suppose you got that idea from the village gossip that went around at the time. But those bloody primitives in Winstead always gossiped about my mother. She was an outsider, which was bad enough in their eyes, but they also condemned her for having come to town unmarried and then having the temerity to run a farm on her own, which she did with much success, by the way. She was a strong woman who was worth ten of any of the mediocrities in Winstead who whispered about her behind her back." Lamb noticed that Tigue had lost his smile. "So no, she had no affair with Sean O'Hare."

"Why did your mother bring you and you brother to Winstead without your father?"

Tigue smiled again, but without the ease he'd shown earlier. "Because my father was dead, Chief Inspector. He was killed in 1917, at Arras."

"I see," Lamb said. He sat back in his chair. "As I'm sure you've heard by now, a murder occurred in Winstead before we found the bones at the farm. The victim's name was Ruth Aisquith, and she was shot to death—shot in the back—in the cemetery next to the church. Did you know her?"

"I'm afraid not, no."

"Did your brother know her?"

"Not that I am aware."

"Were you aware that your brother's wife has gone to her sister's in Chesterfield for the duration of the war?"

"Is that what he told you, then?"

"That's what he's told his neighbors."

"Well, I suppose he had to say something, didn't he?" Tigue stubbed out his cigarette in the ashtray and pulled another from the case, but this time did not offer one to Lamb. He lit it and took a pull. "You see, the truth of the matter is that my brother's wife has left him for another man—a motor car salesman, of all people. I'm not even sure how Alba met the fellow. But my brother's marriage never was very robust. I think Alba married Lawrence because she believed he had prospects. Then he left London and dragged her back to Winstead. Alba is a London girl, you see. She never fancied Winstead. And as much as I hate to say it, I don't think Lawrence ever measured up much as a husband. He always was a bit watery in that way." He shrugged. "Alba had had enough, and so she left. I can't say I blame her, really."

Lamb was not surprised to hear—if indeed the tale was true—that Lawrence Tigue's wife had left him and that Tigue had made up a story to cover his humiliation. But Algernon Tigue's apparent disdain for his brother—his seeming utter lack of compassion for his brother's wrecked marriage—did surprise him, and he found it telling.

"You sound as if you don't like your brother much, sir."

"Well, I suppose one's passions and opinions always are most intense when it comes to blood relations."

"I'm afraid, too, that the body of a tramp was found dead in the wood by Saint Michael's Church yesterday," Lamb said. "Although I haven't publicly released the man's identity, I'm certain that the man was Albert Clemmons."

Again, Lamb wanted to see Algernon's reaction to the bald stating of a fact that might cause him to react emotionally.

But Tigue expressed nothing that Lamb would have called surprise or shock at the news. He exhaled smoke. "I hadn't heard that a tramp had died," he said. "As for whether or not the man was Albert, I'm willing to believe anything. Given what happened to Albert he might very well have become a tramp. He drank a bit when I knew him, after all. That's something that never came out about Albert, by the way—that besides being a pedophile, he drank. My mother frequently had to rouse him out of bed in the morning to get him to do his chores around the farm. A less patient person would have gotten rid of a man like Clemmons, but my mother wasn't like that."

"Does it surprise you that Albert Clemmons had returned to Winstead?"

"Not really." He shrugged.

Lamb waited for Algernon to ask how Clemmons died. When he didn't, Lamb said, "He was poisoned."

Again, Algernon managed to keep his emotions concealed. Lamb could not ascertain if Algernon cared one way or the other about Clemmons's death or the manner in which it had occurred. "Suicide, was it then?" Algernon asked.

"I haven't determined that yet."

Lamb was not prepared yet to tell Algernon that Clemmons had confessed to killing the O'Hares. He remained partially unconvinced that Clemmons had written the note. Lamb moved a bit closer to the table to ask his next question. Again, he was fairly certain what Algernon's response would be and asked only in an effort to crack Algernon's armor.

"Do you think it's possible that someone might have poisoned him because they knew that all the digging out at the farm was bound to turn up the child's remains and that Clemmons knew something about it—perhaps knew the identity of the child and the truth behind its death—and therefore had to be silenced? Because you see, sir, I'm of the mind that the child's body was not placed there since the farm was abandoned, as you suggest. I'm of the opinion that the body was buried there while you and your mother and brother were living in the house, and during that time when Albert Clemmons worked on the farm."

Again, Algernon merely shrugged. "I wouldn't know. As for your opinion and intuitions, I can only repeat what I told you earlier, Chief Inspector—that neither I nor my brother had anything to do with, or possess any knowledge of, the death of the unfortunate child you've uncovered in the house. My mother knew nothing of it, either."

Lamb reached into his pocket and withdrew the figure of General Grant. As he held it up for Tigue to see, he saw genuine surprise flare in Tigue's eyes and noticed him glance quickly at his desk, which was behind Lamb, where the Napoleon figure stood guard.

"Do you recognize this, sir?" Lamb asked. "You seem to."

Tigue shrugged yet again. Lamb could almost sense Algernon calculating how to react. "Should I recognize it?"

"I don't know," Lamb said. "I just thought you might."

Tigue's smile now returned—though this time his eyes held a hint of malice that he couldn't entirely camouflage. "And why would you think that, Chief Inspector?"

"I found the figure among Albert Clemmons's meager possessions," Lamb said casually. "I noticed that you have a very similar figure of

Napoleon on your desk." Lamb turned to glance at the figure, then back at Tigue. "In fact, I'm quite sure that they come from a set manufactured years ago by Britain's—a set of famous generals."

Lamb's producing the figure indeed seemed to have caught Algernon Tigue's attention. In fact, the appearance of the Grant figure caused Algernon to recognize, very suddenly and irrevocably, that his plodding, cautious brother, Lawrence, whom he had always believed lacked backbone and cunning, seemed to have outwitted him. He willed himself to relax and decided that his best—perhaps his only—option was to strike back at Lawrence.

"You're right about the Napoleon, of course," Algernon said after a pause. "It might very well have come from a matched set." He paused as if thinking on the subject, then added, "Lawrence gave me that figurine years ago. As a boy, I was rather smitten with Napoleon; he was one of my heroes, I suppose you'd say. Lawrence gave me that as a kind of token or memento. But as I said that was years ago. As a matter of fact, Lawrence owned a set of figures very much like those you mentioned—famous generals, as you said. He rather fancied toy soldiers."

Lamb returned the Grant figure to his coat pocket and stood. "Well, thank you for the tea, Mr. Tigue," he said and got to his feet. He was finished with Algernon Tigue, but only for the moment.

Tigue also stood but did not offer Lamb his hand. "You're welcome," he said.

"I'm going to ask that you not leave the area in the next few days," Lamb said.

Algernon smiled. "Is that an order, Chief Inspector?"

"It's a request."

"Well, I think I can agree to do so, then."

—⁓—

As Lamb limped back to Vera and the Wolseley, he found himself pondering his situation. He had begun to play with a notion about the significance of the toy soldiers and their possible origin, based on something Ned Horton had said—"every boy owns toy soldiers." And yet, despite all that had occurred in the past twenty-four hours, he'd collected little real, usable evidence to aid in his inquiries. He was chugging along mostly on gut instinct and prior experience—his long knowledge of how the guilty acted and reacted, how they endeavored to maintain control over an unraveling situation, and the ways in which they sought to cover their tracks.

In and around Winstead, long-buried secrets were coming to the surface, and those who had guarded those secrets already had begun to act. He possessed pieces of a puzzle that he was becoming more and more certain were related. But he needed more—perhaps much more—before he could connect those pieces.

TWENTY-ONE

—ᴥ—

LAMB NOW WENT FROM ONE TIGUE BROTHER TO THE OTHER. VERA
stopped the car near Lawrence Tigue's cottage on the east end of
Winstead. Lamb had made no appointment with Lawrence and hoped
to surprise him. He knocked upon Tigue's red front door.

Tigue came to the front window, surreptitiously parted the curtain, and saw Lamb standing on the threshold. He was now close to
finishing his preparations and could afford to answer the questions he
was certain Lamb would ask him. Very soon the answers—whether
true or not—would cease to matter, in any case. He opened the door
with a smile. "Chief Inspector," he said.

"Hello, Mr. Tigue. I wonder if you've a few minutes to talk?"

"Of course, of course." Tigue stepped back from the door to allow
Lamb in. "I was just finishing lunch."

Lamb stepped into the foyer and removed his hat. Tigue led Lamb into the sitting room and bade him to sit on the couch. Tigue took a seat in a chair facing Lamb.

"Well, then, how can I help you, Chief Inspector?" he said. "I'm half hoping you've come to tell me that you've cleared my Webley in the killing of that unfortunate woman."

"No," Lamb said. "We're still waiting on Scotland Yard for that."

Tigue smiled. "I see. Yes, of course. These things take time—they must, of course."

"As I'm sure you're aware, Mr. Tigue, an extraordinary chain of events has occurred in and near the village in the past couple of days, and I was hoping that you could help me sort them out, particularly as you have some connection to at least one of those events," Lamb said.

"Yes, of course. You're going to want to ask me about the discovery of the skull out at the farm, and Albert Clemmons's death."

Lamb found himself unsurprised by the fact that Lawrence Tigue had known that the tramp who had been living in Miss Wheatley's wood had been Albert Clemmons. If Miss Wheatley had recognized Clemmons, despite the man's changed appearance, then it stood to reason that Lawrence Tigue, who had known Clemmons better, also might have recognized the old farmhand. He was surprised, though, that Lawrence readily admitted that he'd known Clemmons's identity.

"You knew, then, that the tramp who lived in Miss Wheatley's wood was Albert Clemmons?" Lamb said.

"Oh, no—well, not at first, at least. I'd seen the man around the village, of course, peeking in dustbins and the like, but didn't recognize him. And he never approached or identified himself to me, though I'm not sure why. I would have helped him if he'd needed it. Perhaps he was too proud—ashamed of how low he had fallen."

"How did you know, then, that the man was Clemmons? I've not released that information."

Tigue laughed—a kind of yelp. "Oh, well, that's easy enough," he said. "I'm afraid the wrong person found his body, as far as keeping things on the QT is concerned, Chief Inspector. Flora Wheatley.

She's incapable of keeping a secret or even a tidbit of gossip to herself. The woman's extraordinary, really—absolutely full to the brim with *schadenfreude*. She delights in other people's troubles and travails. I'm sorry if my knowing surprised you, but I'm afraid that was to be expected. One simply can't trust Flora Wheatley to keep her trap shut. The fact that the tramp was Albert Clemmons is pretty much general knowledge in the village by now, I'm afraid. How did Albert die, by the way, if I'm not out of line in asking?"

"We're still awaiting the results of the autopsy."

"Yes, I see, of course."

The fact that Miss Wheatley might have put it about the village that the tramp was Clemmons concerned Lamb, though he could do little about it for the moment.

"How do you explain a child's skull coming to earth in the basement of the farmhouse in which you lived for so many years?" he asked Tigue, pressing on. He intended to pressure Lawrence in the same way in which he had Algernon, hoping, perhaps, that Lawrence proved an easier nut to crack. Given his status as chairman of the Winstead parish council, Lawrence had more obvious reason to seem cooperative.

Lawrence leaned back a bit in his chair and crossed his legs. "Well, I can't, I'm afraid."

"Do you think the skull belongs to one of the O'Hare twins?"

"I would hope not, certainly. At the time, everyone pretty much concluded that Sean O'Hare had taken them to Ireland. Unless I'm mistaken, no one in Winstead has seen Sean or the twins since." Lawrence moved a bit forward in his chair. "Are you saying, Chief Inspector, that you've identified the skeleton as belonging to one of the O'Hares?"

"No," Lamb said. "We haven't identified the remains yet and might not for some time. I'm merely interested in your thoughts on the matter. As I told your brother this morning, I'm of a mind that the body was not placed there in the past ten or so years, during the time when the farm was abandoned, but was put there during the time that you and your brother and mother lived in the house and Albert Clemmons was your farmhand. Which, of course, very much puts you and your family in the picture, Mr. Tigue."

Lamb wanted Lawrence to know that he'd spoken to Algernon. He'd sensed by the manner in which Algernon had spoken of Lawrence's failed marriage that the brothers held each other in low regard—it was clear that Algernon, at any rate, possessed little respect for Lawrence.

"You spoke to Algernon, then?"

"Yes."

"And what was his opinion on the matter?"

"I'm here to get your opinion, sir," Lamb said.

Lamb's mention of Algernon brought back to Lawrence memories of the humiliations he had suffered at his brother's hands. But he reminded himself anew that he had righted those wrongs—that Algernon had underestimated him, and that he had nothing more to fear from Algernon. He had fixed matters so that Algernon could not gain the upper hand. He wondered if Lamb had inadvertently revealed this fact to Algernon through his questioning. If so, it was too late for Algernon to counter the move. He was certain of that.

"Well, I don't know what to say, really, Chief Inspector," Lawrence said. "I suppose you're right that Algernon and myself are very much in the picture, as you put it—that is if your theory about when the body was placed there is correct, which I doubt it is. I can only give you my word that, however that body came to be buried in the basement of the farmhouse, we had nothing to do with it."

"Did you see the O'Hare boys on the farm on the day they disappeared?"

"No. I was off hunting rabbits in an entirely different part of the farm. I bagged three that morning, as a matter of fact."

"And your mother and brother, sir? Where were they?"

"Well, Algernon was off somewhere playing with his mates, as I recall. Wasn't even on the farm. And my mother was busy around the house. She didn't see the boys that morning."

"Did your mother know when she hired Albert Clemmons that he had a conviction for pedophilia?"

"No. The news shocked us."

Lamb glanced around the room. "You seem to have done quite well for yourself, sir," he said.

Tigue smiled. "Yes. I try, at any rate."

"How long have you lived in the village?"

"Eight years. I lived on the farm with my mother until 1932, the year she died. I then went to London—to seek my fortune, I suppose you'd say. That's where I learned the printing trade and met the woman who became my wife."

"What brought you back to Winstead?"

"Well, I didn't like London—hated it, actually."

"And you now operate a freelance printing business out of your garage?"

"Yes."

"What sorts of things do you print?"

"Well, I print the village newsletter for one, though I don't charge for that. I also do a lot of government work, informational fliers and the like. There's a lot of that these days, as you know. 'What to do if the Germans invade.' That sort of thing." He smiled again. "You seem to know quite a lot about me, Chief Inspector. Not that I mind, of course. It's your job to know these things; I realize that."

"Yes, it is my job."

"Well, just in case you don't know, I also raise chickens and make a bit of money from selling eggs to the people who are developing the farm—though my eggs have gone missing recently. I'd say that's a case for you, but I'd be wasting your time, given that I already know the culprit."

"Who is it, sir?"

"Flora Wheatley, of course. The woman hates me, Chief Inspector, as I'm sure she must have told you by now. She is obsessed with the local songbird population and is convinced that I've been stealing eggs from their nests and selling them with my chicken eggs. It's preposterous, of course, but there it is. I daresay she's already told you the whole sordid story of my supposed guilt."

"Have you seen Miss Wheatley steal your eggs, sir?"

"No, but I'm sure it's her. It couldn't be anyone else. And her cottage is just across the meadow behind us here."

"To whom do you deliver the eggs at the camp?"

"A man named Taney seems to be in charge over there. At times I've dealt with him, though, really, it's whoever happens to be handy about the mess tent when I arrive."

"Did you ever deliver the eggs to Ruth Aisquith, then? She worked in the mess tent."

"No. As I told you before, I didn't know her."

"I understand that your wife has left Winstead to live with her sister in Chesterfield for the duration of the war," Lamb said.

"Yes, well, I'm afraid that last summer did her in a bit. She began talking about it then, but we held off on doing anything since it seemed like such a large step. Then, with the coming of this summer, she became anxious again. I tried to convince her that the Germans were finished with us down here, though I hardly believe it myself, of course." He looked at Lamb. "So, yes, she's gone, Chief Inspector. She left just a couple of days ago."

"I see," Lamb said. "And what is your sister-in-law's name?"

"Mary Hart. My wife's maiden name is Hart, you see. Alba Hart."

"And does Mary Hart have a telephone in Chesterfield?"

"Well, yes, she does."

"May I have her number?"

"Her telephone number?"

"Yes."

"Well, I don't know it from memory. I can go and fetch it if you really think it's necessary."

"If you wouldn't mind."

"Yes, well, if you'll just wait here, then." He rose and left the room. A minute later, he returned and handed Lamb a slip of paper with Mary Hart's name and telephone number on it.

"There you are, Chief Inspector."

"Thank you," Lamb said. He now asked the question he'd asked Algernon: "Did your mother have an affair with Sean O'Hare, sir?"

"Certainly not!" Lawrence said. "And I resent that you should ask that, Chief Inspector."

Lamb produced the Grant figure, which Lawrence instantly recognized. Indeed, Lamb's possession of the figure cheered him; it was further evidence that his plan was working as he hoped it would.

"Do you recognize this?" Lamb asked.

"No."

"It comes from a set of generals made by Britain's toy company that also includes a Napoleon figure. Your brother has a Napoleon figure sitting on his desk in his rooms at the Everly School. He told me that you gave him that figure. Is that true, Mr. Tigue?"

Tigue nearly was overcome with delight. Lamb not only had found the Grant, but also seen the Napoleon in Algernon's rooms. He wondered at the shock that Algernon must have felt in seeing Lamb produce the Grant figure.

"I'm afraid my brother's mistaken, Chief Inspector," Lawrence said evenly. "I never gave him such a figure."

"No? He claims you were an aficionado of toy soldiers, a collector."

"Well, that's curious," Lawrence said. He felt entirely in control of the situation. Neither Algernon, nor Lamb, nor anyone else could touch him now.

"Why is that?"

"Well, it was Algernon who was the toy soldier aficionado, not me." Lawrence looked around the room. "After all, you don't see any figures on my shelves, do you?"

"Would you mind if I had a look in your garage, sir?" Lamb hoped to test his theory on the possible connection between Lawrence and Ruth Aisquith.

"Well, I don't see why you would want to, but go right ahead," Tigue said. "I'll get the key."

Tigue was confident that Lamb would find nothing—though Lamb's asking to see the garage meant that Lamb might be getting close to discovering certain truths. Once again, Tigue reminded himself that, very soon, none of that would matter.

Tigue unlocked the garage. "There you are, Chief Inspector," he said. "If you don't mind, I'll wait out here." He spoke this latter sentence in a tone that suggested he was not pleased by Lamb's snooping around his shed.

Lamb entered the garage. He first had to move around Tigue's 1928 Morris Minor, which, from the look of the dust that had collected on its bonnet, Tigue hadn't driven in some time. Since the war started, most people who owned motorcars had mothballed them, given the scarcity and dearness of petrol. More than any other commodity, save food, the success of England's war effort depended on petrol, the distribution of which the government strictly controlled and rationed. In some ways, petrol had become as valuable as gold.

Lamb moved to the rear of the garage, where he found, hard against the rear wall, a small Adana printing press and next to it a table containing a mimeograph machine. A second table, which sat beneath the window on the shed's north side, contained bundles and stacks of papers, many of which appeared blank. Lamb knew nothing about printing presses and so was not exactly sure what he was searching for other than some evidence that Lawrence Tigue might have used his machine to produce some manner of forged or counterfeit papers for Ruth Aisquith. Lamb had spent a fair amount of time thinking about the large sum of cash they'd found in Ruth's purse and concluded that Ruth had not brought the cash with her to Winstead merely to keep it safe from her bunkmates at the prison site. He believed she had brought the cash to Winstead to pay someone for some service rendered—but a service that did not allow the participants to be seen together without casting suspicion on themselves.

Lamb suspected that Ruth had come to the cemetery so early in the morning not to visit her grandmother's grave, as she had told Taney and others, because Ruth's grandmother wasn't buried there. Indeed, Ruth's grandmother probably wasn't even buried in Hampshire. Lamb's theory was that Ruth Aisquith had come to the cemetery—a normally deserted place on the far western edge of the village, and always very early in the morning—because she had not wanted to be seen. She had needed a quiet, out of the way spot in which to pick up the goods that someone in the village—perhaps Lawrence Tigue—was producing for her. In turn, she left payment for those goods hidden somewhere in the cemetery. However, on the morning of her death she'd been shot before she could complete her covert transaction.

Lamb took a final look around the garage, then rejoined Lawrence Tigue by the door.

"I expect that I will have more questions for you and must ask that you not leave Winstead for the next couple of days," Lamb said to Tigue.

"I've nowhere to go in any case," Lawrence said.

"Very good, then," Lamb said. "Thank you for your cooperation. I can find my way back to the High Street, thank you."

Lawrence watched Lamb disappear around the side of the house in the direction of the High Street. As he did so, he put his hand in his right pocket and felt the head of a tiny general.

TWENTY-TWO

—⁓—

WHILE LAMB INTERVIEWED LAWRENCE TIGUE, VERA STROLLED UP
the High Street in the direction of the church. She found the cemetery
deserted and stood outside its black iron fence for a moment, staring at
the graves. The grave of Miss Tutin still was mounded with fresh earth
but otherwise—and despite what had happened two days earlier—the
cemetery appeared as if no one had entered it for years. The place felt
weighted by a kind of sad shabbiness, Vera thought.

She heard a voice behind her say, "Hello, Miss Lamb" and turned
to find Julia Martin, Lilly's mother, standing behind her holding a
canvas bag of groceries in each hand.

Vera had instinctively liked Julia the first time they'd met. She
smiled. "Can I help you with your bags?"

Julia returned the smile. "That's very kind, thanks." She handed
Vera one of the bags, which contained, among other food, a loaf of the

coarse rationed bread the government called the National Wheatmeal Loaf and a tiny tin of strawberry jam, which had become rare and which Julia had been lucky to obtain. Julia nodded toward the western end of the village and said, "I live just up here."

They walked toward Julia's house. "I wonder if I would be prying to ask how the investigations are going," Julia said. "It's quite terrible what's happened around here in the past few days. First these two deaths in the village and then the discovery of the child's skeleton on the old farm. I'm afraid it's left many of us reeling. It has me."

"Well, I'm afraid I don't know much, really," Vera said. "I went with my father when Miss Wheatley led him to the body of the tramp, and I have to say that I found it all rather sad, the old man dying alone in the wood like that."

"Yes. It is very sad—how someone can become so invisible to the rest of the world."

"Did you know him at all? The man who died in the wood?"

"No, though I saw him about the village now and again. He never came to our door, though I understand he came to Flora's."

Vera knew that her father had released very little information about what the police had found at the tramp's campsite and so was reluctant to say more about it. "Do you remember the trouble with the O'Hares?" she asked Julia.

"Yes, I remember it; I was about Lilly's age then. I lived in Winchester, of course, but we followed the story. They lived in a house that is not far from here."

"How has Lilly been taking the recent upsets?" Vera asked. She wondered if Julia knew of Lilly's nocturnal wanderings about the village, and if she should tell Julia of Lilly's claims of having followed Miss Wheatley and Mr. Tigue in the night, and of Lilly's fanciful theories about the fate of Alba Tigue. Although Lilly might consider it a betrayal of confidence, Vera had felt from the beginning that Lilly would be better off if her mother knew to what lengths Lilly had gone to stave off her loneliness. Even so, she held off saying anything for the moment.

"Well, it seems not to have affected her too much," Julia said. "But you never know with children her age. They often seek to hide their emotions from their parents, unfortunately. We all do it. She's about the village somewhere at the moment, off riding her bicycle. I'm afraid she's a little lonely these days, with her father gone and school out for the summer term. And I've taken a night-shift job working in Southampton." She sighed. "The war has been hard on Lilly—hard on all of us."

With that, the two women became silent for a moment. They walked about fifty meters past the church before they reached a narrow road on the left called Lennox Lane that wound slightly uphill. "This is it," Julia said. "Our house is at the very end."

Tall English oaks lined Lennox Lane, shading it from the hot, midday sun.

"Have you lived in the village long?" Vera asked.

"Fourteen years—since my husband, Brian, and I married. He was born and grew up here. We live in the house that belonged to his parents; his father was the doctor here. His parents both were quite old, really, when they had Brian, who was their only child. We met in Winchester, where I'm from. Brian had come there after studying art at university." She smiled, as if she considered the memory a pleasant one. "I was just finishing secondary school when we met. Six months later we were married." She shrugged slightly. "But life is like that, isn't it?"

Vera was curious about Julia Martin—her life and family, the choices she'd made. She thought that she could do worse than ending up as Julia had, or seemed to have. Julia clearly was intelligent and possessed a kind of quiet elegance, along with youthfulness and an unpretentious beauty. She knew from Lilly that Brian Martin was in North Africa, gone from their lives.

"Is your husband a doctor, too, then?" she asked.

Julia laughed a little. "No, nothing like that," she said. "He's a painter—an artist. He paints portraits on commission and makes a decent enough living at it. He's quite good. We came to Winstead so we could take possession of the family house. His father had passed on by the time we were married, and we came to live in the house with his mother. Two years later, Lilly was born. Then Brian's mother died. That's been ten years ago and we've lived in the house, the three of us, since. That is, until Brian left in April." She looked at Vera. "He volunteered, silly man," she added. "He felt embarrassed in some way, within himself, by the fact that his life has been relatively easy. Most people around here don't lead easy lives, but Brian believes his has been so. He thought it was time that he threw himself into the fray."

Vera wasn't sure how to respond. She thought that being a doctor's son and a painter probably did make for rather an easy life. She was slightly surprised that Julia had told her so much about herself and so soon and all at once, as if she had been waiting for an opportunity to speak of it.

About a hundred meters down the road they came to a large white house. A stone path led from the lane to the front door.

"Well, this is it," Julia said. "I hope you'll come in for tea, Miss Lamb, so that I can repay the favor."

"That would be very nice, thanks," Vera said. "And please call me Vera."

They entered the foyer, where Julia took the bag from Vera and bade her to find a seat in a neat sitting room off the hall. Vera sat on a yellow couch with large, firm cushions.

"Make yourself comfortable," Julia said. "I'll just be a minute." She disappeared in the direction of the kitchen.

A piano dominated the far side of the room. Vera wondered who played and decided that it was Julia. Perhaps Lilly also played. Vera regretted that she'd never mastered a musical instrument. In grade school, she'd played around with the clarinet for a time but had gotten bored and dropped it. She rose from the sofa, moved to the piano, and pressed one of the white keys. It sounded out of tune.

She noticed two framed portraits on the piano. The first was of Lilly at about age eight. The smiling girl in the photo seemed confident and happy. But preadolescence and the war had denuded that cheerfulness, Vera thought.

The other photo was of a man who, Vera guessed, must be Brian Martin. He was nothing like what Vera had envisioned. She had pictured a roguishly handsome man with an aquiline nose, intelligent eyes, and longish hair—an artist, a painter. She thought that perhaps she'd expected this because she considered Julia to be an attractive woman—the sort of woman who would have found it easy to win a handsome man's attention. It was not so much that the man in the photo *wasn't* handsome—he was, in his way. He had a roundish face and dark hair and happy-seeming eyes. She saw signs of Lilly in the shape of his face and the fineness of his hair. But he radiated nothing that Vera would have called "special." But was "special" really the word she wanted? In any case, she had thought that Julia Martin's husband would have been less ordinary looking.

Julia returned carrying a wooden tray bearing a steaming green ceramic teapot, cups, saucers, a small carafe of milk, a bowl of sugar, a plate containing four slices of the National Wheatmeal Loaf, and a small bowl into which she'd spooned strawberry jam. She sat on the sofa next to Vera and poured.

"What do you do in Southampton?" Vera asked.

"I work a lathe, of all things. I fashion handles for screwdrivers out of solid plastic tubing. Lord knows, I never would have thought that I'd work a lathe—I hardly knew what one was before I took this job." She smiled. "But there it is. We need the money and I was lucky to get the job, considering my lack of experience." She smiled a little and added, "Normally, I should be sleeping now, I suppose, but I couldn't, so I thought I would go to the shop."

"Do you like the job?" Vera asked.

"Very much, actually—surprisingly so—though it involves a circuitous bus ride to and from Southampton. I sometimes feel as if I spend half my life these days on a bus. And, of course, it keeps me away at night. I feel guilty about that—leaving Lilly alone. But I tell myself that she's old enough now and that, in the end, it's for the best.

As I said, we need the money." She smiled again—a forced smile, Vera thought. "But we manage. Plenty of others have had it much worse, losing their homes and loved ones in the bombings and the rest of it. I don't like to sound as if I'm complaining."

"I have to admit to snooping about while you were getting the tea," Vera said. "Is the man in the photo your husband?"

"Yes, that's Brian. I miss him. Lilly misses him," Julia said. "I got lucky with Brian. You never can tell with men, can you? So many of them seem to have no feel for children. But Brian is different. He loves Lilly very much, and she most certainly loves him."

"It must be hard for you."

Julia looked at her. "It is." Julia clearly had wanted to talk—to unburden herself—but did not want to come apart, Vera thought. She wondered if Julia worried that if she allowed herself to come apart, she might not be able to pull herself together again.

"But how about you?" Julia asked. "How long have you been your father's driver?"

"Only a few days and only because he sprained his ankle and found it too painful to work the pedals on the car," Vera said. "I shouldn't think the job would last more than a week, maybe two. I think my father is devising ways to avoid me being called up."

"He must love you very much, then."

"He does, yes. But I suppose I want to tell him that I can look after myself—that I *should* look after myself. I'm not sure he's ready for that yet, though he says he is."

The front door opened and Lilly appeared in the foyer, flush from a jaunt on her bike around the village.

"Hello, darling," Julia said as Lilly entered the room. "Miss Lamb has stopped in for a visit."

Lilly appeared stunned to see Vera. They hadn't spoken since Lilly had revealed to Vera the details of her nocturnal spying on Miss Wheatley and the Tigues. Vera knew that Lilly must be thinking: *Has she told mother about me?*

"Hello," Lilly said to Vera.

"Hello, Lilly," Vera said. "Your mother and I were just talking about our jobs."

"Oh," Lilly said. She turned to her mother. "Is there anything for lunch?"

"I've just been to the shop. There's bread and sardines in the kitchen if you'd like. And I bought some strawberry jam."

"All right, then," Lilly said. She abruptly turned and left the room.

"I'm sorry, Vera," Julia said. "She doesn't mean to be rude."

"It's quite all right, really." She smiled. "I should be going, anyhow. My father's going to want to be driven somewhere or another soon enough." She stood. "Thank you for the tea."

"You're quite welcome. I hope that you'll come and see us again."

"I'd like that," Vera said. She had thought it very generous of Julia to have so readily shared her ration of strawberry jam.

As Vera headed back up Lennox Lane, Doris White moved up the path from the village to the church. She'd made up her face in the same way as she had on the previous night, when Gerald had come to her. She was on her way to luncheon with Gerald at the vicarage. Before last night, Gerald had never invited her to luncheon.

The events of the previous night had gone as she'd hoped and planned. Gerald had ravished her by candlelight, just as he had done when she had been his mistress, his naughty secret. Though, once upon a time, he had then set her aside as so much rubbish, she remained drawn to him—dangerously, she knew—like a moth to flame. On the previous night, when they'd finished and were lying together, he had told her that he was developing a plan to rid them of Wilhemina.

He'd told Doris that he'd sent Wilhemina to London, to get her out of the way so that he could have time to think. He was devising a plan, he'd said, and suggested they have lunch at the vicarage on the following day so that they could discuss it—though he'd added that she should dress as if she were coming to clean the vicarage, as usual, in case someone saw her and became suspicious. He'd looked into her eyes and said, "This will be our secret—yours and mine."

Although she'd dressed as Gerald had instructed, she'd defied him slightly by making up her face. She knew that he was right about not raising other people's suspicions, but a part of her was almost beyond caring about such matters. As she strode toward the vicarage, she felt firmly in control of her life for the first time since she'd met Gerald. She was set on taking him back forever.

—⁂—

Gerald peered out the window of his study and watched Doris approach. He'd decided that the time had come for him to start anew. He would have little trouble reinventing himself elsewhere. People liked and trusted him. People were like dogs, easily led, eager for a master. The war had shrunken everyone's opportunities, of course, and the ease by which one could travel from one place to another. And he would have to endure a bit of privation as he regained his feet. But he could no longer endure the alternative—remaining in Winstead with Wilhemina and the hedgehog who cleaned his toilet.

First, though, he must do what was necessary to avoid a scandal and a trial. If he were to see his plan through to its hoped-for conclusion, he first must minimize the damage done in Winstead. He'd begun devising the plan as soon as he'd read the note from Doris demanding that he come to her cottage. The note had stunned him at first, given his belief that he had trained Doris well over the previous three years. Even though he'd soon regained his feeling of mastery in the matter, he'd realized that he could no longer fully rely on Doris staying silent and therefore must be rid of her for good. He opened the door of the vicarage to her knock with a smile.

"My love," he said, offering his hand and inviting her in. That she had made up her face in defiance of his order briefly startled him. But he was expert at masking his true emotions. "You look charming."

Doris took his hand. "Thank you."

Gerald smiled and his eyes came alight with a kind of rakishness. Fending off revulsion, he bent to kiss Doris on the lips. He allowed the kiss to linger as long as he could stand it. When they parted, Doris stood still for a couple of seconds with her eyes closed. Gerald stifled an urge to do away with her in that very instant. He could wrap his hands around her rubbery neck and choke the life out of her. But he must be patient. He must stick to his plan.

"Come in, my dear," he said. He led her to the sitting room and poured them each a glass of sherry, then sat next to her on the couch.

"I suppose you've heard about the tramp," Doris said.

"I have, of course. Poor man."

Doris smiled. "Of course, I couldn't help but wonder if you had anything to do with it."

Again, Gerald hid his surprise. "Now, why would you think that, my dear? The poor fellow was just an old tramp, according to the *Mail*." He smiled at Doris. "Certainly you don't think me that wicked?"

"Of course I do," Doris said. "I believe you're capable of anything, Gerald, especially if you had reason to believe that he might have seen something in the cemetery."

Gerald let the remark pass. He must press ahead. He moved closer to her. "Have you thought about what I suggested to you last night?" he asked.

Doris ignored the question. She sipped the sherry, then put her hand on his knee.

"What have you made for lunch?"

"A vegetable stew," he said, placing his hand on hers. "I hope you like it. I fancy myself rather a good cook."

She smiled. "You're so talented at so many things, aren't you, Gerald?" she said.

He managed a smile. "Yes," he said.

"At lying, too," she said, her smile wide and bright. "You're very talented at lying. I find that exciting. I know I shouldn't, but I do all the same. I wouldn't be surprised at all if you killed the tramp just to confuse the police about that poor woman in the cemetery—to put them on the wrong track. It's exactly the kind of thing you'd do."

He could sense her heating up and his own revulsion rising.

"Yes," he said, smiling and wagging his finger at her. "You do know me and I *am* naughty. And that's why I must ask you again: did you think about what we discussed last night?"

She made a playful bite at his finger. "Yes."

"And what did you decide?"

"I'll do whatever you ask, Gerald. But now, you must do as I ask."

She stood and unzipped her dress. It dropped to the floor around her ankles, exposing her pale, doughy flesh.

"I can be naughty, too," she said, smiling, her lips and cheeks a bright crimson.

TWENTY-THREE

—⚋—

LAMB LEFT LAWRENCE TIGUE'S HOUSE AND LIMPED BACK TO THE
Wolseley to find that Vera had not yet returned from wherever she'd
gone. He decided to make the short walk to the village school to
ensure that Rivers had gotten the incident room up and running and,
hopefully, to find a cup of tea.

He indeed found Rivers in the school, leaning against a wooden
table and sipping tea from a white ceramic cup. The room contained
three such tables, each equipped with a telephone; a topographical map
of the village and the area surrounding it was taped to a blackboard.
The small desks of the students had been shoved to a corner of the
room. Other than Rivers and Lamb, a trio of uniformed constables,
each of whom sat at one of the desks, speaking on the telephone,
fielding leads, occupied the room. Harding and Lamb had given the
press only so much information about the three cases they had before

them. They had not released the fact that Ruth Aisquith had been a conscientious objector, nor that she'd been found with fifty pounds of cash in her possession. In addition to not yet identifying the dead man in the woods as Albert Clemmons, they had made no mention of him having possibly committed suicide. Harding was handling the press, leaving Lamb to concentrate on the inquiries. The three cases had generated the usual glut of leads, most of which would turn out to be useless, and most of which were first screened by the constables who manned the telephones.

Lamb was glad to see a gas ring with a steel kettle upon it sitting on the table against which Rivers was leaning. Near the ring was a black teapot that appeared to be full, along with a small container of milk and, surprisingly, a bowl of sugar. He wondered where Rivers had obtained the sugar, but decided he'd rather not know. Lamb found that the pot contained tea and poured a cup, adding to it a spoonful of the precious sugar. Rivers had not looked up when Lamb entered. Lamb thought that Rivers was deep in thought, but when Rivers looked up at him as he neared the table, Lamb thought that Rivers merely looked tired. Then, too, Rivers normally kept his emotions well concealed.

Lamb nodded at Rivers. "Any luck with the canvass?" He was glad to catch up with Rivers; the rush of events had precluded him from speaking in detail with Rivers, Wallace, and Larkin about the inquiries. During the past two days, Lamb had felt much like the captain of a ship that was under bombardment. He'd had time for little else than issuing orders designed merely to keep the ship from foundering.

Apart from setting up the incident room, Rivers had spent the morning in the village continuing to take statements from residents. Rivers reported the fruits of his morning labor: no one had seen Ruth Aisquith on the morning of her death, and no one knew—or admitted to knowing—much of anything about the tramp. Lamb, in turn, told Rivers of his conversations with Ned Horton and the Tigue brothers.

"Sounds as if the old man bollixed it pretty well," Rivers said of Horton.

"Yes," Lamb said. He sipped his tea and found that it was cold.

"I'm with you on the tramp," Rivers said. "The suicide note is rot. In my experience, the down-and-outers don't do themselves in. Suicide is for people who're convinced they have something to lose, a way to escape the consequences. People like Clemmons already are neck-deep in the consequences. I agree that he was killed because he knew something about what we're turning up at the farm."

"So who killed him, then?" Lamb asked.

"One or both of the Tigues. Clemmons knew something that the brothers couldn't allow to be known—the identity of the child buried in the cellar."

"You're guessing, Harry," Lamb said. "But so am I. We've no real bloody evidence yet." He looked at Rivers. "We need to know more about Ruth Aisquith," he said. "I want you to go up to London first thing tomorrow and find out what you can about her. Start with the Ministry of Labour and National Service, which will have the record of her conscription. She had to have had some history."

Rivers nodded his assent.

Lamb took his tea to one of the desks, removed his hat, and pulled from his pocket the slip of paper on which Lawrence Tigue had written the name and number of his sister-in-law in Chesterfield. He waited for the constable stationed there to finish his call, then took possession of the telephone, dialed Mary Hart's number, and waited as the line buzzed. But no one answered. Feeling frustrated, Lamb hung up the phone, returned his hat to his head and the tea cup to the table from which he'd fetched it, and hobbled back to the Wolseley, where he found Vera waiting for him. Seeing her lifted his spirits.

"I'm going to have a look at the house in which Claire O'Hare died," he said. "Would you like to come along?"

"I know the house," Vera said. "I passed it on my walk the other morning, when I ran into Miss Wheatley toting around her fowling piece. It's along the same path that she led us along yesterday to the tramp's body. It passes her cottage and leads to the house and, eventually, to the road that becomes the High Street by the church."

"Show me, please," Lamb said.

Vera looked at her father's ankle. "Are you sure you can walk that far?" she asked. "There's a lay-by on the road right near the house."

Lamb smiled. "All right, then. Drive on."

They got into the Wolseley and drove up the High Street, past the church and out of the western end of the village, in the direction of the former Tigue farm. Halfway there, they came to the lay-by, in which Vera parked the car. She led the way along the trail to the O'Hare place, then through the bramble and bush to a trio of half-hidden and cracked stone steps that led to the house's wooden front door. They found the door nailed shut, a state of affairs that appeared to have been the case for some time, years probably; the door's white paint nearly had all chipped away.

Lamb peered through a narrow broken window just to the right of the door. The house's interior was dark and emanated a strong odor of rot and mildew. He could just make out the form of an upturned wooden chair in the middle of a long, narrow, low-ceilinged hall that led from the door toward the rear of the house. A small animal he could hear but not see scurried across the hall, from a room on the left to one on the right, startling him and causing him to pull suddenly away from the window. Blackberry bramble had grown to mostly cover the window that looked into the room on the right of the hall.

Wanting to see if the room might be the one in which Claire had hung herself, Lamb tried to wade into the bramble to peer into the window but found that he couldn't without the bush snaring his trousers and jacket in a dozen places, and pricking his hands. He retreated from the window, freeing himself one by one of the petulant little snares.

"Do you want me to try, Dad?" Vera asked. She was thinner and more agile than her father and therefore probably could easily negotiate the bramble.

"It's not that important," Lamb said. "Let's try around back."

They retreated from the front door and followed a narrow, dirt-worn path through the brush to the back. As they passed the right side of the house they came upon another window that looked into a room that appeared to be connected to the one into which Lamb had just tried to look, with both rooms letting out onto the narrow hall that bisected the house. The glass in the window had long ago been shattered out, with the exception of a few small, roughly triangular pieces that protruded from the bottom of the frame, like the jagged teeth of some malevolent animal.

Lamb moved to the window and peered in; the same odor of rot assailed him. The room was dark and empty, save for the natural detritus and bits of trash that lay about the floor. Despite the murky light, he clearly saw a wooden crossbeam that bisected the room along the ceiling. This appeared to be the room in which Claire O'Hare had done her deed, he thought, though of course he could not yet be certain. The other rooms might also contain crossbeams.

Vera had moved up behind him and was peering over his shoulder. "Can I see?" she said.

Lamb moved aside and allowed her to look. "Is this the one, then?" she asked her father, finding the room genuinely spooky.

"I don't know," Lamb said. "But it looks a good candidate."

"What a lonely way to have to die," Vera said, as much to herself as to Lamb. She shuddered, as if picturing Claire O'Hare hanging there.

Lamb actually was entertaining a vision of Claire hanging from the rafter—though his was in the service of forensics. He was trying to figure out if it was possible for Claire to have done what Ned Horton's report had described her as doing. He decided that unless Claire was very short—essentially a midget—she likely could have managed it.

Vera retreated from the window.

"Let's see if there's a door in the back," Lamb said.

They were just about to move when they heard from behind them the sound of someone moving through the brush from the main trail. In the next instant, Lilly Martin stepped onto the hard-worn path.

"Lilly," Vera said.

Lilly pretended to be surprised to see them, though in fact she had been following Vera since shortly after Vera had left the Martin house. She was sure that the man Vera had met by the school must be Vera's father, the detective. When the two had driven away, Lilly had followed on her bicycle at a discreet distance and found the Wolseley parked in the lay-by. She had read that morning's *Mail* and knew of all that had happened in and around Winstead in the past few days. She had not been friendly with the tramp—indeed she had mostly sought to avoid him, finding him smelly and a bit creepy—though she had seen him around the village now and again and knew that he had lived in a lean-to in the wood behind Miss Wheatley's cottage and that he sometimes went to Miss Wheatley's door for a handout.

Once, about a month earlier, she had been walking down the trail at twilight when she had encountered the tramp loitering by the ramshackle chicken wire fence that marked the front of Miss Wheatley's property. He had gestured to her then and said, "Hello," and when she had said hello back, he had suggested that she follow him into the wood, as he had something "interesting" there to show her. But she'd been able to see clearly that he was drunk and didn't trust him. "I'm going to tell my father that you've been speaking to me," she'd said to him—to scare him off—though her father was gone by then. She'd backed away and moved quickly down the trail, and the tramp hadn't spoken to or bothered her again.

She knew the story of the O'Hares well enough; everyone in the village knew something of the story, after all. Since the spring, when she had become so enamored of detective stories and murder mysteries, Lilly had begun to think a bit more about the O'Hare case and even quizzed her mother on it, who had been reluctant to say much in detail about the matter, except to seriously understate the obvious in calling it "unfortunate." Then, too, there was the matter of Lawrence Tigue and his suddenly absent wife and his nocturnal visit to the O'Hare place. So much of interest was happening in the village, and yet she mostly was being left out of it—all of it. That's why she had followed Vera—to see if she could see what Vera saw. Now that Vera and her father were snooping about the O'Hare place, she'd felt as if she couldn't merely hide in the weeds and watch.

"Hello," Lilly said.

"What are you doing here, Lilly?" Vera asked.

"I was looking for you," Lilly said. It was partly true—in a way. But now that she'd said it she had to think of a reason why that sounded plausible. She immediately invented one. "I wanted to apologize for not taking tea with you and going into the kitchen like that straightaway and eating. It was rude of me, I know, and my mum said that I should find you and apologize."

Vera introduced her father as Chief Inspector Thomas Lamb.

"Are you a detective?" Lilly asked.

"I am," Lamb said, offering Lilly his hand. "It's a pleasure to meet you, Miss Martin."

"Thank you," Lilly said. She nodded at the window that Lamb and Vera had just been peering in and found herself saying things she hadn't planned to say. "I suppose you're looking for the place where Claire O'Hare hung herself. Well, you've found it. It was right in there—from the rafter across the ceiling. I can show you the quickest way in if you want. We dare each other to go in. I've been in."

"All right, Lilly, thank you," Lamb said. "Please do show us how to get in."

"It's through the back door," Lilly said.

She led them to a rear corner of the house, which was near an oak tree from which hung an old rubber tire attached to a rope. The ground beneath the swing was barren, from where children had scuffed it while playing on the swing.

"That swing is haunted," Lilly said. "It's been there more than twenty years, since the O'Hares lived here."

"Oh, *Lilly*," Vera said.

"Well, that's what everyone says."

They stood next to two rotted wooden steps that led onto a narrow wooden porch that ran the length of the rear of the house.

"You go in through there," Lilly told Lamb, pointing at the door in the rear wall that opened into the hall. "You'll come to a small mudroom first, then the hall. The first room on the left is where it happened."

Lamb carefully mounted the steps, which creaked beneath his weight. He tried the door and found that it opened easily, emitting a strident creaking noise that sounded, he couldn't help but notice, just like the groaning doors in haunted house films.

With Vera and Lilly following him, Lamb stepped into the mudroom carefully and tested the wooden floor, which seemed solid enough. He was aware that Vera and Lilly were following him but decided that there was no harm in that.

He stepped into the musty room in which Claire O'Hare had committed suicide. In the low light, he could not discern much detail. He moved beneath the central beam and looked up at it but saw nothing that would suggest that someone had tied a rope to the beam and swung from it. Then again, twenty years had passed and the light was poor. A general odor of decay was very strong in the room.

"They say she was hanging right in the middle of the room, swinging like a pendulum," Lilly whispered. She and Vera had squeezed into the room behind Lamb.

Lamb walked a slow circuit of the room but saw nothing interesting. He stopped at the jagged-toothed window, where the light was better. His foot came down on something small and solid. He lifted his foot and saw beneath it a small, dark, human-like figure. He instantly knew what it was—a toy soldier. He squatted and lit a match so that he could see it more clearly. The brief light illuminated a lead figurine of a man Lamb recognized from his youthful history studies as the Prussian Field Marshal Paul von Hindenburg, arrayed in an ornate uniform of crimson, blue, and gold. He recalled Rivers saying that the set of generals included Hindenburg. He picked up the figure. Its size was identical to that of the Grant he'd found among Albert Clemmons's belongings and the Napoleon he'd seen on Algernon Tigue's desk.

"What did you find, Dad?" Vera asked.

"A toy soldier."

Lilly moved close to Vera. Lamb held up the figure in the light coming through the window.

"Do you recognize this, Lilly?" he asked. "Is there a boy in the village who plays often with toy soldiers or who keeps a collection of them?"

"I should think that they all do," she said. "But I can't think of anybody specifically."

"Do any of the boys in the village come into this house on a regular basis?"

"Not that I know of. Most of the children in Winstead believe this house is haunted." She hesitated a second, then added, "I don't, of course. I'm too old to believe that sort of rubbish."

"Of course," Lamb said. He smiled at her. "Thank you, Lilly."

"Is it a clue?" Lilly asked.

"No," Lamb lied. "I'm merely curious." He looked toward the door. "Well, I guess we can go now." When Lilly and Vera turned toward the door, Lamb slipped the figure into his pocket.

He followed them onto the porch. When he looked in the direction of the oak tree he noticed that the tire swing was swaying ever so slightly.

TWENTY-FOUR

—⚬—

HAVING FINISHED THEIR SEARCH OF THE O'HARE HOUSE, LAMB AND
Vera made the short drive to the prison camp. There, they stood on
the edge of the farmhouse foundation with Harding, Captain Walton,
and Wallace, who had just returned from interviewing Oscar Strand,
the man who had sold the farm to the government. Lamb nodded brief
greetings to each, including Walton, who stood slightly apart from
the rest. Lamb had begun to wonder if the slackness he'd noticed in
Walton on his first visit to the camp wasn't purposeful—if the slackness might in some way have served Walton's purposes, along with,
perhaps, those of Taney.

Larkin and the police surgeon, Winston-Sheed, had nearly
finished exhuming what amounted to a full skeleton to match the
skull that Charlie Kinkaid had found. But in doing so, the forensics
man had unearthed yet another conundrum, as Harding promptly

informed Lamb: the skeleton appeared to be that of a very young child, perhaps no older than two or three at the outside. However, in digging up this skeleton Larkin had found another child's remains, just nine inches above the head of the first skeleton. This second child appeared to be older, in the range of five or six. In addition, the first skeleton clearly showed that the child had a clubfoot. Lamb thought of the O'Hare twins. They had been five years old when they had disappeared, though he remembered hearing nothing of either of them having had a clubfoot, nor had Horton's file contained any mention of either of the O'Hare boys as being clubfooted.

Lamb removed his hat and handed it to Wallace, then moved to the edge of the foundation and eased himself into the burial site. Winston-Sheed rose to meet him and shook his hand. The doctor's temples were moist with perspiration. He dug into the inner pocket of his jacket, removed his cigarette case, and offered one to Lamb, who accepted, then took one for himself.

"Do we know the sex?" Lamb asked the doctor. He took a pull from his cigarette, which calmed him.

"A boy. The skeleton looks complete and apparently the body was buried naked, as we've found no sign of clothing in the grave. The man who found it took off the tip of its left index finger with the point of his shovel—that was the first bone he found. On the following day he grazed the top of the skull. He marked the site for us almost perfectly."

"Do we know how the first child died?"

"Strangled, probably. The hyoid bone is broken. It wouldn't have been difficult. Of course there might be other signs of abuse or trauma on the bones. And there's the clubfoot."

"What about the other skeleton?"

"Larkin has uncovered the feet and a portion of the legs so far, as you can see. The child was wearing black shoes—boy's shoes by the look of it—white socks, and tan short trousers. Preliminarily, I'd say that this second child is older than the first by a couple of years."

"So who is this younger child, then?" Lamb said. He was thinking aloud, more than conversing. He had expected the first skeleton to be that of one of the O'Hare twins and reasoned that the other twin was also probably buried there. Now, Larkin had found two skeletons, but one appeared to be too young to belong to either of the twins.

"Have you found any sign of a third skeleton?" Lamb asked the doctor.

"No."

"What are you thinking, Tom?" Harding asked from the edge of the foundation.

Lamb said that he was now assuming that the second skeleton could very well be one of the O'Hare boys. The child seemed to be the right age and had been found with black shoes. "The description that Albert Clemmons gave Ned Horton of what he saw the boys wearing on the morning of their disappearance included black shoes, white socks, and tan short trousers for both of them. One of them was wearing a green shirt, while the other was wearing a blue shirt."

Lamb looked at the larger skeleton—the second one Larkin had found. "If Mr. Larkin uncovers either a blue or green shirt with these remains, then I'd have to say that we've found one of the O'Hare boys, and that if we've found one, we are likely to find the other. As for the other child, I'm stumped."

"It's obvious we have a child killer on our hands here," Harding said. "I've already put some men to the job of rooting around in the records to see if any children other than the O'Hares have gone missing in this area in the past twenty years. We've only two more days to figure it out—and to find out what else, if anything, is buried here. Then it's back to work on the bloody prison camp."

"I should think the army could see its way to giving us an extension based on what we've found here," Winston-Sheed said.

"Don't bet your wages on it, Doctor," Harding said. "Life is rather cheap these days, in case you hadn't noticed. As Taney said, they've a boatload of Italians due, and they've got to put them somewhere."

Lamb climbed out of the hole and rejoined Harding, Vera, and Wallace. During the time that Lamb had been in the foundation, Captain Walton had returned to his tent. Lamb had not yet had time to bring Harding up to the mark on his interviews with the Tigue brothers. He now told the super about the toy generals he'd found in Clemmons's campsite, on Algernon Tigue's desk, and in the O'Hare house. He added that Algernon Tigue had said that Lawrence had given him the Napoleon and had possessed a collection of toy soldiers as a boy.

"But I sensed, too, that the brothers are rivals—or that Algernon sees them in that way, at any rate," Lamb said. "He also claimed that Lawrence Tigue's wife has not gone to wait out the war with her sister in Chesterfield, as Lawrence claims, but that his wife has left Lawrence for another man. He seemed pleased by this and spoke of his brother in a way that made it clear that he feels no sympathy for him."

"What is the meaning of the toy soldiers, then?" Harding asked.

"I don't know yet. But there are too many damned coincidences—or apparent coincidences—popping up in this little village. I think someone might be using the soldiers to point us in a certain direction, though I'm not certain yet whether that direction is toward or away from the killer."

Harding looked into the foundation. "The Tigues sound like good suspects in this mess," he said. He looked at Lamb. "I needn't tell you that we mustn't let them slip away."

"I've advised both of them not to leave the area," Lamb said. "But I have nothing to hold them on yet. They both argue that the children could have been buried in the basement of the house during the ten years when the place lay abandoned, though I tend to believe that the remains are older than that." Lamb looked again at the second, larger skeleton. "If we can positively identify this boy as one of the O'Hare twins, then we should have enough to at least bring them in and hold them on suspicion of murder."

Harding frowned. Lamb considered informing the superintendent of his working theory of the possible relationship between Lawrence Tigue and Ruth Aisquith—the theory that explained why Ruth Aisquith had been found carrying around such a large sum of cash. But he decided that he needed more evidence that the theory was correct before he informed Harding, who preferred the delivery of fact to that of theory and guesswork.

Hoping for better news, Lamb turned to Wallace for a report of his interview that morning with Oscar Strand.

Strand originally had bought the land hoping to develop it into a housing estate after the first war, Wallace said. But the Depression, and then the second war, had intervened. Strand had sold the parcel to the government only the previous year. By then, the farm had lain fallow for a decade, since Olivia Tigue had died and her sons had gone their separate ways.

"He sounded as if he was glad to be rid of the place," Wallace said. "He'd had high hopes for it that never quite blossomed. He rented the farm to Olivia Tigue for ten years and got to know the Tigues pretty well. He said that at the time the Tigues first came to the farm, Olivia Tigue told him that the boys' father had been killed in Arras. He said that he admired Mrs. Tigue; he described her as a strong, hard-working woman who made a life for herself and her sons on the farm. He'd doubted at first that she would last long as a farmer, but she proved him wrong, and he came to respect her for that.

"He came to the farm once a month to collect the rent; Mrs. Tigue always paid on time. Neither of the boys was allowed to slack off when it came to the farm, especially Lawrence. He described Lawrence as shy and quiet—though a hard worker, like his mother—and Algernon as more open, friendly, and self-confident, even charming. He reckons that Lawrence Tigue had to become the man of the house rather early, given the father's death, whereas the little brother was free of those responsibilities. Algernon Tigue also was a bit of a whiz at maths, apparently, even then. According to Strand, Algernon went to university, while Lawrence stayed behind on the farm with his mother until she died."

"What did he have to say about Clemmons?" Harding asked.

"I didn't tell him that we'd found a suicide note near Clemmons's body," Wallace said. "Though I did say that we were considering the possibility that he might have poisoned himself. He described Clemmons as a bit of an oddball and said he wasn't surprised when it came out that Clemmons was a convicted pervert."

Lamb silently assessed his situation. The information Wallace had gleaned from Oscar Strand hadn't been as detailed or as deep as Lamb hoped it might have been. He would have to press the Tigues harder, he decided, and perhaps play one off the other.

He fought off a momentary feeling that events were threatening to swamp him. At the moment he wanted nothing more than to go home to Marjorie and a decent hot meal with a glass of beer, followed by a decent cup of tea. He looked at the western sky, which still was bright and clear. But he decided that he was finished for the day—that he must extract himself from the swirl of events in order to take proper stock of them.

He looked at Vera and said, "Let's go home."

—⁂—

At a little past eight o'clock that night, Gerald and Wilhemina Wimberly sat together at the table in the kitchen of the vicarage.

Earlier that day, Gerald had done everything Doris White had demanded of him; doing so had taken all the willpower he could muster, and many times, feeling humiliated by the way in which she'd seized control of him, Gerald had wanted to kill Doris. He had consoled himself with the notion that her control was only temporary, for he had worked his magic on her regardless and she had agreed to his plan. And so, in the end, he counted himself the victor.

He'd told Doris that he'd sent Wilhemina to London, though, of course, he'd done no such thing. The whole time Doris was in the vicarage that day, Wilhemina had been hiding in the attic. All the while, Wilhemina had known what Gerald and Doris were doing in the sitting room, but she had swallowed her humiliation and remained silent, as Gerald had instructed her to do. Gerald had promised that he would take care of the problem and was doing so.

Now Gerald and Wilhemina sat across from each other, as they had countless times during their marriage, the table barren even of a pot of tea. They had become conspirators rather than man and wife, though Wilhemina would have said that their marital union had come undone many years earlier.

Patiently, Gerald outlined for Wilhemina his plan to rid them of Doris White. He had convinced Doris that the two of them, Doris and he, would leave Winstead to begin a new life together. After midnight, he would go to Doris's cottage, where she would be waiting for him. He would take with him a bottle of port with which he would propose they toast their new freedom—a bottle that he had laced with a heavy dose of rat poison.

A sick feeling threatened to overtake Wilhemina, though she managed to dispel the feeling rather quickly. She had no objections to Gerald doing away with Doris, who was less than worthless to her. Her main concern was that Gerald's killing of Doris would worsen rather than improve their present situation and cause Lamb and the other police to come after them with yet more vigor.

"I've taken care of that," Gerald assured her. "In any case, we can afford to take no chances with her. She knows too much. Eventually, she will hurt us unless we get rid of her."

Once the poison had killed Doris, he would compose a suicide note on Doris's typewriter in which she would confess to shooting Ruth Aisquith with Gerald's gun, which she had stolen from his study a week earlier. Her motive would be jealousy; the note would contain her confession that she'd secretly been in love with him—Gerald—but had not believed it proper to act on this love. Then, when she'd noticed Ruth Aisquith coming to the church in the mornings, she'd become consumed by the idea that Ruth had romantic designs on Gerald, which she could not abide. And so she had acted in a moment of envy and rage. Afterward, she'd admitted to herself the monstrousness of her act and become remorseful and frightened that she would be caught and face a trial and hanging. Therefore, she had ended her life by swallowing rat poison in a glass of port. The note also would say that Doris had hidden the pistol in a place where no one ever would find it because she wanted to ensure that it could no longer be used for evil purposes.

"Once that's done, I will come home," Gerald said. "We will provide each other with alibis. Each of us will say that the other never left the house."

Wilhemina was not certain that Lamb would buy that scenario. Even so, Gerald was right—with Doris gone, Lamb never would find the pistol, and the only other eyewitness to the events in the cemetery would be out of the way forever. Lamb could entertain all the doubts he wanted, but doubts did not amount to evidence.

"It's foolproof," Gerald assured her. He was thinking beyond the deed itself to the new life—the actual one, unfettered by human millstones—that he would begin elsewhere. Initially, he would have to take Wilhemina with him. But he could take care of her in due time. Then he would be free again.

He smiled and touched her hand. "Soon, everything will be back to normal," he said.

TWENTY-FIVE

—∿—

LILLY AWAKENED AT A LITTLE AFTER ONE A.M. FEELING RESTLESS.
She lay awake for ten minutes or so, listening to the empty house creak. The night sounds that emanated from the house's corners and hidden places still upset her, though she had tried her best to harden herself to them. Her mother had tried to pacify her by saying that the sounds merely came from the house "breathing," which she found ridiculous, the kind of thing an adult would say to a very young child. She found it ironic that her mother had concluded that she was old enough to stay in the house alone through the night yet otherwise treated her as if she still were a little girl.

She rose from bed propelled in part by an idea she knew to be odd. Yet it also fit with her desire to face the macabre and learn from it; she wanted to see the place where the tramp had died. She had heard about the discovery of his body, of course. Although the police had yet to announce an official cause of his death, the talk in the village was that the old man had died of some natural cause, a bad heart or consumption, or merely the ravages of age. Yet more interesting—and ghoulish—was the story that had been put about the village that the man had once, long ago, been a farmhand on the Tigue farm at the time of the mess with the O'Hare suicide.

Lilly had gone to bed with her clothes on, certain that she would rise before the night was out. She grabbed a battery-powered torch and set out, moving past the darkened church and cemetery to the edge of the wood, by the path that led into the village. A misty rain fell, though the air remained warm. The night was dark, the sky cloudy and moonless, and the wood darker still. She stood on the footpath, took a deep breath, counted to three, then moved into the wood. The low, wet leaves of the undergrowth touched her ankles and bare calves, putting her in mind of the tongues of an unseen creature licking her as she passed. Once past the fringe and in among the trees, she switched on the torch, finding the rough trail the tramp had trod to and from his lean-to over the past several months.

The darkness of the wood, the dripping trees, and the proximity of the place where the tramp's dead body had so recently lain frightened her in a way she hadn't expected, and she found herself hesitating. But she countered this by quite firmly telling herself that she had nothing to fear from wet leaves and mere darkness. And she reminded herself that she did not believe in ghosts. Such inspirations, combined with a keen curiosity, urged her forward, and she continued along the rough path, pushing the low branches of young trees out of her way, until the beam of her torch caught a small clearing and the outline of a sad-looking lean-to. Although the structure remained, the police seemed to have removed from it all of the tramp's possessions. She had expected the place to feel eerie—and it did, sort of, though not to the extent that she had imagined it would. Mostly the spot seemed empty, almost as if it had been sanitized and she soon realized, to her disappointment, that the spot held little, if anything, of interest to a budding crime novelist.

A drop of water from a sodden leaf struck the top of her head, causing her to utter a muffled sound of surprise. Instinctively, she put her hand on her mouth to calm herself. She suddenly became aware of noises in the wood—small, mysterious sounds of movement, of leaves rustling and twigs cracking. But the same feeling of restlessness that had awakened her—the same keen curiosity—spurred her forward, toward Miss Wheatley's cottage. She had no idea what she might find there, but decided that she was not yet ready to return to the quiet, lonely house.

With the light of her torch she found the path that led to Miss Wheatley's place. She emerged from the wood behind the cottage, which she found to be dark and silent. By then, the misting rain had ceased. As she moved into the meadow, she saw the flash of a torch beam ahead and glimpsed a dark figure moving toward her, out of the wood, from the direction of Lawrence Tigue's house. She turned off her torch and jumped off the path, squatting and sheltering in the brush and remaining as still as she could. She heard the slightly labored breathing of the figure as it approached. Instinctively, she held her breath.

The figure, slender and slightly bent, moved past her with a sense of purpose.

Mr. Tigue. She could not mistake him.

He passed quickly—and just as quickly Lilly decided that she would follow him. She allowed him to get a bit farther down the trail—a safe distance—then emerged from the brush and followed the glow of his torch, which she could see just ahead.

When they reached the O'Hare house, Tigue left the trail and entered the house by the rear door, as she and Lamb and Vera had done earlier that day. She settled in the brush by the trail and watched. She soon saw the faint light of Tigue's torch through the window of the sitting room; the light appeared only for a few seconds before it went out again. Less than a minute later, the beam suddenly pierced the darkness at the side of the house, as Tigue appeared again and walked back onto the main trail. He'd stayed in the house only a minute.

Tigue followed the trail to the lay-by, where he halted and extinguished his torch. Lilly stopped perhaps fifteen meters behind him and again concealed herself in the low brush. From her hiding place, she could see the dark outline of Lawrence Tigue's figure standing at the edge of the road. He seemed to look up the road, as if he were expecting someone to come from that direction, then began pacing from one edge of the brief clearing to another. Lilly watched him for what she reckoned was four or five minutes. All the while, Tigue paced, his movements to and fro as regular as a metronome's.

Lilly heard what she thought was movement behind her; the sound startled her and she turned toward it quickly, expecting to see whomever Tigue seemed to be awaiting bearing down on her. Instead she saw nothing. Her heart began to beat rapidly; she made herself be still and listened for the sound of another step, though none came. Then the murmur of low voices—male voices—came from the direction of the road, drawing her attention back to the lay-by.

A second man had joined Tigue in the clearing. Lilly had not seen from which direction the other man had arrived, though she was certain that he had not come up the path. She'd heard no car arrive. Tigue and the other man stood just apart, facing each other.

She heard the other man say, "Do you have them?" His voice was a deep, authoritative one that Lilly didn't recognize. She watched as Tigue handed something small and compact to the man. In turn, the man handed Tigue something that Lilly could not quite see, though it was small enough for Tigue to stash into the inner pocket of his jacket.

"This will be it," the other man said. "There's far too much going on now."

"I don't care if it continues," Tigue said. "I only want what was promised me."

"Well, that will have to wait, too."

"What?" Tigue said. His voice seemed to rise an entire octave in surprise. "What do you mean it will have to wait? We have an agreement."

"For God's sake man, you must know that this mess changes everything. The police are everywhere now, looking under every rock."

"But we had an *agreement*."

"Well, it's bloody *off*," the man said with obvious irritation.

"But I'm ready. I've spent a good amount of time and effort preparing to go *now*."

"Well, I can't help that can I?"

"You could help it. Appeal to them. There's no danger from anything happening here. None of it has anything to do with that."

"She told me you were a strange little bird, but I hadn't realized how strange. She found you pathetic, mate—but I'm sure you figured that out long ago. For all I know, you killed her because of that, or maybe just because you got nervous."

"*Me*? I didn't kill her! I'd no reason to."

"You'll just have to wait until they're comfortable again. My advice is to keep your mouth shut and be happy with what you've got. If you stumble, they'll make you pay. I can't protect you, and I'm of no mind to in any case." He paused, then added, "If you did kill her, then I might come after you myself one day."

"But you *must* do something. We have an agreement. And I can't wait. I must go now! Everything is set."

"Sod off. You don't give orders, you take them."

"Bastard!" Tigue hissed.

The other man moved very suddenly; he cocked his right fist and hit Tigue squarely in the face, sending Tigue reeling backward and into the mud of the lay-by. As Tigue lay moaning, the other man stood over him. "No one calls me a bastard," he said. "If I didn't have better things to do I'd kill you here and now. Consider yourself warned." The man spit on Tigue, then abruptly turned and disappeared into the darkness up the road.

Tigue lay in the mud for nearly a full minute, emitting a kind of low whimper. Finally, he stood and turned back toward the path. He passed Lilly's hiding place, walking very quickly, his right hand held against his injured face. Lilly considered following him, though the violence of what she'd just witnessed made her hesitate. The other man had accused Tigue of killing a woman. *She*. Was *she* the woman whose body had been found in the cemetery? Or was it Alba Tigue?

Again, the sound of movement just behind Lilly startled her. She turned, heart in mouth, expecting to see Tigue, believing that he'd known that she'd been watching him all along and now, somehow, had managed to quietly double back on her, intending to silence her forever. But a large, round figure—clearly not Lawrence Tigue—moved toward her through the dark. Lilly put her hand to her chest and worried that she would faint and that the dark figure would be the last thing she would ever see.

"Lilly!" the figure whispered.

Lilly gave an involuntary yelp of terror. A second later, the figure was on her and clamped a beefy hand over her mouth. "Quiet!" the figure hissed. "He'll hear you."

In that instant Lilly realized that the hand over her mouth belonged to Miss Wheatley; she was flooded with a combination of shock and relief. Miss Wheatley took her hand away and put her finger to her own lips. Lilly drew in a deep breath, feeling as if she'd nearly drowned.

"Are you all right, my dear?" Miss Wheatley said.

"Yes." Still mildly shocked, Lilly wasn't quite sure what else to say.

"I won't ask you what you're doing out here in the middle of the night, though I think I know. But you heard everything?"

"Yes."

"He's up to something, just as I have always said, and I intend to find out what it is once and for all." She nodded at the O'Hare house. "The first thing we must do is search the house to find whatever contraband he's hidden there."

Lilly wasn't certain that she wanted to ally herself with Miss Wheatley, who was loony. But in this case, Miss Wheatley seemed to be right. Lawrence Tigue clearly *was* up to something. "He killed someone—maybe his wife," Lilly said. "The other man all but said so."

Miss Wheatley looked down the trail toward Tigue's cottage. "I'm not certain he's capable of murder."

"But what if he finds us?" Lilly said.

"He won't if we're careful," Miss Wheatley said. Lilly noticed a shotgun lying on the ground next to Miss Wheatley's squatting figure. "Now, come," she said, picking up the gun and resting it in the crook of her right arm. "We've got to see what he's up to so we can report it to the captain."

Lilly found herself getting to her feet and following Miss Wheatley toward the rear door of the O'Hare house. She'd never even *considered* entering the house after dark. Miss Wheatley produced a torch and played it on the small, rickety porch and the back door. She stepped onto the porch, which creaked under her weight, and pushed open the door. Lilly followed.

Miss Wheatley immediately went into the room in which Claire O'Hare had hung herself. She seemed utterly without fear, or even trepidation, Lilly thought. "Now then," she said, speaking to herself aloud. "What have you hidden in here? I intend to search every nook and cranny until I find it."

Lilly remained silent. Although she was as anxious as anyone to know what Mr. Tigue was on about with his nocturnal wanderings, following Miss Wheatley around the O'Hare house in the dark made her uneasy. She glanced up at the roof beam from which Claire O'Hare had hung herself and found herself wondering if, perhaps, ghosts did exist.

Miss Wheatley crept about the room, breathing heavily, and playing the torch in the corners and along the walls. Lilly worried that if Mr. Tigue had for some reason decided to return to the house, he would see them—catch them out. Something about the way Tigue had lain in the mud whimpering, then in the hurried, angry way in which he'd retreated from that defeat, had frightened her.

"Damn," Miss Wheatley said under her breath. "I can find nothing."

Lilly thought she heard a motorcar approaching; she froze and reached for Miss Wheatley's arm in an almost unconscious gesture to reassure herself that she was not alone in the spooky house.

"What is it, my dear?" Miss Wheatley whispered.

"A motorcar," Lilly said. "Listen."

They stood together in the middle of the dark room. Miss Wheatley also heard the approaching car. They expected it to pass and enter the village. But to their surprise it seemed to pull into the lay-by, its tires crunching twigs and gravel. Miss Wheatley now reached for Lilly in the dark. "Follow me," she said and headed for the back door, toting the bird gun, which still lay opened in the crook of her arm. Lilly followed her into the yard and then behind the large oak tree from which the tire swing hung. They moved just beyond the tree into the brush, where they crouched.

"Has he come back?" Lilly whispered. She worried that Lawrence Tigue actually had seen them earlier—that he'd pretended that he hadn't and now was returning in his motorcar, perhaps with a gun.

But Miss Wheatley did not answer. She was staring intently through the darkness toward the narrow path that led past the side of the house and the window that looked onto the sitting room. Lilly settled in behind her and waited, suddenly conscious that her heart was beating very rapidly.

A minute later, a tall male figure appeared in the darkness, moving along the narrow path. The man stopped at the window and appeared to peer into the sitting room. Lilly could tell from the man's height that he was not Lawrence Tigue. The beam of a torch snapped on; the figure played the torch around the interior of the room for at least a half-minute. He then switched off the torch and began to walk toward the swing. Lilly feared that the man somehow had discovered her and Miss Wheatley's hiding place. She held her breath and felt Miss Wheatley stiffen.

The man stopped at the swing and seemed to examine it. He touched the tire and set it rocking. He then abruptly turned from the swing, mounted the back porch, and entered the house through the back door. Lilly saw the faint light of his torch coming from the window of the sitting room. The light ebbed and brightened, depending on which way the man turned and walked.

"Is that the same man Mr. Tigue was arguing with?" Lilly whispered.

"No—it's Algernon Tigue," Miss Wheatley said.

"What?"

"I'd know him anywhere."

"Mr. Tigue's brother?"

"Yes."

"But why . . ."

Miss Wheatley put up her hand to silence Lilly.

The figure was exiting the house. He stood on the porch for a moment, then began to play the torch around the backyard. The beam swept past the tire swing and oak tree. Instinctively, Lilly pressed herself lower into the brush.

The man switched off the light. He stood for another moment on the porch, lit a cigarette, and took a long drag from it. Lilly saw the orange tip glow brighter. The man seemed to be in no hurry, she thought. Neither did the dark, spooky surroundings seem to cause him any anxiety. He walked off the porch into the backyard and stood there for another couple of minutes, finishing his cigarette. He dropped the butt, ground it beneath the tip of his shoe, then headed back along the narrow path to the front of the house.

"I'm going to follow him," Miss Wheatley said.

Before Lilly could object, Miss Wheatley had risen and was making her way toward the trail. Lilly hesitated only for a second before following. As she rose and made her way through the brush, she told herself that she must be brave—that she must not give into the natural desire to run from danger.

Miss Wheatley moved with what Lilly found to be shocking nimbleness through the dark and the undergrowth to the side trail, where she stopped very suddenly and yet again raised her hand; Lilly nearly ran into Miss Wheatley as she, too, abruptly halted. She looked around Miss Wheatley toward the main trail that led from the road in the direction of Miss Wheatley's cottage. She saw the man stop there for an instant and snap on his torch again. He then disappeared into the darkness down the main trail, toward Miss Wheatley's place.

Without turning to look at Lilly, Miss Wheatley whispered, "Come," and gestured for her to follow. They moved away from the house onto the main trail, staying close to the verge on their left. Lilly saw the beam of the man's torch bouncing ahead of them, about thirty meters distant. She figured that if the man was Algernon Tigue, then he must be heading toward his brother's house, and she wondered why he didn't drive there. She was surprised then when, at a point just opposite Miss Wheatley's cottage, he turned abruptly to the left, toward the wood and the trail that led to Albert Clemmons's lean-to, the same trail that Lilly had followed in the opposite direction less than an hour earlier.

Miss Wheatley's gait quickened, and Lilly sped up to keep pace. Lilly saw the beam of the man's torch play on the trees of the wood as he moved onto the trail.

"Albert," Miss Wheatley whispered under her breath. In April, shortly after Albert Clemmons had taken up residence in the wood behind her house, she had encountered Algernon Tigue in a shop on the High Street, where he was buying a packet of cigarettes. She had assumed that he had come to the village to visit his brother, though she hadn't asked. She had never really liked the Tigues as boys; she'd found Lawrence aloof and sullen and Algernon arrogant and self-centered, rather too full of himself. He had shown himself to be quite gifted at maths at an early age, and Miss Wheatley had concluded then that this had gone to his head and made him vain. Even so, she had told Algernon that Albert Clemmons had returned to Winstead and was living in a lean-to in the wood behind her house, essentially a tramp. She had hoped that Algernon, who was a bachelor and had done quite well for himself, might have outgrown his youthful haughtiness and seen fit to lend Clemmons a hand. But so far as she knew, Algernon had failed to lift even a finger to assist Albert.

Miss Wheatley began to crash through the brush in the direction of the wood; Lilly thought that she moved as if she no longer cared about maintaining stealth. She followed Miss Wheatley onto the trail that led into the damp wood; Miss Wheatley continued to move quickly, her intimate knowledge of the trail allowing her to easily negotiate its dips, turns, and obstacles in the darkness. They stopped about ten meters short of the clearing in which Clemmons had built his lean-to and moved off the trail, to the right, and crouched in the brush. The man stood in the clearing, moving the beam of his torch around it. He approached the lean-to and shone the light within it but did not attempt to enter it. He then abruptly turned back toward them and began moving along the trail back in the direction of Miss Wheatley's cottage, causing Lilly's heart to nearly jump into her throat. She and Miss Wheatley froze as the man passed them, only a few meters away.

Miss Wheatley let the man get only fifteen meters or so ahead before she abruptly set off after him again. Lilly considered staying hidden in the underbrush, but told herself again that she must not chicken out. Besides which—and this sudden emotion surprised her— she felt as if she must protect Miss Wheatley from doing anything stupid that could result in her being hurt.

The man retraced his steps past Miss Wheatley's cottage and onto the main trail, where he turned in the direction of the lay-by and his parked motorcar. Lilly and Miss Wheatley followed him there; they watched him get into the car and drive off, in the direction of Winstead. Lilly noticed that the car was the sporty kind, a convertible.

"They're up to something, the both of them," Miss Wheatley said.

She turned to Lilly and gripped Lilly's arms with her hands. "I want you to go straight home and to bed," she said. "Don't stop for anything. Tomorrow, we'll find Captain Lamb and tell him what we've seen. We can corroborate each other's story, and that ought to be enough to convince him that we're not merely telling tales."

She then let loose of Lilly and moved into the road to watch Algernon Tigue's motorcar disappear in the direction of Winstead.

TWENTY-SIX

—✦—

EARLY THE FOLLOWING MORNING, LAMB AGAIN FOUND HIMSELF
standing on the edge of the farmhouse foundation with Vera, Wallace,
Harding, Captain Walton, and George Taney, who, thanks to the government's sanctioning of the excavation at the prison site, had given
up his opposition to the dig, though he continued to grumble that
it meant that the workers at the camp "were being paid for mucking
about and doing nothing." Rivers had gone to London that morning
to check the government's records on Ruth Aisquith.

Larkin stood in the hole with Winston-Sheed, preparing the site
for that day's excavation. Since Lamb's visit of the previous afternoon,
the forensics man and the doctor had, as Lamb had guessed they might,
uncovered a portion of a third small skeleton, parallel to and a mere
ten and a half inches from the second body. This third body seemed
to be of the same size as the second skeleton—roughly the size of a

five-year-old boy—and the close proximity of the second and third skeletons made it appear as if they had been buried together, side by side. In addition, the two graves contained scraps of clothing that matched the description of the shoes, shorts, socks, and shirts that the O'Hare twins were wearing on the day they disappeared.

Although Winston-Sheed had yet to positively identify any of the three bodies in the foundation, everyone who stood on its rim was now convinced that the two latter skeletons belonged to the O'Hares. The identity of the third, clubfooted body—the one that Charlie Kinkaid accidently had unearthed—remained a mystery.

But this was not the end of the revelations the team delivered to Lamb that morning. Late on the previous afternoon, Larkin also had discovered two nearly identical pieces of evidence. The first he'd found in the grave of the younger, clubfooted victim and the other in the first of the graves of the older children. In each, he'd found buried in the moist earth beneath the bones a lead toy general that was much like the figure of Grant that Lamb had found at Clemmons's campsite and those he'd found in the O'Hare house and seen in Algernon Tigue's rooms. The figure Larkin had uncovered in the grave of the smaller child was of British Great War general Douglas Haig, while the grave of the larger child—the one that everyone assumed contained the remains of one of the O'Hare twins—had contained John Burgoyne, who had led British troops in America during the revolution.

Lamb toted up the generals that had thus far come to earth in connection with his inquiries: Grant, Hindenburg, Napoleon, Haig, and Burgoyne. The only one missing from the Britain's set that Rivers had identified was the Duke of Wellington.

Lamb looked down at the foundation, which had been a fount of disturbing shocks in recent days, and put the figures of Haig and Burgoyne in the pocket of his jacket. If events unspooled today as he hoped they would, he might also have in his possession the Napoleon that guarded Algernon Tigue's desk, and perhaps Algernon and Lawrence Tigue both in custody—though he still was not yet entirely certain about exactly what charge he would be able to hold them on. But he believed he was close to discovering the answer to that question.

Vera drove Lamb and Wallace to Winstead, where Lamb intended to test his hunch about why Ruth Aisquith had been found carrying such a large sum of cash.

They parked by the incident room. Lamb ordered Wallace to head up to Saint Michael's Church to comb the interior and perimeter of the cemetery in search of a spot where Aisquith might have hidden or buried cash for someone to retrieve and where someone, in turn, might leave something for her. That something could be rationed food of some kind or some manner of forged documents—identity cards or rationing coupons for food, clothing, or petrol—that could be sold on the black market for profit, Lamb told Wallace.

"If I'm right, she and someone in the village were trading something in the cemetery. I think the cemetery was a drop point, and, if that's true, then we must find the specific place where the drops happened," Lamb said. "Get on your hands and knees if you have to."

Wallace was about to exit the car when Vera turned to her father and said, "May I go with Sergeant Wallace, sir? I could help him look, and it would save me from having to wait around in the car, feeling as if I'm making no contribution."

Vera normally did not call her father "sir"; she called him Dad. Neither Lamb nor Wallace spoke for a second; each was too surprised by Vera's suggestion. But Lamb was seriously considering Vera's request. Her presence had helped him to discover several troubling events in the village that he might otherwise not become aware of, including the nocturnal wanderings of Lilly and Miss Wheatley. He looked at Vera and decided that he had no valid reason to mistrust his adult daughter and his detective sergeant working together, and that if he was wrong about that—if something indeed was brewing between them—then there was little he could or perhaps even should do to prevent it. It was time that he accepted the fact that his daughter irrevocably had crossed the line into adulthood. He glanced from her to Wallace and back to Vera and said, "All right."

Vera smiled. "Thank you, sir," she said.

Wallace remained still. Lamb winced internally at the repeated "sir," then looked again at Wallace. "All right, then, get going," he said. "Find me something useful."

Wallace nodded. He looked quickly at Vera, who still was smiling, then exited the car.

—⁂—

Lamb walked up the High Street to Lawrence's Tigue's cottage and rapped on the door. He immediately sensed that the place was empty and worried that Tigue might have fled. He silently chastised himself for not paying more attention to Lawrence Tigue, for not recognizing Lawrence's potential importance in the inquiries earlier and not having paid enough attention early enough to both of the Tigue brothers.

He knocked on the door again and waited for a full minute, but no one answered. He walked around the perimeter of the house, to the back, where he found the door of the garage firmly padlocked and its windows covered. He peered through the slender crack between the edges of the two doors and was able to see that Tigue's motorcar still was parked within the shed. This partially relieved him given that, if Tigue had run, he'd likely have taken his car, which would afford him more mobility and concealment than buses and trains.

Lamb returned to the incident room, from where he intended to send one of the uniformed constables stationed there to keep a discreet eye on Tigue's cottage. On this morning, Lamb's favorite uniformed sergeant, Bill Cashen, and three uniformed constables staffed the room. Cashen greeted Lamb as he entered. "Good morning, sir."

Lamb returned the greeting and went to one of the phones that, at the moment, was not in use. He found in his wallet the paper on which Lawrence Tigue had written the name and telephone number of his sister-in-law, Mary Hart. The number rang three times before a female voice answered.

"Hello," Lamb said and identified himself. "May I speak to Alba Tigue, please?"

"I'm sorry, but Alba is not here," the woman said. Lamb heard confusion in her voice.

"Is this her sister, Mary Hart?" Lamb asked.

"Yes it is. How can I help you, Chief Inspector?"

"I'm sorry to bother you, madam, but I'm merely checking out a few things from here in Winstead. Your brother-in-law, Lawrence, told me that your sister has come to Chesterfield to spend the duration of the war with you."

"Alba?"

"Yes."

"Well, I don't know why he would say that. I haven't seen Alba since last Christmas, when she and Lawrence came up on the train."

"When is the last time you spoke to your sister, madam?"

"Well, I suspect it's been close to two weeks. We try to speak on the telephone—to catch up, you know—but don't always get around to it." Lamb heard alarm creeping into Mary Hart's voice and decided not to upset her further, given that he had no evidence that Alba Tigue was in any danger or had been hurt. She might have, as Algernon claimed, left Lawrence for a motorcar salesman, a turn of events that Alba might not yet have been willing to reveal to her sister. Then, too, Alba might have objected to, or discovered, some nefarious activity in which Lawrence had involved himself. In any case, Lawrence clearly had lied about his wife going to spend the duration of the war with her sister.

"Is there something wrong, Chief Inspector? Alba's not in any trouble, I hope?"

"You've no need to worry, madam," Lamb said. He hoped that this was true. "We're merely looking into a few things as a matter of routine."

"Well, all right, Chief Inspector. That sets my mind at ease, at least a bit. If there's anything I can do to help, I hope you won't hesitate to ring me back."

"I won't, madam," Lamb promised. "And thank you."

He hung up the phone feeling yet more distressed and frustrated. Hoping for better news, he inquired of Cashen if any decent leads had come in to the incident room.

"The usual stuff, sir, I'm afraid," Cashen said. "The normal loonies, fortune-tellers and mystics claiming to be able to communicate with the dead, and people claiming to have hush-hush information that you can find in any newspaper account of the crime."

He handed Lamb a stack of about twenty-five slips of paper on which the constables had written the names, addresses, and telephone numbers—if they possessed one—of those who had called with tips, with a brief description of what the so-called tip consisted of. Lamb took a minute to quickly thumb through them and saw that Cashen's description of the callers had been accurate. The fact of the matter was that the overwhelming number of tips the police received in noteworthy cases were useless. And yet each had to at least be briefly examined to ensure that it did not contain at least a nugget of potentially useful information.

As Lamb flipped through the slips of paper he saw a name he recognized: *Markham*. The note said that a woman named Sylvia Markham, in Lower Promise, possessed "information regarding the O'Hares, Ned Horton, and missing boy from Cornwall. Wife of former PC John Markham of Lower Promise, now deceased."

According to Ned Horton's file, John Markham had been the first police officer on the scene of Claire O'Hare's hanging, Lamb recalled. Lower Promise was just over the hill, to the east of Winstead. Lamb had intended to track John Markham down and question him about the events of twenty years earlier, if Markham remained alive. Now it appeared that John Markham indeed was dead, but his widow was eager to talk.

Lamb dialed the number for Sylvia Markham, who answered.

"Hello, Mrs. Markham. This is Chief Inspector Thomas Lamb. I'd like to speak with you about the information you have regarding the O'Hares and Ned Horton."

"When I read in the *Mail* this morning about your finding a boy with a clubfoot in the Tigues' basement, I had to call," Sylvia said. She sounded elderly. She was silent for a few seconds, then added, "We've kept quiet about it, John and I. Kept quiet for too long."

"Do you mean your husband, John, the former bobby in Winstead?"

"Yes."

"Are you saying that you believe you know the identity of the child with the clubfoot?"

"I'd rather speak with you about it personally, if you don't mind," she said. Her voice quavered.

"Yes, of course," Lamb said. "I understand. Can you meet me this morning?"

"I can meet you right now."

"I can be there in ten minutes," Lamb said. "I have your address."

"All right, Chief Inspector. I'm in the last cottage past the church as you come up from the village green."

"Thank you, madam," he said.

After he rang off, Lamb looked again at the note from Mrs. Markham's initial call that the constable who answered that call had made.

. . . the O'Hares, Ned Horton, and missing boy from Cornwall . . .

The juxtaposition of those names made him shudder internally.

TWENTY-SEVEN

—⁂—

WALLACE AND VERA ARRIVED AT THE CEMETERY AND STOOD BY the black fence for a moment. Wallace surveyed the space for a likely spot in which Ruth Aisquith might have hidden something.

"We haven't come very far have we, David?" Vera said, as she stood by him.

Wallace turned to her. "What do you mean?"

"In the inquiry. We don't seem to know much more than we did when we started."

"There's a lot to sort out. Rivers is in London looking into the Aisquith woman's background; hopefully he'll find something useful." He smiled at Vera. "Besides, I've confidence in your father, even though he makes me bloody nervous sometimes. He seems to *know* things, almost by instinct."

Vera laughed. "Try being his daughter. You can't get away with anything—not because he *knows*, necessarily, knows in the actual way, I mean—but because he knows, as you said. I've sometimes thought that he can tell that you're guilty of something just by looking into your eyes."

Wallace found Vera incredibly fetching in her ridiculous uniform. She seemed to him innocent—if that was the word he sought; he wasn't entirely sure—and young, and he felt slightly ashamed of himself for feeling so attracted to her. Then, too, she seemed to possess some of her father's wisdom and patience. Despite her age, she radiated a kind of quiet self-confidence that he was not used to looking for in women. During all of his adult life, he'd found it easy to attract women. Perhaps, though, he'd avoided the difficult ones, those who were unwilling to be summoned. He was sure that Vera was not the easy type, which only kindled his attraction to her. He realized that he was willing to tell her things about himself that he would not normally tell a woman for fear that she might conclude that he was weak.

"I was thinking about what we were talking about a few days ago," Wallace said. "About deferments and nepotism and the rest of it. I'm leaning toward quitting the police and joining up."

This news alarmed Vera—and she found herself surprised at her alarm. Had her feelings for David advanced so quickly? A mere two days ago, such news would have left her feeling concerned for David but not worried that his call-up might separate them for a long period or, perhaps, in the worst scenario, forever. She thought of how much longer she might remain her father's driver. She hadn't fancied taking a job she knew to be the result of nepotism. But now she didn't want to lose that job—not yet. Not before she had a chance to say something to David that she wanted to say. But what did she want to say, exactly?

"But you're needed here." She sounded almost as if she were protesting his decision and felt guilty at having done so. She had no right to keep David from doing what he believed to be necessary. And yet she was certain—she did *not* want him to go.

"I know that," he said. "And yet I can't help feeling as if I'm ducking something." Hoping to make her understand, he told Vera the story of his cousin, Alan. "He bloody went, and here I am, safe and sound."

Alan's story touched Vera, though it also moved something harder within her. She was sorry for Alan, but he was dead. She saw no reason why David should, out of guilt, sacrifice himself on the same altar. She did not want him to go to war. But if he did go, he should do so for the right reasons and with a clear conscience that his work as a policeman had not constituted a way of avoiding his rightful duty.

Before she fully understood what she was doing, Vera kissed Wallace on the cheek, quickly. *This*, she thought, is what she had wanted to say. And now she had said it.

Wallace instinctively put his hand on the place she had kissed, as if checking to see if he could be certain about what he believed had just happened. "What was that for?" he asked, feeling clumsy. With most other women, he would not be clumsy, he thought.

Conflicted, Vera looked at him. She felt embarrassed by what she'd done and yet she was sure that she was right to have done it. "I don't know," she said. "Like I said yesterday, you've no reason to be ashamed of yourself. I'm not ashamed of you."

Wallace put his hand on hers; unmistakable electricity crackled between them. He looked into her eyes. "You're a beautiful girl, Vera, and I like you very much." He smiled, crookedly, which she liked. "But I don't know what to do about that."

"Neither do I."

"Maybe we shouldn't do anything."

Vera moved her fingers so that they became intertwined with Wallace's. "I'd hate that," she said. She pressed her fingers more securely between his.

"I suppose it's not fair that you kissed me and I haven't kissed you back." This was his usual way; he was turning on the charm now. He did not want Vera to slip away. He wished that he could summon a more direct and honest way to communicate to her how he felt. But for the moment he did not know another way.

"It *would* be unfair," she said. She smiled, easing a bit of the emotional and sexual tension that was building between them. "I don't kiss people every day, you know."

"What about your father?"

"He'll have to adjust."

"That's easy for you to say."

"Yes," she said. "It is." She looked directly into Wallace's eyes.

In the next instant they kissed, moving in unison toward each other. For all that, the kiss was brief and even chaste, a product of their shared anxiety that Lamb might appear at any minute and catch them out. Vera squeezed Wallace's hand a final time, then let it go.

She smiled and said, "We should get back to looking for this hiding place." In that moment, Wallace began to reconsider the wisdom of voluntarily signing up to have his arse shot off. Why should he go to war and leave something as seemingly rare and good as Vera Lamb behind?

—⁓—

Feeling now more than ever that he must be in too many places at once—and that he could use more men—Lamb set out to speak with Mrs. Markham in Lower Promise. He decided to make the short drive over the hill alone, so that Vera could continue to search the cemetery with Wallace, and to test his tender ankle on the car's pedals. Soon his ankle would be healed, and he would have to decide whether Vera should remain his driver.

He was about to head to the Wolseley when Miss Wheatley burst into the incident room. She was nearly out of breath, as if she had been hurrying.

"Captain," she said to Lamb. "I'm so glad I caught you; I saw your car. I've important news!"

Lamb offered her a seat. "Come in, Miss Wheatley," he said, gently guiding her toward the chair.

She sat. "Thank you." She looked at Lamb. "I've news of Lawrence Tigue. He came past my cottage last night and I followed him. He met with someone by the road, at the end of the trail. Then Algernon Tigue suddenly appeared and began snooping around the O'Hare house and Albert's campsite."

Lamb was uncertain how to react to this news, given Miss Wheatley's inclination to lay all of what she considered the worst of Winstead's ills and crimes at Lawrence Tigue's door. But he also had grown more suspicious of Lawrence and Algernon Tigue.

"What time was this?" Lamb asked.

"Well past midnight," Miss Wheatley said. "Lawrence Tigue came up the path from his cottage and met someone—another man—at the end of the path. I've long suspected that he's up to something, as I've told you, and now I'm certain of it."

"Did you recognize this other man?"

"No, it was far too dark and I was hidden in the brush. But he was tall."

"Are you sure the man you saw coming up the path was Lawrence Tigue?"

"Oh, quite sure!"

"Could you hear what they said?"

"Oh, yes! The other man asked Mr. Tigue for 'them,' and Mr. Tigue took something from him in return—a packet of something. The other man kept talking about how 'they' couldn't do something for Mr. Tigue that Tigue said they had promised they would do because everything had become 'too hot,' as he put it." She nodded at Lamb. "He meant you and your men being around the village, Captain. Mr. Tigue protested vociferously, saying that he expected this third party to keep its promise to him, but the other man basically told him that there was nothing to be done and that, besides, 'they' might hurt Mr. Tigue if he didn't mind his business. The other man also all but accused Mr. Tigue of killing the Aisquith woman. He's up to something, Captain, mark my words. And he has a co-conspirator!" She touched Lamb's arm. "And I have an additional witness. Lilly Martin."

"Lilly?"

"Yes. She also followed Tigue along the trail—or, rather, I followed the two of them. Once Tigue finished with his rendezvous with this man I approached her—I'm afraid I startled her a bit. I wanted to follow Lawrence Tigue back to his cottage, but Lilly was reluctant. I believe she was a bit scared to follow him, given what we saw and heard. But then Algernon appeared and we hid in the brush and watched him go about his business."

"And what did he do, exactly?"

Miss Wheatley delivered to Lamb a detailed account of Algernon's movements. "He seemed to be looking for something," she said.

"And did he find it?"

"I don't know. At any rate, he seemed to be carrying nothing with him when he returned to his car."

"Did it not surprise you that Lilly Martin was out and about last night?" Lamb asked.

"Of course!" Miss Wheatley said. "But you had told me that someone had seen me nick the eggs from Mr. Tigue's henhouse. And when I encountered Lilly last night, I put two and two together, you see, and figured that it must have been her. I think the girl is quite distressed, with her father gone and her mother working. She's left alone in the house, you see. I'm not surprised that she's taken to wandering around on her own."

"What did you do after Algernon Tigue left in his motorcar?" Lamb asked.

"We went home. I told her that we could vouch for each other."

"Are you sure that Lilly went home?"

"Quite sure."

"Now I must ask you, Miss Wheatley, why *you* were out and about so late last night?"

"Well, I couldn't sleep, you see, and I'd just gone out for a second for a breath of air, when I saw Mr. Tigue pass; I saw his torch light. And then I noticed that Lilly was not far behind him. I could tell it was her by her size."

"So you hadn't gone out to pilfer Mr. Tigue's eggs a second time, then?"

"No, Captain. I swear to it. I told you that I was finished with that." She raised her chin proudly. "I'm a woman of my word."

Miss Wheatley clearly was a terrible liar, and Lamb didn't believe her explanation of why she'd been out in the night. He believed that she likely had been spying on Mr. Tigue, as Lilly had been. Perhaps they had done so together. He would have to look into that, particularly on Lilly's account. He continued to find it disturbing that Lilly was spending so much time outside in the dead of night and apparently without her mother's knowledge. That said, he believed that the balance of Miss Wheatley's tale possessed the ring of truth and counseled himself not to dismiss it. Indeed, the story seemed to confirm his suspicions regarding Ruth Aisquith and someone in the village—in this case Lawrence Tigue—having formed some manner of illicit partnership that profited both parties. If his guess about that was correct, then the mysterious "they" mentioned by the man Tigue had met on the previous night might be an organized gang trafficking on the black market in stolen or counterfeit goods.

Although he was all but convinced that Lawrence Tigue had done a runner, he was nonetheless concerned that, on the chance that Tigue had not yet run, Miss Wheatley might confront Tigue with her suspicions, thereby spooking him for good and all and perhaps even putting herself and Lilly in some danger.

"Thank you for the information, Miss Wheatley," he said. "It's very valuable. But I must ask that you not confront Mr. Tigue with your knowledge or suspicions, or speak to him, or anyone else, of them in any way. That could turn out to be very dangerous to you and Lilly. For those reasons, it is absolutely crucial that we keep this knowledge to ourselves."

Miss Wheatley's eyes widened. "Of course, Captain. I promise."

TWENTY-EIGHT

—␣—

ON THE PREVIOUS AFTERNOON, RIVERS HAD CALLED THE MINISTRY
of Labour and National Service in London and been given over to
a pleasant, youngish-sounding army officer with an upper-class
accent—a Captain Willis—who had said that of course Rivers could
see the records of the female conscientious objectors and that he
would see that Ruth Aisquith's file was ready for Rivers when he arrived
on the following morning.

"Obviously, we haven't many female conchis, given that conscription of women is so new," Willis had said. "They're still a rare species."

Rivers had left for London that morning and arrived at the ministry a bit after ten; Willis met Rivers in the ministry's foyer with a
smile and handshake. Willis walked with the aid of a cane and what
Rivers took to be a permanent limp, since he wore no bandages or
other evidence that his disability was recent.

"Glad to see you could make it," Willis said. "Sounds as if you've a frightful mess down there in Winstead."

Rivers didn't like toffs as a rule but Willis's genuine, open friendliness won him over. "Yes, well, we're trying to clear it up," he said.

Willis led Rivers up a flight of stairs and down a hallway that bustled with busy-seeming people moving to and fro, to his small office, which had a single window that featured a view of the brick wall of a neighboring building. Willis bid Rivers to sit in one of two wooden chairs that faced his desk, which was wedged into the office's far corner, with the window to Willis's left. He handed Rivers the file on Ruth Aisquith that he'd pulled that morning, then moved around the desk and sat in the chair behind it. "Sounds rather a tragic case—the matter with the Aisquith woman," Willis said as he settled himself into his chair.

"Yes," Rivers said absently. He'd explained the situation regarding Ruth Aisquith to Willis on the previous day.

The file was in a cardboard portfolio bound with string. Its contents surprised Rivers as soon as he opened it. The file contained roughly two dozen pages that included Ruth Aisquith's personal information, copies of correspondence between her and the Labour Board regarding her call-up to the fire-watching service, the written decision of the tribunal for the northwest of England denying her application to be excused from the requirements of the National Service Act of 1941 for reasons of conscience, her appeal of that decision and its denial, and the papers related to her subsequent imprisonment in Manchester for willfully failing to comply with the provisions of the act in the wake of the tribunal's denial of her appeal.

Her photo—a standard mug shot—was attached to the upper right-hand corner of the first page with a paper clip. But the unsmiling woman in the photo clearly was not the woman whom Rivers had seen lying dead in the cemetery of Saint Michael's Church. This woman's face was entirely different—round, while the victim's was angular. This woman's hair was light, even blond, whereas the victim's was black. The woman they'd found lying in the cemetery had a dark, Latin aspect to her features, while the woman in the photo was positively Nordic. They weren't even close.

Rivers looked again at the name on the file: *Ruth Aisquith.* He flipped through some of the documents in which he saw the name repeated again and again. The page to which the mug shot was clipped contained a summary of Ruth Aisquith's personal information, each bit neatly typed into its appropriate box beneath the appropriate heading: name, age, height, weight, race, eye color, hair color, date and place of birth, last known permanent address, and the date of her confinement to prison. And here Rivers found something that stunned him further. According to the file, Ruth Aisquith had died in prison two months earlier of "sudden cardiac arrest." She had been thirty-six years old.

Willis saw the obvious look of consternation on Rivers's face.

"Is something wrong, old man?" he asked.

"How many people have access to this file?"

"Well, several, including me. However, the files are kept under lock." He pulled a small knot of keys from his pocket. "I've the key right here."

"Who else has a key to the file?"

"Several people, as I said. What's wrong?"

"The woman pictured here is not the woman who was shot to death in Winstead."

"Oh, dear," Willis said. "You're sure?"

"Yes, I'm sure. Either someone has tampered with this file, or the woman whose background I'm investigating isn't Ruth Aisquith. According to this file, Aisquith died of a heart attack in June."

Willis stood. "Let me see the file, please," he said. Rivers handed it over. Willis looked over the file for several seconds. "What did the woman in Winstead look like?" he asked.

Rivers described the woman he'd thought was Ruth Aisquith.

"Only seven women have gone to prison for willfully defying the conscription act since it passed," Willis said. He held up the key to the files. "I'd say it's time we had another look at the dossiers."

—ᛜ—

Having heard her father tell David to get "onto his hands and knees" in searching the cemetery—which Wallace had not yet done—Vera decided to take the lead. She looked at the blackberry bramble that ran along the rear wrought iron fence of the cemetery of Saint Michael's Church and decided that this was as good a place as any from which to begin her search. The bush was only a few meters from the place in which Ruth Aisquith's body had been found. She carefully pushed away some of the thorny branches growing close to the ground and did her best to peer at the ground beneath the bush. A portion of the space, close to the fence, appeared to have been disturbed. Vera slowly worked her hand through the bramble, snagging her sleeve on thorns here and there, and began to feel around the area. The soil was loose and moist and she found that she was able to dig into it easily with her fingers. She clawed at the spot and found that she easily could clear several inches of soil. Someone seemed to have dug a shallow hole there, then filled it in, she thought. She stood and called to Wallace, who was searching the growth that lay just outside the fence farthest from the church.

Wallace joined Vera at the spot by the rear fence. "What have you got?" he asked.

"I think I found something. The soil here is very loose, as if someone has dug it up."

Wallace eased his hand through the thorns. "Yes," he said, plunging his fingers into the crumbled dirt. He looked at Vera. "Yes, I think you've found it. Why else would someone be digging about beneath a bloody blackberry bramble, unless they wanted to put something there that others would normally steer clear of?"

Wallace rooted a bit farther into the loose soil with his fingers and soon pulled a bit of coarse cloth from the ground, stood, and held it up. In the sunlight he instantly saw that it was a bit of gray canvas fabric that appeared to have torn loose from a bag or covering of some kind.

Neither he nor Vera spoke for a second. Giving into spontaneity, he bent down and kissed her cheek. He held up the bit of cloth. "You're a champ," he said.

Vera smiled. She was proud of herself and knew that her father would be, too. At least now she was earning her keep, nepotism or no, she thought. She considered kissing Wallace on the cheek in response when she heard the front gate of the cemetery creak. She looked there to see her father coming through the gate. Vera wondered if her father had seen what just had transpired between her and David. She decided that it was better that she not take the offensive in an effort to knock her father off the scent—that taking the offensive would only cause her father to smell a rat.

In fact, Lamb had not seen the kiss. Even so, he sensed a kind of forced jauntiness in the countenances of Vera and Wallace, which led him to believe that they'd been up to *something* they'd rather he remained ignorant of. He smiled at Vera. "Do you have good news?" he asked.

"As a matter of fact, yes," she said. Wallace held up the bit of cloth for Lamb to see, and Vera bent and pushed away the blackberry branches. "Someone clearly has been mucking about under this bush."

Lamb took the bit of cloth in his fingers and examined it, then stooped and reached beneath the bush to feel the loosened earth. He stood and smiled again at Vera. "Good work, Constable Lamb," he said.

Wallace smiled very briefly. Lamb noticed this but did not remark upon it.

"Just earning my keep," Vera said.

"Yes," Lamb said.

He then told them of the events that had occurred since they had parted ways—of his call to Alba Tigue's sister-in-law in Chesterfield, of the information that Miss Wheatley had delivered, and of his brief conversation with the widow of the man who had been the local constable at the time of the O'Hare case.

Lamb had plotted out a plan of action in reaction to the information he'd received in the past hour. In addition to sending one of the uniformed constables who had been manning the incident room to stake out Lawrence Tigue's cottage, Lamb wanted to catch up again with Algernon Tigue before he, too, became anxious and considered running—if he hadn't already departed for unknown parts. He told Wallace and Vera that they should return to the incident room, where they would find Sergeant Cashen awaiting them with a car. Wallace and Cashen were to drive to the Everly School and request that Algernon Tigue accompany them to the nick for questioning. If Tigue refused, then Wallace was to threaten him with arrest on suspicion of murder.

"Whose murder?" Wallace asked.

"I'm still trying to figure that out," Lamb said with neither irony nor humor. "But I'm betting on the fact that if you give him a choice between coming willingly or in handcuffs, he'll choose the former. He's smart and very cool. Just get him into the nick, where we can keep tabs on him until we begin to straighten out this bloody mess. If the Tigues are involved in any of this, then they've got to be feeling very nervous. We might already have lost Lawrence. I don't want to lose Algernon, too."

Lamb also had an assignment for Vera; she was to track down Lilly to see if Lilly confirmed the story Miss Wheatley had told Lamb. Then she was to return to the incident room and await his return from Lower Promise.

"But who is going to drive you to Lower Promise?" Vera asked.

"I'll drive myself," Lamb said.

"But what about your ankle?"

"I think I can make it. A bit of a trial run."

Vera looked surprised, and Lamb thought he understood its source. She was enjoying her time as his driver and was not yet ready for it to end. "I shouldn't wonder that by the time I've driven to Winchester and back it will be acting up and I'll need you again," he said, hoping to assuage her disquiet.

"All right," Vera said.

Lamb smiled at her. "I'll see you a bit later." He turned to Wallace. "In the meantime, I suggest you and Cashen get moving."

TWENTY-NINE

—⁓—

THE HAMLET OF LOWER PROMISE AMOUNTED TO LITTLE MORE THAN a northeastward extension of Winstead, Lamb thought, as he eased the Wolseley down the narrow street that served as its main artery, his ankle smarting a bit each time he depressed the clutch. It lay roughly a half-mile from Winstead, on the opposite side of a gently sloping wooded hill that formed the western bank of a narrow, swift stream. The road that led into Lower Promise followed the stream, which was to Lamb's right as he entered the hamlet. After a hundred meters or so, the road took a sharp left, turning into a kind of market square that contained a pub, a small general merchandise shop, and a post office. The central green was small but well kept and contained a black granite obelisk to Lower Promise's war dead—a monument that struck Lamb as unusually large for such a small place. Just beyond this square, on the village's eastern end, stood a small church and cemetery.

The church looked at least a century older than Saint Michael's, and seeing this caused Lamb to realize that Winstead likely had been an outgrowth of Lower Promise, rather than the other way around. First had come the hamlet, hard by the deep, dark little stream, and then had come Winstead on the opposite side of the hill. For whatever reasons—likely its closer proximity to the coast and the port cities—Winstead had prospered and grown larger and more robust than had Lower Promise.

Fifty meters beyond the church lay four nearly identical stone cottages, each well preserved and each with identical green wooden doors and small, tidy flower gardens in front. The last of these was the one in which Sylvia Markham, the widow of former constable John Markham, lived.

The drive from Winstead, as brief as it was, taxed Lamb's sore ankle more than he had expected it to, and he was suffering a mild, dull pain there by the time he pulled the Wolseley to a stop. He exited the car and, with a slight limp, moved up the stone path toward the Markham cottage, past a garden of fading red and white peonies, to the green front door. He was about to knock on the door when it suddenly opened and Sylvia Markham loomed in the doorway. Incredibly—or so Lamb thought—she was just as he imagined she would be. Short, portly, slightly bent, wrinkled, iron-haired, and dressed in a green housecoat, though with a clear glint of vigor in her eyes—that vigor, whatever its source, which had allowed her to continue breathing well into her old age.

"Good afternoon, sir," she said before Lamb could introduce himself or inquire as to whether she was, indeed, Mrs. Markham. "Wipe your feet, please," she added, before abruptly turning from the door and moving deeper into the house.

Lamb did as directed, wiping his feet on a rattan matt just outside the door, before following Mrs. Markham into her small, neat sitting room. She sat on a red couch and gestured for Lamb to take the pink chair that faced it from across a well-polished mahogany coffee table. A bone white ceramic tea service arrayed with delicately painted cornflowers sat on a silver tray in the middle of the table. Lamb noticed immediately that the house was spotless and that everything within it seemed to be in its proper place. Not so much as an ashtray appeared askew.

Lamb sat in the chair.

"Milk and sugar?" Mrs. Markham asked. Lamb still had not yet had a chance to speak.

"Yes, thank you," he said.

Mrs. Markham poured his tea and carefully placed the cup and saucer on the table in front of him. "Thank you," Lamb repeated. "And thank you for contacting me. I'm very anxious to hear what you have to say."

Now that she had poured tea and arranged things in a way that obviously made her feel comfortable, Mrs. Markham seemed to relax, Lamb thought.

"As I said, when I saw the story about the boy with the clubfoot, I had to call." She glanced away from Lamb for a second, and he sensed her discomfort. He said nothing, though, and allowed her to compose herself and continue in the manner that made her most comfortable. "I've kept silent about it long enough, though I did so only for my husband's sake—for John's sake," she said after a few seconds. "I had to—we had to—or else John would have lost his job and reputation. Ned Horton would have seen to that as sure as you and I are sitting here. But John is gone now, and so I've no reason, nor any wish, to protect the others involved in this story." She looked hard at Lamb. "In fact, the rest of them can burn in hell, so far as I'm concerned. They *should* do."

"I see," Lamb said, speaking as little as possible so as not to sidetrack Mrs. Markham from relating her long-held secret.

"The thing really started in the spring of 1919, you see, not long after Olivia Tigue came to the farm with those sons of hers and no father with them. Almost from the beginning, Algernon Tigue developed a reputation as a hellion and troublemaker, which is how John came to know the Tigues. Algernon was the type of boy who stole trinkets from the shops and the like—for the thrill of it, I think—and would lie about it, pretty as you please, when someone confronted him. Most children, when you catch them out red-handed in something, will show some shame and fear of punishment. But Algernon Tigue was different from most boys. As John used to say of him, Algernon Tigue would as soon spit in your eye as tell you the truth.

"A few months after the Tigues came to the farm, someone strung up a cat from a lamp post on the High Street in Winstead, just by the pub. It was quite a terrible thing, as you might imagine. John immediately suspected that Algernon might be the culprit, given the cruel nature of the thing. Then a man in the village told John that he had recognized the cat as one of the strays that had regularly loitered about the Tigue's barn and farm, looking for rats and other vermin.

"But John never really was able to pin the deed for certain on Algernon, and soon enough, it was forgotten. Then, a month or so later, two more cats were hung up from the same post in Winstead, and within just a couple days of one another. The *Mail* got hold of the story then—the ghoulishness of it. In turn, the Hampshire police decided it was worth looking into and so sent a detective out here to investigate. And that detective was Ned Horton."

"And had your husband spoken to Algernon Tigue and his mother about the cats by then—by the time Ned Horton came onto the case?"

"Of course. Or, I should say that he tried to. But Olivia Tigue put him off. Each time my husband went to the farm asking after Algernon, Olivia told him that the boy wasn't home. John very quickly came to believe that Olivia knew that her son had killed and displayed the cats and was protecting him from the consequences."

"So Ned Horton took over the inquiry after the third cat was found?"

"Yes. And 'took over' is exactly what he did. My husband believed that he might give Horton some assistance in the inquiry, but Horton made it clear that he wanted nothing from John. He thought John beneath him."

"Did Ned Horton share your husband's suspicions of Algernon Tigue?"

"Well, if he did, he dismissed them and very quickly concluded that Algernon had nothing whatsoever to do with the matter. That's when Horton told my husband that he needn't bother Olivia or Algernon Tigue any longer. That was the word he used—'bother.' As if he believed John to have been guilty of something, rather than the Tigues. I've no doubt that Olivia Tigue presented the matter to Horton in exactly that way—that John had harassed her and her blessed little boy. In the end, Horton threatened John, told him that if he 'bothered' the Tigues again that he'd see to it that John would lose his posting here in Lower Promise."

"And what happened with the case of the cats?" Lamb asked.

"After the third cat was found, the hangings stopped and the whole thing was forgotten. John was angry about that. He used to say that Ned Horton came in and shut down the case but never solved it."

Lamb believed Sylvia Markham's story. Indeed, Horton's actions in relation to the cats seemed to fit hand-in-glove with his later shoddy investigation of the O'Hares' disappearance.

"And you believe that these events are connected in some way with the death of the boy whom we've found in the farm's foundation—the boy with the clubfoot?"

"Oh, yes," Mrs. Markham said. "Him and the O'Hare boys both, I daren't say."

"You believe then that someone on the Tigue farm, or connected with the farm, killed the clubfooted boy and the O'Hare twins?"

"Not 'someone,' Chief Inspector. Algernon Tigue. That would be my bet."

"But you've no proof of that?"

"Unfortunately, no, though I daresay that Ned Horton discovered proof and hid it away."

"And why would Horton do that?"

"For sex, Chief Inspector. Some men will do anything for it, as I'm sure you've found in your work. Some will throw away everything they've got for it. They become obsessed with a certain woman, and there's an end to it."

"With whom was Horton having sex?"

"Olivia Tigue, obviously."

This assertion surprised Lamb. And yet it explained the seemingly shoddy job that Horton had done on the O'Hare inquiry. Also, Mrs. Markham seemed to be implying that Horton had some knowledge of the boy with the clubfoot. But Lamb had no knowledge that Horton ever had had anything to do with such a case. In any event, Lamb could recall no case of a young boy with a clubfoot having gone missing in Hampshire.

"Are you saying that you believe Ned Horton also assisted the Tigues in covering up the matter not only of the cats, but the killing of this boy with the clubfoot?"

"Oh, yes. Olivia Tigue had Ned Horton wrapped around her little finger, as they say. That is the main reason why I had no doubt that Horton would have made good on his threat to John if John continued to investigate the Tigues—to 'bother' them, as Horton put it."

"Tell me what happened, please."

"The problem with the cats happened in the summer. During the following October, Olivia took her sons to visit her sister in the village of Four Corners, in Cornwall. Her sister ran a farm that, I eventually came to learn, was in the family and that she and Olivia had run together for several years before Olivia moved to Winstead. While Olivia and her sons were in Four Corners, a very young boy from the village there—his name was Tim Gordon, which I shall never forget—went missing on the very morning that Olivia and her sons left the farm to return to Winstead. Olivia's sister had a motorcar, which she lent to Olivia and which Olivia used to return to Winstead. Then Olivia turned right around, quick as you please, and drove the car right back to Four Corners and from there took the bus home again straightaway. All of this came to light later, when the detective from Cornwall who was investigating Tim Gordon's disappearance came to Winstead to interview the Tigues about Tim. Tim had lived with his parents on a farm in Four Corners that neighbored the Tigues' place, and this detective was suspicious of the fact that Olivia Tigue and her sons had left Four Corners—and it seemed, rather quickly—on the very day of Tim's disappearance."

"Do you remember this detective's name?"

"Of course. I shall never forget it, either. Fulton. Inspector Charles Fulton."

"Continue, please," Lamb said.

"The whole matter struck Fulton as suspicious—this matter of the Tigues suddenly scurrying to Winstead in the sister's motorcar and then Olivia turning right around and driving the thing directly back to Four Corners. Fulton wanted to know why they all hadn't simply returned home by train or omnibus the first time around. When Fulton came to Winstead, he had the decency to call on my husband and request his assistance, and he shared his suspicions with John, who told me that Fulton originally had his eye on Lawrence Tigue, as Lawrence was of a more fitting age to have committed such a violent crime than was Algernon. But John told Fulton that if either of the brothers had harmed that little boy, it would have been Algernon."

"And did Ned Horton attempt to steer Fulton away from the Tigues, as he had turned away your husband?" Lamb asked.

"Yes, exactly so, Chief Inspector. Fulton shared his suspicions with Horton, too. After all, why wouldn't he? He believed that Horton and he were on the same side in the matter. But of course they weren't. Horton was on the side of the Tigues—their protector. Before he returned to Cornwall, Fulton told my husband that Ned Horton had assured him that the Tigues couldn't have been involved, but that Fulton remained unsure. Unfortunately, though, that was the end of it. Fulton never returned to Winstead, and John heard later that the matter in Four Corners had withered on the vine there. That's why I had to call when I saw the story in the *Mail* this morning. I've kept the secret too long—for John's sake, as I said. But now my conscience won't allow me to continue to be silent on the matter. I believe that

Fulton and John were right all along and that Tim Gordon's body has been lying in the basement of that wretched house since the day he disappeared."

Mrs. Markham suddenly brought her right hand to her mouth in an attempt to stifle herself from dissolving into tears. Lamb immediately reached across the table to touch her hand. He'd used the method many times—touching someone who was about to cry—and it always had worked in delaying them from doing so until he'd finished questioning them.

"You're right to have spoken up," Lamb said. "For your sake and for John's. And I promise you that if Ned Horton did act in the way that you've described, I'll do my best to see that he pays the price, and I'll see that John's reputation and memory are not tarnished in any way as a result."

Mrs. Markham looked at Lamb. "Thank you," she said.

"But I must ask you to tell me a bit more before we're finished," Lamb said. "I need to know about your husband's involvement in the O'Hare case. Ned Horton's files mention that John was the first policeman on the scene of Claire O'Hare's suicide."

Mrs. Markham put her hand on her forehead and was silent for a couple of seconds before she answered.

"Yes," she said. "John found her and, of course, called the constabulary to notify them that an inspector was required on the scene. And once again the man who showed up was Ned Horton. The coroner ruled Claire O'Hare's death a suicide and everyone accepted that, just as they accepted that Sean O'Hare had abandoned her and taken their sons with him."

"I take it that John was not among those who accepted the coroner's verdict," Lamb said.

"John never saw the suicide note that Ned Horton claimed he'd found in the O'Hare place and which he came to believe was counterfeit. Horton shut John out of the O'Hare case just as he had the matter with the cats. I wish that we had stood up to Horton, but it was just after the war and we couldn't afford to lose John's posting.

It would have come down to John's word against Ned Horton's, and Ned Horton had the rank and the power."

"Did your husband ever discover the identity of the person who called and alerted him to the fact that Claire O'Hare was dead?"

"No."

"Did John have any reason to believe that the Tigues might have had any connection to the events that took place at the O'Hare cottage?"

"He *suspected* them, yes. He suspected them because of what he believed about Algernon and because he knew what Olivia was capable of when it came to protecting Algernon. And so he was suspicious of them. But he had no proof that any of them had had anything to do with the O'Hare matter."

"I've heard that a rumor had gone 'round the village at the time that Sean O'Hare might have been having some sort of dalliance with Olivia Tigue. Did John also believe or suspect that?"

"He believed it possible and even likely. But again, he had no proof of such an affair."

"Did *you* know the O'Hares, Mrs. Markham?" Lamb asked.

"Only by reputation."

"What can you tell me about them?"

"Sean was a reprobate and drunk—though he was good-looking and could be charming, a ladies' man, or so I heard on many occasions. He was one of those men who seemed to have a hold over a certain kind of woman, and Claire, I suppose, was one of those. She was a local girl, you see, and Sean O'Hare was a man of the world, and an older man, twenty or so years older. Claire also drank heavily and was by everyone's account an utter failure as a mother."

"What do you believe became of Sean O'Hare and the twins?"

"I don't know." She shook her head.

"How about John? Did he have an idea?"

"He came to believe what most people around here came to believe—that Sean had gone away with the boys. It was easier for us to believe that, I suppose—easier on our consciences."

Mrs. Markham again looked away from Lamb.

"He was never proud of that, was John—of his giving in to Horton's threats." She turned back to face Lamb, with a look of beseeching in her eyes. "But he didn't want to lose his job."

"It sounds as if Ned Horton gave him little choice but to obey," Lamb said, hoping that this would comfort her.

"That's what I told John. But he never believed it. He believed he'd taken the coward's way out and regretted it for the rest of his life." Tears welled again in Sylvia Markham's eyes. "He was never the same man after that."

THIRTY

—◆—

LAMB HEADED BACK TO WINSTEAD, HIS ANKLE SMARTING AS HE
worked the clutch. He was furious at Ned Horton but told himself that
he must not expend undue energy on Horton until he'd cleared up
the rest of the mess facing him. The information that Mrs. Markham
had given him made him feel for the first time that his inquiries were
finally moving forward. Although he was becoming more certain
that he was correct in his theory about Ruth Aisquith's frequent
early-morning visits to the village cemetery, he remained stumped on
who had shot Aisquith and why. If the other portion of his guess was
correct—that Lawrence Tigue might have been supplying Aisquith
with some sort of forged documents—then Lawrence likely hadn't
been Aisquith's killer, given that Lawrence had something to lose
from Aisquith's death. Unless, of course, Aisquith had double-crossed
Lawrence in some way.

He parked at the school but did not go into the incident room. Instead, he walked up the High Street toward Lawrence Tigue's cottage, where he found the constable he'd assigned to watch the house sheltering in a spot just across from and slightly down the street from Tigue's place. When the man noticed Lamb approaching, he straightened to attention.

Lamb smiled. "At ease," he said. "Any sign of our man?"

"None, sir."

Lamb pulled his packet of Player's from his coat pocket and offered one to the constable, who, surprised, took one. "Thank you, sir," he said.

Lamb lit the constable's cigarette and then his own. He took a long drag and, as he exhaled, eyed Tigue's empty cottage. He again chastised himself for not paying more attention to the Tigues. He smiled at the young constable and said, "Keep on it, then. We'll get you some relief soon enough."

He then returned to the school, where he found Vera waiting for him by the Wolseley.

"I couldn't find Lilly," Vera said. "I'm sorry."

"Don't worry yourself about it," Lamb told her. "We've still time to straighten things out." He felt as if he was trying to assure himself, as much as Vera, of the truth of this notion.

"I'd like for you to drive me back to Winchester," he said. "I'm afraid the little drive over to Lower Promise has left my ankle the worse for wear."

Vera smiled briefly at this, then slid behind the wheel of the Wolseley.

On the drive to Winchester, Lamb remained mostly silent. He did not feel it necessary to fill Vera in on all that he learned that day. There would be time for that as events continued to spool out. Instead, he smoked and attempted to clear his mind of rubbish—of the useless emotions surrounding his failure to adequately recognize the importance of the Tigues and his anger at the way Ned Horton had handled the cases in Winstead twenty years earlier. He closed his eyes and willed himself to relax and was surprised to find, when they arrived at the nick, Vera gently nudging him awake.

He sent Vera to the pub across the street from the nick to pick up cheese-and-pickle sandwiches and tea for the both of them—neither had yet eaten lunch—then went immediately to his office, where he began to fill out the forms necessary to obtain a warrant to search Lawrence Tigue's premises on the grounds that he believed that Lawrence had been producing counterfeit documents on the printing press in his garage. This was a long shot, based on his theory about who might have been conspiring with Ruth Aisquith and why. But he believed they'd collected enough circumstantial evidence of Lawrence's apparent participation in such an operation to convince a magistrate to issue the warrant.

While Lamb was working, Evers, the man at the front desk, put through a telephone call to Lamb from Wallace, who reported that Algernon Tigue was not in his rooms. Wallace had asked around the school but no one he'd spoken to knew where Algernon had gone.

"Maybe they've run together," Wallace offered.

"It's possible," Lamb said. He told Wallace to take over the job of watching Lawrence's cottage from the constable.

When Lamb finished the warrant application, he called a magistrate he knew well and explained the circumstances to the man, who said he would sign the document. Lamb gave the papers to a uniformed constable with instructions to deliver them to the magistrate and return with the signed warrant. By then, Vera had returned with the sandwiches and tea; Lamb took his into his office and ate alone. As he was gulping the last of the weak tea, Rivers, freshly returned from London, appeared at his door.

"Ruth Aisquith isn't her real name," Rivers announced. "It's Maureen Tigue, and she seems to be mixed up with the Irish. She also might have killed the real Ruth Aisquith and stolen that woman's identity."

Lamb sat at his desk for a couple of seconds in silence, trying to digest what Rivers had just said. The information stunned him—and, yet, too, it seemed to confirm the scenario that he'd been building in his mind. Working the case had been like unraveling a tangled ball of string, strand by strand; now Rivers seemed to have loosened a primary knot.

Rivers removed his hat, sat in one of the chairs facing Lamb's desk, and told Lamb the story of his visit to London.

After he'd seen Ruth Aisquith's file and become convinced that the woman whose photo was attached to the file was not the woman who was shot in the cemetery, he and Captain Willis had gone to the file room, where they'd examined the files of the handful of women who had claimed and been denied immunity from conscription on the basis of conscience and at some point afterward gone to prison. All had lost their appeals and had subsequently been ordered to report for duty. When they'd refused to report, they'd been convicted of noncompliance and fined. All had refused to pay the fine and been sent to prison for an initial term of three months, pending a second hearing before the tribunal.

"That's how it works," Rivers told Lamb. "All of them followed the same path of staunch refusal leading to jail. Less than a hundred women have applied for conchi status since the conscription act went into effect. Of those, roughly three in ten were excused from the call-up. The rest, save these seven, gave up the nut at some point in the process to avoid jail. Most men follow the same path; only the hard cases go to prison."

He'd only sorted through three of the seven files when he noticed the name Maureen Tigue on the fourth, he told Lamb. The surname had caught his eye. He opened the file and found attached to it a photo of the woman they'd found shot to death in the cemetery.

"According to her file, Maureen Tigue objected on the grounds that conscription is coercive, undemocratic. Ruth Aisquith had objected on the same grounds. In both cases the tribunal called that bollocks. Aisquith landed in prison four days after Maureen Tigue, in April. Slightly more than two months later—roughly seven weeks ago—Aisquith died in prison of a sudden heart attack, although she was only thirty-four and had no history of heart trouble. The coroner ruled it death by cardiac arrest; the report was in her file.

"Two days later, Maureen Tigue requested a second hearing in front of the tribunal on the grounds that she was willing to forego her application for immunity and would answer the call-up. That hearing was granted and three weeks later she left prison and was assigned to report for duty at the POW camp project in Winstead. But she appears to have arrived at the prison camp bearing the identity of Ruth Aisquith, rather than Maureen Tigue. She must have paid off someone on the prison end to provide her with Aisquith's identity and background. Walton might also have been paid to look the other way. I think it's likely that she was working for the IRA and that they were paying the freight. She was arrested in 1938 for agitating on behalf of Irish Republicanism. She was swept up in what was thought at the time to be a plot to bomb a police station in Cornwall, though nothing much seemed to have come of it. She then seemed to have gone underground until she filed for conscientious objector status. Her file listed her mother as Martha Tigue of Four Corners, in Cornwall. The file says the mother is deceased and that she has no siblings. It also lists her father as 'unknown.'"

Rivers paused and leaned forward a bit in his chair. "I worked a poisoning five years ago in Warwickshire—wife killed her husband for running around on her," he continued. "She put cyanide in his ale and he died of cardiac arrest. She almost got away with it but the police surgeon up there was thorough and found evidence of the cyanide, enough to put down a bloody elephant. The only thing I can't figure is why, once Martha Tigue was out, she went to the prison camp."

"I believe that someone—likely Lawrence Tigue—was providing her with something, some sort of fake documents he produced on his printing press. Identity cards, maybe, or ration tickets of some kind," Lamb said. "That's why we found so much cash on her. She was leaving the cash for Tigue, and he was leaving whatever it was he printed for her. She would come to the cemetery very early in the morning, when no one was about, ostensibly to visit her late grandmother, but actually to pick up whatever Tigue had left for her and leave the money in the same spot. We found a likely drop spot in a corner of the cemetery today. Tigue probably made his drops and pick-ups in the dead of night. If your theory about the Irish is right, then maybe Maureen Tigue was passing these documents to the IRA in some way—and maybe with the help of someone else at the camp."

Lamb recounted Miss Wheatley's story of having seen Lawrence Tigue meet someone on the previous night in the lay-by by the O'Hare house and of how the two had argued.

"What you've found fits with what Miss Wheatley claims was the substance of this meeting Tigue had with this man," Lamb said. "That they were discussing some sort of deal that had come to an end with Tigue believing that he'd been cheated of something he'd been promised. If the dead woman is related to the Tigues—given her actual surname—then she probably knew that Lawrence Tigue had a printing business and could prove useful if the price was right. It's possible they knew each other quite well. Then this project comes up in Winstead and she hears of it in some way, and sees a way to help 'the cause,' and here she is."

"So the mystery man Tigue met by the road might be Taney, then?"

"That's my best guess. His trucks come in and out of the place every day, hauling away the rubbish and the rubble. I saw one of them the first time I spoke with him at the camp. Maybe the drivers take a few documents away with them, too. And you're right—Walton might also be getting a cut. He runs an incredibly shoddy operation out there, and this would explain the shoddiness. Also, I found out today that Olivia Tigue—Lawrence and Algernon's mother—had relatives who lived in Cornwall, near a village called Four Corners."

Lamb took another couple of minutes to fill Rivers in on the information he'd learned that day in his interviews with Ned Horton and Sylvia Markham, and his brief inspection of Horton's files on the O'Hare case.

"So who killed Maureen Tigue, then? If she was the golden goose for Taney, Tigue, and Walton?"

"I don't know," Lamb said. "Maybe she double-crossed one of them. If she did kill Ruth Aisquith to steal her identity, then she had bloody ice water in her veins."

"What about the vicar?"

"I might have been wrong about the vicar." Lamb hated to admit it.

"So which of the three—Tigue, Taney, or Walton—is colder even than she?"

"Lawrence Tigue has done a runner."

"He doesn't strike me as the type."

An image of the seeming spiritless and weak-willed visage of Hawley Crippen flashed through Lamb's mind.

"But you know as well as I do, Harry," he said. "They never do."

THIRTY-ONE

—⚬—

ALTHOUGH THE CONSTABLE LAMB HAD DISPATCHED TO THE magistrate with the warrant to search Lawrence Tigue's cottage had not yet returned, Lamb was anxious to get back to Winstead. In addition to searching Lawrence's cottage, he wanted now to speak again with Taney and Captain Walton at the prison camp—to confront them with the fresh evidence Rivers had uncovered in London. He ordered a second constable to deliver the warrant to Winstead as soon as it was signed and delivered. In the meantime, he, Rivers, and Vera prepared to return to the village posthaste. But even with this, Lamb first wanted to call Inspector Fulton, the detective from Cornwall who had investigated the disappearance of Tim Gordon.

Lamb hoped that Fulton still was on the force and was in to take his call. His luck had not been running too well throughout most of the inquiry, he thought, and yet, it seemed to have changed today.

The duty sergeant in the Cornwall County Constabulary answered his call. Lamb identified himself and asked for Fulton, whose Christian name he didn't know.

"Just a minute and I'll put you through, sir," the man said. Lamb looked at Rivers, who was sitting on the edge of Lamb's desk, and winked. A bit of luck.

A few seconds later, a man with a tired-sounding baritone voice answered. "DI Fulton." Lamb again identified himself and explained the reason for his call. He told Fulton that they had found a small skeleton with a clubfoot buried in the basement of the former Tigue farm, and that he believed that this body belonged to Tim Gordon.

Fulton sighed. The news seemed to sadden rather than surprise or anger him. "Bloody hell," he said resignedly. "I once had suspicions that the Tigues were mixed up in Tim's death, but I never had the proof."

"Why did you suspect the Tigues?" Lamb asked.

"They'd been up here, visiting Olivia Tigue's sister, Martha. Martha was Olivia's older sister; she ran the family farm on which the both of them had grown up. At the time, it hadn't been that long since Olivia had moved from Four Corners to Winstead, to begin her own farm. But they had returned for a visit—Olivia and her two sons—at the time when Tim disappeared. Tim lived with his parents on a farm very close to Martha Tigue's, and Lawrence and Algernon Tigue had known the boy and his family during the time they and their mother had lived here, with Martha. They returned to Winstead on the very day on which Tim disappeared—very abruptly, I thought. I discovered that Martha had lent them her motorcar, though they had come to Four Corners by bus. Then Olivia Tigue returned with the motorcar almost immediately—and then returned again to Winstead by bus just as quickly. The whole thing struck me as suspicious. My theory at the time was that, if the Tigues had been involved, they might have brought Tim's body back to Winstead in Martha Tigue's motorcar and disposed of it there. Now it looks as if that's exactly what they did."

"You came here to interrogate them?"

"Yes, but I got nothing. Olivia Tigue was very much like her sister; both of them could be hard as stone."

"And Ned Horton intervened on behalf of the Tigues? He was a DI down here then."

"Yes, Horton. He vouched for them—for Olivia and the boys. Spun me a tale of how they'd been wrongly suspected of various crimes about the village in the past; said that the local people were unfairly suspicious of them because they were outsiders and had an unusual living arrangement, with Olivia the head of the farm and no man about the place. I thought Horton a bit of an odd duck, to be truthful. The nervous type."

"Did Martha Tigue have a daughter—a girl named Maureen?"

"She did—and the girl was a bit of trouble, besides. Ran away from home a lot. By the time she was sixteen she had developed a reputation as a bit of available goods. A couple of years later, she got herself involved in an Irish plot to blow up the nick here—got caught up in a sting. It turned out that the plot had never really gotten past the talking stages, and that she was involved only on the fringes, though she went to jail for a couple of years. That was fifteen years ago, at least."

"Do you know what became of her?"

"As I recall, she left Four Corners after she got out of jail. I assumed that she went to Ireland, given her affinity for the Republicans."

"We've had a killing down here that I believe might be related in some way to the Tigue brothers. The victim was a woman, a former conscientious objector who gave up her opposition to the draft and was conscripted into a work crew that is building a prisoner-of-war camp down here. It appears that she somehow managed to steal the identity of another conchi, a woman named Ruth Aisquith, who died in June. But we've discovered that the woman actually was Maureen Tigue. Now Tim Gordon's remains appeared to have been uncovered in the foundation of the old Tigue place along with the bodies of a pair of twin five-year-old boys who were said to have disappeared from Winstead more than twenty years ago."

"Five-year-old twins? You mean the O'Hare boys?"

"You know the case, then?"

"Oh, yes; I was a DC at the time here. That story made its way out here, most definitely. Of course, the O'Hare matter occurred the summer after I came to Winstead. But I remember hearing rumors in the village while I was there that Sean O'Hare had taken up with Olivia Tigue and that Sean's wife—whose name I've forgotten—knew about it but didn't care. And I was quite ready to believe that, given my experience with Sean O'Hare and the rumors I'd heard regarding him and both the Tigue sisters, Martha and Olivia."

"You knew Sean O'Hare previously, then?" Lamb asked, frankly surprised. "Already knew of him when you came to Winstead on that first occasion?"

"Yes. Sean O'Hare had spent some time in Four Corners ten or twelve years before all that mess broke in Winstead. This would have been more than thirty years ago; I was a mere PC then. While he was here he developed a reputation as a bit of trouble—a drinker, a brawler, and a charmer of the local females. It was common knowledge in the village that all three of the children born of the Tigue sisters, Martha and Olivia, were bastards. Neither of them ever married. Although it was a scandal, neither of the sisters seemed really to care much about what the rest of Four Corners thought of them. After their father died, they took up running the family farm as a kind of team and made a fair go of it besides, all the while raising their three bastard children together, just as they ran the farm, with nary a grown man about the place. Rumor had it that Sean O'Hare was the father of at least the first child, Maureen, if not indeed all three. Martha Tigue, for one, never took pains to hide her interest in Sean, nor he in her. But Sean was the roving type and he left Four Corners eventually."

Lamb could scarcely believe what he was hearing. "You're saying that Maureen, Lawrence, and Algernon Tigue all are bastards?"

"Absolutely. As I said, that's common knowledge in Four Corners. That's why I say that when, a year after Tim Gordon disappeared and the matter involving the O'Hares hit the press, I thought to myself, 'Well, well. Sean O'Hare again, is it?' When I discovered during the previous year, during my visit there, that Sean had landed in Winstead, it suddenly made some sense to me as to why Olivia Tigue had left the family place in Four Corners and struck out on her own. She and her sister had been making a pretty fair go of the farm here, as I said. And then for reasons that weren't clear to anyone, Olivia suddenly up and left it all behind to go to Winstead."

"What about motive?" Lamb asked Fulton. "Why would any of the Tigues want to kill Tim Gordon?"

"Well, that was just it. At first, I wasn't certain about motive. I checked the boy's parents first, of course, but they had alibis; they'd gone into Four Corners to shop for food and supplies for the farm that morning and had left the boy at home, alone, believing him safe there. They were seen in the village several times throughout the morning. Of course, one of them might have doubled back and killed the boy, but I could find no proof of that, or a reason why either of them would want to do so. Both of them struck me as genuinely broken up by the boy's death. Indeed, it was the boy's mother who first named one of the Tigues as a possible culprit, though I'd already had my eye on them in any case, thanks in part to Maureen's penchant for troublemaking and that they lived on the next farm over. Then, when I went to the Tigue place on the following day and discovered that Olivia and her sons had hightailed it on the previous afternoon, and that a witness had seen them drive away in Martha Tigue's motorcar, I decided that I had better take a little ride out to Winstead."

"Which of the Tigues did Tim's mother name as the one she suspected?"

"Algernon. She despised the boy—told me she'd been relieved when Olivia had left and taken him and Lawrence to Winstead—which is one reason why I took her suspicions with a grain of salt."

"Did she tell you why she despised Algernon?"

"She considered him evil—and that was just the word she used, too. *Evil*. Over the previous year she had found two of her ewes with their throats cut and had suspected Algernon."

"Did she say why she considered Algernon to be evil?"

"Well, she was foggy on that point, which is another reason why I hedged my bets a bit on her accusations. To her it was a matter of merely knowing Algernon, of what he was like. She said as much to me. 'Once you know him, you'll understand.' Words to that effect. But she had no actual proof that Algernon Tigue had cut the throats of her ewes, or any evidence that he'd ever done anything to her or her family in the past. It was more of an intuition, apparently. When I eventually came to Winstead and spoke to the local constable, Markham, he told me much the same thing. That he believed Algernon Tigue to possess a kind of evil streak and that he suspected that Algernon had hung up several cats in the village square during the previous summer, but that he'd never been able to get the goods on the boy, in part because Ned Horton had warned him off."

"What else can you tell me about Horton's actions at the time? Did you suspect that he was putting you off the Tigues as well?"

"Not at first. I took his word on the matter of the Tigues. Even so, I did wonder a bit about his relationship with them. He seemed protective of them. I eventually came to believe that Horton might have been at it with Olivia Tigue—or wanted to be."

"What do you mean?"

"Just that. I could have believed that they were at it; people slide down that slope all the time. It's the most common thing in the world. It was just a feeling I had. She was one of those women who had something about her, you know? But she also was hard as rock, as I said. I could get nothing out of her. She never flinched."

"What can you tell me about Tim Gordon, other than that he had a clubfoot? We're trying to definitively identify the body we've found as being his."

Fulton spent a couple of minutes describing Tim Gordon—his height, weight, hair color, the type of clothing he was wearing at the time of his disappearance, and other distinguishing characteristics. Fulton had never forgotten the case, or its particulars.

"One other thing you should know, Lamb," Fulton said. "I came to believe that Tim was taken in broad daylight from the lane just next to the farm on which he lived with his parents. His mother said that she had just bought him a set of toy soldiers for his birthday two days earlier, and that he had left the house with those. But I never found them."

"Toy soldiers?"

"Yes," Fulton said. "A Britain's set. Generals and field marshals."

THIRTY-TWO

—⁓—

THE LATE-AFTERNOON AUGUST SUN STILL WAS HIGH AND BRIGHT in the sky as they drove down the rutted farm road toward the prison camp tent village, with Vera at the wheel. Wallace remained in Winstead, keeping an eye on Lawrence Tigue's cottage.

The camp workers had finished their duties for the day and were in the mess eating their evening meal. Lamb met with Larkin and Harding, who were overseeing the removal of the unearthed remains to the morgue. Lamb brought the two up to date on the latest developments.

Lamb said that he suspected that Captain Walton and, perhaps, George Taney might have had a hand in whatever operation Maureen Tigue had been running out of the camp under the alias of Ruth Aisquith—Walton because of his obviously lax management of the camp, and Taney because of the powerful and central role he played in the camp's operations. Lamb had found it suspicious that Taney had agreed to give Maureen such generous leave on the morning of her death, and he now thought that perhaps Taney had granted that leave because Maureen's ability to move about Winstead freely also profited him. Lamb suspected, too, that the mystery man Lawrence Tigue had met in the lay-by on the previous night—a man Miss Wheatley had described as tall and who had arrived at the meeting on foot, a man who had angered Lawrence Tigue by bluntly telling Tigue that "they" no longer intended to honor the "deal" they had made with Tigue—also might have been George Taney. But even with that said, he still possessed no proof that Walton or Taney knew for certain that "Ruth Aisquith" actually was Maureen Tigue. He intended to interview both men again—to press and discomfort them this time and to see what that produced. He thought that his doing so might crack Walton, though he was less sure of Taney.

He was about to head first to Walton's tent when, about twenty meters away, one of George Taney's work lorries suddenly started and began to move through the otherwise silent camp up the rutted dirt lane, toward the main road that passed through Winstead. Lamb had just enough time to glimpse Taney at the wheel. As the truck fell into the road's well-worn ruts, it sped up and began to bounce up the rough trail at a rate of speed that obviously was too fast for comfort. Harding, Vera, and Rivers also had noticed the sound of the truck starting in the post-work stillness and had turned toward it.

"It's Taney," Lamb said. "He's running."

Lamb turned to Harding. "Pin down Walton, please, sir," he said. "We can't let him go anywhere for the moment."

Harding nodded and, in the next instant, turned to Rivers and said, "Take my car and get after him; it's much faster than Lamb's old thing." The super gestured to a pair of uniformed constables to get a move on and follow Rivers. "Take these two with you," he said to Rivers, who immediately made for Harding's big black Buick saloon, along with the two constables, whom Harding instructed to "look sharp," at his heels.

Lamb began to limp toward his Wolseley. Taney was just turning right onto the main road, heading away from Winstead. Vera stood by the car with a quizzical look on her face. Having seen Taney's truck pass on the road, she was, only now, gaining a notion of what was occurring.

Lamb knew that he could not work the clutch as he must to keep up with the speeding Taney and Rivers; his ankle still was too sore from his brief jaunt to Lower Promise. He opened the passenger door. "Hop in," he said to Vera, who slid behind the wheel. As Lamb eased into the Wolseley, Rivers and the constables sped past him in Harding's car. "Follow Harry," Lamb said.

Vera started the car, put it in gear, and stomped on the accelerator; the aging Wolseley lurched and she and Lamb were off, bumping and rocking along the dirt access road. She followed Harding's car onto the main road leading out of Winstead. Once on the macadam surface, Rivers sped up in pursuit of Taney. Vera seemed to hesitate for only a second—she had no experience driving a car at breakneck speed down a narrow, country road—then stepped on the accelerator. The Wolseley lurched like a horse that had just had its haunches smacked. Lamb felt his stomach turn a notch; instinctively, he grabbed the dash to steady himself.

Vera shifted into a higher gear and they soon were on Rivers's tail. Although Taney had a head start, the lorry he was driving was slower and heavier than the police cars, and he seemed to struggle to pitch the graceless vehicle through the narrow curves at high speed. On three occasions, its wheels lifted slightly from the ground as Taney attempted to swing it through a tight curve. Rivers followed closely, the saloon's bells ringing furiously. He closed in and nearly rammed the lorry several times. Vera fell in behind this drama at what seemed to Lamb as too close a distance. But Vera was doing what he'd asked her to do.

As they reached a portion of the road in which it straightened and was bounded on either side by meadow, Rivers gassed the saloon and pulled into the oncoming lane, next to the lorry. He blared his horn, then threw the nose of Harding's car toward the driver's side, forcing it suddenly to the left and nearly off the road. "Bloody Christ, Harry," Lamb said under his breath.

Lamb expected Taney to take a retaliatory swipe at Rivers, but Rivers was too quick. Before Taney could get himself straightened again, Rivers nosed the saloon toward the lorry a second time—like a small, quick animal attacking a larger, slower one. This time Taney could not keep his left tires from running off the road and onto the grassy shoulder. He tried to swing the lorry back onto the road, but Rivers was on him a third time and the lorry surged to the left, off the road. Its left tires slid into a drainage ditch, where it came to an abrupt halt, half in and half out of the ditch and listing sickly to port.

Rivers pulled Harding's car to the side of the road about fifteen meters beyond Taney's mired truck; Vera pulled the Wolseley to a stop in front of Rivers. Lamb opened the glove box of the Wolseley and removed from it a Webley Mark VI pistol along with a box of .455-caliber cartridges. Lamb had worn—and used—the pistol during his time on the Somme; he kept it in the glove box for what he termed "emergencies." Although he had faced several situations in which he had pulled the gun from the glove box in the line of duty as a policeman, circumstances never had forced him to fire it. He slid the gun into the pocket of his jacket.

Rivers and the constables had exited the saloon and were crouched and moving toward the truck when a pistol shot rang out; the bullet struck the passenger side of Harding's car. Rivers and the constables dropped to shelter on the ground.

Lamb pushed Vera down behind the front seat. "Stay down and don't move," he instructed her.

"What was that?" Vera said, alarmed.

"Taney has a gun."

Lamb crawled over Vera and opened the driver's side door.

"Where are you going?" Vera said.

"Stay here," Lamb answered. "And don't raise your head over this seat."

A few meters up the road, Rivers and the constables sheltered in the lee of Harding's sedan. Once free of the Wolseley, Lamb moved forward to join them. Crouched and huddled near Harry Rivers, the both of them under enemy fire, Lamb could not fend off memories of the time the two of them had spent in the trenches of northern France nearly twenty-five years earlier.

"Is everybody all right?" Lamb asked.

The constables nodded and Rivers said, "Yes."

"Where is he?"

"As far as I can tell he's still on the passenger side of the truck—though I haven't seen a bloody damned thing since he took a shot at us," Rivers said. He looked at Lamb and smiled, slightly, as if the situation didn't concern him overly much. Lamb understood Rivers's forced nonchalance as a signal that he was ready for action. He thought that the sound of a bullet whizzing toward them must have recalled in Rivers, too, memories of the Somme.

Lamb sat on the road with his back against the front driver's side tire of Harding's car as he loaded the Webley's six-round cylinder with cartridges. He then moved past Rivers and the constables to the rear edge of the saloon. The front of Taney's mired lorry, its engine still running, was only ten meters away. He was formulating a plan of action that was based on the tactics he'd learned as a lieutenant of infantry—tactics he'd employed often in the trenches with Harry Rivers along as his second in command. Before he acted, though, he had to ascertain Taney's exact position on the other side of the truck. The possibility existed that Taney might have moved into the meadow and taken up a position there, preparing to run.

Rivers understood. "Don't get your bleeding head shot off," he said.

"I don't intend to," Lamb said.

Ignoring her father's instructions, Vera exited the Wolseley and crouched behind it, ten yards or so away from the others. She felt safer sheltering behind the bulk of the car; more significantly, though, she was worried about her father.

Lamb pressed his right shoulder against the big Buick. "You're wasting your time, Taney," he yelled. "The longer you resist, the worse it will be for you." He hoped that Taney would give away his position.

"Sod you!" Taney yelled.

"All right, then," Lamb whispered to himself. He calculated that Taney was sheltering by the lorry's passenger-side door. He glanced back at Rivers, who nodded that he understood what Lamb was preparing to do.

"Throw down your weapon and give yourself up," Lamb yelled. "I know what you and Maureen Tigue were on about." This latter statement still was based mostly on a guess—though, Lamb thought, a good guess, one worth betting on.

"Go to hell."

Lamb wanted to take Taney alive. With Maureen Tigue dead, Taney and Lawrence Tigue were his only sources of information about the operation he now was certain that Maureen had been running out of the camp, and therefore they were the only links to the criminal operatives who likely were at its other end. Lamb wanted to identify those men and crush the operation. Also, Taney might know who killed Maureen Tigue and why. Indeed, perhaps Taney himself had killed her.

Lamb moved back to Rivers and the others. "He's against the lorry, by the door," Lamb said to Rivers. "If he doesn't move into the meadow, we've got him." He handed Rivers the pistol. "I'll go behind the lorry and flank him." He nodded toward the rear of Harding's saloon. "Position yourself there and be ready to move once I get his attention and turn him toward the rear of the truck."

Rivers looked at the pistol. He thought Lamb too old for the heroics he understood the chief inspector to be contemplating. "We could wait for help; I could get on the radio," Rivers said.

"He just put a bullet into Harding's car," Lamb reminded him. "I can't risk waiting."

"Why don't you take the gun and I'll flank him," Rivers said. He smiled, slightly. "I'm younger than you. You're too bloody old."

"Only by a couple of years," Lamb said. "Besides, you know the rules, Harry. Never ask someone to do what you aren't prepared to do. Remember?" He spoke before Rivers could object again. "If you have to shoot do your best to wound him, please. He's no use to us dead." He put his hand on Rivers's shoulder. "Now let's go before he figures out what the bloody hell we're up to and we lose our chance."

Lamb turned to the two uniformed constables. He realized that he didn't know either of their names. They seemed to him impossibly young, clearly replacements for the experienced men who had gone into the war. "You two go with DI Rivers and be ready to move when he does. Follow his orders exactly. If all goes well, the three of you will take Taney down."

"Right," one of the constables said. The other merely nodded.

"Now, take off your shoes," Lamb said.

"Beg pardon, sir?"

"Take off your shoes so he can't hear you moving."

The constables complied. Lamb and Rivers also removed their shoes. With that, the four of them moved in their stocking feet to the rear of Harding's saloon. Lamb decided to check a final time to ensure that Taney hadn't moved. "It's better that you give it up, Taney!" he yelled. "We have more men on the way. You can't hold out here like this for long."

They waited for Taney to reply, but he remained silent, which worried Lamb and Rivers.

"What do you think?" Rivers said.

"He's done talking, obviously."

"He might have moved." Rivers didn't like that they no longer knew Taney's location for certain.

"We'll know soon enough," Lamb said. Crouching, he moved quickly and quietly to the lorry and along its driver's side toward its rear; Rivers moved around the rear of the saloon, followed by the constables.

Now, Lamb and Rivers moved very quickly, as they had on the Somme. The two of them had specialized in nighttime surveillance missions across No Man's Land to positions close to the German trenches. Sometimes they merely lay in the cold mud and gained, from keen and silent observance, strategic information about the enemy's positions that was not obtainable in daylight. Other times their job had required them—and the men under their command—to slip into the German trenches and quietly kill whomever they encountered in the course of gaining the intelligence they sought.

On one of these missions, the man who had been Harry Rivers's best friend since boyhood—the man Rivers had gone to war with, Eric Parker—had been killed and for many years Rivers had held Lamb responsible for Parker's death. Lamb had been too careless in his deployment of Parker that night, Rivers had believed at the time. Rivers had nursed that grievance against Lamb even up until the previous summer, when he'd found himself transferred from Warwickshire to Hampshire to help fill the drain of men from the Hampshire force that partly had resulted from the fact that the Germans had so relentlessly been attacking southern England from the air that summer.

Since then, though, Rivers had begun to rethink his enmity toward Lamb—and the self-imposed damage to his own soul that had resulted from his long-nursed hostility—and begun to allow himself to respect Lamb as a police detective. He even had found himself softening toward Lamb as a man and a colleague, though a part of him continued to resist this easing of a trait that had for so long defined him. Now, Rivers found himself worried that Lamb's age and some silly secret notion that Lamb might hold of his own indestructibility might lead Lamb to do something stupid, giving Taney an opening to wound or kill Lamb. But Lamb already was on the move.

—ɷ—

Lamb moved along the side of Taney's truck. Surprise was crucial in the maneuver he was about to undertake—but so was knowledge of the enemy's position. His heart pounding, he willed himself to continue, like a man plunging into water he knows will be freezing. He moved quickly around the rear of the lorry and into the ditch in which it was mired. On this cue, Rivers yelled, "Taney!" Lamb was relieved to see Taney facing toward the front of the truck and crouched against the driver's side door as he rounded the lorry's rear corner. The maneuver had begun. Now everything moved with alarming speed, and from here out Lamb and Rivers acted entirely from instinct and their memories of how they had operated in the trenches.

"Taney!'" Lamb yelled. That was Rivers's signal to move. Lamb quickly jumped back into cover behind the truck. Confused and alarmed by the voices vying for his attention, Taney rapidly turned around to face Lamb, thrusting out his pistol and preparing to fire. In that instant, Rivers moved around the nose of the truck and stuck the barrel of Lamb's revolver against the back of Taney's head. "Move and I'll blow your bloody fucking brains out," he said. "Drop the gun."

Stunned, Taney did as Rivers commanded. "Take him," Rivers said to the constables. The pair moved around Rivers and subdued Taney, pushing him to the ground face first, as Rivers retrieved Taney's pistol—yet another .455-caliber Webley. One of the men pulled Taney's hands behind his back while the other put handcuffs on Taney's wrists.

"We've got him," Rivers yelled.

Lamb appeared from around the back of the truck. "Good," he said. He realized that he was breathing so heavily that he nearly was hyperventilating. He sat against the rear bumper of the lorry, removed his hat, and tried to catch his breath.

The constables pulled Taney to his feet. They and Rivers brought him around to Lamb, who stood and met Taney's angry gaze. Doing his best to pretend nonchalance—for his heart still was pounding—Lamb shook his head, as might a disappointed prefect who was facing a wayward student. "Consorting with the IRA, Mr. Taney," he said. "You'll hang for that, of course, unless you become a bit more cooperative." Again, Lamb was betting that his guess was correct.

Taney said nothing, though Lamb was certain he saw genuine fear flare in Taney's hard, intimidating eyes.

"Take him to the nick," Lamb said. "I'll see you back there as soon as I can."

The constables hustled Taney to the rear seat of Harding's car. Rivers held back for a hitch. He handed Lamb back his pistol and said, "Are you all right?"

"Of course not," Lamb said. "I haven't had to do something that bloody stupid in years." He straightened his back and took a deep breath. "I can't get my heart to stop pounding."

Rivers smiled. "Well, I suppose you did all right, all the same."

Lamb rubbed the back of his neck and tried to relax. "I'm alive, at any rate." He suddenly remembered Vera. He went around the truck to the Wolseley, where he found her waiting, worried and expectant.

She moved toward him. "Are you all right, Dad?"

"Yes." He laid the loaded pistol on the roof of the car and willed himself to be calm.

"What happened?"

"We arrested Taney."

"Yes, but how did you get the gun away from him?"

Lamb smiled, more to reassure Vera that he was unhurt than because he felt like smiling. "An old trick," he said. "One that Taney fortunately didn't know." He nodded at the Wolseley. He wanted to get back to the nick and to interrogate Taney immediately. They had no time to waste. He put his hand on Vera's shoulder.

"I'll tell you about it on the way back to Winchester," he said. He picked up the Webley, opened the chamber, and began to remove the bullets one by one. As he did, he noticed that his hand was shaking.

THIRTY-THREE

—⁓—

LAMB PUT ONE OF THE CONSTABLES TO WORK SEARCHING THE lorry and the stretch of road between the prison and the place where Rivers had run Taney off the road, while the other constable assisted Rivers in taking Taney to Winchester. Lamb guessed that Taney might have tried to dispose of evidence as he fled the camp. He told the constable to do the best he could in the fading light and that he should look especially for a bundle of documents. Once finished, the man was to hoof it back to the prison camp and report in from there.

Lamb and Vera drove to the camp to pick up Harding, and they returned to the nick, leaving Larkin and a half-dozen uniformed men to secure the camp and ensure that no one else attempted to flee. In order to keep Taney tied down for the moment, Lamb charged him with attempted murder for having taken a potshot at them from the ditch. Despite Taney's outward coolness, Lamb was sure that Taney was frightened. If Taney and Maureen and Lawrence Tigue had been conspiring with the IRA, then Taney could face hanging for treason. Lamb intended to use that as leverage in his interrogation.

On the way to the nick, Taney had demanded a solicitor, whose arrival Lamb had to await before he could begin to interrogate Taney. While he waited, Lamb got himself and Vera yet another pair of cheese-and-pickle sandwiches and cups of weak tea from the pub across the street. Lamb ate his meager meal at his desk as he discussed with Harding his strategy for breaking Taney. Lamb said that he intended to proceed as if they possessed evidence that Taney and Maureen and Lawrence Tigue had treated with Irish Republicans—and that he already had planted this seed in Taney's mind when he arrested him.

Harding reported that he had interrogated Walton and that the captain had been cooperative and claimed to have no knowledge of any counterfeiting scheme that might have been ongoing under his nose. Walton had consented to a quick search of his tent, in which Harding had found nothing. Walton had agreed to come in for questioning, and Harding had sent him ahead with a uniformed man. Indeed, Walton was downstairs under the watch of that same constable at that moment, waiting to speak to Lamb. But George Taney was Lamb's main concern for the moment.

While Lamb and Harding conversed, the constable Lamb had set to the search of Taney's lorry and the roadside arrived at the nick. The man indeed had found a bundle of papers in the weedy roadside grass less than a hundred meters from the entrance to the prison camp site. He laid the bundle on Lamb's desk. "Ration tickets for petrol, sir," he said. "There's two hundred of them in that packet alone—at least four hundred pounds' worth."

The chief inspector and the superintendent examined the forged coupons. The IRA could sell such documents on the black market for many times their normal value, thereby turning a huge profit on whatever they had invested in paying off Taney, Lawrence Tigue, and anyone else who was involved in the scheme, which likely included whoever in the prison system had assisted Maureen Tigue in gaining possession of Ruth Aisquith's identity. The Irish also might be using the tickets to suck up as much of the available petrol as they dared, thereby hobbling the British war effort.

Tigue's forgeries were quite good—very clean, crisp, and official looking. They didn't need to be perfect to be serviceable in the general economy; ration coupons for everything ranging from cheese and cigarettes to socks and sweets had become so common since the war began that people hardly noticed them. The only people who closely examined ration tickets were those whose job it was to spot forgeries.

Ten minutes later, Lamb seated himself at a table in the interrogation room across from Taney, who remained in handcuffs, and Taney's solicitor, who came from Southampton. The lawyer was a short, thick, balding, and middle-aged man arrayed in a funereal dark suit who did not bother to introduce himself when Lamb entered. His voice was deep and gravelly and possessed of a Cockney inflection that he managed to camouflage only partially—a vigorous voice, Lamb thought, that didn't match his unimposing physical presence.

"My client would feel less indisposed with the handcuffs off," the lawyer said.

Lamb motioned for Rivers, who had entered the room with him, to remove the cuffs.

Lamb dropped the stack of forged ration coupons onto the table with a thud. As he did so he once again saw Taney's eyes flare with surprise—and fear. Despite himself, Taney's solicitor also could not quite hide his surprise at the sudden appearance of the coupons.

Taney massaged his wrists. Lamb thought Taney was doing his best to seem unconcerned. He was a man who was used to being in control and, indeed, Lamb had spent some time wondering why a man such as Taney—or the man he thought Taney to be—had allowed himself to enter into such a risky situation as the one he'd seemed to have entered with Maureen and Lawrence Tigue. The promise of money almost certainly had been part of it; the IRA probably had paid very well. But there was something else, Lamb thought—something that had gone straight to one of Taney's weaknesses and convinced him to not merely let down his guard but also to cede control and take an enormous risk. He believed that Maureen Tigue had given Taney not only a cut of her operation's profits but something else besides. Ultimately, sexual seduction always amounted to a play for power, and Maureen Tigue had possessed assets—relative youth and beauty—that might have allowed her to gain control of Taney, despite Taney's bluff exterior.

Lamb wasted no time in pressing his advantages, repeating what he'd told Taney when he'd outwitted and arrested him on the road near the prison site. He pushed the packet of forged ration coupons toward Taney.

"You've allowed yourself to fall into a very deep and dark pit, Mr. Taney," he said. "Forgery and the IRA. Your only way to avoid the gallows is to cooperate."

"I don't know what you're talking about," Taney said. He managed to say it with some conviction in his voice, though he did not look Lamb in the eye as he spoke and indeed had failed to meet Lamb's eyes even once since Lamb had entered the room.

"My men found these on the side of the road near where you crashed your lorry as you were trying to escape the farm earlier this evening. I'm certain we'll find your fingerprints on them."

Lamb looked directly at Taney—stared through him until Taney finally, reluctantly, met his gaze. "The longer you stall the more tightly the noose tightens around your neck," Lamb said icily. "I know about Maureen Tigue's background, including her connections to the Irish. You've been incredibly stupid, but my guess is that you found her to be worth the risk. The money was only a kind of icing on the real treat. But she played you, of course—used you. And now she's dead and none of this can hurt her, while you and Lawrence Tigue are left to swing. And you know as well as I that, even if by some miracle you managed to walk out of this nick tonight a free man, the Irish wouldn't waste a minute in hunting you down. You know far too much. So you can help me or you literally can go to hell, Mr. Taney. The choice is up to you."

Tears began to well in Taney's eyes. "I've a wife and two bloody children," he said. He was cracking.

"You should have thought of them while you were at it with Maureen Tigue," Lamb said bluntly. He leaned across the table a bit, closer to Taney. "I believe her death surprised you—shocked you, even. But once it occurred you knew that the operation had to end. You had thought you were in clover—the money *and* Maureen Tigue. Then the whole thing crashed in, with the Irish breathing down your neck. I think it was only then that you realized how bloody stupid you'd been, how thoroughly she'd seduced you. You were the big man at the prison camp; everybody said so, even Walton. But in fact you were on your knees to *her*, and all for the most common of reasons. Was your plan to run away with her—to leave your blessed wife and children to fend for themselves? Is that what she promised you? That you could have her all to yourself?"

Taney banged his fist on the table. "No! It wasn't like that!"

Lamb trained his eyes on Taney like a spotlight on a man cowering in a dark corner. "How was it then?" he asked.

Taney's lawyer leaned in close to Taney and whispered something that Lamb could not hear. But Taney literally pushed the man away and said, "No," and Lamb understood from the look of defeat that crossed Taney's face that he now must be patient and allow Taney to talk.

———

The time was ten minutes after eleven P.M., and under the cover of the late hour and the darkness, several people in Winstead had begun to stir.

Gerald Wimberly stood in the living room of the vicarage, preparing to walk down the path to Doris White's cottage and kill her. He expected to dispatch her quickly.

Wilhemina stood near him, her arms crossed. As Gerald prepared to leave, he said to her, "They won't be able to do anything to us, so long as we vouch for each other. You must remember that."

He was just turning for the front door when it opened, abruptly, and Doris stepped into the foyer. In her pudgy hands, she held aloft Gerald's Webley Mark VI pistol, which she pointed at his chest. He and Wilhemina both immediately noticed the eccentric nick in the gun's barrel.

"My God," Wilhemina said.

Doris wore her best green dress and had made up her face.

"But you said you got rid of the pistol," Wilhemina said to Gerald, her voice frantic.

"I did," Gerald said evenly. He'd fixed his eyes on Doris. Her sudden appearance and the sight of her holding the pistol he thought he'd buried forever stunned and enraged him. But he recovered quickly from his shock and fury—forced himself to put aside those emotions for the moment so that he could focus on what he might do to extract himself from the situation while doing as little damage to himself as possible. His first job would be to disarm Doris. Then he could act in the way that best suited him. He'd always found it easy to seduce and control Doris. He told himself that he must leave himself open to whatever opportunity presented itself and then move without hesitation.

Doris smiled. "You don't look surprised to see me, Gerald," she said.

"I'm not in the least surprised. I see what you are doing." He flipped his head in Wilhemina's direction. "You want to kill her so that she can't bother us any longer. But as I told you, killing her would be too messy. Lamb would be sure to come after us if we left a body behind. Better to do things the way we've planned and make a clean getaway."

"Shut up, Gerald," Doris said, stunning him anew. She raised the barrel of the pistol so that it was aimed at his face. "You do so love the sound of your own voice."

"How could you have been so stupid, Gerald!" Wilhemina shouted.

"Shut up, damn you!" Gerald snapped at Wilhemina—though he did not take his eyes from Doris. He'd quickly formulated a plan. First, he would attempt to convince Doris to give him the gun. If that failed, he would encourage Doris to shoot Wilhemina, then, in the confusion of the moment, wrest the gun from Doris and shoot her. He would tell the police—truthfully—that Doris had broken into their home and shot Wilhemina. Doris had done so, he would say, because she was jealous of Wilhemina, which also was true. He would admit to Lamb that he and Doris had had an affair, but that it had ended three years ago—another truth. He would say that, after Doris had shot Wilhemina, he had been forced to shoot Doris in self-defense. No one would be left to dispute that story. It was not the escape he had planned, but it would have to do.

"Give me the gun, my love," he said. "Then we can get away."

Doris smiled again. "I'm in charge now, Gerald," she said, confidently meeting his gaze. "There's been a change of plan—and unless you want me to shoot you, you'll do as I ask."

A sick feeling—a feeling he despised—filled Gerald. He felt trapped and feeble, like an animal in a snare. And he was so much more than that—so much finer. His intellect was superior to those of Wilhemina and Doris. It struck him as impossible that either of them, but especially the fat little odious hedgehog, might have outwitted him. But she had done, and this realization only increased the rage he felt. He regretted not having killed Doris long ago. Even so, he managed to remain outwardly calm.

"Of course, my dear," he said to Doris. He gestured again toward Wilhemina. "You're right—go ahead and kill her. That way we can be rid of her. I should have seen that."

"You bastard!" Wilhemina screamed. She turned toward Doris, frantic. "He was on his way to kill *you*!" she shouted. "He's poisoned the wine!"

"Don't listen to her, my love," Gerald said quietly.

"He never intended to run away with you!" Wilhemina said. "His plan was to kill you and then type a note on your typewriter that would say you killed yourself because you were guilty of killing the Aisquith woman. He was going to write that you were jealous of her!"

Gerald moved toward Wilhemina, intending to silence her. He raised his hand to strike her.

"Stop, Gerald!" Doris said.

Gerald turned back to Doris. "Kill her," he hissed. "It's the only way."

Wilhemina wailed, then began to cry and quiver uncontrollably.

"Shoot her!" Gerald urged. "Then we can go."

"I told you to shut up, Gerald," Doris said calmly. "Sit on the sofa."

Doris's command hit Gerald like a slap on the face. Even so, he complied. Doris moved a step closer to Wilhemina. Wilhemina's rising sense of terror had begun to twist and disfigure the features of her reddened, tear-stained face. "Please!" she said to Doris.

Doris leveled the pistol at Wilhemina's chest. "Please," Wilhemina repeated. "I'll do anything you ask!"

"Did Gerald seduce her?"

Wilhemina shook her head. "No."

"Then, why?"

Wilhemina looked at Gerald. She hated him with every ounce of her being now—hated what he'd done to their marriage and to her. "Because I wanted to create a mess for him," she said. "Gerald bloody Wimberly, vicar of Saint Michael's. I wanted to create a mess that he couldn't explain away." Staring at Gerald, she raised her chin slightly in defiance. "And I did."

"Stupid cow," Gerald said.

Doris turned the pistol on Gerald again. "I told you to be quiet, Gerald," she said. She had been worried that Gerald had seduced the woman who came to the cemetery in the mornings. Doris had seen the woman numerous times from within the church as she cleaned the chapel. She had not, at first, seen the woman on the morning Wilhemina had shot her, but she had heard the shot from the chapel and gone to the cemetery before Gerald had arrived and found Wilhemina standing over the body.

Now, Doris gazed upon a terrified Wilhemina and found that she enjoyed the idea that Wilhemina was frightened of her. Queerly, too, though—for she wouldn't have thought feeling such an emotion toward her hated rival possible—she pitied Wilhemina. She even found that she admired the way in which Wilhemina had stood up to Gerald—that Wilhemina had "created a mess" for him, as she put it.

Doris turned back to Gerald and aimed the gun at him. "Find some rope," she commanded.

—m—

When Taney finished talking, he slumped in his chair as if he'd just been shot. His confession had exhausted him.

Much of what Taney had said fit with what Lamb had deduced from the other evidence he'd gathered. Lawrence Tigue produced the forged gas ration coupons on his printing press and, in the night, left them buried beneath the blackberry bush in the rear corner of Saint Michael's Cemetery, near the grave of Mary Forrest. Under the guise of visiting that grave, which she had said was her grandmother's, Maureen Tigue came to the cemetery very early in the morning, when no one was about, took the coupons, and left cash for Lawrence to later retrieve. The drivers of Taney's trucks took the coupons to Southampton, where they were handed over to an IRA operative. All were well paid for their efforts. Taney told Lamb that Walton was weak and allowed him to take control of the camp but that the captain was not in on the scheme and had no knowledge of it.

Despite this information, Taney's narrative brought Lamb no closer to understanding who had killed Maureen Tigue and why. Taney had suggested that the killer might have been Lawrence Tigue. He told Lamb that Maureen had spent two weeks at the Tigue farm in Winstead during the summer of 1921—two years after the disappearance of the O'Hares—when she and Lawrence were eighteen and Algernon fourteen. That summer, Lawrence had made a romantic advance toward Maureen, Taney claimed, but Maureen not only had rejected Lawrence but humiliated him by beginning a sexual relationship with Algernon that the two cruelly flaunted in Lawrence's face. "That's why he killed her, I think," Taney told Lamb. "I think he had hated her from that summer on."

Lamb asked Taney if Maureen Tigue had said anything to him about the fate of Tim Gordon or the O'Hare twins. Taney insisted that she hadn't—that he'd never heard of Gordon, knew next to nothing about the O'Hare case, and never had met Algernon Tigue. He had been as surprised as anyone by the discovery of the bodies in the foundation of the farmhouse, he said.

Taney also said that Lawrence Tigue had requested of Maureen that, once the counterfeit ration ticket operation was finished, the IRA would spirit him out of the country, to the Republic, where Lawrence hoped to dissolve into the Irish landscape and begin a new life, and that the Irish had agreed to this request. "But Maureen's killing ended that deal, as it ended the operation," Taney said.

"You and Lawrence Tigue met in the lay-by by the O'Hare house last night," Lamb said. "It was then that you told Lawrence that the counterfeit deal was finished and that his escape plan was off—and that was a message he didn't fancy."

"Yes," Taney said. "He threw a tantrum over it. Maureen always did say he was weak."

A pair of constables led Taney away in handcuffs to a holding cell in the basement of the nick. Lamb was inclined to believe Taney that Walton had no direct involvement in the counterfeiting scheme—though Lamb also believed that Walton must have noticed irregularities in the camp that he conveniently ignored and therefore had been seriously derelict in his duty. But his showdown with Taney—on the road and in the interrogation room—had left him feeling spent, and he felt in no rush to get to Walton. The captain could wait until the following morning.

He had begun to put together in his mind what he believed were reasonable connections between the events he possessed knowledge of—connections that, if correct, would yield a narrative of the crimes that had occurred in Winstead during the past few days and, perhaps, two decades earlier.

And yet his day was not quite yet done. While he was interviewing George Taney, the constable he'd dispatched to the magistrate returned with a signed warrant to search Lawrence Tigue's cottage.

THIRTY-FOUR

―⁂―

LAMB, RIVERS, AND VERA HEADED TO WINSTEAD IN LAMB'S CAR.
Although they were exhausted, Lamb had decided that he could not
leave such an important job to the following morning. A car containing four uniformed men followed them to the village.

Night had fallen by the time they arrived at the school, where
they fetched Sergeant Cashen from the incident room, then walked
up the High Street to Lawrence Tigue's cottage, where they found
Wallace sequestered across the street and sucking on a cigarette. Lamb
saw Wallace catch Vera's eye for an instant and nearly smile before he
realized that Lamb was looking directly at him.

"I take it that Tigue hasn't returned," Lamb said to Wallace.

"No, sir. No sign of him."

Lamb nodded toward the cottage. "All right, then."

He led the small troop across the High Street to Tigue's residence, explaining that, once inside, they should keep an eye out for official-looking documents, such as identification or ration cards, which might be collected in bundles.

When they arrived at the front door, Rivers knocked upon it and yelled, "Police, Mr. Tigue. Open up. We've a warrant to search your premises." He waited twenty seconds; when no one answered the door, he turned to Cashen and said, "Open it, please, Sergeant."

Cashen, a stout-chested, squared-off man of slightly less than medium height, stepped back from the door to get a run at it. He threw his bulk against the door, though it didn't budge at first. He tried again and this time the door shuddered and emitted an audible crack.

"Once more should do it," Rivers said.

Cashen, red-faced, gave the door a savage kick, which finished the job. Just inside the sitting room, to the right of the foyer, lay Algernon Tigue with a neat bullet hole in the middle of his forehead.

—⁂—

Lamb squatted by Algernon's head and stared for a second into the man's dark, dead eyes. Blood had pooled on the rug by Algernon's head and his mouth lay open, as if in astonishment. A white envelope containing what appeared to be a letter was pinned to the front of Algernon's jacket. Lamb picked up the envelope and saw that it was addressed to him.

He sat in the same chair in which he'd sat when he'd interviewed Lawrence two days earlier and opened the envelope. It contained a handwritten letter on high-quality paper. Lamb read it through. The thing *was* a confession of sorts, but also a rambling and some-what disjointed note of self-justification that laid out and explained in detail the reasons for all of the sins that Lawrence had committed in and around Winstead during his lifetime—sins he pinned on the influence, depredations, and humiliations wrought upon him by his younger brother, whom he admitted shooting to death. The thrust of the missive seemed to say that, had it not been for Algernon Tigue, Lawrence would have—could have—lived a normal and perhaps even an exemplary life. At the same time, the note cast Lawrence himself in a positive, nearly heroic, light, as a man who, despite enduring repeated humiliations at the hands of his brother and others, including his cousin, Maureen Tigue, and his wife, Alba, had nonetheless undertaken a series of brave risks that were designed to redefine and salvage his good name, reputation, and character for posterity.

Lamb put the letter in the inner pocket of his jacket. He went again to Algernon's body, where he joined Wallace, Cashen, and Rivers, who was searching Algernon's pockets.

"A confession, then?" Rivers said, guessing at the note's contents.

"Of sorts," Lamb said. He nodded at Algernon's stiff body. "*This* definitely is his work."

Given what Miss Wheatley had told him earlier and what he'd just now read in Lawrence's note, it seemed clear that Algernon must have come to Lawrence's cottage late on the previous night, some time after Miss Wheatley had seen him ghosting about the O'Hare property and the site of Albert Clemmons's killing. Lamb guessed that the two brothers had then discussed—and probably argued about—how best to address the obvious problem that confronted them. With the bodies turning up in the foundation of the house in which they had grown up as boys and the police on their trail, a perverted bond between the brothers—a secret they had kept and shared—had come undone. Lawrence, having killed his brother, had run, probably in Algernon's car. Lamb worried that Lawrence might be suicidal.

"The entry wound looks too small to have been made with .455-caliber," Rivers said. "Not the same gun that killed Aisquith."

"Yes," Lamb agreed.

Lamb heard Vera's voice calling him from the foyer—a sound that initially alarmed him given the urgency he heard in her voice.

"Dad," she said, stepping into the room. She hesitated for only an instant when she saw Algernon Tigue's body lying in the middle of the floor.

"It's Lilly," she said. "She's outside telling a fantastic story. She claims Lawrence Tigue is holding Miss Wheatley hostage in the O'Hare house."

Lilly was standing just outside the front door, waiting for them.

"Please," she said as soon as she saw Lamb. "He's got Miss Wheatley, and he's going to kill her."

Lamb went to Lilly and gently placed his hand on Lilly's right shoulder.

"It's all right," he assured her. "Calm down now and tell me what you know."

"He gave me this note and said that I must give it to you," Lilly said, handing Lamb a neatly folded piece of paper. The handwritten note read:

> *Lamb:*
> *We must speak or I shall kill Flora Wheatley. Come to the window and announce yourself. Once you get the signal from me you are to enter the room alone and unarmed. If you do as I say and I am satisfied at the end of our discussion, I will release Miss Wheatley unharmed. Otherwise, she will die.*
> *Lawrence Tigue.*

Lamb asked Lilly to tell him exactly what had occurred that night. Lilly then told a brief tale that indeed sounded fantastic.

She and Miss Wheatley had met that evening in Miss Wheatley's cottage with the intention of spying on Lawrence Tigue. "Miss Wheatley was desperate to know what he was up to," Lilly said. They were about to set out down the trail to keep watch on Tigue's house when Tigue himself burst into Miss Wheatley's cottage holding a pistol. He took them at gunpoint to the O'Hare house and into the room in which Claire O'Hare had hung herself. He'd already placed a chair and a kerosene lantern in the room. He commanded Miss Wheatley to sit on the floor in the middle of the room and then had bound her ankles and hands.

"Then he told me to go to the school and tell whatever policeman I met there that he wanted to speak with you, Mr. Lamb," Lilly said. "Then he gave me the note addressed to you. I was on my way to the school when I saw the police motorcars in the lane and Miss Lamb standing by the door. He says he'll kill Miss Wheatley if you don't come."

The telling of the tale had brought Lilly to the verge of tears.

"It's all right, Lilly," Lamb repeated. "You've done the right thing." Vera moved closer to Lilly and put her arm around the girl.

"Where is your mother?" Lamb asked.

"At work, in Southampton."

Lamb told Cashen to assign a constable to call Julia Martin's workplace and get word to Julia that she should come home as soon as possible to fetch Lilly and that Lilly was all right. Then the constable was to call Harding and inform the super of the situation.

He turned back to Lilly. "I want you to stay here with Vera until your mother comes from Southampton to fetch you," he said. "She'll be here soon."

Lamb had turned toward the door, preparing to confront what appeared to be a desperate man bent on mayhem when Vera suddenly said to him, "Please be careful, Dad."

Lamb turned back toward Vera. The worried look on his daughter's face made him realize that he'd forgotten something vital. He went to Vera, took her hand, and said, "I will." Then, in an act of unforgiveable nepotism, he kissed Vera on the forehead.

For the second time that day, Lamb retrieved his Webley from the glove box of his car, this time along with its shoulder holster, and loaded it. He put the three uniformed constables to guard Lawrence Tigue's house with orders to allow no one to enter. Then he, Rivers, Wallace, and Cashen headed up the trail to the O'Hare house.

THIRTY-FIVE

—⁂—

TWENTY METERS FROM THE O'HARE HOUSE, LAMB HALTED THE troop and moved into the verge to the right of the trail, where he and the others could see the dimly lit window of the room in which Claire O'Hare had been found hanged.

Lamb first turned to Cashen and instructed him to go to the end of the trail and search for Algernon Tigue's car, which Lamb suspected Lawrence had been driving and likely had parked nearby. Given what George Taney had confessed, Lamb believed that Lawrence Tigue had reached an impasse in carrying out the plan of escape he'd arranged as part of his payment from the Irish for producing the counterfeit ration coupons—the plan that Ruth Aisquith's murder had scuttled. He reasoned that a distraught Lawrence intended to use Miss Wheatley as a bargaining chip for something, perhaps to regain that escape plan.

If that was true, Lawrence would need Algernon's car. When Cashen was on his way, Lamb turned to Wallace and Rivers.

"I'm going to get closer and see if I can get a peek into that window," he said. "Then we can figure out how to handle this. I think he wants something and intends to bargain for it with Miss Wheatley."

"All right," Rivers said. "But watch yourself."

Rivers considered how Lamb already had played the hero once that day and thought that twice was likely pushing it. But he knew it was fruitless to protest.

"I've no desire to become a casualty," Lamb assured Rivers. He pulled the Webley from its holster and put the gun in the pocket of his jacket.

Carefully, Lamb moved to within an arm's length of the window and peeked inside. He saw Miss Wheatley sitting uncomfortably on the floor in the middle of the room, beneath the beam from which Claire O'Hare had hung herself. Tigue had gagged her mouth and, as Lilly had said, bound her ankles and wrists. A kerosene lantern sat by Miss Wheatley's feet, providing the only light in the room. Also on the floor, just in front of the lantern, stood the final figurine from the Britain's set of generals and field marshals: Arthur Wellesley, the first Duke of Wellington, the man who famously had defeated Napoleon at Waterloo.

Behind Miss Wheatley was the room's lone door, which opened onto the narrow hall. Lamb could not see Tigue from where he crouched but reasoned from what Lilly had told him that Tigue likely had positioned himself in a chair in the rear corner of the room.

He retreated to the place where Rivers and Wallace were waiting.

"He's bound and gagged Miss Wheatley in the middle of the room and set up the final figure from the Britain's set of generals on the floor next to her," Lamb told the pair. "It's Wellington."

"His Waterloo, then?" Wallace asked.

"Yes. But he doesn't intend to play the role of Napoleon. That was his brother's part. He's Wellington."

"He'll shoot you as soon as you go in there," Rivers insisted. "He's obviously mad."

Cashen returned to report that Tigue indeed had parked the car in the lay-by and only partly endeavored to conceal it.

"If we don't move, he'll kill Miss Wheatley," Lamb said. "He's come to the end of some sort of rope. He had planned to go away, to escape his life here, but Maureen Tigue's killing stymied that plan. Now he's killed his brother—defeated and outmaneuvered his Napoleon. He's desperate."

"And mad—as I said," Rivers repeated. "Let me go."

"He wants me," Lamb said. "He made that clear."

"But we need a plan," Rivers insisted. "You can't go in there unless we have a way to get you out, hostage or no."

Lamb looked at Wallace and Rivers and made a quick decision that was similar to the decisions he'd made in the trenches of northern France many times—similar indeed to the decision he had made on the night that Eric Parker had been killed, which originally had turned Harry Rivers against him. But given the way in which he and Rivers had acted in concert to bring down Taney, Lamb had seen evidence enough that he could trust Rivers and that, more importantly, Rivers again had come to trust him. For that reason, and because of Rivers's superior experience in matters of combat, Lamb wanted Rivers manning the last line of attack—or defense, if it came to a shoot-out. He was not certain that if the thing came down to Wallace versus Tigue, Wallace could act in the cold-blooded manner it would require to stop Tigue. Also, Rivers, like himself, was no longer a young man, and Lamb needed a strong, youthful man for the role he envisioned for Wallace. The plan of attack that Lamb had decided upon was, like the one he'd employed to capture George Taney, little different from the raids across No Man's Land and into the German trenches that he and Rivers had conducted on the Somme. The difference this time was that Wallace—along with himself—was to act as the bait that drew the enemy out.

Lamb did not relish having to put Wallace in such a dangerous situation; indeed, he had done his best to keep Wallace away from the war and combat. But in addition to being young and exceptionally strong,

Wallace was a trained policeman—and a good and brave one. Lamb was mindful of the fact that Wallace and Vera obviously had formed a mutual attraction and that, should Wallace end up hurt or killed in the operation, Vera might come to blame him for Wallace's death, as Rivers once had for Eric Parker's. But he could not allow such concerns to stand in the way of deploying his men in the best manner open to him. He was certain that Miss Wheatley's life depended upon himself and the others acting with intelligence and dispatch.

He sketched out his plan to the other two. He described for them the layout of the house's interior and the fact that it had but one way in or out—the back door. He assigned Rivers the job of stopping Tigue—killing him if all else had failed. Cashen was to second Rivers. However, before it came to that, Lamb would enter the house as Tigue had instructed and look for an opportunity in which Wallace could quickly enter the house and the two of them could overwhelm Tigue without any harm coming to Miss Wheatley. Wallace would arm himself with Lamb's pistol and would get as near to the house as he dared without alerting Tigue, moving only if and when Lamb gave the signal to do so.

The signal would be simple: Lamb simply would yell, "Go!" Because Lamb would be unarmed, Wallace's first job would be to ensure the neutralizing of Lawrence Tigue. Once that was accomplished, Rivers and Cashen would follow and see first to the safe removal of Miss Wheatley and only then to the assistance of Wallace and himself. Everything would depend on Wallace's initial rush. Simply put, he and Wallace would seek to outflank Tigue, just as he and Rivers had outflanked Taney. Once again, Lamb was to act as the lure, drawing Tigue's attention. In the end, though, if no opportunity arose in which Wallace could enter the house without harm coming to Miss Wheatley, then Wallace was to stand down and await developments with Rivers and Cashen. If Lamb went down, then Rivers was to take command and act as he saw best, keeping in mind that the ultimate goal was to save Miss Wheatley.

Lamb now turned to Wallace. "This job will be dangerous, David," he said. "When you move, you must not hesitate. Your first job is to protect Miss Wheatley's life, then your own, then mine—in that order and in that order only." Lamb fixed Wallace with his eyes. "Do you understand?"

"Yes, sir," Wallace said simply.

Lamb handed his Webley and holster to Wallace and said, "Put this on." He then turned to Cashen and Rivers, who had also armed himself with a Webley.

"I'm counting on you two as well, obviously," he said. "I want to take him alive if we can, but if he wreaks havoc you must stop him."

"Leave it to me," Rivers said. Cashen merely nodded.

Lamb nodded in return.

"Good luck," Rivers said and offered Lamb his hand—the first time he'd done so since the day of Eric Parker's death twenty-five years earlier.

"Thank you, Harry," Lamb said, taking Rivers's hand. Then he turned toward the O'Hare house and said, "Now, I've got to go."

THIRTY-SIX

—w—

LAMB MOVED TO A PLACE JUST BENEATH THE WINDOW OF THE room in which Claire O'Hare had died.

"Mr. Tigue, it's Lamb," he said. "I'm alone and unarmed. I'm going to enter through the rear door."

He still could not see Tigue and hoped that Tigue would answer and give away his position—the same maneuver he'd used in ascertaining Taney's position.

Tigue obliged. "No tricks, Lamb," he said. Tigue's voice came from the rear right corner of the room. "Any tricks and I shall kill Miss Wheatley."

Lamb turned from the house to face the verge and underbrush. He could not see Rivers but knew that he was there, watching and waiting. Lamb pointed toward the rear right corner of the house, signaling to Rivers that Tigue was sheltering there. Rivers and Cashen then began to move stealthily toward the rear yard.

Lamb found the rear porch draped in darkness; its aging boards creaked as he stepped onto it and approached the shadowy outline of the back door. He pushed the door, which opened with an ostentatious creak. The interior of the house smelled powerfully of mildew and other decay. As he stepped into the narrow mudroom, the hall, shrouded in gloom, stretched before him to the front door, littered here and there with dark, indistinct detritus. The door to the room where Claire O'Hare had been found dead was a few meters away, on his left.

"Mr. Tigue," he said. "I'm coming in." Tigue did not answer.

Lamb moved up the hall and stood in the open doorway. He now saw Lawrence Tigue sitting in a straight-backed wooden chair in the right rear corner of the room. The faint light from the kerosene lantern illuminated Tigue's essential shape but little else; his face lay obscured in darkness. Between Tigue and Lamb, Miss Wheatley sat in the middle of the room, her head drooping a bit. She emitted a low, muffled sound from beneath her gag. Then, from the corner in which Tigue sat, Lamb heard the unmistakable sound of a pistol being cocked.

"Put your hands up, come into the room, and stand in the corner opposite me," Tigue commanded. "If you force me to, I will kill you, Chief Inspector."

Lamb did as Tigue ordered. Tigue stood and approached Lamb, holding the pistol. Lamb now saw that Tigue's right eye was swollen and dark—the result of Taney having punched Tigue in the face as they had argued in the lay-by on the previous night. Wordlessly, Tigue patted Lamb down and satisfied himself that Lamb was unarmed.

"Keep your hands up," Tigue said. He returned to his seat in the corner. "Now, Chief Inspector, move to the window and turn to face the room."

Lamb did as Tigue instructed, so that he stood with his back against the window.

Tigue smiled, slightly. "Now, if your colleagues are entertaining any ideas of making a sudden appearance through the window they will have to clear you out of the way first, and I rather think that they'd prefer not to do that."

"Let Miss Wheatley go," Lamb said. "You have me now; you don't need her."

"But you and I both know that you wouldn't be standing here, unarmed, and risking your life, if it wasn't for the fact that I have Miss Wheatley." At this, Miss Wheatley squirmed and emitted another muffled sound—a clear sound of protest and indignation, Lamb thought.

"What do you want?" Lamb asked.

"I want a boat and safe passage to Ireland. Just that—quite simple, I think, for you to arrange."

"The Germans constantly watch the coast. Nothing goes to Ireland that's not in convoy. You'd be risking your life, even in a small boat."

"I'm willing to take that risk." Tigue nodded at Miss Wheatley. "I shall take her with me, of course. And you, as well. As insurance against your colleagues getting any ideas. But I give you my word that once I'm safely on Irish soil I shall release the both of you."

"It can't work. You know that."

"I know no such thing," Tigue said, the tone of his voice rising a bit. He waved the pistol at Miss Wheatley. "It *will* work, Chief Inspector, and *you* will make it work. Or *she* will die."

Lamb intended to keep Tigue talking, to stall and potentially lull him, and give Wallace a fighting chance at entering and besting Tigue. Lamb nodded at the Wellington figure on the floor, by Miss Wheatley's feet.

"You defeated your brother, as Wellington defeated Napoleon," he said. "I read the note you left pinned to his body. I also know what you and George Taney and Maureen Tigue were doing—the forged ration coupons. And I know what Maureen did to you—how she treated you and how that must have humiliated you." He hesitated, then added, "And I know that Algernon killed Tim Gordon."

Lamb counted on Lawrence being proud of his defeat of his brother and therefore willing, and perhaps even eager, to speak of it.

Tigue smiled—a strange, slight, distant smile. He glanced at the Wellington figure.

"The toy generals belonged to Tim," he said. "Algernon took them as a kind of memento of his first murder. He lured the boy to my aunt's farm and strangled him in the barn. Does that shock you, Lamb—that one as young as Algernon was then could have committed such a violent murder and for no other reason than he desired to? But that was Algernon. By the time he was twelve, he'd become extremely precocious—charming, smart, and very cunning, very aware of his own power. The young maths wiz. My mother loved him, you see. And he seduced and charmed her, just as he seduced so many others, including his victims. The only person whom he failed to charm—and therefore control—was myself."

Tigue raised his chin, as if in a gesture of pride, then smiled again. "Algernon was very much like his father, you see," he said. "The apple, as they say, never falls far from the tree."

"His father was Sean O'Hare."

"Yes. I knew, of course, that it was only a matter of time before you began to peel back the layers of the past."

"Sean also was Maureen's father."

"Very good, Lamb. You have done your homework."

"Maureen was cruel, cold, calculating—just like her father and Algernon."

"Yes."

"But you joined her in the counterfeiting scheme."

"I did so only for my own benefit. She was useful to me—her offer was useful. It suited my plans perfectly."

"And Ned Horton?"

"He knew the truth of what Algernon had done almost from the beginning—from the time that he first stuck his nose into the matter of the cats. Algernon began with cats, you see—practiced on them— then moved to children. Horton fancied my mother, and she allowed him to believe that she fancied him in return, even to the point of yielding to him for a time. But she did this only so that Horton would protect Algernon from the consequences of his actions. And Horton did an excellent job as a protector."

Tigue halted his narrative, sniffled, and cleared his throat. Lamb sensed anger welling beneath Tigue's controlled exterior.

"I buried them," he continued. "All three of them. Not that *I* cared whether my brother was caught and punished for his sins. A part of me wanted him to be caught and punished. Then we— Mother and I—could be rid of him. But Mother loved Algernon in the same way as she had loved his father. A kind of blind love. And so I buried them, not for Algernon's sake, but for Mother's. As you might also have learned by now, Lamb, Sean O'Hare was not my father. To my mother, I was merely a mistake she had made with another, different man—a man who was not Sean O'Hare, the man she never stopped adoring."

Tigue became quiet, and for a full minute made no sound. He seemed suddenly to have drifted very deeply into reminiscence, Lamb thought, almost detaching himself from his surroundings. Lamb prepared to give Wallace the signal to enter.

But Tigue suddenly spoke again. "You see, Chief Inspector, I outwitted my brother in the end. He believed me to be incapable of any sort of intrigue, an opinion he held of me to the end. Even years later, when we were adults and I gave him the Napoleon, he didn't catch on to what I was up to, despite his so-called brilliance."

Tigue looked at Lamb wistfully—almost as if he were seeking understanding, Lamb thought.

"Do you know that I drove to Portsmouth today in Algernon's car and spent many hours toting around a bag full of cash along the docks hoping to find some shady character to take me to Ireland? I got nowhere, of course. Shady characters don't make themselves known, do they? You can't simply approach them as if they are shopkeepers with legitimate wares to sell." Tigue smiled weakly. "Do you find that rather pathetic, Lamb? I do."

Tigue sat back in the chair and closed his eyes for an instant, as if hoping to erase the memory of his failure. Lamb was on the knife-edge of signaling Wallace when the sound of a creaking board came from the porch. Lamb, Tigue, and Miss Wheatley all turned toward the sudden sound and in that instant Lamb's heart sunk. He immediately understood that Wallace had given away his approach.

Tigue whirled on Lamb and pointed his pistol at Lamb's head.

"Call him in!" Tigue commanded.

When Lamb hesitated, Tigue rose and went to Miss Wheatley. He stuck the barrel of his pistol into her right ear. Miss Wheatley's eyes filled with terror and she began to emit muffled screams from beneath her gag. "Do it or I'll kill her," Tigue said evenly. "You must have figured out by now that I no longer care, Lamb."

"Wallace," Lamb shouted. "Come in slowly."

The back door creaked; a few seconds later, Wallace loomed in the narrow door of the room. Tigue stood by Miss Wheatley with the pistol still pointed at her head.

"Show your hands," Tigue said.

Wallace complied.

"Do exactly as I say or I'll blow the old woman's brains out."

Wallace had Lamb's loaded Webley lying in its shoulder holster beneath his jacket.

"Keep your hands up, walk to the corner opposite, and remove your jacket," Tigue commanded. Wallace did so, revealing the pistol.

"Pull the pistol very slowly from the holster, open the chamber and empty it of bullets."

Wallace did as Tigue ordered. The bullets slid from the chamber and bounced onto the floor like so many spilled marbles.

"Kick the bullets into the hall and toss the gun there, too."

Wallace hesitated.

"*Do* it, Sergeant," Tigue said. "No need to compound your mistake."

Wallace kicked the bullets toward the hall through the doorway, sending them spinning into the darkness, then tossed the pistol there, too.

"Now, move back into the corner with your hands up," Tigue said.

Wallace moved into the corner that was opposite to the one in which Tigue had set up his chair, to which Tigue now returned.

Tigue turned his attention again to Lamb. "I want a car to Portsmouth and a boat awaiting us there—one that is large enough to get the three of us safely across to Ireland," he said. His voice had lost its dreamy, self-pitying tone and had taken on that of a general barking orders. "You have a half-hour to leave this room, arrange it, and return unarmed. If we're not on the road to Portsmouth in thirty minutes I shall kill Miss Wheatley and the sergeant. The same is true, obviously, if you make any effort to storm the house. I shall kill them before you can get to me." He smiled at Lamb. "And then you'll have a few more bodies to contend with, Chief Inspector."

He pointed the pistol directly at Lamb.

"Now," he said. "I've finished talking."

THIRTY-SEVEN

—∞—

AS THE MINUTES PASSED, VERA'S ANXIETY ABOUT HER FATHER'S safety—and that of Wallace—grew. She could not help but recall the risk her father had taken a few hours earlier in arresting George Taney. She had not realized in how much danger he had placed himself until the incident was finished. In all the years that her father had been a policeman, Vera had never seen him handle a pistol or heard of an incident in which he'd used one. Until today, she merely had assumed—if she thought of the matter at all—that he went about his job unarmed and, in turn, was not normally menaced by armed men.

And David? Did she love him? She was not yet certain. But she believed that she could love him, given time.

The constable whom Lamb had instructed to call Julia Martin and then to call Harding had done so and then left the incident room to position himself by the path that led from Lawrence Tigue's cottage to the O'Hare place, leaving Vera and Lilly in the incident room to await Julia's arrival. But a half-hour had passed since her father and the others had set off in the direction of the O'Hare house, and Vera decided that she could no longer merely sit and wait. She did not know what she could or would do to assist her father and David, but she resolved that she must act regardless.

"You'll be fine here," she told Lilly as she stood to leave. "I'm going to the house."

"I want to go with you. I'm worried that he'll hurt Miss Wheatley."

"You can't go. It's too dangerous."

"But I'm the one who reported them."

"Don't be silly," Vera said. "You must stay here."

Vera turned to go.

"But it's not fair!" Lilly said. "I'm always the one who's left alone—left *behind*."

Vera stopped. Lilly's words pierced her because they were true. Lilly *had* been the one left alone and behind. First her father had gone to war, then Julia had gone to work in Southampton.

Lilly began to cry. Instinctively—for she hardly knew what she was doing at the moment—Vera opened her arms and Lilly flew into them. They embraced, and in that instant Vera understood that she could not leave Lilly in the incident room—that as soon as she left, Lilly would follow, silently and undercover. She could waste no more time arguing with Lilly.

Lilly roughly wiped the tears from her eyes. "I know the house better than anyone there," she said. "You need me."

"All right. But you must do as I say."

Their pact thus sealed, they made their way quickly toward the church, where Lilly said she could lead them to the main path through the wood and therefore avoid the constable who was guarding the path by Lawrence Tigue's cottage. They did just that, passing the place where Albert Clemmons had been killed, and soon were on the path heading from Miss Wheatley's place toward the O'Hare house, where they moved into the verge. From where Vera and Lilly positioned themselves, neither Rivers nor Cashen could see them, and so did not know that the pair had arrived.

The image that Vera saw in the dimly lit window of the O'Hare house shocked her. Her father stood with his back to the window, his hands in the air, his fedora-topped silhouette unmistakable. Still, he was alive. She saw no sign of David or Rivers or Cashen and could only guess at where they had gone, but figured that they must be somewhere near. She tried to think in the way she believed her father would in such a situation—strategically. She recalled how he had first ascertained Taney's position by the truck before moving to capture him. She turned to Lilly.

"Don't move," she whispered. "I'll be right back."

"Where are you going?"

"I'm going to see if I can find out what is happening in that room."

She moved through the verge to within five meters of the window. She could hear the murmur of a voice coming from within the room. The voice was that of a man's, though she did not recognize its tone or cadence, and so she guessed that it must be Lawrence Tigue's.

She strained to see if David also was in the room, but the dark outline of her father's figure blocked her view. She crawled to within a meter of the window and knelt there. This allowed her to see just past her father's left side; and there she saw David standing in the corner with his hands up. She saw a portion of a woman's dress and her knees near the floor. *Miss Wheatley.*

She heard the alien voice say, "Do exactly as I say or I'll blow the old woman's brains out." She watched as David emptied the chamber of his pistol and tossed the gun away—and in that instant a plan made itself clear to her. She moved back to Lilly.

"Do you know where Miss Wheatley keeps her gun? The big one?" she asked Lilly.

"Yes."

"Show me."

Lilly led the way back along the trail to Miss Wheatley's cottage. The front door was open. The two-barreled .20-gauge shotgun lay on the kitchen table near the box of cartridges. Miss Wheatley must have taken the gun down from its rack on the wall by the door earlier in the day to shoot starlings and not returned it to its perch by the time Lawrence Tigue had burst into the cottage and taken her hostage. Vera picked up the bulky gun. She had never fired, or even handled, any sort of gun, and Miss Wheatley's shotgun felt alien and heavy in her hands. Her first instinct was to lay it back on the table and walk away from it. But she understood with an almost perfect clarity that she could not do that. She must overcome her trepidation—her fear—for the sake of her father and David.

"Do you know how it works?" she asked Lilly.

Lilly also knew very little about guns. But since she and Miss Wheatley had formed their partnership, she had seen Miss Wheatley load the gun. "You have to open the barrels to load it."

Vera carefully laid the gun again on the table. "Show me," she said.

Lilly pointed out the lever at the bottom of the barrels, which allowed them to open. "You push that to open it," she said. She lifted the gun from the table and pushed the lever. The barrels cracked open.

"You slide the cartridges into the barrels and then close the gun," Lilly said. "Then it's ready to fire. There's a little lever on the side. If that's on, then you can't fire the gun. It's called the safety. You have to push it so that it's off."

Lilly picked up one of the cartridges and showed Vera how to slide it into the barrel. "You put them in with the metal end up," she said. Vera loaded two cartridges, then snapped the barrel shut and put on the safety.

"Let's go," Vera said.

"What are you going to do?"

"I don't know yet."

They made their way back to the O'Hare house. Her father continued to stand at the window with his hands raised. "Is there another way into the house other than the back door?" Vera asked Lilly. "Other windows?"

"Most of them are blocked by things. And they have little shards of broken glass sticking from them. Mr. Tigue would hear you."

"Is there nothing else, no other opening?"

Lilly thought on the matter for a couple of seconds. "There's the coal chute. It's in the back wall, where the kitchen was. The chute itself has been ripped out but there's a hole there, an opening. It's narrow, though."

"Could I fit through it?"

"You might just."

"Where is it?"

"At the rear of the house—to the right of the back door. I can show you."

"No—I can find it." She looked directly at Lilly. "I couldn't forgive myself if I let anything happen to you."

"I can take care of myself," Lilly protested. "I don't need your pity."

"You're right," Vera said. "I'm sorry. But there's no need in two of us going. The more people creeping about the back of the house, the more likely Tigue will hear us."

"All right," Lilly said. "But please be careful."

"I will," Vera promised. Her heart had begun to pound.

Carrying the gun across her chest, like a soldier on the march, Vera moved through the verge to a spot by the tire swing. The gun was heavy. She thought of Rivers and the rest of them and hoped they were near and organizing a plan of rescue. And indeed at that moment Superintendent Harding was arriving at the incident room in the village with an additional six men and Cyril Larkin.

Twenty meters to Vera's left, dim light leaked from the window of the parlor blocked partially by the dark figure of her father with his hands up. She couldn't wait—mustn't. She moved into the rear yard and along the porch, keeping parallel to it, toward the other side of the house, where Lilly had said the coal chute was.

Rivers and Cashen, who were huddled behind what remained of a long-dead pear tree about twenty meters from the rear door, saw

Vera's dark figure move by the porch. They did not recognize her in the darkness.

"What in hell?" Cashen whispered hoarsely. "Who is that?"

Rivers stared intently into the gloom. "I don't know," he said, believing that the mysterious figure threatened to ruin the plan. He considered calling out to the figure to stop but knew that this would only alert Tigue. And so he watched and readied himself to move if necessary.

Vera reached the end of the house, just to the right of the back door, and there turned toward the opening in the wall that once had contained the coal chute. She crouched by the opening for a couple of seconds to catch her breath, clutching the cumbersome shotgun and trying her best to ward off a rising sense of fear. Her heart thumped so heavily and loudly that she worried that Tigue might hear it.

The opening was just at the level of Vera's chest and perhaps eighteen inches square. She reckoned that she could just squeeze through it, though she would have to ease the shotgun in separately. She slid the gun into the opening barrels first, playing its length through her hands until she felt the tips of the barrels touch the floor. She moved the gun as far to the right of the opening as she could and managed to lean it, stock up, against the interior wall.

To compress her body as much as possible, Vera exhaled and held her breath. Going into the opening would be like diving underwater, she thought, with the main difference being that once she reached bottom she could open her lungs again. She moved the upper half of her body into the opening, plunging herself into a darkness that was more dense than the one she had been maneuvering through. The smell of rot filled her nostrils. She moved into the opening up to her hips with relative ease, the sides of the opening scraping only a bit against the outside of her shoulders. She found the floor and placed her hands against it; the floor was so dirty that she felt as if she was placing her hands in a kind of loam. She began to move the rest of her body through the opening, inching forward across the floor with her hands. Her rump became stuck in the tight space, though it took her only a couple of seconds and a bit of extra effort to free it, after which she carefully eased the rest of her body through the hole.

A sense of relief swept over Vera once she was in the house—and yet, too, she felt exhausted. She turned herself to sit on the floor for a second and regain her bearings. She reached for the place on the wall where she had leaned the gun. She stood, picked up the gun, and turned toward the door of what had once been the kitchen, which gave onto the short, narrow, junk-strewn hall. Just across that hall was the room in which Lawrence Tigue was holding David, Miss Wheatley, and her father. She still did not know, exactly, what she intended to do and decided that the only thing for it was to do as the good guys invariably did to the bad in the movies. She would jump into the room and surprise Tigue—demand as loudly as she could for him to drop his gun and put up his hands. She was not sure what she would do, though, if Tigue refused that order—was not certain if she could bring herself to fire a gun at a living soul.

She took a step toward the door, forgetting to flick the safety lever to "off." As she did so, she heard Lawrence Tigue say, "I've finished talking."

THIRTY-EIGHT

—⚊—

I'VE FINISHED TALKING . . .

The words chilled Lamb. He prepared to strike at Tigue—desperately, blindly, if necessary. He glanced at Wallace, whose eyes were fixed on Tigue's dark figure. If the pair of them could strike together they might have an even chance of overpowering Tigue, though one of them might have to take a bullet in the effort.

"I know you didn't kill Maureen," Lamb said to Tigue, hoping to forestall Tigue into bringing down the curtain on the story of his victory over Algernon. "Taney did." Lamb was flailing; he did not know who killed Maureen Tigue. "You can help me bring Taney down. He and Maureen used you. I can protect you from the Irish. They'll be after you, given what you know."

"I no longer care about any of that," Tigue said. He looked at Lamb. He raised the pistol and pointed it toward Miss Wheatley. "You've just wasted a minute of your half-hour, Chief Inspector."

Lamb was readying himself to leap at Tigue, come what may, when Vera appeared in the door holding the shotgun.

"Stop!" she yelled. Her appearance startled Tigue, who stood and pointed the pistol at Vera. In that instant Wallace threw himself with his full power and bulk at Tigue, propelling Tigue against the wall in the corner.

Tigue's pistol fired; Wallace yelled and recoiled. The pistol clattered to the floor and Tigue slumped to the ground, delirious from Wallace having smashed his head against the wall. Wallace tumbled backward and struck the kerosene lamp by Miss Wheatley's feet as he fell to the floor. The lamp broke and the floor surrounding it burst into flame as the burning wick dropped into a puddle of spilled kerosene.

Vera dropped the shotgun. "David!" she yelled.

"Rivers! Move!" Lamb yelled.

He turned toward Tigue, who lay crumpled and unconscious in the corner. Vera was kneeling by Wallace, cradling his head. Lamb went to them.

Wallace was conscious and his eyes were open, though filled with pain.

"Where are you hit?" Lamb asked.

"Left thigh." Wallace winced.

The fire from the broken lamp was burning the dry, rotted floor and spreading quickly; it licked close to Wallace's left leg and was moving toward Miss Wheatley. Lamb grabbed Vera's shoulder. "Drag him out of here as best you can," he said. "Get your hands into his armpits and pull him. He's going to cry out but you must keep going, despite that."

"All right," Vera said.

Lamb helped Wallace into a sitting position. Wallace winced again and emitted a yip of pain—"Ah! Bloody Christ!" Vera got her hands under his arms and, with some difficulty, began to drag him toward the door. Wallace squeezed his eyes closed against the pain and did not cry out.

Then Lamb heard Rivers's voice above him. "Lamb!" He looked up to see Rivers and Cashen crowding through the door. "Get her out of here and help Vera with Wallace," Lamb said, gesturing toward Miss Wheatley. He felt the heat of the fire growing just behind him, and the room was filling with smoke that stung his eyes.

Rivers dragged the bound Miss Wheatley toward the door, while Cashen helped Vera with Wallace.

Lamb turned back to Tigue. Through the thickening smoke, he saw that Tigue, though unsteady, was attempting to stand. He'd retrieved the fallen pistol and was moving its barrel toward his mouth.

Lamb leapt through the flames and caught Tigue's arm with his left hand, yanking the gun away. The pistol fired and, for a terrifying instant, Lamb expected to feel a sharp pain. But the bullet had missed him. An instant later Tigue pushed him away. Nearly losing his balance, Lamb grabbed for the wall and caught himself.

—⁓—

Vera and Cashen dragged Wallace into the rear yard. Wallace yelped again as they eased him onto the ground. Harding was there now, with the other constables and Larkin, who immediately went to Wallace to give him what medical attention he could. The others leapt onto the creaking back porch to help Rivers with Miss Wheatley.

All of this occurred in what to Vera seemed like a single enflamed, kaleidoscopic instant. She smelled the smoke coming from the window of the twins' room and realized that her father had yet to emerge from the fire.

She yelled, "Dad!" and plunged through the back door into the narrow, dark, smoke-filled hall. As she stepped into the room, she saw her father struggling with Tigue in the corner. The fire was beginning to lick up the rear wall. She heard the shot from Tigue's pistol and saw that her father continued to stand. As she began to move toward her father, her right foot struck something heavy that nearly tripped her.

Miss Wheatley's shotgun.

She picked it up and leveled it at Tigue. "Stop!" she yelled, but Tigue ignored her. She saw Tigue push her father away and point the pistol toward him. She had not been certain that she could use the gun if the moment required it. She had hoped only to frighten Tigue with the gun. But as she saw Tigue point the black pistol at her father, she forgot all of that and yanked on the double triggers.

But the triggers failed to give; the gun failed to fire.

The safety! She had forgotten to turn it. But there was no time to fumble with it. With all of the strength she could muster, she flung the shotgun at Tigue, as if throwing a spear. The gun struck Tigue in the left shoulder and staggered him. For a third time, Tigue's pistol discharged.

Lamb heard the bullet embed itself harmlessly into the floor. In the next breath he tackled Tigue, and the two of them went to the floor. Lamb felt the heat of the flame against the side of his face. Then Rivers suddenly was there. He brought his right boot down squarely onto Tigue's already damaged face, shattering Tigue's nose. Tigue screamed in pain. Rivers roughly yanked Tigue to his feet and locked his arm around Tigue's neck.

"Get the bloody hell out of here!" Rivers yelled to Lamb and Vera.

Lamb found the wall with his left hand and pulled himself to his feet. His head was spinning and he worried that the smoke was about to envelop him. He felt himself slipping. He turned toward the door and saw Vera making her way across the burning room toward him.

THIRTY-NINE

—⁊⁊—

LAMB AND VERA STUMBLED FROM THE HOUSE INTO THE REAR yard, their arms about each other. Lilly ran toward them.

"Miss Lamb!"

"I'm all right, Lilly," Vera said.

Harding ran to Lamb and helped Vera to hold him up. He ordered one of the constables to bring Lamb and Vera water, which they both drank greedily. Harding immediately began to try to convince Lamb to allow one of the men to drive him and Vera to the hospital, but Lamb waved the super off. "I'll be all right," he said. "It's Miss Wheatley and Wallace who need tending." Lamb looked at Vera and said, "Take her, too." But Vera stood her ground. "I'm all right," she said. Lamb hadn't the heart, or the energy, to argue the point.

Harding relented, but he ordered Lamb and Vera to immediately return home and rest. An hour later, the pair returned to Marjorie in the wee hours, filthy, exhausted and stinking of burned kerosene. Marjorie made a fuss over them—prepared them tea and buttered bread—after which they slept, spent physically and emotionally.

The O'Hare house had burned to its foundation by the time a pumper arrived from Southampton later that evening. Julia Martin arrived and took Lilly home. Miss Wheatley was rushed to the hospital in Winchester, where she came awake in bed at six the following morning, confused but safe. Wallace also went to the hospital, where doctors discovered that the bullet that had entered his right thigh had shattered the tibia, which meant that his leg would be in a cast for months.

Lawrence Tigue was to spend several days in the hospital, healing from the blow to the head he'd received when Wallace had dived into him and from the broken nose that Rivers had inflicted upon him to go with his swollen eye. He was charged with treason for his part in the counterfeiting scheme and with murder in the killing of his younger brother. An autopsy revealed that Algernon Tigue had been shot in the forehead at point-blank range with the same .22-caliber pistol with which Lawrence Tigue had shot Wallace and nearly shot Miss Wheatley and Lamb. Taney also was charged with treason.

On the afternoon following the events at the O'Hare house, Lamb woke after having indulged in a long, healing slumber and prepared to go into the nick alone. Vera also awakened and asked her father why he was readying to leave without her. Lamb insisted that she should spend the day resting and that, besides, his ankle had healed well enough for him to drive, which was not true. Vera knew this to be untrue and, in turn, insisted that her father allow her to drive him to the constabulary and to visit David in the hospital. Once again, Lamb acquiesced.

He realized how close he'd come to being shot and initially found himself unable to adequately express his gratitude toward Vera—she had risked her life for him. He had not expected that such a thing ever would have been necessary. In trying to keep her from the danger of the war and conscription, he had placed Vera into an entirely different kind of danger. And she had responded brilliantly. This insight had first come to him quickly, all at once, in the chaos of the moment of the fire itself, and, despite his realization of it, words had failed him. Now, as they settled in the front seat of the Wolseley to drive to the nick, Lamb thanked Vera for saving his life. A part of him was angry at her for having disobeyed his instructions and putting her life in danger, but he refrained for the moment from saying so.

In that moment, Vera also found herself unable to adequately express all that she wanted to say to her father about the events of the past few days—of her fears for his safety, which had driven her to actions that she now saw, in the light of the morning, to have been risky almost to the point of stupidity and, at the same time, the respect and awe she felt at her father's bravery and his willingness to put himself in mortal danger for the sake of another's life. And yet, she also took a quiet satisfaction in her own actions. Yes, she had acted stupidly. But what else might she have done? She was glad she had acted as she had.

As they drove to the nick, Lamb asked, "Do you want me to keep you on for a while longer?"

Vera wasn't certain of her answer. She realized that, despite her misgivings at her father's nepotism, she was not quite ready for this moment in her life—this experience—to end. For one, she didn't want to find herself immediately cut off from regular contact with David. She also intended to keep a discreet eye on her father for a few more days, to ensure that he was as healed as he claimed to be. And she herself needed looking after—to ensure that she, too, wasn't deluding herself about her own steadiness. She was certain that her father would be looking for any sign that she needed tending.

"Can we wait and see for a bit?" she said.

Lamb smiled. "Okay."

―⁓―

Even in the wake of the climactic events at the O'Hare house, threads remained for Lamb to unravel. His subsequent follow-up interrogation of Lawrence Tigue provided him with most of what he needed in order to divine the truth of what had occurred in Winstead, in the present and the past.

Lamb interviewed Tigue as Tigue recuperated in the hospital. Lamb found Tigue surprisingly eager to talk, and continued to believe that Tigue was motivated by a desire to achieve what he considered a kind of clearing of his name—a clearing of the accusation so often leveled at him by his brother and his cousin, Maureen, and eventually his wife, and perhaps even his mother while she was alive—that he was weak, hesitant, easily manipulated, and humiliated, a small person in spirit and vigor whose feelings therefore were hardly worth considering and whose actual intelligence and strength (at least as these qualities existed in Lawrence's own mind) never had been properly recognized and respected.

Lawrence described Algernon as a malignant soul who thrilled to the sensation of choking the life from someone as they stared at him, terrified—as one who enjoyed playing what he considered to be the role of God, deciding who would die and when. According to Lawrence, this seed had been planted in Algernon by his father, Sean O'Hare, a man whom Lawrence described as a "charming but dangerous rogue" who had seduced both his mother, Olivia, and her older sister, Martha, the consequence of which had been the births of Algernon to Olivia and Maureen to Martha. Algernon had been Olivia's second illegitimate son; several years earlier, Lawrence had been the result of a brief dalliance Olivia had conducted with a local boy who had later gone off to the war in France.

Although Sean O'Hare had left Four Corners and abandoned the young Tigue sisters and his children, Olivia Tigue never had stopped loving Sean and had maintained, even in the face of much contradictory evidence, that Sean one day would return to fetch her and Algernon. Lawrence refused to reveal his father's name to Lamb, though he allowed that the man had died in Arras during the war, and that Olivia had used this story to explain the absence of a husband when she'd moved to Winstead with two sons.

"From a very young age, I knew that my brother had a different father, whose name was Sean; my mother told me that much," Lawrence told Lamb. "But I knew nothing of Sean O'Hare the actual man until my mother uprooted and moved us to Winstead so that she could be near him again."

In December 1918, Olivia Tigue had received a letter from Sean O'Hare in which he claimed he'd never stopped loving her, apologized for his long absence, and asked that she join him in Winstead—a letter that, in Olivia's mind, confirmed her assertion that Sean would not forsake her forever. In this letter, Sean admitted that he had a wife and two young children in Winstead, but promised Olivia that he would leave them soon enough and that the two of them could be together. He'd married and had children only to lessen his chances of being called up in the first war and, now that the war was finished, he no longer need worry about that, he wrote Olivia. He also claimed that he wanted to get to know the son whom he had fathered with Olivia. But for all of that to come to pass, Olivia must come to Winstead and establish herself there, the letter insisted.

"My mother was driven by a passion for Sean O'Hare that was like a drug," Lawrence said. "She had the same sort of love for Algernon. Neither could do any wrong in her eyes, which was why I had to be vigilant in protecting her."

Once the Tigues moved to Winstead, Sean began seeing Olivia again, creeping to her bed in the night. And he came to know Algernon and saw in his son the same narcissistic cold-heartedness that was the hallmark of his own personality. But Sean also saw that, in addition, Algernon possessed a wickedness that went even beyond that of Sean's, Lawrence claimed. Indeed, Sean became convinced of Algernon's wickedness during the family's first summer in Winstead, when Algernon killed several of the cats that loitered about the family's barn and hung them up in the village for the sheer pleasure it gave him.

"That first summer was when Ned Horton entered our lives, ostensibly as the man who was going to solve the mystery of the murdered cats," Lawrence said. He laughed—a kind of cackle that Lamb found bizarre. "But Horton was putty in Sean's and my mother's hands. He immediately fell for my mother, you see, and very soon baldly offered her a deal—that he would protect Algernon from arrest and prosecution in the matter of the cats if she acceded to his 'requests.' And my mother did accede to Horton's deal—and with Sean O'Hare's blessing—in order to save Algernon from the consequences of his depredations. My mother wanted to protect Algernon because she loved him blindly, as I said. But Sean also wanted to protect Algernon because he had plans for him. Not only that, but Sean saw right away that a compromised Horton eventually would prove useful to him. And Horton did prove useful. Very useful."

During the family's visit to Four Corners that succeeding fall, Algernon crossed the point of no return and moved from killing animals to children. Tim Gordon had been an easy victim of opportunity for Algernon, who had coaxed the boy back to Martha Tigue's farm and strangled him in the barn, Lawrence said.

"He derived a sexual pleasure from it," Lawrence added. "Afterward, he told my mother and I what he'd done. Even then, he'd convinced himself that he never would be caught and that my mother never would give him up. This was his arrogance, you see, Chief Inspector—the same arrogance that eventually led to his downfall."

"And so you brought Tim's body to Winstead in the boot of your aunt's motorcar and buried it in the basement of the farmhouse?"

"Yes. I buried Tim—to save Algernon for Mother's sake, though Mother never cared for me in the way she did Algernon."

"And Horton covered for you again, just as he had with the cats, and under the same arrangement?"

"Yes, though this time Sean became directly involved. He told Horton quite plainly that if Horton didn't cooperate with him and my mother on the matter, they would make it known that Horton had consorted with my mother while on duty and been derelict in his investigation of the matter of the cats to gain sexual access to my mother. They were taking a risk in doing this, of course. But Sean had read Horton correctly and bet that Horton would conclude that he had trapped himself and had no choice but to comply—that otherwise his career and reputation would be ruined. From then, Sean O'Hare controlled Horton, as surely as a master controls a mongrel."

"Tell me what happened to the O'Hares," Lamb said.

"It was quite simple, really," Lawrence said. "No big mystery—nothing in the way it has been made out to be in the papers. Had any sort of decent detective been on the case, it would have been solved. But, of course, Ned Horton was the man on the job, and so it remained a great puzzle."

"Sean killed Claire?"

"Of course," Lawrence said. "He strangled her and then made it look as if she had hung herself from the rafter of their sitting room. Then he handed over his twin sons to Algernon, who killed them in our barn. Sean had planned it all out, you see, right down to the point of having his oldest son kill his younger ones, thereby leaving his hands clean in the matter, and the lead policeman on the case compromised beyond the point of no return. Prior to this, of course, he'd made the usual promises to my mother about remaining with her for the rest of their days. But that had been a lie, just another part of his grand plan. As soon as the deed was done and he was free of Claire and the twins, he fled, just as he always had done. This shocked my mother at first and, for a short time at least, she considered confessing everything to the police. But that would have meant giving up Algernon, too, and she simply couldn't bring herself to do that, though she knew full well what Algernon had done to the O'Hares, just as she had known what he'd done to Tim Gordon. Eventually, my mother found the courage to send Horton packing. She became convinced—and rightly so—that he never would reveal what he knew."

"And so you buried the O'Hares next to Tim?"

"I cleaned up that mess, too, yes. And do you know that my mother never thanked me for it?" He looked away from Lamb for a second. "Never a word of thanks."

"But you had had the foresight to keep the toy soldiers that Tim had been playing with when Algernon had killed him."

Tigue smiled—a broad, contented smile that left Lamb convinced that the evil seed hadn't been exclusive to Maureen and Algernon Tigue. Indeed, all of the Tigues seemed to have been cursed in one way or another with a dark malevolence at the core.

"Yes, Algernon had left them scattered on the floor of my aunt's barn, and as soon as I saw them I had a kind of instinctual inkling that they would prove useful to me someday," Lawrence said. "You see, Chief Inspector, I never deluded myself that one day I, too, would need to protect myself from Algernon. And so I was able to use the soldiers to show my brother that he could not play God with me, as he had played it with others. In the bargain, I was able to also deploy the generals to point you toward him."

Tigue paused for a second, as if trying to picture something in his mind, then continued.

"I would have liked to have seen the expression on Algernon's face when you produced the General Grant and connected it to the Napoleon that he so proudly displayed in his rooms. In his penchant for underestimating me, Algernon did not guess that the Napoleon I gave him was *the* Napoleon—the one from Tim's set—and that I might therefore possess the other figures in the set as well. After Oscar Strand sold the farm to the government, I knew that it was only a matter of time before the house was torn down and the foundation dug up and the bodies of Algernon's victims found. And so I gave him the Napoleon. I knew that his vanity would insist that he display the toy as a kind of souvenir of his handiwork, even though he believed my story that I'd found the figure in a London shop. But when you produced the Grant and told him where you'd found it, Algernon came to understand that I had trumped him. He came to the O'Hare house that very night, looking to see if I had left others in the set in the house or near the place where Albert Clemmons was murdered. But there were no other figures to find. I had possessed them all and had deployed them for my benefit."

Lawrence then described for Lamb how, after searching the O'Hare house and the wood, Algernon had come to his cottage and confronted him.

"Once he knew the truth, he flew into a rage," Lawrence said. "But I had anticipated his reaction and was ready for him. Even as he came at me, intending to kill me with his bare hands, as he had those little boys, he underestimated me—believed that I, too, was a little boy who would weakly yield to him. Instead, I shot him in the head."

"Which one of you killed Albert Clemmons, then?"

"Algernon. When Strand sold the farm to the government, he began to worry that the bodies would come to light, which I found uncharacteristic of him. But I think he had begun to understand even then that the situation no longer was in his complete control, as Mother and Horton were long out of the picture and could no longer protect him. We both knew, of course, that the only living people besides ourselves who knew the truth of what lay within the foundation of the farmhouse were Horton and Albert. My brother wasn't worried about me—at least not at first—and he certainly wasn't worried about Horton, who he knew would never talk. But he wasn't as certain about Clemmons. And of course, Flora Wheatley made the mistake of telling Algernon that Albert had returned to Winstead, which proved fatal for Albert. I bore Albert no ill will. But as I told you, Chief Inspector, Flora Wheatley finds it impossible to keep her bloody trap shut."

Lawrence Tigue shrugged. "And there you have the story." To Lamb's surprise, he then asked Lamb for a cigarette.

"I hadn't realized that you smoked, Mr. Tigue."

"I don't. But I've decided to start." A brief smile crossed Tigue's face. "Isn't that always a condemned man's final request?" he asked. "A cigarette?"

FORTY

—◆—

ON THE DAY AFTER THE EVENTS AT THE O'HARE HOUSE, LAMB and Vera arrived at the nick an hour or so after lunch. Lamb expected that he would put in a light afternoon completing the paperwork he'd neglected during the previous days, and then return home for an enjoyable dinner with Marjorie and Vera. He had convinced himself that he'd earned that, as had Vera.

However, as soon as they entered the nick, Harding met them to say that thirty minutes earlier, Rivers had taken a call from Samuel Built, the civil defense man in Winstead, who reported that a local man had gone by the vicarage that morning and found the vicar's wife bound and gagged in the sitting room. The man had untied Mrs. Wimberly, given her water, made her comfortable, and then called Built, who sat with Wilhemina to await the arrival of the police.

Rivers had called in an ambulance and gone to Winstead with Larkin and Sergeant Cashen. Lamb and Vera immediately headed once again to the vexed little village, where they met Rivers at the vicarage.

By then, the ambulance had taken Wilhemina Wimberly to the hospital in Southampton. Rivers reported that she was exhausted, dehydrated, and probably in shock, but that she appeared to be otherwise unhurt. She had confessed to him something he'd found extraordinary: *She'd* shot Maureen Tigue to death in the cemetery to "cause trouble" for her husband. She claimed that Wimberly had cheated on her with Doris White and numerous other women throughout their marriage and treated her despicably in other ways. She had seen Maureen in the cemetery on several occasions in the early morning and had come to believe that Maureen was meeting Gerald for trysts.

"I wanted to see how the vicar of Winstead would explain a dead woman in his cemetery," Wilhemina had told Rivers. She'd added that Doris White had seen her shoot Maureen Tigue and sought to blackmail Gerald and her with this knowledge. Doris hadn't wanted money, Wilhemina had said. She wanted Gerald. Gerald had planned to rid them of Doris but, on the previous night, Doris had turned the tables on them.

"Wilhemina believes that the pair of them might have left Winstead together," Rivers told Lamb. "But she said that if Gerald did leave with Doris, he did so only to save his own skin and likely would kill her the first chance he got. He apparently meant to poison her last night with a bottle of wine he'd spiked with strychnine. I was just about to check her cottage."

And so the three of them—Lamb, Rivers, and Vera—descended the path by the cemetery to Doris White's cottage.

—⁂—

On the previous evening, slightly more than an hour before Lamb began his showdown with Lawrence Tigue, Doris White had quietly brought to a close her plan for what she believed was the correct ending to the story that she and Gerald Wimberly had together written.

At her bidding, Gerald had tied up and gagged Wilhemina. Then she and Gerald had gone down the hill to Doris's cottage, Doris walking slightly behind Gerald with Gerald's Webley pointed at his back and Gerald carrying—also at Doris's bidding—the poisoned bottle of wine.

A few minutes later, Gerald sat alone on the couch in Doris's cottage, her prisoner, the feeling of being weak and trapped he so despised threatening to consume him. The bottle of wine sat on the table next to the couch, along with two glasses and a corkscrew that Doris had placed next to the bottle. Doris had lit the cottage's interior with the candles she'd stolen from the chapel. Despite his growing sense of panic, Gerald's mind worked frantically to devise a way by which he could regain control of his fate and kill Doris White.

"We're still going away aren't we, my love?" he'd asked Doris. "The two of us together?"

"Yes," Doris said. She stood behind him, leveled the pistol at the back of his head, and ordered him to uncork the wine and pour them each a glass.

Fear flooded Gerald.

His hand shook as he poured, which caused him to spill some of the wine on the table.

Doris moved toward the table and picked up one of the glasses. "We're going to the bedroom now," she said. She followed Gerald into the room and commanded him to lie on the bed.

"*Please*, Doris," Gerald pleaded. "We can still be together."

"Lie on the bed, Gerald," she said evenly. A pair of pillows lay propped against the headboard. "I've made a nice comfortable spot for you."

Gerald lay on the bed with his head on the pillows. He tried with all of his will not to give into despair. But something—the hard, unyielding remorselessness that was the key to his character—seemed to have broken and fallen away inside him and all that remained was a whimpering, frightened boy.

"Now," Doris said, raising her glass. "I'd like to propose a toast: To *us*." She raised her glass.

"I beg of you!" Gerald blubbered. Tears began to stream down his face.

She aimed the gun at his face. "You really are a coward and quite despicable in nearly every way," she said. "But unfortunately, I love you all the same."

A final instinct of survival bubbled to the surface within Gerald Wimberly. He threw the wine at Doris, yelped like an animal in its death throes, and leapt at her. Doris stepped back and pulled the trigger. The bullet hit Gerald between the eyes.

Doris looked at Gerald. He lay sprawled on the bed, a dark bloody hole in the middle of his face. Her chest heaved and her heart raced and she realized that she had begun to perspire heavily. She looked at the floor and saw the glass she had dropped as Gerald lunged at her. *Empty*, she thought.

She dropped the pistol and picked up the glass. She went back to the coffee table, where she filled the glass with sherry. A fragile warmth emanated from the candles.

She returned to the bedroom and put the glass of sherry on the night table, then opened the table's drawer and removed from it the small blue bottle of perfume Gerald had given her three years earlier, when she had been his mistress. She had wanted to throw the perfume away many times—just as Gerald had thrown her away—but found that she hadn't been able to. She opened the bottle, tipped a drop of the perfume onto her finger, then daubed it behind her ears. The scent filled her, leaving her contented.

She picked up the glass and lay upon the bed. She put the glass to her lips and quickly drained the sherry—all of it. She then turned toward Gerald and threw her arm across his body.

Lamb rapped on the cottage door. "Miss White?" he said. "Police. Open up, please."

He gave Doris White thirty seconds to respond, then tried the knob. The door was unlocked. He stepped inside, followed by Rivers and Vera. His eyes immediately went to an uncorked, partially full bottle of sherry on the coffee table. The many candles about the room had burned to stubs and gone cold.

"Miss White?" he said.

They moved into the tiny cottage; Lamb noticed that the bedroom door was closed. "Miss White?" he repeated.

He went to the bedroom door and pushed it open. His first impression upon entering the room was the faint scent of a cheap French perfume that came in a small blue bottle labeled *Desire*.

ACKNOWLEDGMENTS

OBVIOUSLY, NO BOOK IS SOLELY THE WORK OF THE AUTHOR. FOR that reason, I'd like to express a heartfelt thanks to two people who have been instrumental in making this book and its precursor, *The Language of the Dead*, a reality—my agent, Joelle Delbourgo, of Joelle Delbourgo Associates, Inc., and my editor at Pegasus Books, Maia Larson. Thanks for believing in Inspector Lamb, and in me.

As always, I also want to thank my wife, Cindy, for her bottomless supply of love and support, which sustains not only me, but also the family that we have together created.